# LOOK OUT!

I was feeling most upset. Intruders were disturbing my people's territory—and one of my eyes was late . . .

The midday darkness was fast approaching. All my eyes, but one, were back in their nests tucked underneath my fronds, feeding me the views they had gathered. I retired into my mind to revise my worldview. The new views coming from my eyes now contained images of strange four-limbed creatures. Somehow, the creatures managed to balance on just two limbs and didn't fall down!

My attention was next drawn to a circle of stones that surrounded the yellow horror of a fire that was blazing away in the center. These strangers must be intelligent *indeed* to be able to control fire!

One of the strangers was holding a stick over the fire. Impaled on that stick were a few chunks of something. The creature pulled one of the chunks off the stick and raised it to its naked mouth. I moved my view closer. Then, with revulsion and horror, I recognized the triple-jointed structure of meat and bone, and the few still-unplucked blue-green pinfeathers on the skin . . .

The creature was eating one of my eyes!

## Other Books in This Series

Rocheworld

Return to Rocheworld (*with Julie Forward Fuller*)

# MAROONED ON EDEN

ROBERT L. FORWARD

MARTHA DODSON FORWARD

MAROONED ON EDEN



A Baen Books Original

Baen Publishing Enterprises
P.O. Box 1403
Riverdale, N.Y. 10471

ISBN: 0-671-72180-1

Cover art by David Mattingly

First printing, August 1993

Distributed by
SIMON & SCHUSTER
1230 Avenue of the Americas
New York, N.Y. 10020

Typeset by Windhaven Press, Auburn, N.H.
Printed in the United States of America

## ACKNOWLEDGEMENTS

The authors wish to thank the following people, who helped us in several technical areas: Julie Fuller, Seichi Kiyohara, and Gordon T. Baker, M.D.

The "Christmas Bush" motile was jointly conceived by Hans P. Moravec and Robert L. Forward, and drawn by Jef Poskanzer using a CAD system.

All final art was expertly prepared by the great gang of graphic artists at Multi-Graphics in Marina Del Rey, California.

## Contents

# SAILING

Solitary and silent, the huge starship *Prometheus* sailed through space, propelled by the sunlight reflected from its large circular lightsail of thin silvery metal film. The 300 kilometer diameter lightsail maintained its flat circular shape by a ponderous rotation of the structure about its central axis, like a slowly cartwheeling tinfoil moon passing across the backdrop of a gigantic empty stage. Below the lightsail hung a metallic cylinder, a space habitat, somewhat the worse for the wear it had experienced over the almost half century that had passed since it had left the Solar System. In the weak light of the small red dwarf star Barnard, six light-years distant from Earth, the ship's metal exterior shone a dim, pale red.

Mechanically and efficiently, the optical telescopes, infrared imagers, particle detectors, electromagnetic receivers, neutrino counters, gravity sensors, data analyzers, information recorders, and interstellar communicators under the supervision of the powerful central computer of *Prometheus* performed their myriad and continuing tasks of observation, analysis, and reporting of the physical aspects and the behavior of the various bodies in the Barnard planetary system.

In close orbit around Barnard circled the gas giant planet Gargantua—four times bigger than Jupiter—

with its retinue of nine moons—four large planetoids and five small rocks. Between the circular orbit of Gargantua and Barnard whirled the strange double-planet Rocheworld in its own highly elliptical orbit around Barnard. Rocheworld's orbital period was exactly one-third that of Gargantua's orbital period, so it passed close to Gargantua once every third orbit.

All the moons and planets of the Barnard system had been surveyed from space during the first three years after the arrival of *Prometheus* at the Barnard system, and two of the bodies had been explored by landing parties. Rocheworld was one of the bodies that was visited, not once, but twice. Two different alien life-forms were found there. One, the "gummies," lived in the highlands of Roche, the name given to one lobe of the double planet, and the other, the "flouwen," lived in the oceans of the other lobe, Eau. The third exploration landing had been on Zulu, the innermost large moon of Gargantua, whose ice-covered ocean contained hot-water geysers around which lived colonies of intelligent "icerugs."

Now, *Prometheus* approached the next landing target, the Gargantuan moon Zuni, which orbited between the ice-covered moon Zulu and the smog-covered moon Zouave. A little larger than the Earth's moon, with a surface gravity of only 28% that of Earth, Zuni should have been barren and cold, or at least should have had a hostile environment like Rocheworld or the other moons of Gargantua. Instead, it looked like a miniature Earth, a South Pacific version, with verdant volcanic island chains stretched out over a planetwide blue ocean dotted with white rainclouds. Part of the reason Zuni had been chosen as the target for the last of the four planetary exploration landers that *Prometheus* carried, was to find out why this small moon was so Earth-like.

Within the sheltering metal hull of the space

habitat, the central computer and "brain" of *Prometheus*, James, absorbed the data that flowed in from all over the ship, while at the same time it effortlessly monitored the condition of its equipment, operated the versatile and sensitive motiles by which it essentially ran the ship; and, at least as important, cared for and served the nineteen human beings whose lives were confined within the hull. For, although James collected and correlated the data, the real analyses and discoveries were made by the humans, who studied the information their machines had gathered about these strange planetoids, and struggled to comprehend the meaning behind the complex gravitational, electromagnetic, mechanical, thermal, and chemical phenomena which shaped and activated them.

The crew lived on the lower five of *Prometheus*'s seven circular decks. The decks were connected by a central shaft four meters in diameter and sixty meters long, terminated at each end by a transparent dome which contained science scanning instruments. The shaft contained an elevator for moving massive equipment, and served as an access route between decks. In the nearly freefall environment of the lightsail propelled spacecraft, the humans drifted up and down the shaft like bubbles as they went about their routines.

The top two decks of the seven decks were tucked up under the center of the lightsail. These were the domain of James's primary motile, the Christmas Bush. Those decks contained the "workwall," a twisted labyrinth of foot-wide corridors with walls that were solidly lined from floor to ceiling with banks of miniature machines, each backed up with triplicate spares in storage. The machines ranged from simple free-fall weighing devices, to fermenting tanks, to ultrasonic cleaners, to tunneling array microscopes, to cubic-meter-sized complete biochemical analytical and synthesis machines. Although all the instruments were controlled electronically by James using direct data links, it was the Christmas Bush motile or one of its subunits which inserted the samples to be analyzed and removed the products that had been synthesized.

The Christmas Bush motile had a six-"armed" main body. Each arm hexfurcated into copies one-third the size of itself, and each copy repeated the hexfurcation until the final stage, which consisted of millions of near-microscopic cilia. Each subsegment had a small amount of intelligence, but was mostly a motor and communication system. The segments communicated with each other and transmitted power down through the structure by means of light-emitting and light-collecting semiconductor diodes. Blue laser beams were used to monitor closely any human beings near the motile, while red and yellow beams were used to monitor the rest of the room. The green beams that were used to transmit power and information from one portion of the Christmas Bush to another gave the metallic surface of the multibranched structure a deep green internal glow. It was the multicolored red, yellow, and blue lasers that sparkled from the various branches of the greenly glowing structure that gave the motile the appearance of a small Christmas tree, and thus its name.

James, the central computer in the spacecraft, was the "brains" and the primary controller of the motile, communicating with the various subportions of the Christmas Bush through color-coded laser beams. It took a great deal of computational power to operate the many limbs of the Christmas Bush, but built-in "reflexes" at the various levels of segmentation lessened the load on the central computer.

The "hands" of the Christmas Bush had capabilities that far exceeded those of the human hand. The Christmas Bush could stick a "hand" inside a delicate piece of equipment, and using its lasers as a light source and its detectors as eyes, rearrange the parts inside for a near-instantaneous repair. The Christmas Bush also had the ability to detach portions of itself to make smaller motiles. These could walk up the walls and along the ceilings using their tiny cilia to hold onto microscopic cracks in the surface. The smaller twigs on the Christmas Bush were capable of very rapid motion. In free fall, these rapidly beating twigs allowed the motile to propel itself through the air. The speed of motion of the smaller cilia was rapid enough that the motiles could generate sound and thus talk directly with the humans. Each member of the crew had a small subtree or "imp" that stayed constantly with him or her. In addition to the imp's primary purpose of providing a continuous personal communication link between the crew member and James, it also acted as a health monitor and personal servant for the human.

Between the two work decks above and the five living decks below was the storage area for the robotic explorers which were sent down to explore the planetoids ahead of the humans, and the four large planetary landers that carried down and returned the human exploration crews. Most of the original robotic explorers had been deployed during the initial survey phase of the mission, and continually transmitted back to *Prometheus* the information they were gathering about the two lobes of Rocheworld, the planet Gargantua, and Gargantua's nine moons. Orbiters, communicators, amphibious crawlers, aeroplanes, balloons, rollers, penetrators, and diggers had all been launched in the three years since the humans first arrived on their mission.

And the mission continued, and would continue as long as these explorers, both human and robot, existed. Launched from Earth forty-five years previously, the crew of *Prometheus* intended to explore the star system Barnard exhaustively for the rest of their lives, faithfully transmitting all the information they gathered back to the planet they would never see again. During those first forty-five years, the carefully-selected personnel had experienced most normal human emotions and difficulties, and some not so normal. The life-extending drug No-Die, administered by James to the crew over a span of forty years, made it possible for them to arrive at their destination while still relatively physically young, but at some costs.

Three of the crew were now at their duty stations on the bottom control deck. In the limited space, they were crowded close to each other; nevertheless, through long habit, each spoke automatically only to his or her imp, which connected them directly to the central computer, which in turn connected them with all the rest of the ship, machine and human alike. For most of the crew, their imp rode on their shoulder, like a brightly sparkling six-legged tarantula, with one leg resting lightly on the neck of the person, its laser beams constantly monitoring pulse, blood pressure, and, using reflection laser spectroscopy through the thin skin, blood constituents. Sparkling with constantly moving flashes of blue, green, red, and yellow along its slender extending fibers, the shape and riding position of the benign imps sometimes reflected the individuality of the people they served. In the case of the expedition commander, Major General Virginia Jones, she had chosen to have her imp form itself in the shape of a bejeweled hair-comb, set firmly into her short crop of curly black hair just behind one ear. Here, the imp could not only carry on its health monitoring activities, but, when she was talking, act as a lightweight telephone operator's headset, one arm extended to pick up her every whisper, and another arm fanned out near her ear to verbalize James's response.

"Caroline, double-check status of the amphibious crawler *Bubble*. It's floating in the middle of a small lagoon on an island at the Inner pole of Zuni. It's been instructed to dive and explore the bottom, but it's not doing it." The words were murmured so softly into the twinkling extension of the Christmas Bush waiting at her lips that she could barely hear them herself. But echoed back from James through her own imp into her ear, the command came clear and brisk. James routed the command to Caroline, who was sitting shoulder-to-shoulder with the speaker.

"Double-checking, Jinjur," Caroline Tanaka muttered in reply to the command coming into her ear through her imp. She deftly rearranged the incoming data display with a few quick finger stabs at the touchscreen. "Hmmm. Lack of actual depth record. Malfunction? David, malfunction of *Bubble*'s depth recorder?"

The inaudible question, properly switched by James to the imp standing on David Greystoke's shoulder, arrested David's attention from the screen he had been watching so intently. He switched his screen to the image on Caroline's screen and scowled.

"Hmmm. All other functions of *Bubble* are operating normally. I'll have James send a self-check command to clarify the situation before it proceeds with the dive. Can't understand why that one unit should fail. Damn." Both Jinjur and Caroline heard the little growl of complaint through their imps—James did not edit any spoken words.

As directed, the central computer sent its questioning impulses on their way, while the crew on duty continued with their analysis work. Soon, the voice of James, tinged with the built-in apologetic note it had been programmed to use when data seemed inadequate, addressed them all.

"*Bubble* apparently cannot reach the bottom of that

particular body of water without threat of damage to itself. The reading from its sonar depth gauge is off its range."

"The lagoon is not that big across," replied Jinjur. "How can it be that deep?"

"Might be a drowned caldera," suggested Caroline. "Not surprising, since according to Richard and Sam, all the islands on Zuni are of volcanic origin."

"David. Better have *Bubble* make a few traverses of the lagoon's surface while measuring the depth to the bottom, then run that data, including angle of bottom slope, etcetera, through James's geophysical mapping program to develop a seabottom map and a safe descent route before we send *Bubble* down to explore. Make a reminder note for—let's see, who's coming on science analysis duty next?—Carmen, I think, and George and Richard."

The reminder note was made and stored. The shift period finally came to an end, and the three people pulled the backs and legs of their coveralls loose from the velcro attachment pads of their console seats, maneuvering carefully in the low gravity so as not to bump into each other between the close-ranked consoles.

"Hey, David!"

David looked over at Jinjur as she spoke directly to him without going through the imp-to-James-to-imp interface. "How's the sonovideo show coming?"

David grinned, his elfin face lighting up under his thatch of reddish hair. "Slow but sure, Jinjur—can't hurry us geniuses! Got to go back to it right now . . ." He went quickly from the command room. Writing music for the sonovideo light and dance performances he created was a joy David couldn't, and wouldn't, share with anyone. They would just have to wait for the performance. He considered, dispassionately, how to costume his preferred dancer, the acrobatic Arielle

Trudeau, for the "Dance of the Northern Lights" he was composing. The auroras he had witnessed on the icy planet of Zulu had left him tingling to set them to music, and the quickness, litheness, and fragility of Arielle's body could illustrate it to perfection; but the spare frame of the aerospace pilot preferred a snuggly bunny suit to any other form of clothing, even in the mild, carefully regulated atmosphere of the ship. Tendrils of ribbonlike fabric with the shimmering overtones of auroral emission colors would be appropriate, but Arielle quite possibly would object. As David made his way up the central shaft to the crew quarters above, he swiftly outlined the problem to James, then dismissed it from his own mind. He knew that James would use its Christmas Bush to manufacture something that would be perfectly satisfactory to both composer and performer.

James noted David's requirement for a costume. Within the labyrinthine confines of the two upper decks, a Christmas Branch, a subset of the Christmas Bush, detached itself from the main motile and went silently to work, spinning gossamer strands from recycled threads of artificial fabric, and creating new colors by synthesizing the appropriate chemical dyes. Such a minor task was handled routinely and easily by James, using only a very small part of the giant computer's capabilities. At the same time, the health reports coming in from nineteen imps were analyzed and stored, maintaining a record of all the changes in the well-being of the human bodies James cared for.

In the hydroponics lab, further subsets of the Christmas Bush moved about in their flickering clusters to pick the crops, filter out the algae, harvest the fish, and cut fillets from the meat tissue cultures, "Ferdinand," "Lambchop," "Chicken Little," "Hamlet," and "Pâté LaBelle." They then transferred the harvested foods to the automatic galley, where they were transformed into basic food staples and stored. Meals were normally prepared by the galley imp on demand from the crew, although a certain supply was kept available for the rare times when a human decided to cook.

Since there was no dirt, in the earthly sense, aboard the ship, there was little waste to dispose of. Human fingernails, human hair, and human waste of all sorts was automatically collected, and along with other organic waste from food preparation and cleanup, was reduced to safe organic molecules. These were then recycled to become part of James's feed stock of basic organic compounds for use in the hydroponics tanks.

Lint from worn clothing, bedding, and the looped carpet that lined the floors and walls of the living areas was also collected by the microimps, along with metal and plastic dust that had been rubbed or scraped off equipment. This was segregated from the organic waste, combined with similar artificial fibers, plastics, and metals obtained from worn-out clothing and equipment, and spun or recast into replacements.

As the data streams came in from the orbiters, landers, and other exploration robots spread out over the many bodies in the Barnard system, they were analyzed by James; reduced to tables, graphs, and charts, and stored, ready for instant access by the crew. Images from the various telescopes were scanned, enlarged, and contoured. Aberrations in the incoming reports were instantly caught, double-checked, verified, and the corrected data then added to the memory banks, while at the same time being inserted into the continual data stream being sent back to Earth by a multitude of interstellar laser communicators. Within James's inexhaustible memory were stored not only all of the data that had been collected to date during the mission, but all of the vast libraries of science, medicine, literature, music, history; all ready for instant retrieval by the humans. Although James was contained, physically, within the hull of the vessel, and designed by humans to serve them, in many ways James actually was *Prometheus*, and bulked far larger in activity and importance than all of them put together. The great computer knew no pride in itself nor affection for the human creatures it cared for; it simply continued its multitudinous functions, as it had been programmed to do. Only the flickering lights of the motiles, and the smooth voice of James, were substantial evidence of the computer's activities; never noticed because it was always there.

James noticed that David was now approaching the living area deck. It had been David's habit to have a tea break at about this time, so James had its motile in the galley switch from cleaning to preparation.

David made his way into the galley, where the galley imp handed him his squeezer filled with hot pseudo-tea and a fresh watercress sandwich made with algae-flour bread. The squeezer was monogrammed with his name and a string of multicolored musical notes. Instead of taking his afternoon tea on the communal sofa in front of the large three-by-four meter oval view window in the lounge, David decided to relax up on the hydroponics deck. With both hands full holding squeezer and sandwich, he used his Velcro-bottomed slippers to push on the loop-pile covered handholds built into the main shaft walls in order to propel his way upward. Arriving at the hydroponics deck, he brought himself to a stop at the sofa which had been hauled up from one of the video lounges and placed here in front of one of the larger hydroponics tanks. Twisting his body so that the Velcro patch on the back beltline of his jumpsuit stuck to the looped fabric of the sofa back, his slight form almost lost in the soft cushions, he leaned back to enjoy the sight of the three massive flouwen, swirling dreamily in the hydroponics tank that had been converted for their use. He alone had the color sensitivity which allowed him to see the marvelous gradations of color in the three aliens, which the others called, aptly, Little Red, Little White, and Little Purple. The "Littles" were small subdivisions of the giant intelligent sea-dwelling natives the crew had befriended on Rocheworld. They had been brought along in this tank of carefully engineered construction and precisely balanced fluid, to assist the humans by exploring the ocean depths of the other worlds in their planetary system while the humans explored the land surfaces.

The "parent" flouwen back on Rocheworld were formless, eyeless, flowing blobs of brightly colored jelly massing many tons. They normally stayed in a cloud-like liquid shape tens of meters in diameter and many meters thick, moving with and through the water. The amorphous flouwen were very intelligent—but non-technological—like dolphins and whales on Earth. They had a highly developed system of philosophy, and were centuries ahead of humans in their knowledge of mathematics. The flouwen used chemical senses for short-range information gathering, and sound ranging, or sonar, for long range information gathering. The bodies of the flouwen were sensitive to light, but lacking eyes, they normally could not look at things using light as humans did. However, the flouwen, White Whistler, parent of Little White, had learned to deliberately form a clear imaging lens out of the gel-like material in its body. White Whistler had then taught the eye-making technique to the rest of the flouwen.

In organization, the flouwen bodies were similar to an ant colony. There were no specialized organs. Instead the whole body was made up of tiny, nearly featureless, dumbbell-shaped units, something like large cells or very small ants. Each of the dumbbell units could survive for a while on its own, but had minimal intelligence. A small collection of units could survive as a coherent cloud with enough intelligence to hunt smaller prey and look for plants to eat. When the collection of units finally grew large enough, it became an intelligent being. Yet, if that being was torn into thousands of pieces, each piece could survive. If the pieces could get back together again, the intelligent individual was restored, only a little the worse for its experience. As a result, although the individual units that made up a flouwen body had a relatively short lifetime, the flouwen itself was essentially immortal. David was always awed by the fact that each of the flouwen in the tank had memories that stretched back thousands of years into the past.

Neither Carmen Cortez nor Cinnamon Byrd, entering a few minutes later, noticed David on the sofa. The vivacity which was so noticeable a part of Carmen's personality when the ship embarked from Earth had been nearly destroyed by an emotional trauma from which she was now slowly recovering. This new reserve was like a very thin protective film about her; delicate and fragile, but vital to her, and none of the crew had attempted to come too close, preferring to let her take her own way. The communications systems on *Prometheus* which she controlled with such expertise were her only real link with her fellows, as if distancing herself through an electronic link would insulate her from further trauma.

Cinnamon stopped at the flouwen tank and spread her long slender brown fingers out over the surface, clearly and sweetly crooning a song to the inhabitants, who clustered quickly to her. Cinnamon's imp was divided into two sub-imps, one covering each ear—a glittering pair of personal stereo earphones, quietly playing the music of one of her favorite songs taken from James's music archives. Her black braids swung, as together, human and aliens swayed to their mutual music, an unearthly duet obviously very pleasant to them all. David and Carmen left quietly so as not to disturb them.

Richard Redwing's large frame rarely went anywhere quietly, and in this case he was shouting as he came through the passway that led from the central shaft.

"Little Red! Let's get you out of that fishbowl, buddy, and do something noisy!" Cinnamon smiled at the interruption, and stepped away from the flouwen's tank, returning cheerfully to the hydroponics lab and her partners there, Deirdre O'Connor and Nels Larson.

Deirdre didn't glance up as Cinnamon came in, and Cinnamon was not surprised. Of all the crew, Deirdre had always been the most self-contained. Indeed, the little animal sharing space with the imp on Deirdre's shoulder usually reacted more to what was going on around them than the woman did. The icy green eyes remained intent on the microscope viewer before her.

Nels stood, as he always did now, at the tall desk he had requested from the Christmas Bush when his new legs were grown. The advanced mathematical skills, analytical ability, and large memory of the flouwen had been able to unravel and comprehend the growth regulators in the human DNA and deduce a method which made it possible for Nels to grow new legs to replace the flippers with which he had been born. Nels took secret pride in the long, but very hairy, limbs which now supported him. At Cinnamon's arrival, he moved slightly to one side, indicating a graph on the console screen before him, as he continued his conversation with James through his imp.

"This decline in cell division of the flour-protein algae—possible causes, James?"

The computer began its survey. "Initial diagnosis is

insufficient nutrients combined with a weakening in light intensity. However, the light intensity monitor was calibrated last week . . ."

Cinnamon thought briefly about the algae in question. Her nurture of the all-important crop was as instinctive as it was learned, as were her other multiple skills in piloting and emergency medicine. She stepped away down the corridors lined from floor to ceiling with water-filled tanks, and looked thoughtfully at one of the sealed algae tanks with its microscopic but living occupants. She reached to increase, ever so slightly, the levels of oxygen within one of the tanks. She returned as Nels concluded his conversation with James: "If you say the oxygen sensor is out of spec, then it's probably a slight case of oxygen deprivation. Increase and observe results." Cinnamon said nothing and went on to her next task.

Back at the flouwen tank, Richard, with the assistance of James, finished "pumping" the fluid Little Red out of its tank and into its clumsy but efficient "wetsuit." The wetsuit, custom-built by the Christmas Bush, enabled the aliens to move safely about the ship in the low gravity, while protecting the humans from the ammonia in the ocean water that the flouwen preferred to live in. The wetsuits were made of the same strong flexible metallic glassy-foil material that the human spacesuits were made of. In the legless wetsuit with its rounded bottom, the red flouwen looked like an over-sized version of a child's punch toy. From ports in the neckring of the helmet there extended three short "arm" sleeves ending in three-fingered "gloves." By inserting a thickened, gel-like pseudopod into the sleeves and gloves, the flouwen could point, control James's touchscreen computers, manipulate small objects, and pull itself about in freefall. On a planet, it could swim in the suit using its normal undulating swimming motion, and move about, clumsily, on land surfaces, by rolling or humping like a seal.

Just as a human space suit came with its own imp, the flouwen wetsuits had imps that could pick up the sonic speech of the flouwen and transmit it to James, who then translated the flouwen speech and retransmitted the translated message to the imps of the humans.

Two semi-globular lenses of plastic were molded into the helmets of the wetsuits at the same position as the eyes of a human. With the lenses to focus the incoming light into an image, the light-sensitive bodies of the flouwen could look at things using light, replacing their more normal method of "seeing" things using sonar. Out in space, this was the only way the flouwen had of observing things at a distance. Inside *Prometheus*, there was air to transmit sound, so they could also use their preferred method of observing, which was to "see" things using sonar pulses generated and detected by their bodies. The wetsuit rendered Little Red about the same size as Richard, and through the assistance of James's imps and translation programs, the two disparate beings were able to communicate with each other quite well enough to argue. It was, perhaps, odd, that of all the physical bodies in this little society, the only two that really enjoyed contact were these two, as they disputed passage of a door with only room enough for one.

It was not always so—in the long years of the flight there had been many, many incidents of physical contact between most of the humans—and highly enjoyable they were, to most concerned. But, with James so admirably tending to every human need, and the necessity to work long, hard hours collecting and analyzing data, the people had become more content to pursue solitary interests. And the last journey of exploration, to the frozen wastes of the Gargantuan moon, Zulu, seemed to have left the explorers themselves a little chilly, a little more distant from each other, a little less concerned about each other, than ever they were before.

Shirley Everett, Chief Engineer, concentrating on perfecting the already-smooth operation of the apartment-building-sized spacecraft she helped design, had no room in her thoughts for the several romances she had known on the trip. Her eidetic memory was now focused on mental images of the original fabrication drawing detailing the fastening arrangements for the heavy duty water pump in front of her.

After verifying the position of the bolt holes using the tiny, but brilliant beam of her Permalite, she used her considerable strength to muscle a replacement pump into its position under the flouwen water tank, the seals on the previous pump having failed while handling the slightly corrosive ammonia water that the flouwen preferred. She was assisted by Reiki LeRoux, who held two bolts, ready to insert them when the mounting holes were lined up, while in the crawl space beneath the floor, a Christmas Branch waited with lockwashers and nuts. The Christmas Bush, despite its wondrous abilities, was too physically weak to manage the massive pump itself, and so James often had to rely on the brute strength of the larger humans to carry out some of its more difficult tasks.

As the pump slid gratingly into its tight fitting position, Reiki dropped the bolts into the mounting holes. Underneath the floorboard, the waiting Christmas Branch quickly and efficiently installed the washers and twirled on the nuts. Then it rearranged itself so that its six tough metal main arms were locked into a bracing structure holding the nut.

On the other side, a slightly panting Shirley replaced her Permalite in her shirt pocket and dug out her Swiss-Army Mech-All from its pouch on her belt. She manipulated a control on the side and the rounded blob of memory metal at one end reconfigured itself into a metric wrench jaw that just fit the hexagonal bolt head. She torqued the bolt down, but in the tight quarters, she skinned her knuckles in the process.

"Damn!"

Reiki politely pretended not to hear.

Shirley's personal imp shifted from its normal crescent shape encircling the top of Shirley's thick single blond braid into a more effective six-legged tarantula shape, and clambered down Shirley's arm to staunch the flow of blood and dress the wound, while sending out distress calls to James. A sub-imp came flying in from the sick bay and unobtrusively applied ointment and a patch of Nu-Skin to the knuckle, then took off again carrying the trimmed-off pieces of skin and the coagulating droplets of spilled blood.

Just as Shirley finished tightening down the last bolt and was putting her Swiss Army Mech-All back into her pouch, through her imp, and that of everyone's imp on the spacecraft, came the call that they all had been waiting for. It was from Nels.

"Come to dinner!"

Nels had offered to cook a meal for the entire crew tonight, in celebration of the good news the Zuni orbiters, flyers, and landers were sending up. His own inventions of new algae cultures and variations on tissue cultures were always edible, but he claimed that he and Cinnamon had prepared something really special for them that evening.

In preparation for the dinner, the Chief Lightsail Pilot, Tony Roma, had put *Prometheus* into a "high-gee" acceleration mode to provide them with some temporary artificial gravity in the normally near zero-gee environment. The acceleration wasn't much—a few hundredths of an earth gravity—but it sufficed to keep wine in glasses and napkins on laps. The crew seldom missed the gravity of Earth. The freedom of living in free-fall was a delight, and with the advent of simple medications to counteract calcium loss and other problems noticed during the early space age, people in free-fall were able to stay active and healthy for decades longer than those subjected to the debilitating effects of a constant one gee drag on one's body. Everyone on *Prometheus* had benefitted from this, as well as the age-lengthening properties of the No-Die drug. These, combined with the strong bodily systems for which the crew had been so rigorously screened, made them capable of enjoying the manufactured foods they normally ate. Tonight's dinner, however, was special.

Reiki, obviously delighting in the formality, smoothed the napkin on her lap and quietly lined up her silver with the edge of the table. She elected, however, to use chopsticks this evening instead, in honor of the occasion. Her beautifully lacquered set had been a gift from her great-grandmother when she first left Japan, and she had treasured them all these years.

Everyone was delighted when the serving imps brought out the free-fall wine glasses. Tall and tulip in shape, they had much narrower rims than an earthly wine glass, and just below the inner rim was a narrow film of water-repellant compound that kept the ball of wine inside—unless one became careless.

"I am so pleased to see this instead of a squeezer," said Reiki, holding up her glass to look through it. "This will allow us to partake of our libations in a civilized manner, enjoying the smell and taste of the wine at the same time, instead of merely slurping the liquid directly down the throat through the squeezer straw, bypassing nose and tongue completely." She looked around as Linda Reagan and Katrina Kauffmann joined them at the table, making nineteen in all. "And we're all sitting down together for once, instead of eating alone like hermits. The experience of sharing food is *so* conducive to civilized behavior!"

The serving imps then paraded in with six wine bottles and went through the wine-tasting ceremony using Sam Houston, John Kennedy, Thomas St. Thomas, George Gudunov, Reiki, and Jinjur as their tasters.

"A 2069 Gewurztraminer!" said Reiki, reading the static-stick label on the real glass bottle.

"No need to sniff this . . ." said John, as he put aside the reusable plastic cork with disdain. He took a tentative sip. "But I've got to admit that it beats any Gewurtz' that I've tasted on Earth, despite the fact that there isn't a single grape in it."

Arielle, brought up on French wines, took a small taste, shuddered visibly, and left the rest untouched.

After an appetizer of pâté de foie gras made from the liver tissue culture "Pâté LaBelle," served with crisp algae-flour wafers, the first course was served.

"What is it?" asked Richard suspiciously.

"It's a spinach quiche," replied Nels with pride. "It has a new strain of spinach that I developed that doesn't make your teeth squeak after you eat it, and a new algae pseudocheese with a taste of both mozzarella and parmesan."

"Real men don't . . ." started Richard, then spluttered as his quiche was spirited right off his plate.

"I was waiting for you to say that," said Shirley, who now had a slice of quiche in each hand and was taking alternate bites from both of them. She then saw the disapproving look in Reiki's eyes and handed Richard back his quiche, slightly diminished.

"Now the piece de resistance!" said Nels somewhat later. "The first harvest of Cinnamon's new contribution to our real-meat meals. I have to hand it to our resident ichthyologist. She has managed to manipulate the genes of our standard hydroponics fish and created a delicately flavored 'ponics-Trout that you would swear just came from a high mountain stream."

The dinner finally drew to a close with dishes of

strawberry sherbet made with real strawberries, followed by more white wine and after-dinner drinks of various ports, sherries and liqueurs, all from James's versatile chemical synthesizer. George raised his wine glass in a toast to the new world they were soon going to explore.

"To the wild winds!" said George, who had been monitoring the patterns of the almost constant storms on Zuni below.

"To the restless waters!" said Shirley, who had worked out the complex tidal charts for the planetoid.

"To the roaring earth!" said Richard, who had determined that each one of the ninety-five island continents on Zuni was the top of a submerged active volcano.

George was in high good humor and opened another bottle of wine with a flourish. "The landers gave us excellent reports from the surface! The flyer, *Orville*, was really busy, flying over island chains to open water and back again, in and out of thunderstorms—plenty of weather down there!"

"Selecting the best spot for our own landing is going to be interesting," said Jinjur, holding out her glass, while George shook a gobbet of wine into it. "With all the different sorts of weather we're seeing perhaps we can pick out a region less . . . hectic? After the problems we had with the waterfall on Rocheworld and the geysers on Zulu, perhaps we ought to look for a quieter place this time."

"It's not going to be easy," said George. "Zuni always has a great deal of weather activity. We're going to have to time things very closely to get the rocket lander down to the ground during a lull between storm fronts."

"Each island is a volcano," reminded Elizabeth Vengeance. "And they all become active during the three-moon conjunctions every twenty-three Earth days."

"Well, Red, then find me a nice large island with a big beach far away from the central caldera," replied Jinjur. She looked at a stack of blue-green and white colored electrorase prints on the center of the table.

George picked up a print from the top of the stack. "Here's a candidate at the East Pole. . . ."

"*East* Pole!" said Jinjur. "Which of the poles is that?"

"East when you're looking at Zuni from Gargantua," said George. "The 'Leading pole'—the part of Zuni which is always facing in the direction that the moon is moving in its orbit around Gargantua. Besides that, and the North and South spin poles, there's the 'Inner pole' which always faces *toward* Gargantua, the 'Outer pole' which always faces *away* from Gargantua, and the 'Trailing pole' which faces in the direction opposite to the motion of the moon in its orbit."

Cinnamon held a print, almost reverently, up to the lights, her fingers careful to respect the surface.

"It's beautiful," she murmured. Her enjoyment of the compliments of the crew on her 'ponics-trout contribution to the fine dinner had given her, unusually, the confidence to take part in the conversation. "Like a beautifully colored marble, or like the Earth! This one, in particular, taken from so far away."

"I took that myself with my electrocamera, from the sunside science dome," beamed Thomas. "Glad you like it."

"That superficial resemblance to Earth could be dangerous," warned George flatly. "We've got to avoid the trap of unconsciously assuming a similarity that doesn't exist in fact."

"That blue-green color may indicate Earth-like photosynthesis, but the light from Barnard is so poor, the plants would have to struggle for it." They all turned to look at Deirdre; her voice was heard so seldom, everyone tended to overreact when she did speak.

Richard and John put down their forks, and carefully wiped their hands before reaching for the stack of prints. Richard ran a finger along what had all the appearance of a storm front.

"Clouds, that's a glare from lightning, I'm sure . . . rain . . ."

"And a strong wind blowing, just there," John noted. "Real weather: it'll seem odd being rained on, even though we're in suits."

"Golly! Remember umbrellas?" Carmen spoke the word, and there was an instant's silence. How strange and ancient a thing! And yet all understood, and recalled, wistfully, the forgotten sensation of water falling freely on bare skin.

John growled, "Yeah, and don't forget to remember puddles, and mud, and slush, and ruined shoes . . ."

Arielle chuckled. "John always look on bright side!"

Shirley spoke thoughtfully. "It's too early to be sure, of course, but the reports I've been studying about the atmosphere below are certainly reassuring. There is plenty of oxygen for us to breathe, and except for a slight excess of volcanic-type gasses, nothing harmful in the air. Our suits are vital for safety, of course, but we might be able to do without . . ."

Jinjur interrupted with absolute authority. "No, and that's final. Not one sniff of strange air, no matter what the analyzers say. All it takes is one undetected virus, one microbe, and either we're in trouble, or one of the alien life forms on Zuni are in trouble . . ."

They all knew she was right.

"Still, even in suits, we may be able to explore it just like a new country on Earth," Shirley said. "Those clouds really do seem to be water, and so do the lakes. The temperature averages between thirty and forty celsius. Pretty warm, but we should find some cooler spots in the shady regions."

"Sounds great," grunted Richard, taking a third

helping of the remains of the salad Cinnamon had harvested only two hours ago. "I won't mind if I'm never cold again." He knew what it meant to be cold—he'd lost both small toes to frostbite during an Alpine rescue. "But why is it so warm? Barnard and Gargantua certainly can't be supplying all that much heat."

George leaned back in his chair. "Tidal action," he said briefly. "The same thing that warms Rocheworld. All those tides. Gargantua raises a huge tidal bulge that shifts slightly as Barnard and the other moons rise and set. Then there are those short, but really high tides when Zuni and Zouave get together in the same part of the sky . . ."

"It's not just tides sloshing around," added Red. "I've been modeling the composition and chemical reactions in the atmosphere. Zouave, the moon that orbits Gargantua just outside Zuni's orbit, loses some of its nice fertile smog into space every day. The smog just sits there in space near Zouave's orbit. Most of it gets picked up as Zouave comes around again, but some of it expands inward to Zuni's orbit and Zuni comes by and scoops it up. Same thing with the water from the geysers on Zulu, which has an orbit inside that of Zuni. Some of the water vapor from the geysers on Zulu gets thrown high enough to go into space, where it forms into a sort of doughnut-shaped fog bank centered around Zulu's orbit, the outskirts of which also fall in on Zuni."

"And all that infalling water and smog pours down out of the sky onto the Leading pole," mused Nels, bent over the closest picture to that area. "Which is why we see a large region of permanent high pressure centered at the Leading pole, spawning storms off its perimeter ranging from hurricanes to super-dense fogs."

"I remember a strange little valley in China," mused Reiki. "It was a lovely, peculiar place, richly green, and so thickly layered with moisture-saturated air that the slightest vibration, like a sharp clap of the hands, caused a tiny shower. I wonder, will this strange world have such fascinating micro-climates?"

There was a long pause in the conversation, and Reiki took the opportunity to take her leave.

"Excuse me," she said softly. John smirked slightly; his tolerance for polite behavior being somewhat limited. Reiki picked up her wine glass, being careful not to disturb the quivering ball of white wine resting in the bottom, and withdrew to her apartment on the upper crew quarters deck to insert the day's events into her electronic journal, and to consider thoughtfully all the implications of an exploratory journey to a new world.

# INTRODUCING

Comfortably alone in the sitting area of my personal suite, I've paused in my entry into my journal to take a brief sip of the evening's wine. This particular "vintage," which of course has never been anywhere near a grape, has a nice color and clarity; I always enjoy the fruity aroma more than the actual taste, which is a bit flinty. The Christmas Bush, as a vintner, tries to please us all—something no earthly vintner would attempt.

Gazing out at Rocheworld is even more refreshing. Although it is far distant from *Prometheus* at this time, it is always under observation by one of the ship's large telescopes, and I have had James arrange so that its telescopically magnified image twinkles on the large viewwall in my room. From here, the strange shape of that fascinating double-world looks even more than ever like a colorful, elongated figure "8," a veritable infinity symbol, traveling its unique and elongated orbit around the dim red sun—Barnard's star—which attracted us all here so many years ago.

On the other viewwall, I can see an image of the moon Zuni, which is pursuing its orderly way around the immense diameter of the giant planet Gargantua. We are becoming as familiar with all the çelestial objects in the Barnard planetary system as we once were with Sol's planetary system, but there is still more to learn than we will ever be able to, a humbling realization which I personally find a trifle irksome to accept.

But, then, I remember . . . that is nothing new.

"Miss LeRrroux!" The Scottish burr rumbled the name lengthily, while the fierce blue eyes glared at me. "Your essay on the failure of the Jacobite uprising is thrrree times as long as it needs to be—and is not enhanced by your careful analysis of the kilt-folding techniques of the time!"

I have always been too easily lured from sober-fact-noting to fascinating side-issues. Even here, lightyears away from the Earth I wandered over with such avid curiosity, I continue to read the ancient Victorian rules for the language of the fan with as much interest as the recent updating of the alien language of the flouwen. The joys of a huge library have been mine from an early age, and at school I had been accepted as a permanent fixture therein, attending classes only to surpass my classmates in exams. One of the most exciting prospects of my present mission has been the opportunity to have at my disposal an almost infinite multitude of scientists, historians, writers, musicians—all more important to me than the limited human minds living around me. And, not only easier of access and dismissal, but also requiring neither tact nor discipline; Mozart never objects when I frivolously use his glorious creations as background music!

"Here" has been our home for so long; the mighty space ship *Prometheus*, which set out so bravely from Earth long ago. How ignorant we were then! And how much we were sure we knew! What we continue to discover is, how important it is to go and find out.

I began, then, to resume these daily journals. The

habit was instilled in me from my first year at the small school in the far north of Scotland, where my Japanese family had sent me, with much love and a sincere relief at my no longer being part of their daily life.

My mother's lovely almond eyes were full of tears, as they looked hard into my round ones, and her slender hands were clenched tightly in my stubborn black curls.

"My precious Reiki! You know you can always depend on us—and you know your father's family will give you anything you want! But you must be as weary as I am, with the curious stares and the nosy questions! Even your little step-brothers are tired of explaining. . . ." I had, indeed, listened with sympathetic amusement as young Ko explained to a new and unusually inquisitive servant that my exotic appearance was due to an illness—which he thought might be contagious! His own sturdy frame was as like to his father's—my stepfather—as my slender height was to mine, even at that time, when I was barely ten.

"I know, dearest mother. And how glad I am to be able to go freely! I'll not forget you—or dear grandfather—or any part of Japan—but I am so eager to be on my way!"

The freedom I began to enjoy then, I cherished, and never surrendered. Continually fascinated with the complexities of intelligent interaction, I explored many cultures and tried my hand at many skills and occupations, learning from everything, but always ready to move on.

As I pursued a kaleidoscopic range of interests, my journal became ever more valuable to me, as a means of sorting through the various disciplines I was absorbing. A custom model of my own design, my journal is no larger than a filing card and no thicker than a coin, but it contains within its electronic files over sixty years of memories and musings, and has room for many decades more. The electrochromo display, which covers one whole side, lies just above the photoelectric cells that power the electronics. If there is sufficient light to see the image on the screen, there is sufficient light to charge the slim battery.

I normally use voice input for these daily entries, but if I don't have the necessary privacy, I can key in my words with subtle chordic squeeze patterns of my fingers on the touch-sensitive pads along the edges on the front and the back sides. A journal is not complete without an occasional picture, so the back side unfolds into a simple solid state video camera with the display on the front side serving as the viewfinder. I normally keep only selected still frames, although I do have a few short video segments saved, which mean much to me. My slim little computer journal contains my most precious memories and it goes with me everywhere.

The skilled use of computers was taught to all of us as a matter of course in school. My classmates, as well as I, absorbed the intricacies of computer programming with the intensity of children learning a new game—which in many ways it was. For me, however, it was more than a game, and my orderly, somewhat perfectionist attitude toward life turned me into a professional programmer—one of the best, I might add, although like many programmers, my interests are varied and wide. Even my name, in Japanese, reflects that. My mother, grieving for my father's death and contemplating this strange-hued infant, her firstborn, had put together a series of syllables odd to Japanese ears, but which included vague hints of long life, thought, peaches, and, strangely enough, etiquette, which ultimately turned out to be a passion of mine. Very early in my childhood, surveying the hurrying crowds far below in the streets, I had seen how the pleasant-faced, smiling throngs shared the sidewalks with the ease of schooling fish, and had reflected that a bad-tempered shove would have had absurdly far-reaching results, and how fortunate it was that everyone was being so polite.

For ordinary purposes, I am called Reiki—Reiki Momoku LeRoux, to be precise, which my mother insisted upon, although the family had a dreadful time with that last name! Although I never knew my father, nor indeed any of his Cajun family, their financial support was unstinting during my youth, and I bear their name proudly. My parents had met and married when he was stationed in Japan. I have seen many pictures of my father, and I can understand how his easy smile, and slouching grace, would have been captivating to my shy and dainty mother. His tragic accidental death soon after their marriage had sent her fleeing homeward, mourning, but she was far too young and lovely to remain unmarried long. As for me, I enjoyed the idyllic babyhood of all Japanese children, loved and spoiled unconditionally. The few letters I received from the LeRoux family, far off in Louisiana, seemed like missives from another world—and set me, even then, thoughtfully studying the huge globe in my grandfather's room.

Some of my friends are puzzled by my using such an obsolete and limited technology as a personal journal. For, after all, we on *Prometheus* have James, the most sophisticated and intelligent computer the human race could construct when we left the solar system some forty-five years ago. My own imp is so much a part of my being now, that I would feel quite lost without its gentle lights and soft sounds next to me. Robots they are, of course, but not unattractive companions, for all that. I like to use mine to hold one of my bits of lace around my throat—both useful and ornamental. With the imp always observing everything, and James recording anything of importance, there is no need for anyone to keep a journal or to take pictures. But I do; I'm not aware if anyone else does.

*Prometheus* has been home to all of us for so long that I am surprised at how accustomed we have become to such an artificial, from Earth standards, existence. It is more like living in a seventy meter tall cylindrical apartment building than in an interstellar space vehicle. Our personal quarters on the two crew decks in the middle have taken on the characteristics of each of us, while the working decks on each end of the ship, and the large commons rooms on the Living Area deck remain impersonal, similar to an office building or a comfortable hotel lobby. It is perhaps a restricted existence, but we have grown to like it well enough, and rarely notice the lack of a larger sphere. It's fun, with a nose as acute as mine, to detect from a lingering fragrance when a fellow crew-member has been lounging in the commons. Once, while in school, I had been reading in a secluded corner of the stuffy library when a classmate had wandered in, sniffed, and said, "Been playing hockey?" The actual explanation was that I'd developed a stiff neck, and the school nurse recommended a particularly pungent liniment; but the remark had led to my enjoyment of this harmless hobby. Harmless, that is, if one has the sense to keep such detection strictly to oneself! Few people would be pleased to know that the ship's air-conditioning system has not instantly eliminated all traces of coffee, or garlic, or whatever. And sometimes there are odd combinations which lead to rather startling speculations—but discretion is another habit of mine, and I never speak of my discoveries. And, truly, it is only of interest in the living quarters.

Of course, most of the huge ship is taken up with other things, and much of the area on the top decks where the Christmas Bush operates is essentially inaccessible to us; I've never been there at all. I'm much more interested in the hydroponics section, the top deck of the five living decks. Of course, the primary purpose of the hydroponics deck is to supply us with the food we eat, but it is also an aid to those times when we feel a primordial tug, and need to see things green and growing. The sharp smell of a tomato leaf is a scent that is treasured among us—it is real and comes from Earth—as we have.

The hydroponics section is in the capable hands of Cinnamon, Deirdre, and Nels; very typical was the scene today when I looked in; Cinnamon singing to herself, as she moved about the rows, touching a leaf gently, adding a minute amount of carefully controlled fertilizer, her personal imp configured into earphones that play music for her to sing to. Nels stood proudly at his tall desk, toes tucked into the free-fall foot restraints, and fingers moving alternately over the touchscreen display and the keyboard as he manipulated the tunneling array microscope and recorded his findings in James's nearly inexhaustible memory.

"I say, Cinnamon, this new tissue culture may lead to something. Maybe not as good as my Chicken Little or Ferdinand—more on the lines of fish—rather like salmon, maybe."

"Nels, if you can even come close!" she sighed. "My mother used to smoke the catch on wooden frames—it was heavenly!"

"Didn't we sometimes have smoked salmon at Goddard Space Station? I think I remember that, but I can't recall if it was good."

"Because it was dreadful! Adding liquid smoke to a can of canned fish is *not* the same thing!"

With which I most heartily concur. Fresh salmon was a joy in Scotland—bought from the fisherman himself, who might say apologetically that it was caught early this morning, but then adds earnestly that it's been on ice ever since! My schoolmates and I headed towards the sea like lemmings at every brief holiday to get away from the boredom of institutional meals.

"Now look, Cin, let's take this culture and add . . ." The conversation become severely technical, as the two heads bent over the desk, staring intently at the screen—Nels' blondness a striking contrast to her tight black braids. I left them, and moved down the corridors between the rows of foliage and the walls of water in the hydroponics tanks to my checkout task. But I sincerely hope their new project might prove successful! Along the way I came upon Deirdre, silent as always, nearly obscured by leafy foliage. I went around behind the plant—Deirdre is a valued friend—to see the massive bloom she was pollinating with a tiny brush. I said only a word; a soft, "wonderful" and was rewarded with a quick glance, and a flip of the tail from the tiny animal perched on her shoulder. Deirdre doesn't waste words, and I passed on, not expecting any. Her voice, like her eyes, is so beautiful, and so revealing of her emotions, that I think it attracts more attention than she can bear, and she maintains her privacy with silence and downcast looks. But when she chooses to be with someone she trusts, her thoughts are a joy to share. Foxx, the small pet, is a privileged creature; he clings as closely to Deirdre's shoulder as her imp, and I believe the two of them have had to work out a rather painful compromise! But his antics sometimes—rarely—make Deirdre laugh, and that is a sound worth hearing.

By far the largest portion of *Prometheus* is virtually empty. It is the forty meter section between the two top decks and the five bottom decks. There were originally four planetary exploration spacecraft stored there, but there is now only one left. Called the Surface Lander and Ascent Module—the initials of which result in an unfortunate acronym—the spacecraft consists of a four engine liquid oxygen-liquid hydrogen rocket-powered stage for landing the ten person exploration crew on a planetoid, an aerospace plane stage called the Surface Excursion Module, for exploring the surface of the planetoid, and a single engine Ascent Propulsion Stage for returning the exploration crew to *Prometheus*. We plan to use this lander to explore the Gargantuan moon, Zuni.

The first of the four SLAM landers was used to explore Rocheworld. After landing the rocket, the crew let down and assembled the aerospace plane—the *Magic Dragonfly*—with our incredible Arielle at the controls. I've heard, from all the members of that expedition, the account of their near-fatal attempt to leave the planet and return to *Prometheus*, and genuine respect comes into their voices as they describe this tiny lady, becoming quieter and calmer as more danger was threatening the little plane. She is almost more bird than human, and eats like one as well—meaning almost continuously! How well I remember the evening when she and David put on their fantastic performance for us all, to celebrate the arrival of *Prometheus* at Barnard. Arielle's acrobatic free-fall dance to David's inspiring sonovideo composition was a hauntingly lovely combination of light, music, beauty, and passion, all evocative of flight. I have James play those scenes on my viewwall again sometimes, and each time find some new joy in Arielle's soaring glides and David's genius for both sight and sound.

I am anticipating with pleasure David's next production inspired by the last exploration trip down to Zulu. What little I've heard from Arielle seems to indicate it might be quite a different sort of story. I've actually learned more from the flouwen about that icy planet than from my crewmates. The flouwen seem to have more time to talk, these days, and are more willing to do so. Sometimes I think, for all our close proximity, we humans are all living farther apart than we used to.

Halfway down the hydroponics corridor, I looked up. There is an airlock in the ceiling at that point, and it was open. Arielle was on the other side, in the control room of the remaining SLAM rocket lander, getting ready to check out the long-dormant airplane attached to the lander's side. This last lander had been named the *Beagle*, after the sailing vessel which Charles Darwin used for his voyages of exploration. Arielle had a squeezer of chocolate algae-shake in one hand and was using her other hand to operate the airlock controls leading from the *Beagle* to the aeroplane, *Dragonfly*. I followed her as she disappeared upward through the passway to the engineering deck on the *Beagle*, which allows access to the aeroplane, and caught up with her as she was opening the windshield of *Dragonfly*.

"Hello, Arielle. Shall we proceed with our check-out?"

Arielle turned wistful brown eyes to me and patted the control panel. "O Reiki, how brave my old ship flied! We were like real dragonfly! You know that bug? Shiny, and quick, and so fast!"

"Yes, I know dragonflies, and you are right. But we still have this one left—perhaps you will have the opportunity to fly it on Zuni—and it will be like it was before!" Normally, one wouldn't promise such a thing, even vaguely, since the makeup of the next landing party has not yet been decided, but the pilot smiled. The first *Dragonfly* plane had been destroyed at the conclusion of the initial expedition, and we had been fortunate to get the crew home safely.

Arielle's fingers silently played over the bank of control switches in the cockpit, gleaming silver in the gloom, just lightly touching them with practiced familiarity. In this low gravity she barely seemed to touch the cushion of the pilot's seat.

"Just wait for me!" she purred to the silent machine. "We will fly again!" Emotion, like so many things, makes Arielle hungry, and she slurped noisily from the squeezer, then exhaled a chocolatey breath.

I quietly began the routine of the checkout. We were soon joined by a Christmas Branch, looking like a six-armed chimney sweep brush. James had dispatched the motile to assist us in the checkout, and it moved smoothly on three of its six arms over our heads to the engineering console.

"I am ready to assist in the checkout of Surface Excursion Module Four," came the smooth tones from the vibrating cilia in the "head" area of the robot. The bunches of fibered fingers, with their flickering cilia, glowed red as they moved closer to the control console. The rest of the arms emitted laser-lights of blue and yellow, keeping Arielle and me under surveillance and reporting constantly to James everything that it saw. Arielle put down her food as her own imp's configuration shifted from headband to earphones. While Arielle spoke, one tiny section of her imp silently reached out to capture a misplaced drop of chocolate algae-shake oozing from the straw on the squeezer, detached itself from the main body of the imp, and flew off to dispose of it.

"Right. We start up airplane, you do *Dragonfly* workwall."

The fuzzy metal robot shifted its jointed limbs, and proceeded down the length of the airplane to the rear, where it fastened itself, like an illuminated starfish, to the surface of the workwall. Its flickering lights intensified as it operated the miniature controls on the various analytical machines and reported the results of the readouts to James and to us. I took my seat at the computer console at the middle of the plane, buckling myself in, since the seat was set at right angles to the low gravity. Arielle remained up front in the pilot seat, waiting until I brought the semi-intelligent airplane alive. Right now the central computer was idling, waiting for instructions. I tilted my head forward and looked down at the glittering bit of imp jewelry holding the collar of fine white lace around my throat.

"Self-check routine zero," I commanded my imp, which is connected through its laser beams not only to James, but to every computer in the ship.

A mechanical voice answered through my imp. "Seven-six-one-three-F-F."

"That is correct," said the voice of James, coming from both my imp and the Christmas Branch at the rear of the ship.

"Self-check routine one."

This time, the voice which answered through my imp no longer had a mechanical tone. Instead, it had the distinctive voice and personality of Josephine, which I had designed as the persona for the computer that operated *Dragonfly Four*. Its rather husky precision is, of necessity, easy for us all to understand and recognize instantly. This simple method of varying the voice pattern of the different computers makes it easy for us to know which computer is speaking to us.

"Surface Excursion Module Four going through systems check," said Josephine. There was a pause. "There is something blocking the motion of the left scan platform."

Arielle was waiting patiently in the cockpit for me to inform her that Josephine was healthy and she could exercise the piloting part of its program. I would now have to ask her to unstrap herself and go back to the science section to check out the scan platform, but instead of tilting my head toward my imp and having James transfer my message, I turned and called down the corridor.

"Arielle, I'd like your assistance, please. Would you mind going back and checking out the left scan platform? Josephine says there is something blocking it."

Arielle reached up in surprise to touch her earphones. "Imp not talking?" I could hear her imp whisper busily. She turned to smile down the corridor at me.

"You like asking 'please' yourself?"

"Yes," I replied. "I didn't mean to confuse you."

We've not had too much interaction in recent months, and our habits are different from each other.

She unbuckled the restraining straps and moved down the aisle in a single swoop to the recalcitrant scan platform. Through the air I could hear the soft muttering of French swearwords, which I firmly prevented my imp from translating. Josephine and I continued to prepare the little plane for its eventual mission, once landed on Zuni and made operational. Following the precise directions engineered for us by the designers, we issued commands to various subsystems and actuators and checked to see that they were indeed obeyed. The heaters were turned on, to return the ship by no more than five degrees Celsius per day to the higher temperatures it would experience on the warm planetoid below. We enabled the battery-discharge regulators, and directed the emergency backup nickel-cadmium batteries to recharge as soon as they were warm enough and energy from the reactor in the rear was available. We warmed the roll, pitch, and yaw thrusters, but awaited Arielle's return before doing any test firing simulation.

Arielle had gone to the galley amidships for a squeezer of Coke and an algae-cookie. The still-secret recipe for the famous cola drink had been entrusted to James's encrypted files upon our departure, and periodically the Christmas Bush would use that recipe to brew a new batch of syrup in the chemical synthesis portion of its workwall on *Prometheus*.

Temporarily satiated, Arielle swooped back from the galley down the aisle of the airplane, passing my head like some small pink dragonfly herself, and settled into her seat again with a satisfied grunt. We continued amicably on through the checkout procedure, chatting impersonally about Quebec during the lulls when Josephine was busy on some long, tedious task. I had spent some months in her native city, ostensibly to study the possible impact of Quebec's secession from Canada on the children of those fierce but genial citizens. Actually, I was observing how the two cultures, French-Canadian and English, with so little mutual respect, had let that disrespect show itself in sly ways of rudeness, with the inevitable result of a complete break between them. Now, all Canada, except Quebec of course, is part of the Greater United States of America, and there are sixty-one stars in the blue field of that ancient, yet ever-modern "stars-and-stripes."

After completing the checkout of the *Dragonfly*, powering the reactor down to maintenance level, and buttoning up the access ports, we went back down through the airlock onto the hydroponics deck, just as Cinnamon and David were coming up to check out Joe, the persona for the computer in the rocket lander. Arielle went off to the central shaft and dove downward toward the living area deck—no doubt to get more food. I went around to another corridor. There, one of the hydroponics tanks has been converted into a most exotic aquarium. There also is a long sofa, hauled up from the lounge of the Living Area Deck, where we humans can sit and watch the activities of our alien friends as they sport in their little home away from home.

As a result of our second exploration visit to Rocheworld, we now have with us on *Prometheus* three "buds" of the natives of that world, the flouwen. Although the aliens prefer to spend much of their time exploring our ship in their own spacesuits, they return to the tank for feeding on the plants and animals, which Nels brought up from Rocheworld and installed around artificial volcanic vents which provide optimum nourishment for rapid growth and reproduction. The flouwen swim with apparent pleasure in the strange mixture of chemicals in the tank. Roughly equal parts of water and ammonia, with traces of methane and hydrogen sulfide, the "water" would be deadly to us, but it is what they are used to on the ocean-covered Eau lobe of the double-lobed planet. Since their home ocean varies from nearly pure water in the hotter parts of the ocean near the volcanic vents where they feed, to nearly pure ammonia in the colder portions where the water freezes out as ice, the flouwen have developed the ability to adapt to various mixture ratios by controlling their internal body chemistry. Nels suspects that they can probably adjust to pure water oceans, provided they get periodic doses of ammonia to keep their body chemistry balanced.

The flouwen are extremely intelligent, and each of us has some private feeling for them. Cinnamon has a special rapport with them, as she does with all living things. Jinjur finds them relaxing to watch, and she appreciates that. The responsibilities of being commander sometimes weigh heavily even on shoulders as sturdy and straight as hers, and the sight of the smoothly swimming animals, like giant jellyfish, is a source of genuine pleasure for her. She prefers to watch them in silence—I remember well how impressed I was with that silence when I first met the lady! It had not been often I had encountered someone whose comfort with stillness matched my own. She listens to all of us with an open mind, and invariably selects a course of action which has our best interests as its top priority. Her public manner of waving her arms about and shouting abuse which so narrowly avoids actual profanity gets her instant attention, which, of course, is why she uses it! I find her an excellent commander, and her words and gestures secretly amusing.

George, our second-in-command, views the water-tank full of colorful flouwen and the panoramic vistas of black space visible from the floor-to-ceiling glass viewport in the lounge, with equal satisfaction. It must be highly contenting to him, after all his years of working to get our mission literally off the ground, to see how successful we have been in making contact with this new universe. The creatures in the tank are very different from anything on earth, and the scene out the viewport in the lounge is both calming and stabilizing. That is reality out there—immense, beautiful, and existing long after we are not.

Richard looks on our small flouwen buds with what has all the appearances of paternal indulgence. In their eagerness to learn, the flouwen are always asking questions and frequently getting in the way. Little Red seems to feel a special affinity for Richard, and learns fastest of all from him as they yell affectionate insults at each other. I heard them at it this morning.

"Move, Little Red, damn it! You keep creeping up, closer and closer, like a damn cat or something, until you're practically in my damn lap!"

"Cat? What is cat?" All senses in the red alien are alert at the new words. ". . . and lap? What is . . ."

"Cat is . . . Oh . . . a pet sort of thing, and lap . . ."

"Pet!" Little Red was shouting at the implied insult. "I not pet! Pets *dumb*!"

Richard laughed, and said, "Then stay out of my—uh—chair."

"Wait! Before you said, 'lap'! What is that? Dumb too?" The tones were suspicious.

"No, no, no . . ." The man tried to define "lap" to the alien. I did notice, wryly, that Little Red had had no trouble with the "damn." Even such short acquaintance with humans had familiarized the alien with the regrettable overuse of that and other slipshod adjectives. One of my own obsessions is that of selecting each word with care, rather than resorting to monotonous slang. Sometimes I think I am setting a good example; at other times I despair. A moment's idle gossip invariably sends me speeding off to the fine minds waiting patiently in my library!

Communication between these creatures and ourselves is overseen by Carmen. It is good to see her restored to some health! None of us, except perhaps John, knows what caused her to retreat so far from us, but I think she is back with us at last. I'm glad to see her responding to the occasional inquisitive question with an aloof raising of an eyebrow—I couldn't do better myself! Her introspection has a different look about it now—I feel she is changing, and growing, after so many years of simply being agreeable.

My own feeling toward the flouwen, I find, is very similar to my attitude towards children; kindly, never angry, but quite prepared to do my part in their education. Their self-sufficiency and easy way of life has resulted in their having no manners to speak of, and they communicate with others with the simplicity and directness of children. There is no need for me to concern myself with this, but as we work with them, I hope, by example, to help them understand the simplest of courtesies—if only to lead to increased interaction and friendship between ourselves. The differences between our two species are so vast that without good will and endeavor on both sides we will always remain enigmas to each other.

It is amazing that with all of our adventures and mishaps, only one of our original crew of twenty has died. That came about during those forty years we all spent as very young children in adult bodies, the result of our use of the drug No-Die, which slowed our physical aging by a factor of four so that our forty year journey to Barnard only aged us ten years, but which lowered our IQs by the same factor of four.

I had struggled very hard, at first, to resist the loss of my own excellent mind, only to succumb to the drug as did the rest, to wearisome play, and then the insidious infectious cancer, which struck without warning. We were all so very ill with that cancer—and its violent cure by chemotherapy! But all of us survived, only to find, when we were allowed to return to our adult minds, that the disease had taken our beloved Dr. Wang, who had not taken the chemotherapy in order to be better able to treat us. I'm not sure quite how the others remember him, but I think of him as a saint.

It is late and I have the early shift tomorrow. I finish my wine and before I bring the glass down from my lips, the room imp is there, ready to take the empty glass off to the galley to be cleaned. I climb under the tension sheet on my bed, and before James has dimmed the lights, I'll be asleep.

# PREPARING

Eager for my next shift, I was ready early. I'd chosen one of my favorite sets of lace, which formed a delicate edge to the crisp neckline and sleeve edges of the practical coverall I generally wear. Fragile though it looks, lace is tough and durable, and I have no fear that my own collection, gifts from many thoughtful friends, will not last as long as I. This set in particular is snowy white, in sharp contrast to my dusky skin. I remember an early lover's self-satisfaction with finding a color match; we were sharing a blissful breakfast in Kashmir, and the smiling Hunza woman brought us a bowl of ripe apricots.

"That's it!" he said, holding one up to my cheek. "You're just that color!" Fanciful, but not inappropriate to that happy time. Trimly regulation in the rest of my appearance, I pulled myself smartly around the last handhold on the central shaft and swung into the big control room on the bottom deck. When he saw me, David got up silently from the computer control console, and I took his place.

Two other members of my shift, George and Sam, were already there, settling down at their console screens. George had the *Prometheus* in hover mode at the L1 point between Gargantua and Zuni, so with little to do, he had switched his pilot console from the normal lightsail navigation display to a science analysis setup. Carmen came in to replace Caroline at the communications console. Neither one looked at the other.

"Carmen. Zouave will be going behind Gargantua in about half an hour," said Caroline through James as she got up and left, talking as she went, with Carmen hearing her clearly through their imp-to-James-to-imp connection. "*Tweedledum*, the high-pressure exploration balloon, is getting some excellent views of a region of Zouave it and *Tweedledee* have not visited previously. Before Zouave disappears, you'll want to set up a bounce relay link through the commsat we placed at Zouave's L4 point." She had disappeared up the central shaft long before she finished talking.

"Right," replied Carmen through her imp, as she wrapped her legs around the console chair stand and readjusted the icons around the comm screen to the left-handed arrangement she preferred.

"George?" said Sam. "Nearly all the data on Zuni collected by the crawlers has been closely analyzed by James and the science analysis gang, correlated with the pictures taken from above by the orbiter, and collated into various files. If you'd like, I think I can run a condensed version of the highlights for you. It ought to give a pretty clear picture of what the two crawlers found before they were lost to accidents."

"Great, Sam. It's good to have all that information, like having an encyclopedia, but getting something out of it is like trying to *read* an encyclopedia!"

I quietly switched my own screen to Sam's so I could watch too.

The reports from the amphibious crawlers *Burble* and *Bubble* had indeed been voluminous. For years they had crawled in and out of the oceans and islands on Zuni below, their webbed tracks working as treads on the land, like paddles in the water.

"Plant, similar to that found in image 74698, color similar to shade 173, structure similar to number K91, located . . ."

The descriptions went on and on, and each find had been plotted on the increasingly detailed maps being developed in the archival memory of James. Of course, when most of these reports were actually coming in, we had been busy elsewhere in the Barnard planetary system.

We had learned of the loss of the robot scouts via brief communications from *Bruce*, the science orbiter which had brought the two crawlers and their aeroshells down close to Zuni so they could land, and who stayed in orbit to act as a communications relay between the crawlers and *Prometheus*, and to collect what data it could from orbit with its video cameras, microwave, infrared, ultraviolet, and gamma-ray scanners, and various science instruments including a gravity gradient field mapper. Soaring high above Zuni, *Bruce's* unemotional voice had reached us with the announcement of the loss of the first semi-intelligent robot.

"*Burble* is experiencing technical difficulties. *Burble* is submerging rapidly off the southern tip of island 105 east, 35 north. *Burble* has ceased communication." There was a pause. "All indications are that *Burble* is no longer operational."

We had all been too busy to respond with much more feeling than *Bruce* had displayed.

"Right, *Bruce*, you and *Bubble* carry on," was, I think, about the extent of it from George at the time. And there was not much more excitement at *Bruce's* equally laconic statement after the loss of *Bubble*. One of our many tasks on Zuni's surface will be to see if we can find any part of *Burble* and *Bubble*. If they are in any way salvageable, it will be well worth our work to return them to *Prometheus* where the Christmas Bush can make use of their parts.

If, now, Sam could begin to summarize all this information in a readable way, I would appreciate it as much as anyone. The scenes on the screen began to sharpen, images narrowing down to focus on some detail, then widening out to encompass a whole valley or bay. By now Carmen had switched her screen too, and some members of the previous shift had drifted back down from the dining area on the deck above to see what was going on, some of them going to spare consoles and bringing up replicas of Sam's screen. All of us watched with interest as Sam began to form vivid panoramas of the land below us, switching from overhead views taken by *Bruce* to the closeups of the same views taken by one of the crawlers.

Zuni looks, with obvious discrepancies, rather like parts of the Earth's South Pacific. It appears to be mostly water, with islands of all shapes and sizes, over ninety-five large ones, and thousands of smaller ones, dotting the surface in such profusion one would think it would be difficult to miss hitting one, landing at random. However, such a move would certainly be disastrous, as the appearance is deceptive, and miles of water separate each morsel of land.

David stopped the display on his console in mid-scene.

"Here's a funny thing! I'm looking at two views of the same small area taken by the orbiter *Bruce* just a few days apart, but they look different! I'm sure it's the same spot, because of that strangely shaped granite knob in the middle of both images, but the pattern of vegetation has changed, and see the color difference?"

He displayed two pictures which we all pulled to our screens. There was a collection of trees in a complex pattern, and the pattern *had* changed significantly between the two pictures taken a few days apart, but, frankly, I could see no difference in the colors of the plants.

"Yes, the reports from *Bruce* do say shade 043 and shade 045, but *I* don't see any difference! *Bruce* is as persnickety about color as you are, David!" Jinjur straightened to her full diminutive height and ran exasperated fingers through her crisp black hair.

"The whole place seems to have nothing but those same bushes. Where's any significant difference?"

"What do you mean, no difference? Look there . . . and there!" David's bony fingers prodded sharply at the two images, pointing to the sets of bush-like structures to one side of the granite knob. His touch-sensitive screen produced green circles on our screens.

"Can't you see how much bluer those plants are in the second image?"

"No," snorted Jinjur. There was a general murmur of agreement.

"Wait, I'll make it clearer," David said impatiently, and began to increase the color difference by stretching the spectrum. The onlookers, an opinionated cluster of individuals, began to come as close to argument as they ever did.

"I do believe I can see . . ."

"Obviously it's just a different time of day!"

"They were taken at the same time of the day," David reminded them.

"Much more likely a seasonal variation—that's why the pattern is different too."

"A major change in color and position in just a few days?" David retorted sarcastically.

"To coin a phrase," said Jinjur tartly, "I think you're barking up the wrong tree."

This, of course, set Richard off.

"Ash-ly, I don't want to go out on a limb, but are

yew holly qualified to judge, Jinjur? I mean, until we syc'more information, I think we should go with the willo' the poplar majority! It's oak-kay with me to leaf the whole thing to David—he walnut be stumped! And as fir my o-pine-ion . . ." Here, fortunately, George ordered him to shut up.

I shifted my own console back to the original picture, and pulling other views of the same region taken by *Bruce* in its daily orbit of the planetoid, began to run it through a time-lapse sequence. Fortunately, the region was near the north pole, so that *Bruce* obtained a picture of the same region practically every day. As the images changed, and time passed, the pattern of plants in the picture slowly began to shift. Of course, that would normally be the case—plants do thrive and then wither. I increased the display rate . . . Suddenly, I stared in shock. As the patterns of vegetation moved and shifted, definite lines of action began to form, almost as if the plants were advancing and retreating! I slowed the pace to a daily rate, and the action became invisible. But sped up, so that weeks were scanning by in a few seconds, it was easy to see—tendrils were moving out from established plants, new growths were beginning, and even more startling, the mass of growth changed with what had all the appearance of deliberate purpose, from the parent plant to the new growth! My gasp of amazement had caught David's attention, and he instantly brought up what I had on my console, roiling in its fast-moving action.

"There's a battle going on!" exclaimed Richard. "The bushes are moving around, and fighting each other!"

"Plants can't move around," said Jinjur. "Don't they always have fixed root systems?"

"Not these plants!" Nels was excited. "Look at that . . . that . . . spider plant there!" He was right, there was a resemblance of this alien plant to those common plants frequently seen barely surviving in some neglected corner of a student's room. "It's just sent out shoots towards that spot where there's more space, and now the little plant on the best spot has shot up to overshadow the neighboring ones! And what's really amazing is that the parent plant is dwindling, obviously sending the offshoot all of its nutrients!"

"You mean the parent plant is sacrificing itself?" It was difficult for me to accept the notion of altruism on the part of a plant.

"No, no, Reiki, it's not sacrificing anything, it's just moving! See, all the other little tendrils are shriveling up too, while that first offshoot is absolutely thriving and becoming the new parent body!"

It was David who spotted the even more aggressive actions of the foliage.

"Watch those little vines! They're trying to strangle each other!" It was true. At this high rate of speed, the sinewy runners looked like furiously battling snakes, coiling viciously around each other, struggling to break their opponent's grip on the soil, trying with obvious intent to crush the life from each other. Amazed, we watched a larger offshoot slide quickly to the top of an apparently established plant and begin to grow strongly, only to be ruthlessly severed from its parent by a branch of the stronger plant.

With quickened interest we focussed our attention on the structure of these peculiar shrubs. The large central portion is very bushy, and almost always there are six tendrils out and about, searching and exploring, setting up new bushy offshoots in a tentative way, until a position is found that permits rapid growth. Then that growth is phenomenal! With the rest of the runners and the parent shrinking into nothing, the successful shoot attains full growth and vigor, and begins to send out little tendrils of its own! The change and warfare seem to be unending. This deliberate slow-motion battling makes us more curious than ever about the planet we hope to explore.

The information we have is tantalizing, to say the least. Although it is totally different from Earth, Zuni has many characteristics to which it is easy to relate. Because its gravity is twenty-eight percent of Earth's, walking will feel almost normal, but lifting heavy weights should be simple, as, for instance, fifty kilos will seem like only fourteen. The length of the "day" is a little over thirty hours, due to the fact that Zuni is tidally linked to Gargantua. The light, what there is of it, comes from Barnard, and is cut off from Zuni by the huge mass of Gargantua in an eclipse, every day, for nearly two hours. At nighttime, Gargantua itself is being illuminated by Barnard, providing more than enough light for us to move around safely. The only real darkness comes during the eclipse; I can easily find attractive the idea of an enforced siesta! Our years of relentlessly scheduled shifts have made me, just a little, resentful of their rigidity.

Eagerly we followed *Bruce's* updated descriptions of the land beneath him, tallying them with the lengthy explorations of our earlier scouts.

"Island 128 East 20 North: small saline lake at south end. Vegetation predominantly similar to more primitive bushes. Seaweed-type vegetation common. Island not visible above water for 1.5 hours around local noon and midnight. Not recommended for exploration."

"Oh brother!" sighed John. "As a tour guide for would-be explorers *Bruce* is a master of understatement. A place that is underwater for three hours every day would not, I agree, be a whole lot of fun."

"These tides," said George slowly, "are going to have to be reckoned with. Bring up the tide table Shirley compiled."

I pulled up the tide table and looked at it and the

accompanying graph of tidal height versus time. The tides are indeed worthy of consideration. The tides on Zuni are not smooth and slowly varying, like Earth tides. Instead, superimposed on a small rising and falling pattern, there are short, sharp spikes of high water at seemingly irregular intervals.

"Gargantua is big and close," explained Shirley as she moved her finger across the touchscreen and a green circle imitated its motion on all our screens. "And its tidal pull is the strongest, of course, but as Zuni faces it all the time, the pull is constant, so all Gargantua does is make a large permanent bulge about twenty-six kilometers high in the ocean and the crust. Barnard, not being a very large star, only causes a modest rise in the ocean surface of one-and-a-half meters, about the same size tides as those on Earth. They come, naturally, twice a Zuni solar day, or about once every fifteen hours.

"Zulu, when it comes past between Zuni and Gargantua, causes a short, sharp tide that is three times stronger than the Barnard tide, or four and a half meters. This occurs during a three hour interval once every twenty-nine hours, a little oftener than once every Zuni day. Zouave's tide is even stronger, six and a half meters, and lasts six hours, but it only comes every seventy-eight hours, or once every two and a half Zuni days.

"But look what happens when the moons line up every eighteen Zuni days. Then we'll have tides of over eleven meters! And, when Barnard gets into the act, lining up with the rest of them, the tides will be nearly thirteen meters, that's forty feet high! The tidal surge then will be bigger than the biggest Earth tides at the Bay of Fundy. Those whoppers only come at the yearly spring tide there. Here on Zuni, it'll be every fifty-four Zuni days and it happens everywhere on the planet, not just in one peculiar bay! Not an effect we can afford to ignore, if we're going to do this mission safely."

"Well, we'll simply select a landing area on an easily accessible hill for the lander that is higher than the highest tide, but close enough to the water that the flouwen can easily get down to it," said Jinjur briskly.

"Right," seconded Shirley. "It might be best to come down over the surface of the water first, so we don't blast the vegetation too much, then slide over to the shore and up onto the top of the hill. With all these islands to choose from, we're bound to be able to find one that's close to perfect."

"It's vital that we do," said George, more seriously than we had heard him for some time. "This mission has me concerned. We have no more landers, and if anything happens to this one, there is no way those on *Prometheus* can rescue the landing party."

This flat statement had a brief chilling effect on us all, but it was brief indeed. I know I, as well as most of the rest of the crew, am secretly hoping to be part of this adventure!

At this point, the three flouwen came surging into the control room in their wetsuits, asking endless questions and crowding the working screens so closely that those who had things to do elsewhere went off to do them. The wetsuit with the vermillion-colored helmet pushed close to David's screen, accompanied by an astringent smell of ammonia.

"Big waves? *Any* waves? Look! There's a good one!" Little Red, like Loud Red, his distant larger portion left back on Rocheworld, was always interested in surfing.

"Big, yes, but look how it crashes onto those rocks. You'd have to drop out, just as it got exciting," said Little White. As Little White "spoke" to Little Red using sonic chirps generated by his body, the chirps were translated by James and the translation sent to us through our imps.

Little Red's desire to play with the actual controls of the computer, set up in fascinating array before him, was so strong that he moved in front of David, slowly pushing the man's arms to one side. Richard, behind David, gently but firmly intervened his own bulk in the opposite direction, but Little Red's attention was still on the flickering pictures before him.

"You're making the picture? You're seeing far away?" The question was wistful.

"I'm not actually seeing, these are old pictures, and we're just putting them together in a time sequence." David wondered how much of that was comprehensible to the flouwen. Little Purple, more content to observe from a comfortable distance, said, "Yes, you know, Little Red, like big wave comes, grows up up up, we slide down down down, then big splash! All in long, long picture!"

"Hunh!" was Little Red's dubious response—his own milder version of the emphatic "Dumb!" of Loud Red. It seemed a good time to change the subject.

"We're looking for the best time and place to go there," I said distinctly. "We need to find a spot where we'll all be able to see and find out more about this new place."

"Yes!" shouted Little Red. "Find good things to eat in the water!"

"That, too," I agreed. "We'll have to share all we learn with each other."

"Share?" A new word.

"Taste," said Little Purple firmly. "Same thing." He was right, for the flouwen can share each other's knowledge with the physical transfer of memory chemicals in a process much like tasting.

"It would probably be a good idea to find a relatively enclosed area of water, for these pests here," said Jinjur. "Nothing as confining as a lake, but we don't want them bounding off across miles of ocean in the few months we plan to be down."

We resumed scanning the terrain. "Here's a bay, but the vegetation seems sparse here."

"We'll keep looking," decided George. "If possible, we should choose a place near the Inner pole. That way the nighttime period will always be illuminated by the light from Gargantua, making it easier to explore. The only really dark period will then be the two hour eclipse around noon. James, divide up the Inner pole area between the leading and trailing poles into thirty degree sectors and the five of us will each take a sector, marking possibles as we search."

I was pleased at being included in this exercise. My own classification, as anthropologist, is somewhat ambiguous to the rest of the crew. It was so, simply because I had hastily selected the field as my first major, years ago, when an apologetic but insistent administrator had extracted me from the library. "You must choose something, from all these fields, to put down on the necessary papers!" I had been pleased at my own choice; so many interesting subjects can be reasonably included in this elastic discipline. With glee, the next term, I added "The Origin and History of American Quilts" and "Celtic Place-names" to my studies; my advisor only waved me wearily away as I happily explained how they fit into such a major. Since then, my studies and explorations had become almost too numerous to list, but George and especially Jinjur were very much aware of them all. They arranged quietly to have me around when I could be of help, either as technician or catalyst.

In the area assigned me I could find nothing promising. There were several islands with lagoons, but most of them were extremely small. We need to have a place large enough to contain a fair representation of all of the most common lifeforms. The largest island had no bodies of water on it at all apparently, except for the lake in the gigantic volcanic crater near the center. It looked like Mount Fuji after a few million years of heavy rain, which, I guess, is exactly what had happened to it. The rest of the island was a sloping volcanic shield ending in black sand beaches, on which the breakers crashed with steady regularity. Little Red, peering over my shoulder, obviously thought this was ideal.

"Good!" he shouted, and then launched into some jargon with his compatriots, apparently describing the curl of the wave which would allow then to travel parallel to the shore for long distances on a single wave. Firmly I moved the scanner inland, away from the attractive coast, and Little Red, disappointed, went off to lean on Richard's stalwart back. The flat fields I was surveying were not very interesting to me either. They reminded me of the "flow" country of northernmost Scotland, whose bleakness had impressed me even in the dreary charts of the agricultural handbook I had picked up one day in that much-loved library. Ostensibly a guide to making a living from those barren lands, it was really more of an encouragement to emigrate, but I had gleaned from it the possibilities of existence anywhere.

It was Caroline who found it. We'd all been working in silence for more than an hour. Her quiet—"here"—contained so much satisfaction we all instantly switched in our consoles to her screen and delighted in the configuration she had outlined. It is a large island, located five degrees west and five degrees north of the Inner pole (which had already been picked as zero-zero) with a central volcano and a number of subsidiary calderas, probably coming from the same magma chamber. On the shore itself is a nearly circular lagoon, probably a drowned caldera, with only a narrow opening to the open sea. It is well suited to our purposes, I think.

"Looks like St. Vincent island in the Caribbean," said Thomas. "Except the Crater Lake on this island is connected to the sea. I guess we should call it Crater Lagoon instead."

"Yes!" said Jinjur, her finger on the touchscreen producing a green blob overlay on the image. "This looks like a good choice. The lander can come down above the center of Crater Lagoon there, slide over to the base of that low volcanic dome there and go up that gradual slope to the top, putting it well out of the reach of the tides. We can then set up camp and get going!"

It sounds almost too good to be true. George probed the reports for further details. The crawler, *Bubble*, had been through the lagoon and had made a traverse of the less forested portions of the island. "The water looks clear, there, and the bottom was too deep for the scout to record, so there is no danger of the tides uncovering anything below the surface. We'll continue to check it out, but temporarily, make it so!"

The continuing reports were favorable. Richard noted, approvingly: "The surrounding volcanoes are even taller—they'll provide protection from the prevailing storm winds. And from what we've seen of the local weather reports, that may be a very real advantage!"

The lagoon is big enough so the flouwen will have room to hunt, and the opening to the ocean is small enough to make it clear what is off limits to them. The microclimate seems to be as moderate as any here, located near the equator midway between the leading and trailing Poles, so that Gargantua is always in the sky, providing some light at night. Indeed, it seems evident that we will be able to see well enough to walk about and work at all times, except during the midday eclipse. That fact is both comforting and daunting! The pressure to get the maximum amount of data during our few months stay is unremitting. Fortunately, we will be able to concentrate fully, having no need to deal with any sort of domestic chores; the Christmas Branches on the rocket lander and the *Dragonfly* aerospaceplane will handle those.

The flouwen, of course, know they are destined for this mission, and are joyous over each step in the process being completed. Among the rest of us, however, a certain unavoidable tension is growing. Selecting the crew for each mission is strictly up to George and Jinjur, and their decisions have not yet been announced. It is entertaining, as well as enlightening, to observe the behavior of various individuals attempting to ensure they will at least not be overlooked! When I mention that Linda, our bouncy little astrophysicist, and tall Elizabeth are both to be found constantly in the exercise room, ostentatiously jogging on the treadmill wearing a spring-loaded hip harness (Linda's specialty) and furiously cycling (Elizabeth's long legs pedaling with amazing speed), the picture is clear. It would be funny, if one didn't sometimes catch a glimpse of the fire that can flash between those two pairs of green eyes as they each race to better their personal goals from yesterday!

David, Arielle, and I have no time to spare for any posturing, even if we were so inclined. All three of us are determined that whoever flies this last lander will find every command response from the lander's computers, Joe and Josephine, quick, clean, and absolutely perfect. Of all the variables on the mission, the computer system is one which we can control, and we intend it to be as reliable as we—and James!—can make it. Joe and Josephine are in constant communication with James, absorbing all the information the central computer has collected about the surface of

Zuni. The satellites to be deployed to provide global communications for the landing party are also undergoing our painstaking examination, as well as the solar-sail levitated statites to be placed in a hovering position over the polar regions. Our work occupies our entire shift, and we are ready to relax when it is over, since James relieves us of any personal housekeeping tasks. I use my time to enter the exciting events of the day into my electronic journal. I am more than ever pleased with the adaptability and speed of my little recorder—I can enter as lengthy an account of the day's doing as I like, either with the lightest of finger pressures on the chordic keypad, or if I am really tired, simply by rambling along, out loud. As its designer, it is a source of much satisfaction to me that it can live in my pocket, as personal to me as my imp. If I have the good fortune to be selected for the mission, it will certainly go along with me . . .

I am going to Zuni! It was difficult to control my delight when Jinjur told me, but I managed, just barely, to restrain it until I returned here to privacy. It is the most marvelous news! It will be wonderful to be in a new place again, quite apart from all the discoveries which we will certainly make! And, like the rest, I too long for the freedom to move about a large and unfamiliar area—imagine having the possibility of tripping over something! Not that it would be pleasant, but for so long we have known every inch of our floors and walls, kept so immaculate by the Christmas Bush. And to think of looking up and not seeing a ceiling!

Jinjur summoned me through James, just now. I was not expecting this to be "the" summons, as of course James is virtually our PA system, and I had thought the announcement to the mission crew was to be a private matter. However, I reckoned without Jinjur's instinctive leadership technique—she takes no significant action covertly.

When I walked into her room, I knew instantly, and a thrill, almost electric, shot through me. There was no mistaking the message of that huge grin! I'm sure I mirrored it, nearly, as she said, "Yep, that's right! You're going to Zuni, and what's even more important to me, so am I!" This was surprising, and I reacted to it even in my excitement.

"Are you really? George . . ."

"Quite agrees, thank goodness. This mission looks to be the closest thing to a fine adventure as we'll be having in the foreseeable future, and I want to be part of it. We plan to leave in fifteen days."

"Thank you for including me—I'm absolutely thrilled!" I said, just to make sure she understood that. It's important to get those words actually said, and when I calm down a bit I shall write a note to her and to George, as a matter of record. She then told me why I'd been selected, and once again I was grateful for the sudden urge which had led me to speak up in my own behalf so many years ago when the committee was considering me for the Barnard mission. General Jones, as I'd thought of her then, had asked, "Ms. Leroux, why do you think this large array of disconnected skills . . . pearl diving . . . costume design . . . would be of any use to us?"

"Such a variety of accomplishments," was my tactful way of rephrasing her query, "surely suggests an adaptability of mind. I've sustained myself, unaided, in countries and cities—not the least of which is here, in Washington! I control myself, and am content with myself. In addition, I have, to a pronounced degree, the ability to interact successfully with anyone, humans as well as computers. Such a skill should certainly be in demand on a mission such as this."

"Anyone?" The strong brown face remained cool.

"Years of absorbing the manners and customs of other people, along with an instinct to listen, have taught me to establish an easy working relationship almost instantly. Normally, I would not speak so frankly, but it will help you to know what I can do as quickly as I can tell you."

That had been all, at the time, but I had long suspected that my selection had been as much for those few words as the official reason. The announced decision, that while my excellent computer programming skills would no doubt be useful, an anthropologist was desired to assist in analyzing any alien life forms we might encounter, struck me as amusing. Jinjur's words to me today substantiated this.

"Right now, it doesn't appear that there will be any life on Zuni intelligent enough for you to analyze, Reiki. But there certainly may be a need for a peacemaker, as I try to keep a leash on this exploratory party!" It was not, strictly speaking, my business to ask who else was going, but happily, Jinjur was in the mood to rejoice with me.

"We've chosen Nels and Cinnamon, both," she said. "They outperform as a team better than both of them separately, if you can follow that! And there will certainly be plenty of interest to them in these weird plants. Nels will enjoy stretching those new legs of his," she added knowingly. I caught the tiny wince of remorse—she had, for so long, felt an antipathy for his flawed physique. "That will leave Deirdre in charge of the hydroponics lab—she'll enjoy that. But it sure will be quiet on that deck while we're away."

"Carmen is going too. I know she was unwell, but she's better now than I've ever seen her, and anxious to do outstanding work. I think she can." I agreed, silently.

"Then there's going to be David . . ." I was pleased with that. With both David and me on the mission, the vehicle computers would perform exceptionally.

"And Richard . . ." I liked that too. Although his person is certainly attractive, it's his sense of what is funny which I most enjoy. He has that trick, which I suspect is a gift, of punning with ease and speed on almost any subject. The others groan, but as an appreciator of words, I find this talent irresistible and am reduced to helpless giggles, though of course I conceal that carefully.

"Shirley's going too . . . ." That was not a surprise. Jinjur and Shirley were a smooth-working team of long standing, and Jinjur knows she can rely absolutely on Shirley's integrity and capability as an engineer to keep the exploration spacecraft operating.

"And John as medic. That makes ten." I was a little less pleased with this last selection, particularly when I considered Jinjur's confrontations with him herself! But I shall try to be optimistic about their desire to cooperate. Quickly I tallied up the list.

"Ten? I counted nine . . ."

"Oh, and Arielle. She can pilot the last airplane. She'll like that," she said positively, and I was almost as thrilled as I'd been for myself. It will be so good to see her at the controls of another *Dragonfly*! I understood, now, the radiant smile Arielle had given me as she passed me in the corridor—I had thought it was due to the size of the piece of cake she was carrying.

This morning has been an exciting one. Those of us who have been selected are striving to conceal our elation, and those who are staying aboard *Prometheus* are vocal in their disappointment. Elizabeth, particularly, who's had no training in military obedience to orders, is openly unhappy.

"George, dammit, I really wanted to go on this one!"

George did his best. "I know, Red, I know. Think

I don't want to go too? But we took the choices one by one, and I think we've got a crew which will make the most efficient use of that few months. Don't get too steamed up, old girl. We've still got lots of smaller moons to visit with almost no gravity to cope with, like Zoroaster, Zwingli, and Zeus. We can reach those easily with one of our left-over Ascent Modules, and your asteroid prospecting experience will be invaluable for exploring those bodies. Also, some day we will need to return the Littles back to the rest of themselves on Rocheworld. We'll certainly need your piloting experience then, to fly an Ascent Module down to the zero gravity point between the two lobes, and rendezvous with *Dragonfly Two* with its crew of flouwen and gummies. There's explorations ahead for *all* of us—enough to keep us busy for the rest of our lives!

This statement of the obvious made all of us, drifting near in the hall, feel better. The crew, intelligent, well-trained, and chosen for compatibility years ago, are in no danger of succumbing to envy. Those of us to go are soberly planning our work and preparing for our needs, and those remaining behind are able to put aside their disappointment enough to help prepare the *Beagle* for its voyage of exploration.

I had, already, privately decided what I would most assuredly take with me if I were selected. I suspect we have all done that! Certainly the task of packing our personal belongings aboard the *Beagle* has gone with amazing speed—and it is a curious coincidence that these personal bundles fit precisely and neatly into the compartments on the second of the three compact decks comprising the crew quarters of the *Beagle*. I have just time to make a brief inspection of my own living area before returning to my shift. The next few days are going to be very busy indeed.

* * *

And they have been! Over this last week we have kept up a steady flow of traffic through the docking port. Our errands range from the important—Nels in particular is literally weighing up the amount of supplies he will need to keep us fed, as opposed to the equipment that he wants for his investigations of the surface vegetation—to the trivial—my own return to the row of bunks on the *Beagle* to see if the space there was really as small as it had looked at first! And it was. Although there is plenty of room for all we need, it seems spartan after the roomy luxury of the two-room suites with a private bathroom we enjoy aboard *Prometheus*.

During the initial phases of the mission, while we are setting out the communication satellites and statites, then carefully surveying our landing site from low orbit prior to landing, all ten of us must be bunked on the rocket lander. But since all that time will be in free fall, we do not need horizontal bunks. Instead we have ten vertically oriented sleeping racks, stacked around half the perimeter of the middle crew quarters deck. Once the rocket has landed and the aeroplane has been lowered and is ready to fly, six of the crew will go to live on that vehicle, and the ten small vertical sleeping racks will be rearranged into four roomy horizontal bunks, plus a good-sized sick bay.

On the other side of the small corridor that leads to these racks are two small zero-gee toilets and a zero-gee shower. The shower will get little use during this trip, since the water storage tank in the consumables column has been shortened to make room for the flouwen. The rest of the crew quarters deck has a small galley, and a cozy lounge with a two-meter-diameter viewport on the outer bulkhead and an equally large viewwall on the inner bulkhead.

Of course, just as James looks after our every need on *Prometheus* with the Christmas Bush and its various detachments, Joe and Josephine and their Christmas Branches will make sure we are equally free from any personal caretaking on the *Beagle* and the *Dragonfly*. We shall, however, certainly be in closer contact with each other than any of us are used to.

We shall be busy on the first few orbits mapping our landing region in great detail from every angle, setting out the communications satellites and statites, and only when they are all working satisfactorily will we descend to Zuni. We anticipate no real problems with the commsats, but we need to see how their relative positions are affected with time by the gravity tugs from Zulu and Zouave as they pass by, and the infall of smog and water vapor "wind" from the gaseous toruses that exist around their orbits.

Once on Zuni's surface, we plan to spend our working shifts outdoors, returning to the *Beagle* for meals and sleep. The information we gather throughout the day will all be entered and stored by Joe and James, so we will be able to pursue our tasks independent of each other. This is the way in which we are accustomed to working, but I have long felt it would be more pleasant and productive if we spent more time in serious discussions of our work. We have got in the habit of relating all of our findings and experiments only to James, so that, for instance, while I know of Nels' results in the creation of edible substances by eating them, I haven't any real grasp of how he got to that stage! And, while I could procure the data from James, on that or any other work in progress, it has always seemed to me to be uncomfortably close to reading another's mail, and I notice we all scrupulously avoid it. Living in such close proximity, we relate more intimately with the central computer than with each other, and while it does make for easier harmony, it sometimes seems to be unnatural. However, it may well be that on the surface of Zuni we find some exciting things to share, and being in a sense "away from home," our own enthusiasm will lead to interesting conversations. I hope so!

Our flouwen have no reticence at all about their eagerness to begin the trip. They will spend the orbital survey time in a portion of the tank which runs from the bottom of the docking lock down through the center of the next two decks. This space was originally designated for the storage of replacement air and water, and was designed with plenty of extra capacity. Now we must recalculate our requirements with great accuracy and only take as much as we need. Shirley and the Christmas Bush shortened the length of the high pressure air tank and the low pressure water tank by half, leaving the top half of the column free to hold the flouwen in the ammonia-water mixture they prefer. A glass window now replaces the metal inspection and cleaning port, and we can peer in at our colorful alien comrades as we step off the passway ladder rungs leading from the engineering deck onto the crew deck.

The flouwen have their own waterproof touchscreen connected to Joe, which allows them access to views seen by the Christmas Bush, any of our imps, or any of the lander's outside sensors, so they are not limited in their sensory input. It is cramped quarters for all three flouwen, however, so they take turns floating about the *Beagle* enclosed in their wetsuits, bothering the crew with their continual questions, and only going into their tank to rest and eat. They make the switch from their wetsuits to the tank via a flexible transfer tube Shirley rigged from their tank to the inside of the docking airlock in the center of the upper deck.

The flouwen go into the airlock in their suits, open their zipper, and stick the end of the transfer tube into their bodies. Joe opens an electronically controlled valve in the transfer line, and sucks the flouwen out of their suits and into their rest and relaxation center. The valve closes, and the airlock opens to the outside vacuum for a short time to vent the ammonia fumes away, then closes again. When the flouwen are ready to come out of the tank, the process is reversed, except that the spilled ammonia in the port is vented to the outside after the flouwen has filled up the suit and zipped it closed, but before he enters the portion of the *Beagle* occupied by humans.

In addition to air and water, the mass of food needed for three extra-large and extra-hungry companions is a concern. John's computations of our individual calorie rations have been ruthlessly meticulous. Arielle's needs are much higher than my own, a fact of which I am well aware.

"You're an easy keeper!" was the remark of a horse-breeder I had once loved in Argentina. He'd accompanied the words with a beautiful smile and an affectionate pat, but I'd left the next day.

During our shift, David and I began, with James, our strictest examination and checkout of the computer controlled systems aboard the *Beagle*. While the Christmas Bush surveyed, inch by inch, the exterior and interior of the plane, David and I started with the launch sequence. We were proceeding steadily, when, in almost apologetic tones, James interrupted.

"The Christmas Bush informs me that latch 0079 will not open."

We looked at each other, then at the screens, in dismay. Quickly we drifted upward to examine the faulty latch, which had jammed shut a storage compartment.

"Damn!" said David. "It's not serious, but it didn't show up on my routine scan!"

"Nor on mine," I agreed regretfully. Together we pried open the latch with tools from the in-flight maintenance kit. This compartment is important to have accessible, as it contains the spacesuits needed for outside repair work and the launching of the commsats.

"Now, we've got to get the thing relatched and workable. I'll get Shirley," David decided. This was a good choice; no one is better than she at repairing this sort of thing so that it *stays* repaired. Then James summoned us to another possible problem, this time in one of the landing jets.

"Arielle's the one we want for this," we decided, and once again, we were successful in correcting the problem.

Arielle looked at the outputs of the engineering sensors for the recalcitrant jet, and fired it three times in quick succession, which cleared it beautifully.

"Vapor bubble," she said succinctly, and drifted back to the galley.

Thus our tests and inspection continued, and will do so right up until launch. Every seal, every filter for air and water, every measuring device and evaluating recorder need to be in the perfect condition they were originally, although the lander has hung here unused for nearly fifty years. We must be sure nothing has deteriorated or altered, even so slightly that, as with the latch, no indication of malfunction had registered with James.

At the conclusion of my shift today I was satisfied that every part of the computer system aboard the *Beagle* is in excellent working order. David and I have gone through the sequences, from our launch, through the deployment of the satellites, to our landing on Zuni, and our return to *Prometheus.* Shirley and Arielle have gone through the same procedures, independently, and James has monitored every step.

When I came off duty I was ready for a quiet meal. I elected to have the comfort of a bowl of porridge; perversely, I had become fond of this innocent food when I discovered how it freed me from the nuisance of hunger in a busy day, and a supply of the humble grain was part of my personal stores, periodically renewed by means of a special planting by the hydroponics crew. Along with an equal supply of barley, and the fiery chili with which the Christmas Bush could supply me on demand, my needs were met most fully. I took the bowl along the corridor, and hearing no sound, went into the big lounge area on *Prometheus*. I was surprised to see George there, alone on the big sofa, staring out the three-by-four meter window. The panoramic view was spectacular—Zuni below, Gargantua to one side, and nearly all the moons visible and fully illuminated by Barnard behind us. He glanced quickly at me and smiled as I settled slowly down beside him.

"Well, Reiki! I hope that's one of your special meals you have there—if all continues well, your next may be one of the camping creations aboard the *Beagle*."

"I'll enjoy that," I said sincerely. "Are we as nearly ready as that?"

"Everyone says so except Jinjur," he grinned. "And I expect she'd say so too, if I could get her attention. I really think she has launched herself, and is too many miles away to hear me. I miss her already!"

He returned his gaze to the swirling cloud patterns of Zuni visible through the viewport. I have been so absorbed in getting ready to make this trip, and I know we will be so busy on the trip itself—it felt strange just to sit and stare, with quiet detachment, at our destination. So must early explorers have felt, as their small ships headed close inshore to foreign lands. Gradually most of the rest of the crew joined us, content to share in the silence.

It was late when George slowly rose, stretched, and said in his most ponderous tones, "Explorers of Zuni, I sincerely trust you will follow the magnificent precedent, set so long ago by the dauntless explorer Joshua Slocum, after he waded ashore on the small uncharted island he discovered off the coast of South America . . ."

We sat, stunned, searching our memories. Richard said, slowly, "Wait. Didn't he put up a sign . . . ?"

"Yes," said George firmly. "Keep Off The Grass!"

It was time to go to bed.

# LANDING

The launch this morning of the *Beagle* from its docking berth on *Prometheus* went like the beautifully planned exercise it was. With Shirley and Cinnamon in the pilot and copilot harnesses, Jinjur and Carmen at the command and communication consoles, all the rest of us firmly strapped into our sleeping racks waved cheerfully at the monitoring cameras as we watched the hull of *Prometheus* slowly slide away on the individual viewscreens built into the Sound-Bar doors of our compact cabins. Our leisurely glide out to an equatorial orbit where we are to deploy the first commsat has been an entrancing panorama of the moons. As the *Beagle* moves among the moons, and they continue their various orbits, the view is constantly changing for us. First Zouave, then Zuni, then Zulu move into a position where Barnard's light illuminates the hemisphere facing us. Using the large telescope mounted on the topside of the *Beagle*, we can spot various features in the landscapes of each. There is a tall mountain rising up out of the everpresent smog, near the north pole of Zouave, as sharp and pure of line as Mt. Fuji, and although I have never been homesick, it seemed to blur for an instant in my sight. And there is what appears to be a lake on Zulu that is so perfectly triangular we all chuckled—it looks as though it has been carefully dug!

We're near the first commsat deployment site now, and John and Carmen have lifted an orbiter from its temporary berth on the engineering deck, taken it through the airlock, and tossed it gently into space. I can hear their terse comments, through my own imp, and visualize what's happening as they talk to the robot.

"OK, *Russell*, you're on your own now," came Carmen's voice. "You can start your deployment sequence."

"Right," came the distinctive, yet mechanical voice of the commsat. "My solar array is going out. Moving . . . moving . . . at full extension . . . now."

"Looks good to me," said John.

"High-gain antenna, unlatched," said *Russell*. "Command to track back and forth . . . done. Are my gimbals working? My sensors say so."

"Very smooth," replied Carmen. "But my imp reports that James says the communication with *Prometheus* is intermittent."

"Try again," suggested John. "Bring it back. May be a procedural error."

"OK," said *Russell*. "Out again. Up. Command."

"Still intermittent," reported Carmen. "Try B transponder."

"Switching to B transponder," said *Russell*.

"James says it's perfect," said Carmen. "Try A transponder."

"Intermittent again," reported Carmen. "An electronics failure in A. Let's go with B."

"Right," said *Russell*. "B transponder commanded. After I get into position, while B keeps up the link, I'll use my motile to see if I can correct A."

* * *

It's fascinating to listen in, and the level voices continue as the deployment is completed, with the communications satellite sliding as smoothly into the planned orbit as if there was an invisible slot waiting to receive it.

The next commsat, *Scott*, had no trouble with its communicating transponders, but one of the placing thrusters was just sufficiently stronger than the other to produce a torquing moment on the satellite. The satellites must of course be positioned in exact station-keeping cycles, to ensure communications coverage from any point on Zuni. I listened intently as *Scott* began with an east burn of eight minutes six seconds, producing a delta-V of seven meters a second and reducing the drift rate from five degrees per day to two point nine degrees per day. Then John performed an inclination correction maneuver using the north thruster—I had worked carefully on that part of the satellite program myself, and was pleased when the maneuver, nearly twelve minutes in length, produced the correct delta-V of fifteen meters per second. The drift rate was reduced again, and the final station acquisition thrust positioned the satellite exactly where the station-keeping cycle began, working perfectly. Some time later, we left the third and last commsat, *William*, with the good feeling of having three securely working orbiters in perfect position, 120 degrees apart, in an exact equatorial orbit. These commsats would allow communication from almost any part of Zuni's globe, except for the polar regions. To supply communications coverage to those points, we needed spacecraft which would sit in space over the polar regions and neither rise, fall, nor orbit—not the usual satellite, but a statite—a stationary spacecraft.

Carmen and John took the first of the statites through the airlock and pushed it out. It looked like a large metallic hockey puck, two meters in diameter and one meter thick—just the right size to fit through the airlock door.

"Wait until you get a good distance away from the *Beagle* before you start sail deployment, *Bob*," Carmen said.

"I am programmed to orient my axis toward you, so you can watch deployment," said *Bob*, as gyros whirled inside the spacecraft body and slowly turned the base of the satellite toward the open airlock door containing the two spacesuited humans. "Deployment commencing." Slowly, four collapsible booms started to unfurl from the central package, drawing with them a thin wisp of finely perforated aluminum foil. Although the film was highly reflective, it was so thin it was almost transparent, for I could see the bright reddish globe of distant Mars-like Zapotec shining right through it.

"Looks good," said John, surveying the emerging acres of lightsail for tears or wrinkles.

"Deployment completed," said *Bob* an hour later. "No indication of any malfunctions." The statite, now being pushed to higher and higher speeds by the light pressure of the photons from Barnard, started to drift away from the heavier rocket lander.

"Perfect!" said Carmen. "You look very pretty all lit up like that—and so big. Like a butterfly coming out of a cocoon."

"Now that you've got wings, you can fly to your position over the north pole," said John. "Check in with James when you get there."

"Will comply," radioed *Bob*. Then the voice channel went dead as the statite moved off to a position over the north polar region of Zuni where the light pressure on the sail from Barnard would exactly counterbalance the gravity pull from Zuni. The sail would also adjust in effective size and angle to compensate for the smaller gravity tugs from the other moons.

The process was then repeated for the second statite, *Arthur*, whose designated position was over the south pole of Zuni. Now, with two statites to cover the poles, and three orbiters to cover the equatorial regions, we would be in constant communication with *Prometheus* no matter where we traveled on the multicolored globe of Zuni in the *Dragonfly* VTOL aeroplane.

With our communications network set up, the next task before the actual landing is a complete, detailed survey of the landing area to make sure there are no surprises. We have excellent maps and images of St. Vincent island and Crater Lagoon taken by the science orbiter *Bruce* and Linda's large telescope on *Prometheus*, but the resolution was not as good as it should be, so Shirley put the *Beagle* into a elliptical orbit with its perigee right over Crater Lagoon, and a period almost exactly equal to Zuni's sidereal rotation period. By making slight orbital adjustments at apogee, she expertly shifted our time of arrival over the lagoon from early in the morning on the first day, to late in the afternoon on the fifth day. The different illumination and shadows from images taken at different times of the day will help in interpreting the scene and allow an estimation of the height of the various topographic features. During the low level flyovers of the landing site, most of us stay in the lounge, looking out the large viewport built into the hull of the lander. The viewport had been installed just for this purpose—to allow the crew to look out at the strange worlds to be found around Barnard. During these last hours, I welcomed my own time at the science console, monitoring the various instruments imaging the electromagnetic spectrum; the work helped to dissipate the suspense that is gradually building. I could see both Richard and David were also eager to take their stint in turn, and the pilots and copilots were equally quick to work. We are all striving to be accurate as we complete the detailed survey of our landing site and transmit all of the information to James, but we are eager to land!

Finally, came the electric words from Joe: "General announcement imminent!"

There was a brief pause, as Joe interrogated the personal imps to make sure everyone was listening, and then Shirley's voice, a little tense, warned: "This time around we're not going to fly by! Prepare for gees in fifteen minutes!"

"OK!" came Jinjur's voice. "Everybody who doesn't have a landing assignment get into your sleeping racks."

With alacrity, we moved to restore all the items drifting freely about the cabins, and to pack away the food trays. Arielle carefully wrapped a large sandwich in film and stuffed it into her pocket, no doubt to sustain her during the long moments of landing! I made sure the galley surfaces were clear, and followed her to the row of vertical sleeping racks. We strapped ourselves in snugly, and settled down for the long-awaited show on the viewscreens in the Sound-Bar doors. Through the imp, I can hear Shirley and Cinnamon, hanging in their stand-up harnesses, talking back and forth to each other as they prepare to land the ship. Jinjur and Carmen, strapped into their console seats, are talking quietly, surveying the weather map being transmitted down from Prometheus.

"There's a weather front approaching," says Carmen.

"That's nothing new on this planet," Shirley replies. "We're lucky we don't have to come down through cloud cover. Switch it through to the bottom left of my display, Cinnamon." I switched my viewscreen to the same map. The front is a large one, with nothing but thick clouds behind it stretching beyond the curve of the horizon. If we don't make a landing now, we won't be able to see the site again for many days.

"What time will that front get to the landing site, Joe?" says Shirley.

"About a half-hour after our scheduled landing," replies the computer.

"Good enough," says Shirley. "Down we go!"

The main engines are roaring into life, slowing the massive lander down, and letting it fall toward the approaching distant island. Someone groans as the unaccustomed tug of gravity begins.

"That was only a half gee," says Shirley. "We'll hit three gees before reentry. Got to get rid of those excess vees somehow."

As the heaviness pulls down on my body, I am grateful we won't have full Earth's gravity on this expedition! Although I know we will soon adjust to our increased weight, and indeed find it useful, the first reaction to it is always this dreary sensation of the slow drag one feels in dreams, when running becomes such an effort.

We are now approaching our chosen site on Zuni! As we come down closer and closer to the surface of the lagoon, we can see the waters begin to ripple outward from the force of our descending jets. Nels is trying to catch a glimpse of aquatic life, while I have my own viewscreen focussed on a view of the strange shoreline taken through one of the secondary monitor cameras outside the ship. Through the walls I can hear the flouwen crooning their pleasure at the sight on their viewscreen of the sliding seas beneath us. The variable and intense deceleration forces of landing have now been replaced with a constant and pleasant gravity force, and I readjust my body in its harness. As we hover here, balanced on our landing rockets, we can see the storm front we have been observing, moving slowly toward us. Shirley will now slide the *Beagle* sideways on its jets, over the water toward the beach, then onto the top of the . . .

My, what a peculiar noise!

We're falling!

I think I must still be in shock. I think we all are. I don't know how I look, but the faces around me are blank and empty as we slump here on the shore, heavy rain pelting down on us from thick gray clouds. In a split second, our lives have been totally changed—for we are vulnerable now—stranded—all those lost and frightening words—and, from being so careful to protect this world from us, and ourselves from this world, now we are exposed to it and must wrest survival from it, for as long as it takes.

Perhaps if I try to recall the events of the last—how long has it been? An hour? Two? It's unbelievable that I can't even determine that! Oh! It has just occurred to me, with a relief out of all proportion to its importance, that my recorder contains an accurate chronometer, and I see that it has been three hours and thirteen minutes since our disaster. I think it is vital that I keep as accurate and rational a record as I can. It may be helpful to us at some future time, and it will certainly help me to feel, in some small way, detached from my helplessness. And, in the course of an unpredictable future, my record may be important in establishing what actually caused the accident.

There had been a whistling roar, followed by a deafening explosion and the crash of the lander. All I remember is the intense noise, and the dizzy feeling of whirling and falling, helplessly, down and down, then a crushing blow from the wall of my bunk as the lander struck the water. When my vision cleared, the only thing lighting the close quarters of my bunk was an emergency light illuminating the latch for the door.

My viewscreen was dead, and so was my imp. It was still in its place, holding today's piece of lace around my collar, and its colorful lights were still shining, running on its internal batteries, but it was silent, as dead as the central computer, Joe. I stared at it for a second, sick with horror at my loss. I don't remember unbuckling my straps, but I suppose sheer instinct guided us all to free ourselves and make our frantic way down the corridor to the passway ladder that leads to the two docking ports.

One look down the passway to the engineering deck below showed there was no escape in that direction. Water was rushing in through the broken airlock windows and rising rapidly up the passway. The massive viewport in the nearby lounge was miraculously unbroken, but there was a line across the middle which indicated the division between water and air—and the line was rising rapidly up the window as air escaped and the lander continued to sink. We scrambled up the passway to the docking port on the top deck.

When I got there, I could see Shirley in the opened airlock, struggling with the latch to the outer door, while Cinnamon was still trying to get untangled from her copilot's harness. I knew instantly why Shirley was having problems with the airlock door. Having been designed for safety, it wouldn't open until the inner door was latched and secured. If we had to go through the complete airlock cycle each time, only a few people could make it out the exit before the lander sank. I went to the pilot's touchscreen. It was operating on emergency power and was obviously in an emergency backup mode, since the normal touchscreen display had been replaced by an archaic operating system prompt. Using the keyboard, I tried to raise Joe—there was no response. Dredging up seldom used commands from my own memory, I gained access to the airlock control subroutine, and programmed with frantic speed around the safety block. By now, most of the crew had made it to the top deck. The water was rising up the passway and was ankle deep on the sloping floor. I finished the changes, and hoping that I had not inserted a bug, restarted the program.

"I *got* it!" yelled Shirley. "It finally worked!" Although the door was now unlatched, she still had to struggle to force it open because of the water pressure outside.

The lights were now dimming as the salt water got to the emergency power supply—that was horrible, and I was becoming terrified! Richard moved forward into the airlock next to Shirley and I saw his shoulders bulge as he added his strength to hers, and the outer airlock door opened. Water came pouring in over the sill and we fell back, but Jinjur began shouting then. Even in my fear I could hear the anger she was putting into her commands, to make us move and obey. Richard and Shirley forced their way out through the hatch, and then clung to the outside, reaching arms back through to grab us in turn and tug us out into the water. Galvanized by Jinjur's furious yells, I stumbled forward with the others and was seized and pulled outward, somehow managing to move with a large bubble of air attempting to escape upward through the incoming water.

An awful sensation—the shock of being completely immersed! It has been forty years since I last swam—the water roared in my ears, and filled my mouth, and stung my eyes, and all I wanted to do was escape from it! I was not consciously swimming, but was kicking frantically. It must have been only seconds before we were all bobbing on the surface, staring around at each other. The air smelled peculiar, and the water tasted odd—everything was as strange as if we'd just been born. I filled my lungs with the atmosphere, desperately thankful that it did not hurt to do so. I could hear Jinjur counting aloud, and her gasp of relief as she breathed, "Ten!"

Then Richard swore, and dove straight down into that alien water. Shirley said, "The flouwen!" and dove after him. I followed instantly—I was a strong swimmer when young, and the urgency of freeing the flouwen sped me down into the dark fluid. But then I could go no further, and I gave up, exhausted, to float to the surface again. Richard and Shirley were already there, gasping in the strange air, obviously filling their lungs preparatory to diving again. Jinjur started to bark an order, but cut it short. I think it was then that we began to realize something of the enormity of what had happened to us, and that if the air or water is deadly to us there is nothing we can do about it. I felt suddenly very small and alone, as I realized my imp was useless, and all communication with James had stopped. I grabbed at my pocket then, and realized with a surge of relief that my precious recorder was intact, firmly buttoned in, and waterproof.

"It's sinking! It just keeps going slowly down. . . ." gasped Shirley. Grimly, Richard continued to pull air into his lungs.

Jinjur commanded: "No! I forbid you to go down again, Richard!" I'm sure we all felt the same sudden dismay. Richard is the strongest among us—if he couldn't get to the flouwen, who could? I saw in Jinjur's face that realization also, and aloud we began to think, to some purpose.

"All they need is an opening. . . ."

"But the valve to the transfer tube is electronically controlled!"

"Break the porthole glass?"

Shirley pulled her Swiss Army Mech-All knife from its pouch on her belt, made an adjustment to it, and holding up the now pointed end with a sparkling tip, spoke fiercely. "A diamond scribe. Now if I can get *down* there!"

Silently, Richard put out his hand. With a sound like a sob, Shirley smacked her precious tool into his palm. "Scribe a big triangle, then punch one corner with the point." We watched in hope and dread as he sucked one last breath, tucked the scribe into a belt pouch and dove, deep and strong, out of sight.

The next minutes were awful. Shirley dove again and came back up exhausted. Arielle was splashing awkwardly, and Carmen was sobbing. I know I was holding my own breath, and trying to see beneath the surface, and diving down to see further, and babbling silent pleas, for what seemed like hours. Suddenly I saw a dark shape below me, rising rapidly and surrounded by blobs of color.

Shirley and I plunged to them. We grabbed Richard, who was dreadfully limp, and hauled him to the surface. His eyes were closed and he was a ghastly color. Together, supporting him between us, we all swam hard for the shore. The instant Nels felt the shelving land beneath his long legs he grabbed Richard about the middle, hauled him onto solid land, and began the rough but efficient resuscitation treatment. We all straggled dripping up the beach and watched anxiously as John bent over Richard, pumping air into the half-drowned body. The desperate minutes dragged on, and Nels took over the rhythmic contractions, as John worked grimly on Richard's head. My fear mounted until I was ready to scream, and then, suddenly, I heard two wonderful sounds—air whistling into Richard's lungs as his ribs lifted of their own accord, and, out in the lagoon, a joyful singing. I slumped, exhausted, onto the sand.

We sat there for some time, each of us trying to come to a comprehension of our situation. As Richard's breathing eased, his color improved, and finally his eyes opened and he sat up.

"I kicked in the glass," he said hoarsely. "The scribe worked, but the glass wouldn't give to pounding. So I grabbed the passway rungs on each side and kicked as hard as I could before passing out."

Obviously, the flouwen, once free, and back in their own element, were able to rescue their rescuer. Richards eyes wandered down to his fist, still spasmodically clenched. He opened it, and we stared at Shirley's Mech-All lying in his palm. Silently, he held it out to her. Was that little tool and my recorder all the technology we had left to us? After all the years of James' silent caring for every need, usually before we even noticed it, were we any longer capable of living on our own?

Jinjur stood up then, slowly and carefully drawing herself fully erect, almost visibly taking charge of herself and reasserting her command. Her heels moved together, disregarding the shifting sand, and her voice snapped briskly. "We're all here, and we're going to survive, blast it!" she said, reasserting her command. "Were any of you injured?"

In some surprise, we hastily surveyed ourselves, and found no physical mishaps beyond a few rising bruises. "Right! Then the first thing we'd better find is fresh water—we're going to have to take a chance on it, I'm afraid, because the salt in that ocean . . ." She broke off, coughing. I realized suddenly that my own throat was raw and sorely burning, and instantly I was horribly thirsty. Without a word I scrambled to my feet and hurried up the beach, hunting for one of the springs our landers had indicated were numerous in this location. Behind me I could hear the others, spread out among the rocks and various likely-looking hollows. Even at the time it seemed so strange—not to have water always available, to have to search for it so desperately, knowing that when I found it, not only was I unable to verify its purity, I hadn't even a container from which to drink!

David's cracked voice suddenly rasped "Here!", and I made my way to him at an eager trot. Clear water bubbled generously out of a little cleft in the rocks here, and ran off into the sand below. We gathered to hold our cupped palms under the flow, and drank avidly. It tasted wonderful! I sincerely hoped it was clean enough, and drank again and again. When that first fiery thirst was assuaged, I helped the others arrange a series of rocks with natural declivities in them to form a small basin. It filled quickly, and certainly looked clear and wholesome. In fact, it looked beautiful, and I sat down abruptly to look at it, and rest. Gradually the others did the same, and we encircled the little pool, weary and quiet. The rocks were heavy, and irregularly shaped—my palms tingled with the first abrasions they had known in years, handling something that was not carefully shaped for their grip. Nor was my imp tending to the soreness with instant attention and the proper medication.

The shock began to wear off, I suppose, and I was left with a feeling of such loneliness and despair as I had never known. The people around me seemed like strangers, as helpless as I was to do anything about our bleak desolation. I looked down at my imp, still entangled in the bit of lace, now motionless and stiff, and lacking the colorful laser lights that normally glittered from its extremities. My robotic companion was dead. Now, without James and the imps, without supplies, without even any means of obtaining supplies, we were as shipwrecked as any mariner has ever been. We were even denied the sight of our possible salvation, for shortly after we had crashed, the storm front had come through and a drifting mist of rain had started. *Prometheus,* overhead, was now hidden behind a thick pall of dark gray storm clouds. I huddled into misery within myself. I had nothing—could do nothing—and was helpless and frightened and weak and alone.

Suddenly, I felt a hand—Cinnamon's strong brown hand had closed over mine. It was startling—the warmth of another life, not so different from my own—gripped me. Instinctively I tightened my grip on her hand, and reached out to Nels, next to me. I grasped the limp hand on his knee, and he turned, as startled as I had been, to stare at me. Then he grinned, and reached out his other hand, to Shirley. The warm handclasp spread.

Jinjur had not observed this sudden, silly linking—she was sitting slumped, with her head resting on her propped hands—and I saw with sudden compassion how small she really is. She looked up, astonished, at the touch of the hands on either side of her. Then she straightened, smiled, and put out her own hands. The whole foolish group of us was joined, embarrassed, but more alive and hopeful than we had yet been.

Then we coughed, or muttered something, and dropped hands. I realized then, with a little shock, that we are all *shy*! How absurd . . . we've known each other for years! But we have lived solitary lives, for all our proximity. With the imps to take care of our every personal need, and our own private apartments to escape to, we have developed very little intimacy. Now, abruptly, we are *dependent* on each other, and none of us know exactly how to handle that.

In addition to the realization, I was becoming aware of an increasing need of my own. Cinnamon had been glancing sharply at me, and now began to say something, but stopped. It is best to begin as you mean to go on! That archaic Victorian injunction floated into my mind, and I spoke into the silence, calmly but definitely.

"Personal hygiene is a matter which I feel merits our attention almost immediately, if you don't mind. Shall we arbitrarily designate a latrine area, and some arrangement for privacy there? I should like to suggest a place quite near the shoreline, in the absence of anything I have seen suitable for tissue."

The practical question broke the emotional moment with some speed, but as I say, I was becoming rather uncomfortable. After a moment's consideration, Nels asked, "Why not just use the sea itself?"

"Why not, indeed?" said Shirley. I was momentarily surprised—Shirley was always the most rigid among us about contaminating an alien surface, and about the risk of being contaminated. "I did notice, as we landed, the shoreline outside the entrance to this lagoon. It slopes away from the point, and there are long beaches along the northern side."

"Right!" said Jinjur briskly, getting to her feet with renewed vigor. "But we'll go together, this first time. Safety in numbers, I hope!"

We marched up the beach and over the point of the lagoon, a pathetic gaggle of humans heading for a comfort station. We found the long beach ideal for this humble purpose; plenty of space to spread out along it for sufficient privacy, even for me, and I waded desperately into the warm salt water as deep as I wanted . . . Oddly I had to remain there for some time—the habits of civilization are not easy to discard, even when the need is imperative!—but finally we were all back on shore, and began trudging back to the little spring.

"What happened to the flouwen?" Richard's sudden anxiety startled us.

"That's right, you were still unconscious," remembered Nels. "We heard them—at least one of them—singing out there, just as you began to get your breath back."

"Singing? What was there to sing about?" said Richard indignantly.

"Well," snapped Cinnamon, "They were free, thanks to you! I imagine it felt pretty good to be out of that little tank, down there in the dark!" It was good to hear the feeling in her voice—a return to a more normal state for at least one of our numbed minds.

"We'll get in contact with them later," Jinjur stated. "First, let's see just what we've got among us."

On a flat rock, near the spring, we put our pitifully few possessions. David and Arielle found some food in their pockets, but it had been ruined by the salt water. Shirley's Mech-All knife and my recorder were still in good shape. Shirley had lost her Permalite and it was no doubt at the bottom of the lagoon along with the lander. Cinnamon produced a small carving of a little animal, in ivory. She said it was her good-luck piece, a statement that was greeted with silence. Nels had, of all archaic things, a pencil—he explained that he liked to draw, a fact which none of us had known before. There was nothing else. From having all technology at our disposal, we were now confronted with two small tools. Shirley spread her strong hands on the rock, and gazed at them in dismay.

"If only we'd worn our suits!" she mourned. "We'd have a lot more to work with . . . like a radio to contact *Prometheus* with!" That was a fact—even the wiring in them might have been usable. But long ago it had been determined that spacesuits were more a hazard than a help to pilots attempting to land on a strange planet. Our clothes are in good shape—due to the constant ministrations of James and the drowned imps, but hardly suitable for an alien environment. One fortunate circumstance is that we are all shod in the light-weight but tough slipper-stockings we wore around the ship when in free-fall, so we can walk without difficulty.

Jinjur spoke with her customary authority. "All right, troops. We're all sound and strong, and we have water that so far seems harmless. We must continue to survive, and we must find some way to contact *Prometheus*."

The sound of the familiar name made us all look skyward, trying to spot the light, if not the shape, of our homeship. The cloud cover had thickened considerably, and there was no sign of the ship.

"Too far away." Arielle's statement was harsh.

"The quicker we can adjust to having nothing, the faster we can begin to solve the problem," said Cinnamon. "At least I hope so! I keep mentally expecting my imp to do things for me!"

"I wonder what the possibilities are for retrieving something—anything!—from the lander," said David.

"If the damn thing stops going down, I might be able to dive to it when I'm rested," said Richard.

"I was thinking more of enlisting the flouwen's assistance," said David. "D'you think there's any way we can get across to them what we want? It's pretty basic."

"How can we talk to them at all?" Shirley wailed with fresh dismay. "Our imps, the translator program, all the computers are gone along with the lander!"

John cleared his throat. "I don't like to be even more discouraging, but it's possible they've left the area for good. Without the ship and its equipment, they may feel they're on their own."

This chilling thought was countered by Carmen. "I don't believe that," she said firmly. "If nothing else, simple curiosity will bring them near fairly soon!"

The talk went on, not smoothly, but brief phrases uttered as the speaker felt compelled. Struggling to comprehend this desperate situation, searching for some sign of hope, feeling physically tired, and uncomfortable, and wet—and having to articulate our thoughts—I know I felt exhausted by the efforts I was making. And yet we kept on talking. It was a new shock, after an hour or so, when there came from the sea a loud and eerie ululation. We went to the edge of the water, and could see, well enough, the familiar forms of our alien friends, floating in the shallows.

"I don't even know how to begin!" said Cinnamon grimly. "If I wave, will they 'see' that?"

"I'm going to try talking to them," said Richard, and suited action to word with a roaring bellow of sound. "HELLO THERE!"

The keening stopped, and I was astounded to hear a strange voice—one I'd never heard before, but clear and sharp. Familiar as I had been with the computer-generated translation of the flouwen's "speech," I listened to this new sound in shocked amazement.

"Why you shout?"

"I understood that!" breathed Cinnamon.

How long had the flouwen been quietly absorbing our words on their own initiative, and how had they managed to duplicate our speech? This was an exciting development, and completely unforeseen!

"Can you hear and understand us?" called Jinjur, slowly and loudly.

"Yes," said a different voice, somewhat huskier than the first. "Like Little Red say, if talking sticks not work, we can talk human."

"Could you do this before?" asked Shirley. "We never knew! Why didn't you say you could do this?"

The third voice was much lower than the other two. "We think you prefer talking sticks. We not talk human good."

A spontaneous cheer broke from us all.

"You talk fine!" shouted Arielle encouragingly, and I agreed, heartily. The grammar can come later, if at all; the important thing is to establish comfortable and open conversations with the flouwen, who are so much at home here. They can be a very real aid to our survival, that is obvious. Not only can they retrieve vital objects from our crashed lander, they can help us procure information about the life on this planet that will keep us from harm. A powerful surge of joy swept through us all. Here was real hope! Our former condescension to the aliens was instantly transformed into appreciation—and I, at least, no longer felt quite so alone.

We moved into the ripples. Richard said warmly, "I owe my life to you, friends. Thank you." Little Red came near his friend to speak. "You let us out of tank. Hard work for you. You swim down to us! That surprise us!"

"We thought we had these creatures analyzed," said John softly. "But it didn't even occur to us that they were intelligent enough to learn to copy our speech. I wonder how much else there is to learn about them, and the rest of this planet, that is going to seem painfully obvious when we find it out?"

Shirley was full of questions, and she and Jinjur kept up a steady flow, "Is the water going to suit you? Is there food here for you? What is the lander doing, still sinking? Can you get back through the airlock? Can you bring things up? How deep . . ."

Little Purple answered patiently. "Water okay. Needs something—(the next word was unintelligible to us).

"Ammonia, I'll bet," muttered John.

"Plenty food here, different, but okay."

"GOOD!" said Little Red.

"Little Red lucky, found (another unintelligible word)" explained Little White. Obviously we have much to learn about each other's languages still!

"Is the lander still going down?" repeated Jinjur,

"Yes. Not fast now. It slide down hill. Long way to bottom." The tone was unconcerned, but the words are bad news for us. With dismay I recalled that our exploratory robot *Bubble* had been unable to reach the bottom of this particular lagoon, and we had selected it for that reason, ironically, as being the landing area where we would do the least damage to the environment.

I had a suggestion. "Can you show us, here on the top of the water, how far down the lander is?" A brief touch, one to the other, and Little Red sped off to one side, with Little White going in the opposite direction. At an appalling distance from each other, they sang out:

"Here!"

"To here!"

About half the width of the lagoon, or about 200 meters, straight down.

Urgently, Cinnamon, Richard, and Carmen began to try to describe to the flouwen the things they thought most important to retrieve, if possible.

"Anything that's loose and floating," said Shirley.

"Anything you can *get* loose!" added Jinjur.

"Anything you can break off . . ." Richard was going on to suggest more destruction, I suspect, but John stopped him.

"Wait. If they just go smashing around down there they may damage something we can eventually recover. It's not as though they are using our judgement—at least, I don't *think* so!" I believe it's the first time I have ever heard self-doubt from John!

As the others continued to offer suggestions for likely places to search and useful objects to bring up, I listened with little to add—these people all know their work so well!—but I did interject, whenever possible, a very sincere "Please!" Perhaps the word was alien to the flouwen now, but I was determined they should learn it happily. At length, armed with instructions, the flouwen sank from sight and we have been trying to relax, while waiting.

"I'll be glad of anything they can bring us," sighed Jinjur, "But if I had any say at all about it, I'd want some way to link back to Prometheus first of all. What I'd give to hear that dry voice of James's!"

There seems to be no answer to that. None of us has any say in the matter at all. It's starting to rain again, steadily. Fortunately, it's warm rain, but we seem to have been wet for all of our time here.

The flouwen returned rather more quickly than we expected, struggling with our badly crumpled food locker between them, and bearing disquieting news. The extremely high water pressure at the bottom of the deep lagoon has crushed most of the equipment, including the spacesuit backpacks, which were designed to withstand vacuum, not high pressure. With salt water all through them, the computers, radios, and power supplies are damaged beyond repair.

Nels inspected the food locker. "That's the supply of special frozen food that was to last us for the duration," he said quietly. "The rest of our supplies were freeze-dried items, no doubt saturated with salt water now."

"Well, let's haul this out and use what we can," said David briskly. "If we can consume it before it spoils, we'll get some good out of it." Nels and Richard tugged the thing out of the water and up the shore. There's no way we can even use the chest for much else, unless we can get some more tools.

Little Purple was obviously pleased with the small additional find he'd procured. "Stuff for helping when needed!" was his very creditable translation of the *Beagle's* emergency medical bag. It is damaged, but the vials of emergency pain-killers and antibiotics are intact.

Shirley was pacing up and down the beach, finally stopping to face Jinjur. "If the flouwen help me, I can get down there!" she said intensely. "And when I'm there, I know I can get into the *Dragonfly* and activate Josephine. With her help we can make a real try at separating the aerospaceplane from the lander. There's bound to be pockets of air for me to breathe long enough to do that, and you realize if we can get the *Dragonfly* up here, we can use its engines and rockets to get off this moon and back to . . ."

"No, Shirley." It was John who said it. "*Dragonfly* is at least two hundred meters down! Even if the flouwen sped you there and back as fast as they can go, the pressure would cave in your chest and kill you before you reached the lander—and the bends would catch you if you tried to come back up. It's just not humanly possible to get down there!"

"*Dragonfly* is thing with wings like Pretty-Smell that fly through the nothing?" Little White queried, having flown in *Dragonfly Two* back on Rocheworld.

"Yes!" said Arielle eagerly. "Is it OK?"

"No." The flat negative was chilling. "Tail broken. Not swim in nothing anymore. Warm though," he added thoughtfully. Arielle gave a single, heartbroken sob, and David reached for her.

Shirley groaned. "Dormant, that's what it is," she said. "We had the system powered down for the landing. If the flouwen can detect warmth, it's because Josephine is keeping the nuclear reactor at maintenance power level. But with a broken tail, that means part of the radiator system is gone and we'll never be able to run the nuclear reactor at operational power levels. From a technology point of view, *Dragonfly* is as far out of reach as *Prometheus*."

Involuntarily I looked up again. The sky was heavy with gray cloud, and only through occasional breaks could I see through to even more cloud, moving swiftly. No chance for the watchers overhead to send anything to us, and no way for us to signal them.

After a brief conference, we have decided to obtain

as much from the lander as the flouwen are willing to bring us, and then rest. Jinjur stepped to the shore to issue orders, and I moved quickly up beside her. She listed aloud the special things to look for—containers, tools, food, bedding from the sleeping racks, and I continued to interject my softening words, changing the orders to requests. When she finished, she stared at me in exasperation. "D'you really think this is the time and place for manners, Reiki?"

"Never more so," I replied firmly. "And it's one of the few things we have left, isn't it?"

We are settled for the night, and I have the first watch. The flouwen worked hard, bless them, and so did we all. Some of the items retrieved from the sinking lander had never seemed important to us before; Shirley pounced with a whoop of delight on her cutter-pliers, and set them out on a rock under a leaf to dry. Most of the items we carried up the beach, out of reach of the tide, and piled them in heaps under the shelter of the line of straggly trees. This is where we have decided to sleep tonight. I had feared it would be sodden, but Nels made a happy discovery.

"See these thick leaves? Of course I've no idea what the plant is, but look at the ground around the base of the trunk. It's bone-dry sand! It looks like the big leaves absorb every bit of water that hits them!"

"How curious!" said Cinnamon. "Look, even the bottoms of the leaves are dry! It's as though the water is all taken into the plant itself."

"Perhaps the water also provides food for the plant?" Carmen speculated. "I don't know much about plants, but those clouds of smoggy atmosphere we saw on the images of the leading hemisphere could have been full of elements the plants use."

"I think that's a real possibility," Nels agreed.

"Perhaps the rain is like food and drink to the plant, so none of it is allowed to go to waste."

The rain continued, steady but not hard, as we worked on.

Cinnamon and Carmen took special care to set out, in an open area, what few objects of salvage were capable of holding rainwater. John has impressed upon us the necessity of boiling our drinking water as soon as we can find a way to do so, although none of us have complained so far of any discomfort resulting from the spring water we have consumed. It was another strange thing, in a day of strange things, to hear Jinjur's order: "If anyone feels sick in any way, I need to know immediately!" I'm sure everyone's first thought was my own: "What business is it of yours?", followed by the much more humble, "Of course." The private monitoring of our physical well-being by James through the imps is now gone, and for our mutual well-being it is now essential that we share our concerns. Such interdependency is going to come very hard to me—I hope very much that I continue to stay healthy, not least because I find it so intolerable to complain aloud!

We had begun by seizing the retrieved articles haphazardly, and stowing them just above the water. I don't recall just when a sort of system crept in. Nels and Richard, standing waist-deep, collected the flotsam from the flouwen, and described it, and one of what was becoming a fairly efficient bucket brigade bore the object along to someone who put it in a more reasonable place, announcing, tersely, where it was. So, after a time, our drenched belongings were more or less arranged, and all of us knew the order. It was dreary, tedious work, and no one enjoyed it less than I, but, in a way, it was satisfying to take from one pair of hands, and pass along to another, yet one more precious remnant of our vanished life.

Throughout our labors, we noted occasionally and spoke of some small creatures, about the size of housecats but looking like nothing on earth, who scuttled out from the bushes long enough to survey us, apparently, and then disappeared. They never came close enough for us to see any details of their structure, but they are a not unpleasant shade of blue-green, and vaguely fuzzy in appearance. The most singular thing—literally!—that we have been able to detect, is that they seem to have just one eye! It is so startling that it gets our attention for the brief glimpse we have of them, and then they are gone.

After some time, as we worked, the rain began to feel cool, in contrast to the warmth of the sea. I was more tired than I have been in years, and began to think dreamily of just floating in the warm water. Fortunately, Jinjur either spotting our increasing fatigue or sharing it, called a halt.

"Little Red! Little White! Little Purple! This is Jinjur. We're going to rest a while. Stay together, don't go far, and don't try anything new until I tell you!"

Silence from the water. Then, "You tell *us* . . . ?" The flouwen's voice sounded surprised. Throughout the months of computer-translated communication, such niceties as mutual respect had been automatically dealt with by the translation program. I had believed, as had Jinjur, that the flouwen had never been able to understand Jinjur's somewhat flamboyant methods of command. Now, in direct communication with the aliens for the first time, weary and worried, she instinctively reverted to early training. There was an echo of boot-camp sergeant in Jinjur's parade-ground bellow: "That's an order!"

I waited, aghast, to hear how our only allies would respond to this arrogance. It was a tremendous relief to hear, out of the rainy dark, only a soft, three-fold shuddering splutter—the flouwen equivalent of a giggle. And to see Jinjur smack herself, smartly, on her own forehead, and turn away.

Wearily, we humans stumbled up the beach one last time. We drank from the little basin again and picked up something from one of the salvaged food lockers. The cold food was unappetizing and tasteless, but we ate whatever it was hungrily, while the rain rinsed the salt from our drenched bodies. By the time we had collected our own choices of sodden bedding or springy tufts and leaves for pillow or cover, and hollowed our selection of sand into comfortable niches, we were too tired to feel anything more than the need to sleep. As I scooped away the soft earth, I saw that our little group had spread itself over a remarkably small area. In the single stroke of our crash, we had changed from maintaining our individual privacy at any cost, to something like a huddle of puppies. I said nothing, only thankful for the sound of other humans breathing, so close to me. One of the few fortunate aspects of our situation is that the air is so warm; as I lie here, propped up on an elbow, the breeze is not even slightly chilling on my damp garment. Indeed, the gentle darkness is balmy on my skin, and brings the strange and spicy scent of the crushed herbs beneath me.

The sound of the rain on the leaves is soporific, as is the gentle wash on the shore; the occasional purposeful rustle among the dark bushes is less so. Overhead, other sounds are in the air; strange little calls and squeaks. There is nothing inherently alarming about the noises, but it will be much less disturbing when we know the source of the sounds, or so I sincerely hope! It is time for me to wake the next watch. I have only managed to stay awake by recording this, and by contemplating the white, pure line of lace around my wrists, and wondering how long I can keep it intact.

# RAINING

We were awakened, this "morning," by a shriek from Shirley. I think all of us had been drowsing, half-awake, for some hours, but were not fully aware in the soft light and gentle rain of what time it might be. Muscles sore from yesterday's unaccustomed strenuous activity were aching all over me. Shirley's scream brought us all to our feet, but to my horror she lay flat, thrashing as though confined. She looked unharmed, but then I saw that her thick braid of blond hair was tightly held down by a thick tendril of vine! We tried to pull her free, but the plant was as tough and strong as wire.

"My Mech-All!" Shirley spluttered. "It's in my back belt pouch!"

She twisted her body violently on the ground, managed to grasp the precious tool, and held it up. She manipulated a control on the side of the handle and the metal blob at the tip reconfigured itself into a serrated knife. Nels knelt, seized the knife, and sawed through the vine with difficulty. When it was severed, Shirley was able to rise, and we could pull the marauding strand down along the braid and off; however, the little tendril remained tightly coiled and rigid, like a spring. I looked at the cut-off end and remembered the sped-up sequence of pictures we had all observed—with such clinical detachment!—back aboard *Prometheus.* This was obviously one of those warlike plants.

"It must have been trying to strangle my braid!" Shirley said, her hands moving from the thick plait to her throat. "I think, if we have to spend another night here, I'll find a spot on the beach!"

Mentally, I decided to do the same, and I saw Cinnamon run a thoughtful hand along her own braids.

Nels picked up the end of the vine from which we had freed Shirley, and gave it an experimental tug. "Humph! Considerable resistance there." I looked along the visible length of the vine—it disappeared underground within a few feet—and was surprised at how thin it was; nowhere near as thick as the coil.

"Why do you suppose the vine is so thin, and then expands at the coil?" I asked,

"Don't know," he said. "Unless it was sort of exploring, and then when it detected something, it enlarged somehow to deal with it." Shirley looked at the difference between the fragile root and her attacker, and shuddered.

We turned to regard the mass of undergrowth with increased respect. Suddenly . . . "Look there!" said David softly. Regarding us from under cover of one of the giant leaves was a single, large, bright eye. Arielle slipped silently towards it, and stopped. In an instant, the eye had vanished, and we heard the now-familiar rustling fade away.

"Did you see it clearly?" asked Cinnamon.

"Too fast." Arielle turned to us, her own eyes wide. "But the legs—like bug? I dunno!"

That is interesting; we'll have to try to get a better look at the little creatures. It might be possible to pursue one if the undergrowth were not quite so thick and soggy.

For it is still raining. Not a downpour, just the slow, steady sort that can fall from leaden skies for days. Morning, after our much-needed rest, brought us the renewed optimism it usually does, and we breakfasted more heartily among our peculiar provisions. Arielle's determined rummaging among the disorder reminded me how hungry I really was, and I joined John in the dividing of a cold but meaty sandwich, while I saw Jinjur munching on an equally cold pseudo-sausage. Not really cold, of course, but I did find my thoughts turning speculatively towards fire.

I was not alone in this, I learned. Jinjur opened the discussion.

"The first thing we must do, as soon as possible, is to get a message to *Prometheus*. They'll know we've crashed, of course, but they won't know if, or how many of us have survived. I think the quickest way to signal them is by a precise pattern of fires along the beach."

This was a startling thought to me—it sounds so primitive! But I could think of nothing more effective to hand, and even this ancient tool was going to take some ingenuity to achieve.

"We can only hope all the dead plants around here are really flammable," said John. "And that we can find anything dry enough to ignite."

David had been scanning the sky intently, shielding his eyes from the raindrops.

"I'm all for a fire," he said. "But I don't see any real break in the low clouds; they're just sitting overhead and pouring. When I do get a glimpse of the higher layers they're moving fast."

"That's bad," grumbled Jinjur. "Any fast-moving cloud will not only obscure our message, it makes it really tough for *Prometheus* to respond so that we can detect it."

"How is that?" I asked.

"Well, if we make some precise shape in fire, it's going to be lost if it's intermittent."

"Tough, too, to keep a fire going for any length of time in this rain," added John, with his usual cool realism.

"And," said Carmen, "what sort of answer can we expect from *Prometheus?* They could try to send some landers down, but those high winds would blow their aeroshells and parachutes far away from us, even assuming we knew they were coming!" The daunting facts of our isolation are, I realize, beginning to sink in. We all know, all too well, how truly desperate is our plight, but we cannot admit it, even to ourselves.

Jinjur decided, arbitrarily. "We need a fire, so let's get going on that first. The meat I ate just now would definitely have been improved by being heated, and I think it would be safer, too. Once we have a small fire, we'll just plan to wait until the weather improves enough to try to send a clear signal. How are any of you at fire-building?"

A wave of dismay swept the faces around. Even as children, or students, we had taken such an elemental tool for granted. Indeed, open fires are a rarity on Earth at present—so primitive and energy-wasteful they are.

Cinnamon volunteered hesitantly, "I did it once, at home, just to see how it was done. But it took me hours!"

"So be it," said Jinjur firmly. "Hours are one thing we've got. Richard, you and I will go back down to the shore and see if we can get the flouwen back to salvage duty for us. The rest of you help Cinnamon." The two of them moved off, Jinjur's short legs taking two steps to his one; I watched them for a moment. Her brown face, at about his elbow level, looked up at her companion with a grin. It is not difficult to see that our diminutive commander takes a very feminine pleasure, even in these hazardous circumstances, in the strong arms still under her command!

I followed the others toward the strange plants, and began looking under the sheltering leaves for dry tinder. At Cinnamon's direction we collected a variety of possible fuels—some very small and others more massive. The slim brown hands sorted through the offerings we brought her, and began to arrange them in separate piles on a flat rock, temporarily shielded with big leaves. While we patiently shredded quite a lot of stuff into very fine fibers, she bent some more limber twigs into a curious shape with painstaking care. When she was ready, we moved to assist her, using the broad leaves to protect her and her work from the rain and the steadily increasing wind. I watched, with great interest, as she bent over the sticks on the dry stone. Faster and faster she spun the little bow she had contrived around its fellow. Of course, if this method failed, we could eventually collect a spark from a lightning-caused blaze, but it seemed important to us all that this should *not* fail—I think, as humans, we want to feel "in charge" of our situation again!

Then, I thought my eyes were mistaken, but no, truly, a thin line of gray drifted up from Cinnamon's busy hands. She bent closer, and gently laid the finest of fibers from the pile near her across the arc. It blackened, shriveled, and more smoke arose! Tenderly, carefully, she added the tiny fibers, and suddenly, there was a tiny flicker of light. None of us dared move, or breathe too deeply, lest we endanger the little fire, but it grew steadily. It was incredibly beautiful! None of us has seen an open flame for years, nor, honestly, have we missed seeing one, but the warmth and life and beauty of the little yellow flame held our gaze. It was amazingly bright compared to the dull red light from Barnard that we had become accustomed to. As the fire grew, and shifted, and began to crackle on the larger fuel, we became aware of the smoky smell, achingly familiar and yet sharply new. It was acrid, and made Arielle cough as it drifted into her face, but it was also deliciously spicy, and the thought of hot tea floated into my mind. The crackling sparks sounded sharp and clear, and then drifted upward with their ancient loveliness.

Easily, now, we added fuel, and propped our protecting leaves with stones and sandpiles, to keep the fuel stack dry and to keep most of the wind and rain from the blaze. Cinnamon stood, and stretched, and grinned proudly at us. Nels took a long step to her side and hugged her tightly.

"Good job, Cin! We're proud of you!" We joined in, in exuberant congratulation. John said suddenly, "Makes me feel independent again!"

"Right," agreed David. "We're on our way now."

"Like Prometheus," I added. Carmen looked puzzled. "The original one, I mean," I said. "The one who gave men fire."

"That's right," said John. "And went on to encourage science and skill."

"The essences of civilization," I said. "We really are back on a path." It seems rather grandiose to attach so much importance to this humble little blaze, but we feel amazing fondness and pride for our—creation! That is what it is, and we shared our moment of triumph in a brief enjoyment of the warmth.

I thought it curious, our behavior—even as I shared it! We are all strangely silent about the future that confronts us, although I suspect we have all thought about it a great deal in the last day, and even more so in the night. We face the very real possibility of living the rest of our lives on this strange and beautiful world, and whether those lives will be days, months, or years longer is speculation about which we cannot even be logical. But none of us is willing to say anything aloud! Partly, I suppose, it is our habits of independence; partly a desire to alarm no one unnecessarily; and partly, a sensible feeling that we can only await developments. For whatever reasons, our conversations have focussed very much on the immediate present. It does no good to discuss how the crash occurred, and we have abandoned the topic. We all are wholly aware of the resources left to George and the rest, and the lack of any real rescue mission they can possibly mount. We know the futility of lamentations, and when, I think, each of us feels a twinge of fear, we are heartened by the resolution of the others, and then we do our own share of heartening. Those last few cautious words around the now flourishing fire are the first which acknowledge the facts beginning to face us. Slowly, but with genuine pleasure, I looked at the faces in the firelight. There are strengths here, and courage, and competent minds and hands. I too am capable, and together we can do much.

At that point, Jinjur and Richard trudged up the beach to join us, laden with soggy flotsam the flouwen had hauled forth.

"The lander has slowed down, Little Red says, but is still going slowly toward the bottom. Sounds like the deepest part of the lagoon is pretty much in the center, and the sides the lander is sliding over must be smooth enough that it doesn't hang up on anything. From its shape, I'm now certain it's the crater of a volcano, like the rest of the place, only this volcano is on the side of an even bigger volcano that makes up the central mountain on this island. And, that being the case, if they are the right kind of volcano, we might find something really useful, when we have time to look around a bit for it."

"Useful?" Arielle queried.

"Obsidian," he answered briefly.

Carmen's face brightened. "Obsidian? That could be very useful indeed! There was a whole display of antique knives and axes in the museum in San Diego—beautiful, it is, but more important, it can be chipped to a really sharp edge!"

That's true, I remembered. Obsidian was used so early on by primitive tribes that it's not known when they began, but obviously they recognized, as we now do, the value of a substance that can so easily be made into a good, sharp knife.

Jinjur looked with pleasure, then, at the fire, her eyes softening. "A gradely sight!" she murmured. "I remember . . ." She broke off. All of us had done some remembering, when the small flames had settled down to their steady dance. I straightened briskly, and set off down the beach.

With Shirley's capable help I pulled a soggy roll of blankets from the creaming shallows where the flouwen had left them. Between us, we managed to twist the fabrics and squeeze the water from them.

"As we went to Necessary Beach this morning, I saw what looked like a pond off to the left—did you see it?" I asked. (I am being stubborn about the euphemism for that beach; it's clumsy, but I prefer it to the much more Anglo-Saxon epithet with which David had startled me!)

"No, I didn't notice," answered Shirley. "But if it's fresh water we could rinse these blankets out—or shall we just let the rain do the job?"

"Might as well," I admitted. "Although, if we do that, it will probably stop raining! You know how cooperative weather is!"

Awkwardly, we draped the thick blankets over rocks, to rinse and drain, if they will. The rain shows no sign of letting up, so perhaps it will do some work for us. Jinjur glances skyward all the time, I notice—searching for some break in the clouds.

Those heavy blankets, after their soaking in salt water, are matted, and smell most peculiar. We are all noticing this; after so many years of filtered air, our olfactory senses are almost overburdened now. As David said, cheerfully, "When I smell that water I realize I'm getting used to the air!"

The "salt" water in the lagoon, to distinguish it from the springwater, is definitely not the same as our oceans on earth. Between us, we have swum in many seas, and we agree on that point.

"I spent a summer near Annapolis, once," John reminisced. "And we did a lot of swimming in the Bay, where the rivers come in. Thick as soup, the stuff was—you couldn't see far enough ahead in it to avoid the jellyfish, sometimes, and it tasted . . ." He apparently couldn't think of an apt comparison. "But you get used enough to it not to mind particularly, and . . ."

"Why did you even try to swim in it?" Shirley interrupted, curiously.

He shrugged. "Gets pretty hot and muggy there in August." I remember that, myself, having spent the summer in the Capitol awaiting the start of the Barnard mission. In many ways, I realize, this climate is similar. I never notice heat, but even I am grateful for the access to both sea and pond.

"At any rate," John concluded, "*this* water tastes worse than *that* water, and while I might get used to it, I doubt if I'll ever like it."

Cinnamon and Carmen have retrieved many containers through the efforts of the flouwen, and have arranged them in a long row according to no other criterion than size. Some of the things can be used for water, others have no immediately recognizable value to us here, but we cannot afford to discard them; we may have to contrive some very basic necessities. Some of the stored foods from the lander are still sealed in their tough wrappings, and we will be able to use them. I was surprised and pleased to observe, among these, several large packets of the oats and barley that had been among my personal stores.

"Look, Cinnamon!" I said. "These came through intact—we'll be able to have porridge, or soup, or something!" She looked at the packets with a curious intensity, and took them from me without a word. However, other foods, such as the fresh fruit, were less carefully stowed, and are sodden and spoiled. For the time being, we placed these in a separate pile, to be destroyed later. Jinjur's command is adamant: "Our rule has always been to disturb an alien planet only as much as is absolutely necessary. We are already doing much more 'disturbing' than I like, but we'll keep it to a minimum, understand? At least," she added in sudden doubt, "for now." We are all complying, though privately wondering how long we can continue to be so scrupulous.

As I was returning to the stack of discards with a very salty bit of overripe fruit, I saw a sudden movement—one of the little creatures was examining the stuff! It was so intent on its survey that I was able to move quite close, silent and undetected. I observed the blue-green fuzz which covered it, and saw that it has six appendages, which it uses like four legs and two arms; these are stiff and jointed, very like an insect's. When it turned towards me I saw that it does indeed have just one eye, and that very large and dark and bright. Instantly, it clutched an overripe strawberry in its front legs and scuttled off on the other four, looking so like an insect that I understood Arielle's simile. It made no attempt, that I saw, to put anything into its mouth—in fact, I didn't even observe a mouth—but it certainly was quick of movement.

I reported my observations. Nels was most intrigued. "We need to catch one, I think. Just to take a closer look!" he added quickly, as Jinjur frowned.

Cinnamon had joined us in bringing up armloads of stuff from the beach, but by common consent she has returned to the care of our fire. None of us is willing to let it go out, even though we are not cold, and we have quickly learned that it can be a temperamental element. I happened to be nearby, when, as I thought, it needed fuel, so I tossed on several large pieces. To my dismay the coals rolled apart and began to smoke dismally. Fortunately, Cinnamon was close by and came running to sweep the coals together and coax the flame anew, but I resolved not to interfere again. Indeed, I watched with sympathy, later, as Arielle, in similar circumstances, added such tiny twigs that they were instantly consumed, and she had to hurry back and forth for half an hour while the fire continued to languish. It was in sad state by the time Cinnamon came to the rescue again. We were both relieved when she announced she would take care of it. Indeed, what with the constant search for more fuel she will have no time for other work, at least until we can build up a reserve of suitable size. Carmen and John seem to be nearly as adept at nursing the thing along, so she can share the chore.

It all seemed well worth while as the inky hour of eclipse approached at noontime. We are all weary—the constant warm shower of rain from the gray sky above is enervating, and we are finding the changed gravity adds to our fatigue. It was a joy to both mind and body to head for the yellow firelight, flickering there under the sheltering leaf, and to eat something hot. We've had some precious minutes of relaxation and rest, as we wait for the light to return. When it does, we shall be busy, as Jinjur, as much from exasperation as anything else, I suspect, has decided we should erect some sort of temporary shelter.

"We'll all take a break from salvage operations, and do something to get us out of this frabbled rain!" was the way she put it. "Can't send a signal, can barely keep the fire going, and durned if I want to sleep wet!"

"I'd just as soon stay out from under those trees," added Shirley, glancing at the dark line of forest.

Carmen was rubbing her ankles in the pleasant warmth. "I think I'd rather have a floor I can walk on without my slippers than a roof over my head," she said.

"A roof would be nice, though," said Cinnamon. "Out of the smoke, if that's possible."

"Wall, please? Wind blows sand—and smoke—in my eyes," requested Arielle.

"Here it goes, you see," grumbled Richard. "Give 'em a tropical Eden, with a warm ocean, sandy beach, a good spring—and they want carpets and furniture."

I closed my mouth; I'd been about to suggest erecting the structure above the rock a step or two, to escape the sandy grit under our slippers. Oh, well—we shall see how this little effort proceeds; Carmen has apparently had some experience in make-shift construction, when she survived the Salamanca earthquake all those years ago, and several of us have camped out in various locales. I myself worked for a construction firm in D.C. briefly, but had left as soon as I'd mastered the new computer. Privately, listening to the discussion around me, I anticipate the shelter will resemble most things built by a committee! Curious, Richard's mention of Eden—it's the last word I'd have selected. The feeling I have is that of being a castaway on a desert island, with no preparation or warning. Indeed, recalling the enormity of the disaster, I am a little surprised at the recovery we have already begun. The natural instincts to survive are doubtless driving us, and although this place so far seems relatively benign, we are working hard at ensuring our mutual safety.

It was indeed a strenuous afternoon. Selecting a site

for a temporary shelter was simple; we are all loath to leave this gentle slope of beach, with its open visibility in all directions and at a reasonable distance from the unknowns in the forest. There is plenty of wood available in the forest. From a hasty survey, it looks like bare-trunked saplings, thin and strong, but we think the poles are actually downshoots from the mammoth trees, which support the heavy branches and their massive leaves. The leaves themselves, wide and stiff, would serve almost as boards, but they are very irregular in shape, and of course we have nothing to cut them with except Shirley's knife, which makes slow work of them. Nor have we fasteners, except for the long snaky vines and roots, which even Jinjur has agreed to use freely as lashings.

Eventually we collected enough material to begin. How awkward and difficult it was, to make even the simplest plan! Accustomed, as we all are, to plenty of charts and graphs and measuring devices, as well as to having James coordinate instantly all ideas, we were now reduced to talking, explaining, describing, waving arms and hands around; even, primitively, drawing in the sand! Like children, we find our dream castle becoming humbler and humbler, as the difficulties of construction become apparent. Somewhat discouraged by the evolution of the building into a sort of shed, I went off with Cinnamon and Carmen to begin fetching supplies.

I had cut several lengths of vine, using Shirley's knife, when yesterday's blisters began to burn. "I'll take a turn, Reiki," said Carmen kindly, and gratefully I handed her the tool. Shortly, she too was glad to pass it along to Cinnamon. By taking turns we were able to continue cutting, gathering, and carrying the vines. "George would be shocked, you know," said Carmen. "Only one tool between us, and so painful to use we give it up happily!"

"George would soon find out for himself," I said tartly. The blisters were becoming raw.

Finally, by dint of much trial and error, we succeeded in erecting two sturdy towers, connected at their top by a ridgepole made of the tallest sapling we could find. Along that support, and with its back to the strongest winds, we laid a lean-to sort of arrangement, alternating bases and tips of the saplings, and covered over with layered leaves, lashed down well by the vines. While Jinjur shouted directions from below, countermanded at nearly every step by Shirley—"Wait! I have a *better* idea!"—David crouched patiently at the top of a tripod, supported at its base by Richard and John. Like the spider monkey he somewhat resembles, he clambered agilely about, seizing the tips of the wavering saplings Nels extended, grunting, to him.

"Stay up there, David, and keep twisting those vines around that beam, while we make another support!" And he did wait, while the architects dithered about the exact spot for the second tripod. But when Arielle climbed to the top of the new one, she found the vines too stiff for her to knot. David swung to the ground, then, and replaced her at the job. Both of the slender workers compared palms later—there is considerable blood in the construction!

The structure is necessarily sturdy, because it must stand against these strong winds; it is also both wide and tall, as the slender trunks are surprisingly long and stiff for their weight—somewhat similar to bamboo. Both ends are enclosed, so that the whole affair is about seven meters deep and ten meters wide, and rises some three meters at the front. We covered the "floor" with as many springy softer branches as we had the patience to cut, and they make a welcome cushion between our bodies and the sandy rock. Viewed dispassionately, it is the most miserable "building" I have ever seen, but it feels wonderful to sit inside, out of the rain! To feel the warmth of the fire, and stare at the fresh blisters and scratches on my hands and arms, and sip from a steaming cup—while the thin fabrics in my clothes toast themselves dry! It couldn't last, and soon we were hard at it in the shallows again, sorting debris.

John said, "I'd really like to have something soothing to put on everyone's skin—the Christmas Branch could supply us with just the thing from its chemical synthesizer! But, in the absence of ointment, this seawater is probably just what's needed to keep your wounds clean and toughen up your skin. Fortunately, we probably don't have to worry about dangerous bugs in the soil, like tetanus, anthrax, and staph. There may be alien equivalents to them in the dirt, but hopefully they don't know how to attack anything as alien as our cells." The seawater treatment stung, but pretty soon our blisters and welts began to recede.

The rain stopped, briefly, about mid-afternoon, and we all paused in our labors to stare upwards. Alas, although there was no water falling from those thick clouds, they were roiling ominously; the winds above must be even stronger than they are here on the surface, and there is no hope of their being penetrable by a signal fire yet.

"If I'd known it was monsoon season, I'd have stayed home," grumbled Jinjur. Oddly, there popped into my head the ancient tradition of the Emperor of Japan decreeing, officially, the beginning and ending of the rainy season; I chuckled, and told Jinjur about it. "Oughtn't you to have that right, Jinjur?" I asked.

"Of course!" she responded. And in her most authoritarian tones, she proclaimed, "I hereby declare the rainy season over! Signed . . . Me, the Me!" To no one's real surprise, the slow drops began to fall again.

With occasional breaks for their own needs, the flouwen continued to bring items from the drowning lander. With commendable patience, they gathered up all the small items which were drifting about, and we harvested quite a crop of dead imps and housekeeping motiles which could be disassembled into pins, nails, and fasteners; coffee squeezers, drink flasks, spoons—I for one had no idea of the number of spoons we'd had with us! A great many more useful items we normally kept secured, either by straps or in compartments, and we left them for the time being, reluctant to instruct the flouwen to start pulling on things below. They can be very strong, when they can get sufficient purchase to tug, and their capacity for destroying something we might be able to obtain somehow, sometime, in better circumstances, was very real.

One of the treasures secured by Little White was the plastic bag in which I had packed my laces for this trip! There were a dozen of the ones I like best, and I was foolishly delighted to have them back. After rinsing, I hung them in the shelter of the trees, and they make a rather startling sight, their crisp elegance outlined against the rough bark.

With fire and water, Nels was able to mix together a large communal pot containing several sorts of our fast-thawing frozen foods, in a vessel I had never seen before. "Don't ask," he had said with a grin when he saw my look of inquiry.

It seemed to take a very long time for the pot to get hot enough to cook sufficiently, and while it was slowly getting to that stage we were able to smell the aromas of cooking—for the first time in how long? Arielle was increasingly fascinated, and rummaging through the small tins and bottles of the few retrieved seasonings, pounced on several which she insisted on adding to the mixture. The smells became even more savory, and by the time the meal was pronounced ready, our appetites were also. Indeed, with the unaccustomed exertions of hauling supplies, dragging wood, climbing and bending, I was very hungry, and the aroma from the stew made me dizzy. We have no means of preserving any of the meal, but that was not a problem as there was not a trace of it left.

Once more sipping some marvelously comforting tea from the cut-off bottoms of our squeezers cups (and what a nuisance they are! It takes a polishing with sand to remove the last traces of stew in order not to spoil the tea-flavor—I was surprised, for the cleaning imp in the galley had always taken care of that detail for us before), we lounged in the front of our lean-to to stare at the flames and plan for the morrow.

"It's tough not to be able to make any long-range plans," fretted Shirley. "And by long-range, I mean a week!" she added.

Carmen smiled, her tiny dimple darkening in the firelight. It struck me again, how lovely she is without a trace of her cherished cosmetics! "We had plenty of long-range plans. Maybe we still do. They're just on hold, and counting."

"Right," agreed Jinjur. "We need to stay alert, ready to take advantage of a situation, or to protect ourselves, but in the meantime establish some sort of working routine. I've been in campaigns like that! So, we'll continue to stand watches, we'll keep on salvaging and sorting whatever the flouwen can bring up, and we'll keep the fire going. Eventually, this rain will let up enough for us to signal. We'll keep using the food we brought with us—no experimenting with anything that might be edible here—yet." The final word was soft, but flat. "Now about this signal fire—our options are still limited. With all the lightning-caused fires we mapped before landing—we need to make it clear this isn't a natural fire."

"How about a geometric shape? A circle, or square of several fires?" suggested David.

"A circle would look like one big fire from that high up," objected John. "And a square would have to be so precise; I'm not sure, without anything to measure with . . ."

"Possibly a long straight line?" asked Shirley.

"In Canada, forest fire sometimes make long line," said Arielle. "So straight, look like road."

I thought of what primitive tribes and clans might do under the same circumstances. They were almost as destitute as we. Then I remembered, the clans used to call their gatherings with a burning cross! I explained, eagerly. "They used a wooden one standing on the top of a hill, but we would need to make a series of fires in two rows. They needn't be exactly straight, for if we can get the whole thing going simultaneously, the configuration won't be like anything which would naturally occur."

To my surprise, Jinjur frowned. "A fiery cross . . . that's not a very civilized symbol, as I recall," she said levelly.

"A cross is a very ancient symbol of civilization," I maintained. "And the Celts used it, burning, to gather all the families for important meetings. It was an honorable symbol between allies, and the misuse of it by the vile Klan"—I practically spat the "K"—"couldn't permanently debase it!" The rest agreed, and Jinjur was persuaded. The long-dead Klan certainly means nothing to this planet, or this century, and the simple device will make as clear a message as we can send, with our limitations.

We began to succumb to weariness. The light, drenching rain makes little sound against the rough thatch of our overhead, or on the wet sand surrounding us. Our thin clothes, after steaming visibly in the warmth of the fire, are dry and comfortable, and we are feeling both exhausted and secure. The moaning wind only deepens the comfort of being under shelter, and the breathing of my sleeping companions is inaudible. I'm glad my watch is nearly over and I can stretch out for my share of oblivion!

# EATING

Incredible though it seems, it has now been raining for more than a week. Occasionally there is a brief cessation of the drops, but the high gray clouds continue scudding steadily, obscuring any sight of the distant sky. We are growing accustomed to being so constantly damp, and it certainly keeps us from the unpleasantly grubby sensations of earthly camping trips, but we are more than ever grateful for the opportunity of an evening to dry out by our faithful little fire, and to sleep under cover. The roof of our lean-to is saturated, of course, but as long as we avoid touching it, it doesn't drip.

We have tried to stay busy during this time, with some result. The last of the free-floating items have been salvaged by the flouwen, and Little Red made no secret of the fact that he was tired of the job.

"Stuff! Too much stuff!" he shouted.

Jinjur insisted: "C'mon, Little Red, look around a little more down there! Can you open the tool locker?"

Little White was as definite as Little Red, though more reasonable. "We look, poke, tug. Nothing more loose, *now*." We were puzzled by the curious emphasis on the last word. Little Purple's explanation was not reassuring.

"Time, tides, waves—shake things around, maybe more to find, then."

Reluctantly, Jinjur dismissed the aliens. "Okay, start looking around. I want to know everything you find out about the plants, animals, rocks—whatever's down there!"

Cinnamon and I started to speak at once, but Jinjur cut us off with a loud, "Please! And thank you for all you've done—we need your help very much! Happy hunting!"

Cinnamon and I looked at each other in delight. Jinjur caught the look, and growled, "Can't very well confine 'em to quarters."

While we systematically used up the deteriorating frozen food, we began to prepare for the eventuality of finding replacements for it. Carmen and Shirley set off together early one day, and returned late and very tired, carrying a large crate slung between them. It was full of shards of black, shiny, glasslike rock.

"This obsidian is better quality than the stuff around home in Mexico," said Carmen. "I'm going to see if I can make a sharp edge or two." Some of the others joined her in the task, using a variety of techniques; pounding the edges with flat stones, grinding, heating in combination with all the other methods. However, Carmen seemed to catch the knack instantly. With glancing, short blows, she transformed one after another of the fragments of shiny material into crude-looking little tools with at least one wickedly sharp edge on each. They are not unpleasant to use just as they are, but we have decided they need handles.

"Umph!" said Arielle, followed by something muttered in French as she sucked her bleeding thumb. "Which edge is blade and which is not?"

We took to arranging the little knives with care, all

the sharp edges facing in the same direction, and to protecting our hands with clumsily tied-on bits of bark or rags. (The smaller towels from the lander are rapidly disintegrating into very good rags, with the constant use we make of them!) Once again, it was necessary for each of us to be aware of the system, and follow it. I've never been camping with such a talky crew! But with ten of us busy about a variety of tasks, and no James to spare us from any of them, we learned very quickly to keep in communication.

"I'm through with the Mech-All!" is a frequent shout, and someone is always eager to take it away, for it is a far more familiar and useful device than the best obsidian blade.

"Still," as Carmen declared, "it's miraculous that there is obsidian available to us struggling survivors!"

All of us continue to keep watch on the various fauna and flora, as we move about. The strange whistles that disturbed our first night are still sounding, although we hear them so constantly they are beginning to seem familiar. Unlike birdcalls, these are at the same time more varied, both in pitch and duration, and more uniform—like speech.

"I wonder . . ." David speculated. It is apparent he has been aware of the sounds all the time, even when busy at something else. "There are tribes on earth who communicate with whistles, aren't there?"

I remembered then. "Yes! Mostly tribes who live in very mountainous . . . one of the Canary Islands, I recall. It's easier, over their deep chasms, to get messages across by whistling." We all, I think, tried to pay more attention to the sounds, but forgot them again in the stress of daily duties. But David, obviously, didn't—or couldn't. It's the way he's made, to be aware of tone almost unconsciously, and occasionally he will interject suddenly a reference to the sounds which we have ignored.

"Hear that? It's repeated that one bit for the last five minutes!"

The rest of us also are gathering useful information. Shirley remarked, one evening, "I tried twisting one of those sapling-things, just at the length I wanted it, and it snapped right off! It was one of the pale-colored ones, and was surprisingly brittle." (Shirley, I suspect, is a born architect; she already wants to enlarge our crude shelter!)

"Now, that will be useful to know," mused Jinjur. "It'd be a good idea, when anyone spots something like that during the day, to pass it along when we're all together. And Reiki!" she added. "Put that sort of thing into your recorder, with some sort of notation so we can find it again! I don't suppose you have an index?" She grinned.

"I've not needed one before," I explained. "All I need to remember is the date I entered something."

"What if it's a long time ago?" asked David.

I shrugged. "I just remember. I don't have to work at it—it's just a sort of trick in my mind. No credit to me," I added hastily. "I've always done it." Shirley nodded understanding—her own memory is unique—and I was grateful, for the others were more skeptical, and I had to dredge up half a dozen old stories before they would believe me. Finally I offered, "I'll set up an ordinary file, for things we might all want access to, and show you how to find it." They were agreeable, and it was easy to teach them quickly. However, I later set up a password to guard the rest of the recorded accounts, having no wish to share quite everything with my friends!

Those "saplings" are indeed peculiar. More careful observation has revealed that they do seem to serve as supports for the massive branches. The central trunk of the tree is enormous, many meters in diameter, and the branches spread far into the distance, heavily covered with the spongy, spicily aromatic leaves we are finding so useful. Periodically, a supporting slender trunk emerges from branch to ground, consisting of little more than a strong, straight tube. As they continue to bear weight, they become slightly thicker, and paler, but we've not found any very massive, or more complex at all—indeed, the big tree seems simply to put out more supports rather than to enlarge the ones it has. Nels has a hypothesis: "Lots of leaf mass, not much trunk mass. If the trunk is the 'main' part, and the leaves are the feeders, all it requires of those stalks is minimal support."

In spite of all our private and desperate worries, none of us can resist speculating on the strange aspects of life here. How do the plants manage to survive on the most barren-appearing soils? And why are they so arranged as to let no drop of water escape? It would seem there is plenty of water available as such, so perhaps there *is* something very precious in the rain. These, and other observations, are tantalizing to us in their alienness.

"Be careful not to assume anything that exists here is similar to something we were familiar with on Earth," had been Jinjur's strong injunction before we crashed. Even as we struggle to survive, we are kept very much aware of our ignorance of the life-forms here.

We have discovered, and made use of, several ponds of fresh water, ranging from a wide, shallow pool with a clean sandy floor, to a deeper, steeply-sided bowl alive with quick-darting fish, but with most unpleasant-smelling water. We use the ponds as well as the lagoon for swimming; both are pleasant, and I particularly enjoy going dripping from one to the other. The buoyancy of the ocean and the pushing of the waves is exhilarating, but the clean warmth of the ponds is refreshing afterward. John stared thoughtfully into the surface of the deeper lake for quite a time one day, wading in the shallows and stooping over to look, like a meditative heron. That evening, as we relaxed, he pulled forth a length of slender vine, and two sticks, which he had apparently rubbed smooth in the sand—they had quite a polished look about them. He began to manipulate the vine along the sticks, and then looked up at our astonished faces with some pride.

"My old granny taught me to knit," he explained. "Both of us hated to wait, and it helped to have something to do with our hands. We had to do a lot of waiting." He grimaced. "Politics."

I know he never shared his famous family's fondness for the political arena—it must have been dreadfully boring for his young mind to watch.

"I'm going to see if this stuff can work up into a net, of sorts," he went on. "Might be useful." It would indeed! I watched his hands move along the vine, slowly, but with rapidly increasing speed and sureness. To my admiration, a widening strip of mesh began to drop from the flying sticks! I was quick to praise this accomplishment—not only were the nets going to be practical, the creation of them put me in mind of my precious laces—perhaps I can learn a useful skill? I sincerely hope so, because, to my intense chagrin, I find myself a perfectly dreadful cook. One of the few fields in which I have never felt any interest whatsoever is that of culinary preparation. But, I reasoned, when it was my turn to tend the pot, what could be simpler? Simply a question of time and heat, was it not? Much to my dismay it turns out to be more complex than that. Covertly I began to study the others at the same job—even timed them!—and tasted and tasted, only to discover that my own efforts tasted as bad to me as they obviously did to the others. With outward resignation and secret shame, I excused myself all but the simplest cooking duties—not the least reason being that I simply could not manage the fire. Either I was overzealous and produced a conflagration that turned food to coal, or I forgot the thing entirely, and we were all reduced to raw dinners. It was humbling to see David, or even John, produce a meal we all relished, while my own best efforts were treated with the wicked ever-so-politeness that has such a sting. I found I even preferred Richard's roaring insults: "Wow! A good big drink of this . . . roast?—and I'm a new man!"

However, today has produced a change. Last night we consumed the last of the thawed food that was remotely edible. In the interests of health and safety we simply incinerated the rest, and it smelled vile for a mercifully brief time, and then vanished.

This morning, Jinjur made her pronouncement.

"It's time," she began rather grimly. "I don't want to wait until we're hungry enough to be desperate, as we were for fresh water. We've got to find out if there's anything here we can eat, and we're going to do it systematically and safely. To begin with, we'll stay in pairs. Keep track of where you are and how far you've traveled, because we won't expect everyone back for . . ." A spasm of irritation crossed the brown face. None of us can keep accurate time, except me! ". . . several hours," she finished rather lamely. "And another thing; you must not taste anything—not once!—until we're all back. I'm not taking any more chances, and it'll be me who does the testing."

This was disturbing. "But, Jinjur," protested John, "If you taste more than one item a day, and get sick . . . or something, we won't know which item was the culprit. And we ought to try things more rapidly than that. Let's divide them up."

Cinnamon agreed, adding, "I'm quite sure we'll find at least ten very different things to try—I've been watching some fruits that seem to be ripening—and if we each sample one, we'll know pretty soon if any of them are toxic."

"How about cooking everything? Isn't that safer?" Carmen wanted to know.

"Yes." Nels was definite. Some things may taste better raw—like oranges—but we must go slow trying that." Accordingly we split up, and set forth.

With an eagerness that indicated they had been longing for just such an opportunity, David and Arielle headed for the tallest nearby trees, around which long vines are wrapped. There are vaguely globular objects half-hidden in the high branches, which we have seen, but none of them have fallen to the ground. I had forgotten how agile the two are, until I saw them leap upwards in the low gravity, David only fractionally behind the lithe woman, and they began to climb swiftly, testing the vines for support but using them mostly for balance.

The skin on all of our hands has toughened with the rough work, and the two called cheerfully to each other as they climbed.

"Did you bring knife, David? I forgot!"

"Yup, got it in the last of my pockets—hope it doesn't cut through!"

"Getting stuff down be tricky, maybe!"

"Just shout, and drop 'em, if they're tough. If not, well . . ." The voices dimmed, and they disappeared from sight.

With equal determination, Richard seized a pouch of stones from a private cache; obviously, carefully selected stones, gathered over several days' time—smooth and round, and uniformly sized.

"C'mon, Cinnamon," he said. "Let's go hunting." Several times, overhead, we have spotted flying creatures. They seem to be curious about us, because they fly directly over, surveying us with an enormous dark eye, and then fly off on blue-green wings. I suspect they, as well as the little creatures who find our discarded food so interesting, are now considered Richard's prey.

Jinjur determined otherwise, however. "I want to know more about these animals," she said as we prepared to move. "I'm going to set a few traps along those faint trails into the undergrowth. But anything we capture must not be harmed!" she added firmly, glaring at Richard. "We're not in any hurry to start eating the natives!"

She and Shirley conferred briefly, before selecting a few of John's nets, and some other containers, and then moved quietly into the forest. I watched with approval. As a child, intrigued by stories of the American Wild West, I had practiced the art of moving silently over any terrain, and it had long since become a habit with me; I was glad to see Jinjur and Shirley could be reasonably quiet also.

Carmen and John headed for the thickest parts of the forest. As we've moved around, looking for fuels among the vegetation, we have all been struck by the diversity to be found. When we were exploring by remote-controlled robots, the impression received by all of us (except David!) had been that the plant population was all very similar. Now that we can look more closely, we see infinite variations. There are a great many thorny bushes, some very large, and while they are apparently individual plants, as we can see their trunks growing into the soil, they tend to grow in dense thickets, and we get tantalizing glimpses of quite different plants in the centers of these hedges. Some of the inner ones are tall, with an upper canopy of rather pretty blue-green fronds. The thorns prevent us effectively from entering the interiors, but the views are enticing.

It is peculiar how one's viewpoint changes! Up until

now, I had regarded this landscape as alien and fascinating, when I didn't feel it to be bleak and hostile. Now, I found myself solely concerned with its edibility!

Nels and I were preparing to head for the tidepools. There are several of them which contain quantities of some sort of large shellfish. However, we had barely outfitted ourselves with containers and some sturdy chunks of obsidian when we heard a triumphant shout from Richard, quite nearby, and moved quickly to see what had happened.

He had caught one of the flying animals! He was holding it in a firm embrace, as it struggled. It put me in mind of an owl, because of the one large dark eye regarding us with silent astonishment. It seemed to have no legs at all! Cinnamon reached to assist Richard, and they spread out the strong bony wings between them, displaying the three skeletal supports in each. The little creature struggled even more frantically in their grasp, and then went suddenly limp. Although it's appearance didn't change, its whole attitude was lifeless. Nels took the animal in careful hands, and turned it about slowly. On the back of the little body, if the eye was on the front, was a small hole, an apparent sphincter. That, and the eye, were the total of its features!

"Most incomplete animal I ever saw," muttered Nels. He made a tiny, tentative cut in the covering fuzz. There was no change in the flaccidity of the specimen, and he proceeded with a deft dissection. The creature was quite dead, and the simplicity of its structure was amazing.

"It's like it's only part of an animal!" Nels was truly puzzled. "There is the large eye, and quite a large brain behind it. But see, no lower limbs, only a minimal gut, and if that's a mouth in back of the eye, it has neither teeth nor tongue! What can the thing live on? I can't figure it out."

Richard laid the little carcass gently on the stones near the fire. Although there seems little flesh to the animal, it will only be practical to consider its food value. I hoped fervently it would not fall to my lot!

We left camp again, Nels and I retrieving our collecting tools and heading for the shore. I had been admiring, without attempting to touch, the clustered shells in the tidepools; the prettiest among them were deeply rounded inverted cups, vaguely hexagonal in outline, and in every possible variation of the color pink. There were wild designs of stripes and patches, dainty borders and neat plaids, all in tone on tone striations of palest pearl to deepest maroon, and gaudy others nearly scarlet. The tiniest ones were particularly lovely, making the floor of the pool look like a thickly flowering rosebush. Now, however, we were after the larger specimens so, selecting a fine neatly striped one, Nels inserted an obsidian blade beneath its rim and lifted, gently. To our amazement, the creature rose and fled from us at great speed on six pink legs.

"Catch it!" shouted Nels, grabbing unsuccessfully at the scurrying little animal. I made a frantic, splashing jump and felt my hands close around it, only to recoil, and drop it immediately.

"It's got claws! I gasped. "Scratchy, horrid, wiggly . . ."

"Oh, hell! said Nels. "Are you hurt?"

I considered my fingers hastily. "No," I had to admit. "Let's try again."

Warily we approached another tidepool, and probed the knife blade swiftly under a likely subject, ready for its dash for freedom. I clamped my hand down firmly over the upper shell and lifted it swiftly into the air, avoiding the wildly waving legs and holding it so that we could see it clearly. It was actually a delightful creature—the upper cup, so shiny in its glowing colors that it looks like an enameled paperweight, fits snugly to the flattened lower plate, leaving only room for the extension of the legs. These are long, jointed, and of a bright salmon color, armed at the tips with quite serviceable pincers. Enchanted, I observed the row of gleaming tiny dots along the rim of the upper shell; they were regularly spaced, and of a deep and glowing coral.

"Look, Nels! Those must be its eyes, like a scallop's!"

He grunted, tentatively agreeing it might be so. The animal regarded us with what I considered very reasonable malevolence, continuing to brandish its weaponry in our direction; but we disregarded that, and stowed it securely away. Then we began to develop a simple technique. We found, very quickly, that it helped to examine each pool quietly for some minutes, staying out of the direct light. Then, a quick and decisive push and flip with the blade and we had success. If we were slow, or tentative, the little creatures were able to grasp the rocks so firmly we could not reach under the shell to scrape them loose.

We worked steadily up the beach, with mixed results, until our backs ached. At least mine did! Nels seemed tireless, and his big hands were still quick with the knife long after mine were sore and scratched. At last we stopped to rest, and looked out to the open water. The flouwen were nearby—they had been observing us quietly for some time. "What you do?" Little Red was curious as usual.

"Hunting food." That, of course, was instantly understood.

"You like those?" Little White flowed a white pseudopod into one of our containers and inspected our catch with interest.

"We don't know. We'll taste them and see." Nels explained.

"They okay," said Little Purple critically, "But too small. Big ones better."

"Yes!" Little Red shouted. He proceeded to rattle off what I presumed was a list of various creatures he had found to his liking.

"They sound delicious! Do you think you could catch one and bring it to us to taste, please?" My polite request was apparently startling.

"*Humans* eat fish?"

"Well, we'd rather like to try, if you can help us. We'd like any help you can give us!"

The flouwen hovered together in the water for a few seconds, and then apparently decided to cooperate. They swam away, and we stood, up to our middles in the warm sea, waiting patiently to thank them, when and if they returned with fish. Finally tiring of the delay, I waded back to the tidepools, and was busy retrieving a large shellfish which had elected to run rather than cling, when the flouwen returned to Nels. I stood to watch, for they had indeed brought him a slippery-looking creature which he was struggling to confine in his net, rather hampered than otherwise by Little Red's shouted advice, apparently. I was too far away to hear their talk, but various explanations were obviously in progress. Suddenly, from the flouwen, there came a squeal—of apparent delight—and then much more talk ensued. Intrigued, I stood watching as Nels turned away and came up to the shore. He clutched the closed net with both hands, while the fish within flopped about. To my surprise, I saw that he was deeply flushed.

"Are you all right, Nels?" I asked. "You look badly sunburned!"

"'S all right," the big man muttered. "Nothing to worry about. Look at this fellow! What do you make of him?" We supported the net between us, so that we could more closely examine the captive.

"It looks like a whale!" I said. "What makes me think that?"

"The shape is whale-like," Nels said slowly. "But there's more to it than that. Funny shape to the flippers, isn't it, and no blowhole on top of the head, but the mouth . . ."

"That's it," I said. "Look at the width of the mouth and the shape!" Upon close examination it became apparent that our prize had a toothless mouth. Instead of teeth there were well-developed bands of very flexible strands, which together formed an effective sieve. It looks like the creature takes in water and strains out food from it.

"Nuts," said Nels, disappointed. I was surprised. "It's a filter feeder. Means no fishing with a line, or bait," he explained. "We'll have to net 'em."

The little recorder's alarm rang, not long after, and we gathered up the various containers we had stowed along our way with their precious contents, and headed back to camp, to add them to the collections of the others.

It was a most unappetizing buffet, spread out on the flat rocks. There were more than we could divide for one "meal," and we put aside, for the morrow if all goes well, a number of seeds and grains which are dry. David and Arielle had obtained several objects which might be fruit from the tall treetops—they are soft and spongy, but have no aroma to us. They had also gathered a lot of long pods of sorts from the hanging vines. When opened, they turned out to be full of fat little things like beans. John and Carmen had found some fruits and several varieties of nuts and grains, and with commendable patience had kept them carefully separated. In addition, they had managed to pull up some thick roots and bring them along. Dubiously we surveyed this assortment, while Arielle and Carmen brought containers of water to simmer close to the fire.

"It's really hard, knowing so little!" sighed Shirley.

"For all we know, these might be absolutely delicious, toasted ever so slowly and then fried, or something. And don't they bury some delicacies in Japan for years before they're ready to eat?" This to me—but I had to confess my ignorance. "Cheese, now, that has to age, doesn't it?" I suggested.

"No matter," Jinjur said firmly. "Before we begin boiling stuff, I want to take a quick look at our trap, Shirley." They hurried off, and returned almost instantly from the thicket. The trap had succeeded! Together we inspected the struggling animal, holding it by the strong and scrabbling legs. Covered with not unattractive blue-green furry fluff, it had a single large eye on the front of the head, and a small toothless opening on the back. Nels grasped on of the upper limbs and looked closely. "Look at that! These digits are opposable! That's how it manages to hold stuff and carry it off."

"And look at the long claws," added Cinnamon. "I've noticed them digging, and pulling things up to take. But I've never seen them actually "eating" anything!"

Surprised, we all thought back carefully. None of us has seen these creatures do anything other than retrieving. At this instant, without making a sound, the little animal collapsed, and with dismay we realized that it, too, had died.

"Certainly low tolerance for shock," Nels said grimly. "Or restraint," I added, thinking. Once again Nels performed the necessary explorations. He and Cinnamon are seriously puzzled; the little creatures have no digestive system beyond the very minimal; it seems certain they are incapable of eating the things we have seen them take with so much enthusiasm. Unlike the "owls," these little beings have tiny brains. Reluctantly, we added the scrawny carcass to our assortment. Operating strictly by guess, Arielle arbitrarily began the cooking of each, sniffing cautiously at the vapors beginning to emerge from the pots, and commenting occasionally.

"Beans and roots probably need more time," she decided, prodding the things with forks which she kept separate in each pot. "And I think meat and fish better grilled." The shellfish she cooked quickly, and removed when their shells opened. The bits of flesh from the animals and the gift from the flouwen she skewered on sticks, and cooked over the coals. This was a peculiar feast before us! And while we prepared to sample them, I thought with private relief of the remaining dry food from the lander; we will not have to rely entirely on these odd items just yet.

"Now," instructed John, "the safest thing we can do is rely on our own bodies. If your particular item really tastes awful, spit it out. Don't eat a lot, and tell us everything you can about each thing. Ready? I'll start." Resolutely, he spooned up some of the long-simmered beans. They had a rather pleasant, oniony aroma, and he pronounced them somewhat like boiled beans at home.

"They taste like . . . a . . . vegetable," he concluded somewhat lamely. We watched him eat with an intensity which would have been funny if it were not so critical.

One by one, we took our turns. Carmen thought the fruits, which were her allotment, had possibilities, but that boiling had not been the best treatment for them. The tubers which fell to my share proved to be very bland in taste, mildly and surprisingly rather sweet, but of an agreeable consistency. I reported as well as I could, and hope the things do turn out to be harmless—not only for my own comfort!—but also because I have a feeling they might be very good, if our cooks can experiment with them. The grilled meats were quite good to their tasters, although the land animals provided scanty fare. All of us watched, repelled yet fascinated, as Jinjur grimly opened the shells of one of the shellfish, looked inside, and gulped audibly. I have seen her do many brave things, but nearly the bravest was the firm way she squared her shoulders and downed the shell's pink occupant. Then her look of determination was replaced by a startled expression.

"I *think*," she said carefully, "that that was good!" She paused, and opened the next fat shell with cautious hope. This time she investigated more carefully, dividing the meat into several bites which she ate with obviously increasing pleasure.

"Well! A slice of lemon, or a bit of tartar sauce, perhaps—anyway, not bad. Not bad at all." She patted her lips discreetly and smiled contentedly.

Nels' taste of the large fish was reassuring, if less evocative of a gourmet delicacy than Jinjur's. He stolidly consumed a healthy portion, commenting only on its tenderness and mildness.

None of us felt any urge to wander off for the next hour or so, preferring to lounge around, waiting to note the effects of these unique ingestions. I know I found myself concentrating on what was happening inside me with such uneasiness I began to feel rather ill; fortunately, I realized this was probably more due to my own qualms than anything toxic I had consumed. Indeed, as time wore on without any dire symptoms appearing, we all became more cheerful. Arielle and Cinnamon fell to discussing seasoning possibilities, and the other women joined in. Having absolutely nothing to suggest in that line, I was free to observe the men talking, very softly, off to one side.

Nels seemed to be describing something to the other three, and their interest was evident. His story progressed, almost inaudible to me, when he suddenly said, loudly, "More!" Then his voice dropped again, and, bewildered, I saw David's shoulders begin to shake.

Suddenly Richard threw back his head with a great shout of laughter, in which John joined. I watched, baffled, as all four turned to regard us with a peculiar mixture of merriment and concern. They then turned back, to confer in low voices again.

Jinjur had been watching, with growing impatience, and now called, "Hey! Front and center, you four! What's so funny?"

The men came slowly, to stand, rather ill at ease, before her.

"It's a bit of a problem," began Nels slowly, looking at the ground.

"But we definitely have the solution," added Richard more firmly, and then chuckled and stopped.

"The thing is," said John with determination, "the flouwen are experiencing difficulty in the ocean; the chemical mixture is such that they can adapt to it, but it lacks something. Similarly, we could live on a restricted diet here for a while, but if there's no—for instance—potassium in the food, we'll eventually become ill."

"I'm aware of that danger," said Jinjur grimly. "It's facing us right here and now. Do the flouwen know what chemicals they lack?"

"Well, that's it, you see. Apparently, what they require is a small amount of ammonia to keep their internal chemistry properly balanced, and by sheer accident—here Richard spluttered again but was instantly silent—they've discovered we can supply them that! If we cooperate," he added hastily.

Jinjur frowned. "Well, of course we'll cooperate. We need to keep them as allies in any way possible. But where do we get ammonia? I don't . . ." She stopped, her eyes widening, as Carmen emitted the first real laugh I have heard from her in months.

"Am I right?" Carmen asked Nels, her eyes dancing. "They want urine?"

I gasped, but it transpired that she was correct. Urine is the human body's way of handling the toxic ammonia produced during some metabolic processes. Two ammonia molecules are tied up into a less toxic compound, which is then disposed of. The flouwen had learned (how, was tactfully not described) that human urine supplied them admirably with the very chemical needed to balance their system's internal chemistry, and it behooves us to share it with them. With careful choice of words, we addressed the problems of supply and demand, and finally decided to set aside a certain very shallow section of the beach for providing the flouwen with that which they need.

Nels said, "We'll need to work out a signal for them, to let them know when . . ."

But I flatly refused to do that. "Of course, I shall do my part," I said firmly. "And happy to help. But I don't intend to make a loud announcement each and every time . . ." I broke off, but the others seemed, mostly, to agree. I'm sure the flouwen, intelligent as they are, will be quick enough to learn when to visit that beach.

As the evening wore on, and we continued to experience no distress from our unusual meal, we became more relaxed. Nels and John had carefully studied the two small creatures we had, apparently, killed, and described their curiously incomplete structures. We puzzled over that to no avail. From there, the conversation ranged to the wide variety of life-forms we have already observed, and a bit of useless speculation about what we have yet to learn. We had fallen rather quieter, when David suddenly produced a wonderful surprise. He had, during the past days, been selecting bits of stick and lengths of sapling for some private purpose of his own. Now, he reached behind him and pulled forth one of the sapling tubes and put it to his mouth. To my incredulous delight, he produced a soft and lilting bit of melody.

"Oldest instrument in the world—any world!" he chuckled at our amazement. "Nothing to it!" And, indeed, it looks simple—but even with the best intentions, I could never have placed the little holes, and the curious little bit of leaf, at just the right position to create music.

"There's more!" he said, putting down the flute. Moving to the shadows at the back of our lean-to, he felt around, and brought out a harp with an odd, boxy frame. It was fitted with little pegs, and strung with tightly wound tendrils from the strangling rootlets. I listened, entranced, as he struck several individual notes in rhythm, and then brushed the entire surface for a gentle chord. "Can't tune it, of course!" he said cheerfully. "And the vines don't work very well. But it's a start!" He snatched up the whistle again, and played a very simple thing of four notes, but with a joyous jigging rhythm. David's pleasure in his own music is revealing; how vital it must be to him, to work so long and patiently to create it! The four sweet notes set up an insistent beat; repeated steadily, but altering slightly at each repetition.

Suddenly, Shirley seized a nearby cooking pot, upended it, and began to beat out a complex tattoo in counterpoint to David's whistling. She has never done such a thing before! I watched in amazement as her face bent to the task, intent and absorbed, while her fingers and palms danced with a life of their own. Quickly, Carmen stood, placed her hands on her hips, and held her body straight and still while her feet flew over the rushes in an intricate pattern.

"My God!" said John softly, his eyes glowing. "It's Amateur Night!" But he didn't move, and I was watching the three with such pleasure I paid no attention to him.

Then, Carmen's foot slipped on the uneven surface, and she stopped. The whistle sounded a final note and was silent, and Shirley's hands clattered a triumphant cadence, and stilled. The hush sounded very quiet for an instant, and then the rest of us applauded madly until our hands ached!

We're all drowsy now, hoping to feel as well when we awaken, and are eager to begin further exploration and food sampling. Although we have still been unable to build our signal fire or to receive any message from *Prometheus,* we are more cheerful this evening—for very little reason!

"It's not such a bad little old world, after all," murmured John. The trite old phrase took on new meaning, suddenly. I considered what we've found, and seen, and done in this hectic time.

"Could have been worse. And still could, too." Nels was realistic.

"Still . . ." Shirley's voice was drowsy, but content. "I don't know . . . it's been kind of fun. . . ."

Arielle yawned unself-consciously. "Good place to swim . . . warm . . . plenty to do . . ."

"And a *terrific* place to sleep!" Carmen purred, and curled even more tightly into her own nest.

# DISTURBING

I was feeling most upset. Until now, the season had been progressing smoothly. The jookeejook were safe in their pens and loaded with ripe fruit, the thook barrier around the tribal compound was thick and tightly sprung, and everyone in the tribe was contentedly busy with their carving, or weaving, or teaching the children how to pict and view and hunt. Even the Toojook tribe on the northern part of the island had been keeping their distance. But now, intruders were disturbing my people's territory—and one of my eyes was late . . .

The midday darkness was fast approaching. All my eyes but one were back in their nests tucked underneath my fronds, feeding me the views they had gathered, while their tired bodies in turn rested and fed on the nourishment teats inside the nests. When the darkness came and my last eye had not yet returned, I was forced to realize that it had been lost. I activated a replacement nest, but it would be many days before I would have my full complement of six again. With darkness upon me, and new views to add to my worldview, I put away the sharp blackglass knife I had been using to cut a notch around one end of a log for a fishing raft I had been making, closed up my fronds, and retired into my mind to contemplate my worldview with its now disturbing features.

As any tribal chief should do, I first viewed the periphery of the thook barrier around the tribal compound. All was secure. I replayed the exits and entrances of the members of the tribe through the three gates. All were now safe inside the barrier except the two young stronglimbs, Beefoof and Haasee, who had taken their fishing nets east to Sulphur Lake some days ago. They had been successful, for already some of their gatherers had returned with armloads of fish wrapped in watersoaked peethoo leaves, then had scampered off again to Sulphur Lake for more. Watching the view of the fresh fish being brought in reminded me that I was hungry, and I sent one of my gatherers off to the tribal fishtank for my midday meal.

I continued my viewing, going in the general direction of the southern beach. Something flickered near the base of a tall boobaa tree as I viewed past. I returned my view to the boobaa tree and looked carefully all the way around it in an old view. Despite being alone, without the protective help of others of its kind surrounding it, the tree was doing well. I would need, however, to send someone to prune back the choker vines climbing the trunk. Up under the fronds at the top of the tall smooth trunk were a number of boobaa fruits, slowly ripening. I switched to a later view, and the fruits were gone!

Down at the bottom of the tree, one of my eyes had recorded a view that showed a strange creature picking up the boobaa fruits that were now lying on the ground. The later views showed nothing, neither creature nor fruit—both had disappeared in an instant. Amazed, I stepped the worldview backward in time until I found the one glance from the eye that had contained the view of the strange intruder.

The creature had only four limbs, and its fronds, instead of being long, blue-green leaves branching up into a decent canopy, were short, curly brown threads drooping down over a bulbous swelling at the top of the trunk. Two of its eyes were in their nests, with the rest out probably gathering views, although I couldn't see the empty nests—most likely hidden under the drooping brown canopy. The mouth opening was in a strange place. Instead of being low on the trunk where the gatherers could get to it, it was up near the eye-nests above a constriction in the trunk.

The most amazing part of the view was that the strange creature, instead of standing on three limbs and picking up the boobaa fruit with its fourth limb, was balanced on only two limbs, while using the other two limbs to pick up fruit. I half expected to see in the next view that the creature had fallen flat on its mouth, but the next view showed nothing, for my eye had flown past. Now severely disturbed, I went on through my worldview, erasing old views, condensing multiple views of stationary scenes, and updating the worldview with new scenes as my eyes continued to feed me the views they had collected.

My gatherer returned, climbed one of my limbs into my mouth, and placed a fresh lakefish in my crop. I lowered my mouth apron, and contentedly ground away with my gizzard at the still flopping flesh, swallowing the juices and bits of flesh with pleasure, while my gatherer fed itself from one of the teats in my mouth.

While I enjoyed my midday repast, I continued my journey southward through my worldview. The further I viewed, the more confused and disturbed I became. Drastic changes were taking place in the scenery in no time at all. Many sections of the worldview made no sense. A peethoo tree viewed from the north looked perfectly normal, its large spongelike leaves sprouting from massive branches supported along their length by slender support trunks that dropped down to the ground. Yet, a view from the east showed the same section of the same peethoo tree as devastated. The slender support trunks had been cut off at the base, the main branch had fallen, and the larger of the leaves had been stripped. It was the same branch—but viewed from different directions it looked completely different. I finally realized that the view showing the damage had been viewed by one of my eyes at a slightly later time than the view showing no damage. There must have been a whirlwind for so much damage to have occurred in such a short time.

I continued on south, looking through my worldview for more signs of whirlwind damage. I finally saw the missing peethoo support trunks and leaves. They were being used to make a structure, somewhat like a storage shed, but larger. In one corner of the structure was the missing boobaa fruit. But the rest of the view was highly confusing, with objects appearing and disappearing from one glance of my eye to the next. There were more of the strange four-limbed creatures, and they kept appearing and disappearing.

Finally, two of them stayed in one place long enough that I was able to look at a series of views over time. What I viewed was most amazing! Somehow, the creatures managed to balance on just two limbs and didn't fall down! It must have been difficult though, for their other two limbs were in constant jerky motion, while their mouths were moving all the time.

All of them had only two eyes, and the eyes were always in their nests. I was forced to conclude that they only *had* two eyes, and those eyes never left their nests. They also seemed to have no gatherers, but instead gathered things themselves. Despite their deficient and deformed bodies, it was obvious that these creatures were intelligent beings. They wore clothing of many different colors, with a weave so fine that the threads were just barely visible in my worldview. The two that were standing together were trimming the missing peethoo support trunks to a uniform length. One of them had a standard blackglass knife, although of very crude construction, while the taller one with the yellow vine down the side of its head had a knife with a shiny luster unlike anything I had ever seen. If these creatures used tools, they were certainly not animals, and lacking gatherers to do their talking, the low growling noises coming from their rapidly moving mouths no doubt was conversation between the two creatures.

My attention was next drawn to a circle of stones in the sand. Nearby was a pile of broken sticks from dead trees that had lost their battles and had been sucked dry. Both the circle of stones and the pile of sticks were new, for my worldview showed nothing but sand the previous time one of my eyes had surveyed that section of territory. I updated my worldview and looked with care at the scene. There was a fire in the center of the stones, kept alive by the occasional addition of dried sticks by one of the strange four-limbed creatures. My body twitched in sympathy as I watched the all-devouring yellow horror licking at the fractured bodies of its prey. Despite the fact that the fire was safely fenced in by stones, I was sincerely glad that we were deep in the rainy season and everything was soaking wet. These strangers must be intelligent *indeed* to be able to control fire! I *must* arrange to meet with them and learn how they are able to do that.

I then expanded my view so I could see what the strange creature was doing with the fire. It was holding a stick over the fire. Impaled on that stick were a few chunks of something. The creature pulled one of the chunks off the stick and raised it to its naked mouth. I moved my view closer and expanded it more so I could find out what the chunk was made of. With revulsion and horror I recognized the triple-jointed structure of meat and bone, and the few still-unplucked blue-green pinfeathers on the skin . . .

The creature was eating one of my eyes!

I was so nauseated by the view that I could no longer keep down my midday meal. Although there was still plenty of juice left in the lakefish in my crop, I regurgitated what was left and one of my gatherers took the juicy ball away. The jookeejooks would feed well today.

The midday darkness was soon over, and my eyes fluttered nervously about their nests, eager to resume their viewing. I was resolved to learn more about these strangers. I generated scanning paths for four of my eyes that would cover the territory to the south where the strangers resided. The paths were designed to be high in the sky so these eyes would not be caught by the strangers. One by one, I fed a simplified updated worldview into their brains, along with the scanning path that each was to follow. They took a last nourishing sip from their nest-teat and flew off. I kept one eye in its nest to serve me until the replacement eye opened.

I activated one of my gatherers and it scampered out of my mouth to my storage shed and soon returned with a tablet of moist writing clay. After the gatherer had returned to its teat and was connected back into me, I used its front claws to inpict a proclamation to the tribe, for I would be away many days.

"I, Seetoo, Chief of all the Keejook, am leaving on a journey to Circle Bay on the south shore to meet with the strangers who have appeared there. In my absence, you shall heed Tookee as you would me."

I had the gatherer place the pictotablet on Proclamation Rock and whistle a call to the tribe. Each member of the tribe sent an eye over to read the message. Beefoof and Haasee would get the message later in the day when they sent one of their eyes in this direction to update their worldviews of the trail back to the tribal compound and the scenes inside the compound thookwall.

I stumped my way to my storage shed and used my nested eye to look carefully at what I had stored there. Balancing on three limbs, I used the roots on my other three limbs to pull out those things that I would take on my journey. I took out my travel net and tied it to my fronds so it hung conveniently at my side. This would be a long journey, lasting many days, so I packed my travel net carefully. Dried fruits and meats, wrapped in waterproof feebook leaves, lined the bottom of the net for those days when the efforts of my gatherers were not sufficient to supply my needs. On top, for use during the first few days of travel, were fresh fruits and steaks from the latest jookeejook slaughter. It would have been nice to top off my food supply with a fresh fish, but after a single day of travel, the taste of the fish would no longer be appealing to my gizzard.

I added some pictotablets, for often strangers from other tribes could understand written pictographs better than the local dialect of the whistles from one's gatherers. For presents to give to the strangers, I selected some gold baubles strung on a piece of tentacle-twine, some strings of pretty peekoo-shell beads, and some of the better blackglass knives that Weehoob had flaked. If the blackglass knife the stranger had been using was typical of their tribal knife-maker, they would certainly be impressed with Weehoob's work.

I added some mouth aprons. I would have to teach these strangers that unless one was a seedling, it was impolite to eat in the presence of others with an uncovered mouth. The mouth aprons were made of the finest white cloth with designs of crawler vines woven with purple threads that had been dyed with the new color extract the weaver Hoonee had obtained from soaking peekoo shells in the gastric juices of lakefish.

By the time I finished filling my travel net, Tookee had made his way across the compound so we could converse, gatherer to gatherer. Tookee was still grinding his midday meal, so his mouth apron was lowered. From behind his mouth apron Tookee's gatherer whistled a greeting.

"I am honored that once again you have chosen me to act in your place, Chief Seetoo. I promise to take good care of the tribe in your absence. Would you like for some of the younger stronglimbs to accompany you on your journey to meet the strangers?"

"No, Tookee, that would not be wise. A single person approaching a group of many persons must of necessity have peaceful intentions—but many persons approaching could be interpreted as an attack. Although these strangers have injured me by killing and eating one of my eyes, which is normally considered an act of warfare, they are so different from us, in both physical form and behavior, that I must excuse their actions as being due to a lack of knowledge of our customs. It is obvious to me that they are quite intelligent, and know much that we do not know. We could learn much from them. I will go alone, but please have some of the tribe keep an eye or two on me during my journey. . . ."

"It will be done, Chief Seetoo."

". . . and make sure the teacher Teeloot keeps Peebeek working on his pictographs. It is fine that the seed of the Chief is an accomplished stronglimb in wrestling and running, but he must also be literate. The pictographs on the last tablet of his I saw when I visited the school were so distorted that I could hardly tell his selfsign from the scratches of a jookeejook."

I replaced my royal-red frond ribbon with a clean new one, and tied it in place with the bow hanging down my back. I then donned a clean white mouth-apron with the crest of the Tribal Chief embroidered in royal-red thread. Leaving my spear in its rack, I strapped on my belt-scabbard that held my favorite blackglass eating knife and stumped my way to the exit.

As I approached the thook barrier, I had my gatherer whistle, "Open for Chief Seetoo." Obediently the thorny coils curled back from the path, and I stumped through, the coils rolling back into place as I passed. The Daylight God was setting as I went down the trail to the south and the clouds in the sky were glowing a royal red. As darkness set in, my eyes fluttered back to me along the trail from the south and settled one by one into their nests. With my worldview fresh, I moved with confidence along the darkening trail through the forest. My replacement eye had opened, and although it would not develop wings for a number of days more, it was already useful for scanning the dark path ahead so I could correlate its view with my worldview and keep to the center of the path.

I came to a clearing where a lava flow from the Great Mountain Hoolkoor had flowed through the forest, killing all in its path. By now, the Nightlight God had opened its eye nearly all the way, and though it was hidden behind the thin, high, cloud cover, there was enough light with which to see. I looked up in the sky to check the positions of all the gods. Off to the right were the eyes of Groundshaker and Oceanriser, also fully open. It would be sixsix plus four days before the eye of Oceanriser grew large and glared down from the center of Nightlight's eye, whistling insults at the Great Mountain Hoolkoor, while Groundshaker went around to the back side where it could use its spear to poke the irritable Hoolkoor from behind. Together, the two would annoy Hoolkoor until it regurgitated a terrible flood of burning lava from its crop, spreading death and destruction over the forest. At the same time, the oceans would rise and flood the lowlands with salty water. I would want to be back safe in the tribal compounds before that time came.

Since the last lava flow had been only twosix days ago, the crusted surface was still hot. I sent out my gatherers to collect peethoo leaves and soak them in a nearby stream. They placed them, three at a time, in front of me, and I ran as fast as I could go over the steaming leaves. By the time I finally reached the other side, Oceanriser had moved in front of Nightlight and its shadow was traveling across the giant lobe, its eyelid slowly closing as morning approached.

Exhausted from my rapid trip across the lava, I rested on all six limbs for a while, while one of my gatherers dropped jookeejook fruits in my crop and I slurped down the good juices and regurgitated the seeds. The winds arose, and clouds gathered. The rain fell in refreshing torrents from the sky. As I lifted three of my legs to continue on my journey to the south, I could hear the rain sizzling on the hot crust behind me.

When morning came, the Daylight God was hidden by the clouds, but my eyes were anxious to be on their way. I sent out three of them to update the view to the south, since no doubt the fast-moving strangers had made many more changes since I had last viewed the territory they occupied. One of my eyes was sent back along the trail to view the tribal compound and check on the lake where Beefoof and Haasee were fishing, since, as Chief, I was still responsible for the welfare of the tribe. The fifth eye was sent ahead along the trail to look for fruit or game, while the new replacement eye served to view my way along the shadowed path through the forest.

The fifth eye returned shortly. It had found a wild jookeejook. After identifying it, it had circled the jookeejook to view it from all sides and had returned to its nest. I looked at that portion of my worldview containing the wild jookeejook as the eye fed me the images.

The jookeejook was eating a small tentacle from a keekoo tree, while some distance away, a large and dangerous tentacle writhed impotently at the end of its thread. The jookeejook had discovered the tentacle-thread running along the ground before the tentacle-thread had noticed the jookeejook was there. The jookeejook had placed itself safely at a distance, then sent one of its gatherers to rush up to the thread and use its sharp digging claws to sever it. This activated the thread, which made the keekoo tree, some distance away, pump nutrients down the thread, causing a tentacle to start forming at the point where the thread had been cut. But before the tentacle got large and powerful enough to attack the jookeejook and its gatherers, the jookeejook had sent in another gatherer to cut the thread again, between the tree and the growing tentacle at the end.

The gatherers had then picked up the small isolated tentacle and were now stuffing the wriggling worm down into the crop of the jookeejook. Off in the distance, the cut end of the thread was now a large and dangerous tentacle, searching about blindly for something to grasp and crush, so it could drag it back to be fertilizer for the roots of the keekoo tree.

I realized that since the jookeejook was coping with a large mouthful, it should be easy to hunt down. I sent my eye on ahead and stumped as rapidly as I could down the trail, my gatherers spread out before me in a hunting pattern. As I came around a bend in the trail, I could hear the whistles of my gatherers and the frustrated screams of a cornered jookeejook, all of its six eyes, out on their springy umbilical stalks, flapping their tiny wings as they tried to keep all my gatherers in view. My gatherers had surrounded the jookeejook. The jookeejook had its own gatherers out to protect it, but unlike my gatherers, who were free, the jookeejook gatherers were permanently tied to the jookeejook through the prehensile umbilical cords attached to the inside of the mouth.

The knife-like claws of my gatherers made short work of the smaller gatherers of the jookeejook. One snip of the umbilical cord and they fell, mindlessly twitching about on the forest floor. Now wishing I had brought along my hunting spear, I raised my forelimb, drew my eating knife from its scabbard, and rocked forward, three-and-two, toward the wounded creature, while my well-trained gatherers kept nipping at the roots of its rearlimb every time the jookeejook attempted to raise the rearlimb in an attempt to escape. A few jabs of my knife-point to the trunk just below the fronds caused the jookeejook to topple, and it was all over. My gatherers cut the eyestalks and the jookeejook was blinded and helpless. Thanking the Rain God again for his gift of food, I pushed the point of my knife into the brainknob hidden behind the leafy fronds and put the poor animal out of its misery.

Since the eyes don't stay fresh very long, they were the first thing my gatherers put in my crop. While my gizzard ground away on the deliciously soft and tasty morsels, my gatherers used their sharp claws to attack the joints on the six legs of the still twitching gatherers of the jookeejook. It didn't take long to turn them into crop-sized pieces, while I cut the main jookeejook trunk into steaks. I and my hardworking parts would eat well for the next few days. No groundworms or dried rations for us!

By the time I had finished butchering the jookeejook and wrapping what the gatherers couldn't stuff down my crop, the Daylight God was high in the still cloudy sky. Filling my travel net with steaks, I continued down the trail to the south, stopping only to gather my eyes during the midday darkness when the closed eye of the Nightlight God hid the always open eye of the Daylight God, and the stars came out in the sky, although there were no stars this midday darkness, just more clouds. I took the time of rest to update my worldview.

The tribe was secure in the compound. Tookee was gatherer to gatherer with Teeloot the teacher, while Peebeek listened attentively at one side. Beefoof and Haasee were still on their raft at Sulphur Lake, Beefoof poling the raft along the shores while Haasee pulled aboard and emptied the long net with its woven pouchtraps, each with at least one fish.

To the south the view was even more disturbed than in previous worldviews. I was now more used to the rapidly moving strangers and their effect on the landscape, however, and was not as confused as I had previously been by incompatible views of a scene seen from different directions. I updated my worldview, and secure in the knowledge that it gave me, started off down the trail in the midday darkness, with my eyes still feeding in their nests. The Daylight God soon came out from behind the Nightlight God and my eyes fluttered off on their assigned viewing routes.

It was much later in the day that I finally came to the edge of the deep forest and entered the stretches of sand made salty from the incursions of the ocean during the high tides caused by the close approaches of Oceanriser and Groundshaker. Here only a few hardy grasses grew. As I stumped across the shifting sand dunes, I whistled to my eyes and had them give me their latest views. Keeping two eyes in their nests, and sending out the others on short trips high above my projected track, I was able to keep my worldview updated often enough that I could actually observe the activities of the strangers. One of them was resting on a rock not too far away. I could now see that its limbs had joints, somewhat like the forelimbs of my gatherers. The two lower limbs were crossed in an impossible fashion, but those two limbs and the bottom of the trunk portion gave it a relatively secure three-point stance on the surface of the rock.

The creature was dressed in unpatterned but colored woven fabrics that covered part of its trunk and the upper portion of its four limbs. Around the constriction in its trunk was an intricate weaving in white thread. I had never seen anything like it before, and had one of my eyes make a permanent impression of its detailed weave. Perhaps it was the creatures' mouth-apron. If so, I would have to acknowledge that it and its fellow creatures were civilized beings.

The upper two limbs of the creature were holding a thin tablet, but it was made of some reflective material rather than damp clay. The mouth of the creature was moving, and growling sounds emerged from its mouth. In the previous worldviews that I could remember, this growling activity had occurred only when two of the strangers were close to each other. Now, however, this stranger was growling at the tablet it held in its limbs. A most puzzling form of behavior, as if whistling at a pictotablet could make marks on it. Taking my time, and aware of the semi-savage behavior of these strange creatures, I approached in a slow walk, three-on-three, taking care to hold up and extend the roots of my three moving limbs at each step, so the stranger could see that I was carrying no weapons. As I approached, one of my gatherers whistled the Peace Greeting with each of my steps forward.

"Welcome! I come in Peace. May your worldview never see strife."

# MEETING

Well, I have been "forgiven," at this point, and the irksome magnanimity of charity is especially chafing since it turned out rather well. No credit to me, however, I must admit.

Since none of us suffered the slightest repercussions from our peculiar meal of the night before—indeed, we all felt refreshed and well—we determined to collect more, and to try the rest of our samples. It's too soon to judge, but our hopes are a trifle brighter about the prospect of surviving in this strange place. Less like terrified castaways, and more like inquisitive investigators, we considered the hours of daylight ahead of us. Jinjur had insisted on our scrupulously recording time spent, so far, in every endeavor. This morning she added a further item to the file.

"The tide rose, during the night, but I've no real idea how much. I think we'd better start keeping track."

"Back on *Prometheus*, I only glanced at the tidal charts James had made," confessed Shirley. "If I had looked carefully at them once, I might now be able to recall them clearly, but I was counting on being able to ask my imp to bring them up in my helmet display any time I wanted to consult them . . ." A quick glance around brought no enlightenment: all of us had assumed we'd have the charts to hand when needed.

David said, "All I do remember is that there were wide fluctuations in the height of the peak tides, depending on how accurately the moons and Barnard were lined up during the quadruple conjunctions, and that some of the tides are really big."

"It doesn't help that most of the time the rainclouds keep us from seeing where Zouave and Zulu are," I added.

"Nothing to do but start from scratch. Literally," said John, moving to arrange a line of stones down the slope of the beach and descending into the rippling shallows. A few minutes search brought a wide variety of colors in the stones, and Nels recorded the arrangement on the back of a smooth piece of bark with his precious pencil. The crude bark tide table was stowed safely, the first entry dutifully made. I stored a duplicate in my electronic journal and set a timing clock running so the time between this reading and the next would be recorded along with the height of the water. The length of the day here was about thirty and a quarter hours, or almost exactly 108,800 seconds. I would later set the zero time for the tide table when the rainclouds parted and at some midnight hour I could see the shadow of the moon we were living on reach the center of the gargantuan planet that hung overhead. It seemed strange to be thinking once again about seconds and hours, for under the primitive conditions we had been living in, a fraction of a day had been sufficient accuracy for any planning activities.

The tide markers set up and recorded, we sorted our various containers, and prepared to search for food. Before setting out, Carmen laid out a quantity of as-yet-untried beans she had found the day before. "There's lots of these," she remarked hopefully. "I hope they turn out tasty, because they're easy to get!"

Cinnamon ran them thoughtfully through her hands, and sighed. "I wish I could try a few things, but I know it's safest to stick to the boiled routine." Richard was awaiting his hunting partner with his usual patience.

"Hurry up, Cinnamon! I want to go down those cliffs today!" He is, apparently, fearless about heights, and I was glad she was willing to watch from a position of safety while he trotted lightly along sheer precipices. He attributes this nonchalance to his Mohawk heritage. Cordially invited to come along, several days ago, while he scouted the cliff-faces for animal dwellings, I had been petrified to see him jump carelessly from one crumbling rim to another, with a drop below of more than a hundred feet! I had sat down, with assumed fatigue, and looked resolutely out to sea until he clambered up to my side again, grinning and not even slightly out of breath. I suspect he is secretly enjoying our misadventure hugely; certainly he has taken to padding silently about the forests, and reporting the activities of some of the smaller native animals with a precision which indicates a great deal of careful observation.

Cinnamon swung the bean pot towards me apologetically. "Will you get the water for me, please, Reiki? If you're going in that direction, that is?"

I was indeed planning to return to the shallow tide pools—the little clams had looked good to us all, and we were anxious to share a taste—and my way passed our little freshwater spring. Cinnamon hurried into the woods, and I hefted the heavy pot thoughtfully. Then I carefully pushed all the beans into it, and set it handy to the glowing coals—I am all too apt to become distracted from a cooking chore, and if the pot was where I would notice it, it would be safer. I selected a large, but much lighter, container for the water, along with a net for my catches, and went quietly down the beach.

My slippered feet made no sound on the soft wet sand, and when I saw one the little six-legged scurrying creatures busily exploring our collection of food, I stopped and watched it. It never looked in my direction, and when it finally picked up a fruit and trundled off I was certain it was unaware of my following presence. It moved rapidly and purposefully down a narrow, almost invisible trail, and seemed unaware of both the noisy rustling it caused among the bushes, and my own silent progress. I was concerned, as we were approaching some thorn thickets, but the little animal's speed never slackened. To my amazement, I saw the thorny branches divide before it! The animal hurried through without pausing, and I was able to follow before the aperture closed again. I noticed with some dismay that it did reclose, and the way behind me was as thick and thorny as ever, but my curiosity was growing with every step, and I postponed worry about my eventual return. In any case, our destination seemed to be so far ahead that we went into and out of many thorn thickets; my small guide was pursuing a beeline, and as long as I stayed quick and quiet behind it, I could follow, and then select my own way home. We traveled thus for nearly an hour, through dark forests, across a still-warm crusted tongue of lava from the nearby volcano, and we had penetrated a larger and thicker forest of thorns than I had yet seen when I suddenly saw a clearing ahead of us, and a spot of bright color.

Thus warned, I hesitated, and stayed motionless as the little animal continued on, straight ahead, up to and into a hole in the trunk of the strangest tree I have ever seen. With instinctive caution in the presence of such a large and peculiar plant, I sank into the shadow of a convenient boulder and watched. The tree is at least four meters tall and very thick in diameter—about one meter, at an estimate. The leaves atop it form a dense canopy, of a softer shade of the ubiquitous blue-green. Suspended from these upper regions are six small structures, like hanging nests. One of the nests quivered from time to time, as though it contained a living occupant. The small animal I had pursued scampered up one of the large roots of the tree into a smoothly rounded hole and disappeared. I watched for its return to sight for many minutes, but nothing happened.

All at once, I heard the whistling which has become so familiar to us, and ducked instinctively as one of the little "owls" fluttered into view and dove immediately into one of the flaccid nest-like structures. Once again I waited, watching, and noting how sturdy are the thick long roots which support the trunk—there were six of them, curved and long.

The glimpse of color which had caught my eye was red, and shaped like a curious decoration, entangled in the leaves of the canopy. In addition, hanging above the little hole in the trunk is a fabric-like banner, creamy in color, and curiously patterned in red. The trunk is girdled with a series of pouches—I was not close enough to determine if they grew from the bark or were simply hung along the surface, but there were things inside them, of varying contours. I watched closely, but caution kept me from approaching nearer—I didn't want the little owl-things to spot me while I was so far off on my own.

The thought of passing time startled me, and I realized I had better leave this fascinating tree, bedecked as it appeared to be for some celebration—by whom?—and report to the others. Accordingly, I turned back, and patiently fought the thorns in silence until I was free of that thicket and could run around the rest, back towards the beach.

By the time I reached the little spring my steps had slowed considerably, and, when I trotted up, I saw with horror the water container I had dropped. Those wretched beans! In urgent haste I filled the jar and fled towards the fire, trying desperately to think how long I had been gone. I quailed when I saw all the others there, busily carrying wood, while Cinnamon bent sadly over the pot of now-roasted beans.

"Reiki, I'm afraid you burned these even before you cooked them!" she said mildly. Comments from the others were less gentle.

"Did you say there were lots of these, Carmen?" asked Jinjur. "So, maybe, we can try again with them when someone is willing to pay attention?"

"Well, yes, there's plenty," Carmen sniffed. "But the branches are stiff and scratchy; *someone* else can go for the next batch!"

"I don't suppose you had any extra time to collect clams, either, Reiki? Hope you're all willing to try boiled roots tonight, folks!" taunted Shirley.

"Gack!" said Richard, with feeling.

"Too late to do anything about that now. C'mon, Reiki, help us hustle for dry wood—haven't you noticed the sky?" David's importunate query caught my ear. Of course I hadn't noticed the sky, having been far too interested in my strange tree. Now I looked and saw that the rain had stopped, at least for a while, and the sky above was clearing. It was near noon, and the darkness was falling as Barnard slid behind Gargantua. Beautifully, magically, the elliptical light of *Prometheus* shone in the darkening heavens through the thinning clouds! My whole self ached with the glorious sight, so familiar and dear, and containing everything I knew of home!

Hastily, I sloshed the useless water into the bean pot and hurried to help. We had, several days previously, formed a huge cross on the sand, as straight and true as possible with the naked eye, and built up a wide ridge of sand along the lines. This sand was quick to drain dry, and along the ridges we hastily and evenly piled our tinder, bringing it from the big supply we kept under shelter. We worked quickly in the fading light, for ominous clouds were gathering again. Then each of us took a portion of the burning coals, and at Jinjur's signal we bent to set our bonfire alight. Rapidly, the dry wood caught, and the flames spread along the bisecting lines, even, straight, and burning brightly. It was a splendid fiery cross! We watched it burn, in silence, and willed our thoughts upwards with the sparks. For half an hour we kept it flaming, sending its clear signal of life and hope. Then, with planned precision, we snuffed it out, as close as we could do it all at one time. This too is part of the signal, indicating we are in some degree of control, at present. As we extinguished the last embers with sand, we were all quiet. We have done what we can, and just about all we can, to reestablish communication with our parent ship. The next move will be up to them. Pensively, wearily, we drifted slowly back towards our campfire as the next storm front moved in and it started to rain again.

Suddenly, Carmen, in the lead, sniffed twice. "What's that I smell? It smells like . . . no . . . it can't be . . . coffee?"

The scent coming on the rising little breeze was not coffee, really, but it was not unpleasant; it was toasty, and warm, with a definite character. Arielle broke into a run and hurried to my steaming bean pot. She and Cinnamon bent over it hopefully, and found spoons to taste.

"Reiki!" said Carmen, her eyes glowing in the firelight. "It's not coffee—yet! But with a little more careful roasting than *you* gave it, and grinding of course, I think we can come up with something pretty close!" She took another sip. "It's already better than we had on *Prometheus*!" she enthused. I remembered when our original stores had been used up, and how disgusted she had been with the Christmas Bush version of the brew. I smiled happily at her, noticing again how pretty Carmen is now that all the makeup she wore has vanished.

Quickly the others tasted, critical, but genuinely appreciative of my serendipitous concoction. I've never been a connoisseur of coffee, and to me it tasted both weak and bitter, but perhaps that can be bettered when the cooks are in charge. At any rate, it helped to make up for the meagerness of the rest of our meal, for which I was grateful!

"You know, Reiki, in the normal course of events, you'd never have had a thing to do with beans, or fire, or even making mistakes," said Shirley thoughtfully. "Of course I'll be only too happy to turn everything back over to James, when we can, but . . . it's really rather exciting, doing things for ourselves."

Jinjur grinned, her white teeth bright in the firelight. "So far we've been lucky," she said. "We're still just blundering around, without really knowing what we're doing."

David glanced up at the leafy roof above us. "Well, considering, I agree with Shirley. I never helped raise a roof before, never thought I would, but it's up and doing the job, and we sure did every bit of it ourselves."

"After all the high-tech apparatus built into my standing desk in the hydroponics lab, *this* is a definite come-down! But it works," Nels admitted. "This" is a long, narrow, flat-topped work area, consisting of leaf-planks lying on simple saw-horse arrangements. It accommodates Nels's lanky height as well as Arielle's small stature by the simple expedient of going uphill, and each of us has found a spot upon it that suits us.

While we ate, and rested through the remaining dark hour of midday, I completed this entry into my journal, but said no word of the discovery of the decorated tree. I don't know why I am keeping that to myself, nor why I am determined to return to it as quickly as I can. It's unlike me to be secretive, but, in this case, the secrecy is compelling.

Would the bizarre interview have concluded less happily, if I had not kept my discovery to myself? I flatter myself that it might have indeed, but of course I cannot be sure.

Before the light had advanced even to dimness, I slipped off, heading silently back to the strange tree I had found. I made good speed, although the light was still gloomy in the slow rain. I had gone well over a mile when I heard, ahead of me, the peculiar whistling we had been puzzling over, and I hid behind the trunk of one of the big banyan-like trees; if this approaching "owl" was communicating with anyone, I wanted no warning of my presence to be communicated. The "owl" flew past me, and I went warily, from cover to cover, hoping I might find who, or what, had been decorating the tree.

Ahead of me I could hear strange new sounds—sounds unlike any I had ever heard before. Keeping out of sight as much as possible, I approached the final thicket where I had last seen the tree, peered through the thorny foliage, then stood, absolutely transfixed. The strange "tree" was MOVING! I cannot express my shock, at seeing the long, thick roots alternately lifting, three at a time, transporting the "plant," slowly, ponderously, with very definite intent, in an elephantine but effective march!

As I stared, dumbfounded, several of the little "owls" emerged from the nestlike structures in the canopy, and flew off in various directions. Their strange cries instantly began again, whether to signal each other or the big "tree" I had no way of knowing. The moving green giant had now reached the edge of the thorny barrier. With difficulty, I remained quiet, struggling to assimilate the meaning of what I was seeing, as the spiky coils rolled back upon themselves, and the "tree" continued its plodding pace, through the opening in the barrier!

Keeping out of sight, I followed the slow progress of the incredible traveling plant. I was fascinated to see that the method of locomotion, while tediously slow, provides maximum stability for what must be considerable weight. The front "leg," as that is what it seems to be, moves in unison with the back side pair for a single massive step; then the trunk is balanced on those three legs while the front side pair and the rear leg move forward in the next step. It is a series of smooth, slow movements, seemingly hydraulic in nature. They were carrying the beast smoothly along the trail; with yet another shock, I realized that the trail was one that led directly to our camp!

I ran ahead to find a good vantage point where I could watch the trail without being seen. It was hours later, and well into the afternoon, when the tree finally ambled into view. It stopped at a thorn thicket just off the trail, and, after a whistle which somehow produced an opening, it went inside. In about the center of the thicket, the "plant" paused in its motion.

In increasing disbelief I watched as one of the roots rose, slowly and smoothly, to the belt around its middle and, without fumbling, removed from a scabbard what certainly looked like an obsidian blade! Two other legs rose to a net hanging down from the blue-green fronds to remove and unwrap a package containing a chunk of something. Using the sharp blade with precision, and an economy of movement that told its own story of sophistication, the amazing creature cut the contents of the package into segments. Some of these segments it swung up to the opening in the "trunk" where they were taken by the small creatures inside. The remaining segments were rewrapped, equally slowly and exactly, in what looked like a thin waxy leaf and placed back into the carrying net.

Then, carefully, the roots lowered the red-embroidered, apron-like cloth until it covered the hole in the trunk. From behind the cloth I could hear soft but definite crunching noises, and I concluded that the segments were being consumed in some fashion.

The thing had been standing still while this took place, but it now resumed its ponderous progress. I began to think, as hard as I could, and swiftly. The strange decorations on the "tree" were, even from this distance, both bizarre and formal, and immaculately clean; it was impossible to mistake a genuine intent in this steady advance; nor could I overlook the obvious intelligence concealed somewhere in this alien creature. We were soon to receive a most unusual visitor!

Quickly, I considered my options. At the rate the giant "plant" was moving, it would be a number of hours at least before it would come near enough to our small camp to meet any of the others by chance. I would have plenty of time to warn them—if that was what was necessary here! But I waited, thinking. This approach had much of stateliness about it, and nothing of hostility. A native of this world, of such size, with unmistakable technical abilities, with appreciation of adornment for its own sake, with apparent control over at least some other species extant here—all of this indicated an emissary worthy of our own most civilized behavior. In an initial confrontation, it was vital that our behavior be not only civilized, but universally understandable. I stood, and took a deep breath.

I felt, very strongly, that I was better suited to make the first tentative step towards amity than most of the others, if not all. I hoped I might be able to provide a peaceful liaison between this incredible being and the weary, worried members of my group. At any rate, I resolved to try.

Still keeping myself concealed from the "owls," who did indeed seem to serve as advance warning for the "tree," I hurried ahead some distance and began to look for a suitable meeting site. It was important that I appear calm and ready for the greeting, and neither hostile nor servile. I found what I was looking for, a few feet off the creature's direct line of march. It was a large rock, to the top of which I was able to climb with a few easy steps. Here I sat, straight, and as still as I could hold.

The moving tree came steadily on. One of the small flying creatures, returning, caught sight of me and emitted such a startled squeak of sound that I nearly laughed. It circled me twice and then flew back to its nest on the animal. After moving about inside for a short while, it returned to the opening in the nest and stayed there, its large eye focused directly upon me. The giant creature stopped, and from the surrounding forest, two other "owls" emerged, returning immediately to their "nests," from which all three surveyed me unblinkingly. I sat motionless, except for speaking softly into the recorder, while I was examined, and commented on, apparently, for several minutes.

Then, slowly, almost formally, the tree started walking toward me. With each step it raised its moving legs high, and spread the roots at the tips of the legs, as if to show that they were empty of weapons. One of the small scurrying creatures, poised in the trunk opening, whistled a melody different from any I had heard before. It was brief, and repeated several times. There was no doubt in my mind that I was being greeted in a most formal and peaceful manner.

Before it had come much nearer, I stood up on the

rock, put the recorder into my pocket, extended my own arms and opened my empty hands. I remained standing tall for a minute, my head nearly level with the top of the fronds on the alien, and then, carefully and precisely I stepped from the rock and lowered my arms. I wanted to make it clear that while I could move with much greater speed than the being before me, I chose not to do so at this time. With slow and steady steps I approached, stopping about five meters in front of the now motionless creature. As slowly and formally as I could, I bowed low. This elicited a ripple of movement from the creature. I straightened, and began to speak in my normal voice.

"I and my friends have come in peace to visit your land. We mean you no harm, although we find ourselves in need of sustenance and shelter, which we have made bold to take for ourselves. We hope that our visit will be beneficial to us, and at least harmless to you. Perhaps we can learn much of value from each other. Certainly, if that is the case, it will be in our mutual best interest to pursue the ways of friendship."

Of course I knew my words would mean nothing to the intelligence before me, but I have long observed that the tones in a human voice convey infinitely more subtle messages than words. The fact that I appreciated and was impressed by the awesome presence of this being would inevitably be communicated if I spoke sincerely, and, more importantly, at some length. I paused, and then, as nearly as I could, I repeated the little tune of greeting.

My heart was pounding, but I soon controlled my breathing and was quiet again. The little animal in the opening vanished suddenly, which caught my eye. It was instantly replaced—by a different one? I could not tell. It began whistling something—neither song nor speech, but with something of each—which went on for nearly a minute. As it was concluding, I saw, with some trepidation, one of the long "legs" rising slowly towards me. It came steadily on, until it was in the air, midway between us, when it stopped. Carefully, slowly, I extended my hand, and, with the lightest possible touch, put my fingers on the outstretched root of the alien. It felt as much like a plant as it looked, but nonetheless real, and I withdrew my hand slowly, my mind tingling as my fingers were not, at the unbelievable meeting.

Which seemed to be over. It was late in the afternoon and it was getting dark. The small animal disappeared inside the trunk, and the enormous legs began their strange shuffle toward a nearby thorn thicket. One of the small creatures in the mouth of the alien gave a whistle and the thorn bush opened to allow the alien in. I turned and sprinted off down the trail toward our camp, as the owls returned to their nests.

It is now the next morning, and I have narrated as clearly as I can all that happened yesterday. I have gone back up the trail and checked, and the creature is back out of its thorn thicket and is obviously on its way here. My recorder is on now so that I won't have to repeat our plans, and so that the upcoming encounter can be entered as it occurs. I'll try to keep our comments identified, so that when we can get this account to James it will be clear. (Fortunately, I can enter my own comments with my fingertips, unheard.)

"How far away is the creature by now, Reiki?" (This was Jinjur.)

"As near as I can judge, about half a kilometer. That'll take it a couple of hours, but we'll see it well before that."

"We've got to be ready for an attack. There's absolutely no reason to count on this being a friendly visit." (John, ever wary!)

"On the contrary—I think we ought to assume it *is*

friendly until we have good cause to think otherwise. For it to have met Reiki in such neutral circumstances, and stayed benign, is a pretty good sign." (Nels, with quiet firmness.)

"For Reiki to have deliberately confronted the thing was stupid!" (Richard, growling.)

"And dangerous. I'm furious about that, Reiki!" (Jinjur is angrier with me than I have ever seen her. I shall speak in my own defense, and in that of the giant—I must succeed in this!)

"I know it was not only not stupid, it was not dangerous. You will see, and feel, as I did, the lack of hostility in this . . . this giant, when you meet it, if you are willing to wait, and remain calm. That's why I wanted to prepare both you and it. And why I ask you, please, to be ready to greet it peacefully, and move slowly and tranquilly. It has come a long way with great patience, to seek us out; I suspect that through its seeing eye owls, it already knows a great deal more about us than we do about it. And the fastest way we can establish a bond we can grow with, is to slow down to its speed, paradoxical though that sounds! We must demonstrate that we are civilized aliens, so we can learn if it too is civilized—for it certainly is alien!"

"Can you repeat that first tune you mentioned, Reiki?" (David's question, as he brought up his whistle.)

"I'll try." (I did, and David quickly copied it, although I'm afraid I got a couple of the notes wrong.)

"Shall we all stay, or some hide?" (Arielle, looking speculatively at the tall tree trunks around us.)

"I'm pretty sure it knows exactly how many we are. Those little 'owls' have been about us all along, and I think they have a symbiotic relationship with the tree—or a relationship of some sort."

"Which is it, Reiki, plant or animal?" (Carmen's question.)

"I don't know. You'll see it, you decide which it is!"

(And here it comes in sight! We are lined up, two formal rows at attention, with Jinjur at our head, and all as still as possible, while the creature slowly advances. I hear gasps of amazement, and even I am newly amazed at this unbelievable sight. The blue-green fronds atop the tall creature move in the wind, and the empty "nests" swing freely. All the little "owls" but one are busy in flight, keeping us all under surveillance. The amazing roots move slowly but efficiently, and one of the small animals suddenly appears in the opening. It's the greeting-song again! David gives me a reproachful look—I had indeed got the tune wrong! But he slowly lifts the flute to his mouth, and responds with a very accurate imitation of the melody. The huge being almost ripples! As we agreed, I step forward, slowly, with Jinjur, until she is within reach of the long legs.)

Speaking slowly, I extend her hand: "May I present our commander, Jinjur."

(The small animal vanishes, is replaced instantly, and a new sound comes forth! Sounding amazingly similar to my tones, the speech is:)

"Maaee preeseent oor coommaandeer jeenjuur."

(Wherever this being maintains its intelligence is a mystery, but its existence is very obvious! With more self-confidence now, Jinjur takes another step, slowly indicates herself with both hands, and states:)

"Jinjur."

(The massive "foot" begins to rise. Jinjur, without flinching, extends her hand, and touches the strong extending "root." From yet another little "mole" comes a new sound—a soft, whistling.)

"Jeenjuur!"

* * *

It's once again late, and my watch. We continue to maintain one, although we've seen nothing to cause us alarm; Jinjur's military training goes too deep to allow her to relax her vigilance on our behalf, and in addition, we are still anxiously awaiting a break in the weather which might bring us a return signal from *Prometheus*.

I have much to think about, as I gaze at the scudding clouds. Our meeting with the giant plant lasted for hours. At some point early on, the creature (which makes most of its sounds through the little animals we have seen gathering food!) emitted a deep noise which sounded startlingly like a chuckle. I very much doubt that it was anything of the sort, but it sounded so like a deep, human laugh that Richard exclaimed, involuntarily,

"Ho, Ho, Ho? Is it a Jolly Blue-Green Giant?"

The name stuck, I'm afraid. To me it sounds both inaccurate and condescending, but the others now refer to the immense creature as a Jolly, so I shall go along with it until we learn more.

And there is vastly more to learn! It proved surprisingly quick to copy our sounds of speech, and to learn the meanings of words. It is apparently eager to learn, and the first symbol it desired to share was the idea of "fire." We must acquire a large vocabulary to communicate more, but the few facts we have gained, with tantalizing slowness, about the way in which the Jolly exists, have been stunning in their complexity and in their total difference from anything we have ever encountered.

"Eyes," indicated the Jolly, with the smoothly moving tip of one limb gliding up nearly to touch my own, then off to touch, equally lightly, one of the little owls!

Cinnamon, moving with extreme slowness, stood on a nearby rock to peer deeply into one swinging nest without presuming to touch it. Her ready empathy with all living things stood her in good stead, and the Jolly never moved as she stepped down.

"There's nothing in there but a single protruding thing, like a teat. It would just fit that opening on the back of the owl, but I don't know . . ." Here, one of the owls returned to that nest, and Cinnamon said, judging from its position, it was indeed on the teat, with its large eye regarding us from the nest opening.

"This is much more than symbiosis!" exclaimed Nels. "That tiny thing is more like a free-flying extension of the Jolly!"

Similarly, the long slow exploring limb, which behaves somewhat like the trunk of an elephant in its massive yet precise movement, touched my mouth, and then the opening in its body. We were unable to see within, partly because the little animals we have seen were inside, and partly because the opening itself was occupied by one of the same animals, emitting sounds more and more like our words. Curiously, there is a covering for that hole which is obviously made of some other material. It appears soft and fine, and elaborately decorated with colored threads. It hangs above the mouth most of the time, and we have no idea what its purpose is.

From the manner in which the small animal-like creatures darted away from, and quickly back to the opening, it appeared they are not the guiding intelligence of the creature; their activities have the appearance of messengers receiving instructions, and communicating with outsiders. Their alacrity and single-mindedness indicate a great dependence on, and trust of, that central intelligence; indeed, that seems true of the owl-like creatures also. Nels especially strove to maintain a scientific position of detached observation; this was wise, as some of the rest of us tend to leap to anthropomorphic conclusions which frequently are erroneous! Our original assumption, that the owls and animals were individuals in their own right, became drastically altered, as we realized they are actually no more independent than our own eyes and hands. We struggled to understand how a structure that is so like a plant, even to the extent of using photosynthesis to some extent, can have evolved into a tool-making animal!

The Jolly's incredible speed at assimilating and using our own speech patterns was in vivid contrast to its slowness of movement. Indeed, as the urgent questions began to fly from Jinjur and John I felt compelled to intervene.

"Excuse me!" I said rather loudly. "We've begun in well-meaning fashion, and it's obvious there's more for us to learn here than we can possibly do in one meeting. This noble creature may be the key to the entire ecology of this world! But I am sure you see that while the intelligence is even quicker than our own, the motions are necessarily very slow, and it is the essence of diplomacy, more than etiquette, to respect that pace, particularly as we are the unwilling intruders in this country!"

Jinjur looked thoughtfully at me, and to my relief, nodded curtly and sat down quietly; the little "eye" which had been fluttering to keep her in sight returned to its nest.

For the next several hours we worked very hard; studying the Jolly's appearance, formulating hypotheses, framing questions, struggling to simplify the questions enough to be understood, listening to the brief answers and then discussing them quietly.

Finally, we humans became tired and hungry. David, in particular, had been sitting crosslegged in front of the Jolly, listening intently to the whistled phrases passing between "eyes" and "hands"; he copied them, constantly correcting himself, on the little flute, and had interpreted meanings for many of the sounds. When he finally stood, it was slowly and painfully.

"I'm not being mannerly, I'm stiff!" he grimaced.

"And I'm hoarse," croaked Cinnamon, who had been doing most of the questioning—her level tones seem to be the most easily understood by the Jolly, and we had been passing our queries through her.

"How shall we end the conference? Ring a bell or something?" asked John.

"David can!" suggested Arielle. "Try first song!"

That was a good idea—since it was undoubtedly ceremonial in nature, perhaps it would serve as temporary farewell also. Jinjur and Nels seemed about to protest at this termination of our interview; however, as they got to their feet also their expressions revealed surprise and discomfort. We have not remained immobile for so long since our arrival! While the rest of us gathered ostentatiously in a neat row, David repeated the first song we had heard from the Jolly. With some relief we heard the answering repetition, and then we all moved off at our own speed. Once again, the huge roots began their curious plodding pace, and the alien creature moved majestically into the welcoming shelter of a nearby thicket.

Jinjur put Shirley to keep first watch, and the rest of us turned to the routine of preparing a meal.

My own part of the job, to which I am philosophically resigned, is the ongoing collection of fuel; I have become skillful enough to have an effective routine, and one which leaves my mind free to reflect. All the new information was seething so busily in my head I paid little attention to my customary path beside the bustling stream which fell from the hills. I climbed steadily, stopping occasionally to stack pieces for my return trip downhill, or to toss large bits to float downstream for most of the distance. I was thinking so intently of the strange life-form we were studying, that the sight in the soft earth of the brookside gave me a physical jolt. It was only my own earlier foot-print, but now I realized how "alien" it was.

How recently I had been fully engaged in a highly technological mission, remote and detached, in sophisticated surroundings, maintained in every respect by intelligences only slightly more artificial than my own! Could there be anything more complete than this present reversal? As the days have gone by, there has been less and less hopeful talk about the possibility of our ever returning to *Prometheus.* I think each of us has gone round and round in our own minds, searching for a way in which that might be done, and have come up with only pessimistic conclusions. The lander under the water may still provide us with tools, possibly even some means of communicating with the ship, but the difficulties inherent in physical transportation are immense and we know them all.

Are we prepared, or even willing, to consider living out the remainder of our lives in these primitive circumstances with only each other for company? No wonder we are so avid to explore all the intricacies of the creature we met today! How interested Katrina and George would—at this point I missed that former life with a very real pang. But each day, I realized, as I continued to muse, the faces here become more real and precious to me. I think the Christmas Bush and its imps did as much to keep us isolated from one another as they did to keep us carefree and comfortable. Since we had no need for the companionship of others, we had gradually become unmindful, even intolerant of closeness. Certainly I had!

Now, it is becoming easy and pleasurable to talk with each other; and I have heard stories of the backgrounds of my friends I never would have imagined! How Shirley had discovered her passion for drums in early adolescence and joined an amateur band, and, with typical enthusiasm, practiced so assiduously her fingers bled daily! How Nels' meticulous laboratory drawings had led to idle sketches of fantastic creatures, and fired his imagination of other worlds. Carmen's sorrow for her mother's sorrow, when Carmen left her knowing she would never return—there were tears when she told us that, but our quiet listening soothed her, and there was new calm in her face as she sighed, still. And what a joy it is to hear a human laugh—it doesn't happen often, but when it does I hear it with such a lift of the heart! I should, I think, regret losing that, if somehow we could return to the world of James. There always seems to be much to say among us, and we are now sharing our thoughts like our labors.

"It's funny," mused John, one evening. "I never bothered to really listen to Jinjur, I just obeyed orders, and did my work, and let my imp do all the communicating. Now I find, when she hollers or whatever, both the words and the holler have meaning, sometimes contradictory." Interesting, if John really has begun to listen! "And the odd part is, is that I get the message quicker than I did through the imp!"

That was a real delight to hear. The easy intimacy of our communal life is becoming a bond, and our interdependence rests lightly on us all.

I was more than ready for the meal ahead. We have been widening our exploration among possible foodstuffs, and when Arielle and Shirley take their turn as cooks the results can be delectable. Indeed, there are several culinary specialists among us. Cinnamon's way of skewering alternate chunks of fish, clam-meat, and a flavorsome small vegetable on well-soaked slivers of wood, to be grilled slowly, basted frequently with the juice freshly squeezed from the fruit we call a mango, results in a brown, crisply glazed portion, tender and succulent. With rapid and vigorous chopping, John transforms the primrose-colored flesh of the large roots we've dubbed yams into a creamy mass, smooth and mellow, which slides effortlessly down the throat, tasting faintly of sweetness. And David collects, high among the canopy, a tiny, fiery berry whose spicy heat adds welcome flavor to some of the safe but stodgy tubers we find most plentiful.

Two of the new items today had been collected by John, who hovered over them with some concern. One of these is a dark-leafed plant which grows in profusion along the many little streambanks; the other is a thick-skinned small fruit, and he had asked both peel and flesh be cooked. He seemed to have some very definite object in mind, but was reluctant to explain, possibly for fear of influencing the tasters. I think that concern is now unnecessary; as we accumulate a wide variety of edible choices, our comments on new tastes have become remarkably candid—Richard's description of the flavor of David's little "pepper" being noteworthy.

Accordingly, I watched curiously as the small dark leaves were gently steamed—they almost instantly darkened in color, and John looked hopeful. Arielle took a tiny taste of the stuff and looked thoughtful.

"Strong! But not bad." She tasted again, more generously, and chewed slowly. "Tough, too," she commented. "Tastes like . . . like . . . greens."

John was obviously delighted, to my puzzlement. "Great! Give me the rest, Arielle, and I'll run some tests. It's vitamin C I'm after," he explained then. "Good old ascorbic acid—our bodies can't make it, we didn't bring any, and without it we're in for real problems, but that leafy stuff may be an answer!"

As he spoke I turned to watch Shirley approach the steaming fruit which was to be her portion. It smelled rather pleasant, and responded to her knife tip. She took a spoonful; instantly her expression twisted into one I would not have thought humanly possible! Without ceremony she spat the offending morsel straight into the fire and reached for the water bucket, dousing her entire face and gulping frantically.

"No good?" asked Arielle, rather unnecessarily.

"Sour!" gasped Shirley. "I never tasted anything so sour!" John responded with a whoop of glee.

"Terrific! Sounds great! Here, try again!" Quickly he spooned up a tiny portion of the fruit juice, which had turned pink in the cooking, and sprinkled it with a small bit of white powder.

"Try this!" he urged, holding it out to Shirley. She hesitated, but then complied, gingerly. Her apprehension changed to interest then, and she was quick to say, "That's much better!"

John was still excited, but explained "Sour may mean vitamin C too, and I'll test it. It may be as close as we can come to citrus here; all I put on was sugar, but you know how little we have of that, and no way to get more. Unless we can find some of that, too."

We shared his hopes, but I am privately dubious. My own hope is that the Jolly will be able to provide us with information we can use much more readily than this hit-or-miss technique. With this in mind I turned to see if our visitor was where we had parted from it.

The Jolly was not visible in the gloom, but without any real worry I rose to search for it. A moment's reflection led me to the thorn thicket, and peering through the tightly interlaced branches I beheld our guest, motionless and quiet, secure within the protection of those spiky defenses. If we had landed as planned, and conducted our explorations encased in spacesuits, and flying in airplanes, we might have posed a real threat to this native. As it was, we met on much more equal terms! Rather more pleased than otherwise, I left the Jolly undisturbed. The quiet talk around the fire centered on all we had learned from our visitor, both by observation and the halting struggle of conversation.

How achingly weary I am! It was exciting beyond belief to meet this new creature, and to try to absorb so many new ideas, but exhausting. How strange—I have given no thought to *Prometheus* or its crew for hours. Now that I consider the heavy clouds above us, I can only wonder when some message will come. The ship itself is invisible tonight. It is time to awaken the next watch.

When shall I glimpse our soaring home again?

# FINDING

Unbidden, the dream played itself out again. First the scream from Shirley: "We're spin . . ." cut off in mid-cry. Then, the interminably dry voice of James: "Engineering telemetry reports left rear rocket engine has burned through. *Beagle* is now sinking in Crater Lagoon. . . ."

"George! Wake up George!"

I awoke in my dark bedroom, lit only by the soft laser lights of my imp, who was trying to comfort me as best as it could. "Your heart beat had risen to dangerous levels and I thought it best to try to wake you. Was it the same dream again?" asked the solicitous voice of James.

"The same one I have every time I try to go to sleep these past few days. I feel so helpless and useless. I'm in *charge* and there is *nothing* I can do!"

I wearily got out from under the tension sheet as James raised the lights in the bedroom. I was still dressed in the wrinkled coverall I had worn when I turned in. I stopped at the bathroom, avoiding the bleary-eyed and unshaven grisly-gray face in the mirror as I took care of the necessities. I was too impatient to hold still and wait while my imp gave me a shave, pulling up and snipping off each whisker in turn, so I palmed my way out the door of my apartment, dove down the central shaft, and swung out onto the control deck of *Prometheus.*

The night shift crew was busy at their consoles and did not look up. Tony was managing the lightsail, keeping *Prometheus* balanced over the inner pole of Zuni, where the *Beagle* had gone down. Linda was monitoring the communications console—silent except for the occasional engineering status report from one of the orbiting commsats around Zuni. At the same time, she was continuing to use her astronomical telescope to look down at Zuni in a search for the missing spacecraft. From the image on her console screen, there was little to see except layer after layer of dark rainclouds, which had not broken since the *Beagle* had crashed.

Sam was at the science console, evaluating the floods of data still pouring in from the robotic orbiters and surface vehicles scattered all throughout the Barnard planetary system. Despite the tragedy that lay below us and the desires of everyone to help, someone had to keep working at the primary reason we had been sent to this distant star—collecting scientific information about the Barnard system and transmitting it back to Earth—six light-years away.

When Sam saw me appear he murmured to his imp, "He looks terrible, James! Tell him to go back to bed and get some sleep!"

"Can't sleep," I replied grimly back at James. I turned to look hopefully at Linda's console screen. "Has Linda seen anything yet?" I asked James.

Linda avoided looking at me. "Nothing but clouds," came back her reply through my imp. Then, knowing full well what the next question was, she added. "Nothing over the radio but lightning static. The cloud cover is starting to break up, however. If I could only predict the weather, I might be able to forecast when the clouds will part enough to let us get a glimpse of the crash site."

"Weather is what I'm good at," I said, finally relieved to have something constructive to do. I swung around her console and sat myself in front of the second science console. My fingers flew about the touchscreen, setting up the icon menu. "Bring up the weather map for Zuni, James," I ordered.

An hour later I allowed himself a weak smile. "In about six hours there is going to be a break between two low pressure fronts. There is a good chance we will be able to see St. Vincent Island for about three hours."

"That will be around high noon there," came Tony's response through my imp. He was looking at the three-dimensional space navigation display in front of him, which showed the placement of *Prometheus* with respect to Barnard, Gargantua, and its moons. The display also contained computer generated lines that outlined the invisible shadow cones of the giant planet and the moons, for knowing the position of those shadow cones was essential in piloting a spacecraft powered by sunlight. The shadow cone of Gargantua was approaching the orb of Zuni. "It's going to be dark for almost two of those three hours."

"Damn!" I said, feeling frustrated again. I sent out orders through my imp. "Linda. James. Have the Christmas Bush get the infrared detector array ready to substitute for the visible photoelectric array in the telescope. The resolution won't be as good, but something is better than nothing."

"You forget I have a searchlight," said Tony. "By the time the break comes, I could have *Prometheus* just outside Gargantua's shadow cone and in position to reflect some sunlight on the landing area. I won't be able to hold the sail in position for the whole two hours, but I should be able to cover most of the eclipse period."

"I was planning on using both the visible and the long infrared arrays at the same time, anyway," injected Linda. "I just have to insert a wavelength selective mirror in the ray path to pull out the infrared portion and send it to the infrared detector array. That way I can look for infrared signatures from objects warmer than the background, and correlate them with any visible spectrum signatures that match typical vehicle, spacesuit, coverall, and skin reflectance spectra."

"Skin reflectance! Are you going to be able to see individual people?" I asked.

"Sorry, no," replied Linda, again avoiding my eyes and speaking softly through her imp while her fingers flew over the touchscreen. "I'm afraid not. To keep the sail out of Gargantua's shadow, Tony is going to have to put *Prometheus* at least one Gargantuan radius from Zuni. That's a hundred thousand kilometers. The best resolution I can get with my ten meter telescope aperture at that distance is ten meters. But the *Beagle* made a careful multispectral survey of the beaches around Crater Lagoon before it went down to land, so we know what infrared and visible spectra to expect. If we see any sections of beach that are significantly different, then there is something new there. And if that something new has the right spectra and is far enough away from the high tide line, then someone escaped from the crash and is on the beach waiting for us to see them."

"I hope so. . . ." I said soberly, and turning my eyes again to my screen I felt the command responsibility weighing heavily on my shoulders again. "Although if they got out, why haven't they radioed us?" I asked my imp. No one answered.

I got up from the console and headed for the lift shaft.

"I think I'll go up to the kitchen and get some

coffee so I'll be awake when the break in the weather comes."

"No, you don't!" Sam yelled behind me. I turned to see him looking at Tony. "Tony—you're technically commander of *Prometheus* during this shift. You tell that bleary-eyed, baggy-suited, bone-weary, blowzy-bearded bum to go back to bed where he belongs. We'll wake him before the action starts."

"Sam . . ." protested Tony. "He's a Colonel and I'm just a Captain. . . ."

I interrupted. "Sam's right, Tony. I'll go to bed like I should. Besides, now that I have something positive to look forward to, I'll probably be able to get some decent sleep this time. We don't know *what* we'll find when we're finally able to see the surface, but at least the uncertainty will be over."

Five hours later, the whole crew was on the control deck, either operating a console or looking over the shoulder of someone who was. Tony was flying *Prometheus* while Katrina had taken over the communications console. Linda was operating the main telescope at maximum resolution. She had three helpers, each one monitoring one of the magnified images the telescope obtained in different parts of the spectrum. Sam and Red watched the long- and short-infrared images and Thomas the visible image, while Linda glanced occasionally at the long ultraviolet display in case anything interesting showed up there.

Caroline was operating the laser ranger. She was set to scan the smoothly sloping beach areas around Crater Lagoon, looking for bumps in the topography that hadn't been there during the initial careful topographic survey of the island and lagoon. The laser wavelength had been carefully shifted to the short-infrared band to avoid any possible eye damage. Deirdre was operating the microwave sounder. Any strong returns from that instrument would indicate highly reflective metal objects. I manned the weather console. The display on my screen showed the actual multispectral cloud cover image superimposed on a computer map that indicated the positions of the various islands on the ocean-covered planetoid below.

"The last clouds of the front are starting to move past the location of St. Vincent Island," I said through my imp. "What's the time to eclipse, Tony?"

"It's starting right now," said Tony. I watched as the shadow of Gargantua began to take a bite out of the mottled blue, green, and gray marble on my screen. The eclipse darkness passed swiftly over the location of St. Vincent Island before the front cleared.

"I see a large circular glow through the clouds in the short-infrared," said Red.

"It's in the long IR too," said Sam. "That must be the lava in the central caldera of St. Vincent Mountain. It matches up perfectly with the caldera in the map overlay."

"Now that the rain has stopped, I'm starting to get decent returns out of the microwave sounder even through the cloud cover," reported Deirdre.

"Any returns?" I asked eagerly.

"None that weren't there before," said Deirdre, switching frequencies and repeating the scan. Every green blip in the return matched up perfectly with the faint blue outlines in the microwave reflectance overlay map that had been generated during the initial surveys.

"Damn!" I said, feeling the frustration set in again.

"That just means there's no metal on the beach," said Red encouragingly. "That doesn't mean there aren't people on the beach."

"What's that glow under the clouds to the south of the volcano?" said Thomas, whose sharp eyes had caught something in the visible display.

"Must be lava in another volcanic caldera," said

Sam. "St. Vincent Mountain has a number of secondary calderas, and they're all potentially active."

"Nope! It's not!" said Thomas in an elated voice, as the cloud cover finally passed away and Crater Lagoon came into view. "Volcanic calderas don't come in the shape of a giant X!"

A half-hour later the clouds were covering St. Vincent's island again, and we switched our consoles to a replay of the action that had taken place during the short break in the weather. Sam was busy combining the output from all the instruments that had been looking at the scene. We had already seen one run-through and were about to repeat it with a different multispectral mix.

"Play it again, Sam," I said eagerly. . . . A sense of deja vu floated through my fatigued brain. The answers to three trivia questions rose—unwanted but insistent—into my tired mind . . .

*Ingrid Bergman said it; not Humphrey Bogart.*

*She said only; "Play it, Sam." There was no "again."*

*The tune was, "As Time Goes By. . . ."*

I shook my head to clear it of the unwanted memories and continued my sentence. "I want to make sure the count we got the first time is correct."

"OK," said Sam. "As I roll the video record again, James will put a circle around each blob whose infrared emission spectra and visible reflectance spectra matches a man-made surface or human skin. During the first run, there were definite matches with coverall spectra and hints of skin spectra, but no indications of metallic or spacesuit spectra."

"Which is why they didn't radio," I said. "The lander must have sunk so fast they didn't have time to put on suits. The atmosphere must not be too bad for them, if they've been able to survive this long. The main thing now is to find out how many of the crew made it to shore."

"By having James follow the blobs as they start the fire, tend it for a while, and then put it out, it is possible to gather information along the way that allows James to tighten the error bars on the size of the blobs, and determine how many objects were in each initial blob. Then, once Caroline's laser ranger passes over a blob, James can use that range data to pick out the highest point in the return from that area and get an estimate of the height of the person to within a centimeter. That's good enough to identify specific people, like Richard and Jinjur. Now watch again and count. I'll have James put a number by each blob as soon as it feels certain that the blob contains one distinct individual."

"One, two, three . . . four . . ." I counted as the computer generated numbered circles around the scurrying blobs that moved up and down the fiery cross. Some of the circles split in two, and all of them became smaller and smaller until a number appeared next to them. Sometimes the number was joined by a set of initials as a particular individual was identified.

". . . seven VJ. That's Jinjur, all right. Standing near the center of the cross and telling everyone else what to do. Eight . . ."

". . . and ten," completed Sam a little later.

"Ten *SE,*" I added, feeling the massive but unseen weight of responsibility drop from my shoulders. "Once Richard was identified, the next tallest one had to be Shirley."

"So, it looks like all ten made it," said Sam. "In addition, there are indications from the visible spectra that a segment of the lagoon is redder than normal, with a spectra that matches Little Red, indicating that at least one of the flouwen escaped."

"I wonder how that happened?" asked Katrina.

"They were sealed in the central water tank on the *Beagle*. If the crew didn't even have time to don suits, then they certainly didn't have time to release the flouwen."

"Somehow they did." I paused and took a deep breath. "Well," I continued grimly. "They're alive. For how long we don't know. Now . . . How are we going to get them out of there?"

No one had an answer.

"James!" I said to the imp on my shoulder. "Keep an eye on those clouds and let me know if they show signs of breaking again." I looked around the control deck at the eight faces waiting for my next sentence. "Let's all adjourn to the view lounge upstairs with a squeezer of coffee and have a brainstorming session. There must be *some* way we can rescue them."

"It's just as you told Jinjur when they left," concluded Red, a few hours later. "If both the *Dragonfly* and the Ascent Module fail, there is no way the exploration crew can return to *Prometheus*. We can't pull the same trick that we used on Rocheworld. There's no zero-gee point for the Ascent Module to descend to, and besides the *Dragonfly* plane is at the bottom of Crater Lagoon. Unless someone thinks of something new that this brainstorming session failed to find, they are marooned on Zuni until the follow-on expedition arrives some twenty-five years from now."

"If they survive that long," I muttered, beginning to feel weary again.

"If there was something drastically wrong with the atmosphere, they would have been dead by now," said Katrina. "Of course, there is the problem of food. Even if they can find something non-poisonous to eat, there is the potential of long term malnutrition due to lack of proper vitamins and trace minerals."

"Thanks for reminding me of that," I said, somewhat sarcastically I'm afraid.

"We could send down one of our exploration crawlers with a load of food, medicine, and vitamin pills," suggested Tony. "They can carry up to fifty kilos of cargo if the cargo is compact enough."

"The first thing we need to do is get them a radio so we can establish contact and find out what it is *they* think they need," I replied. "Fortunately, the crawlers have an outside microphone as part of their exploration sensor suite. Unfortunately, we'll have to wait until the weather clears completely before we attempt to drop in a crawler. The high winds in the jet streams could cause the crawler aeroshell to tumble and burn up, while the updrafts in the storm clouds could cause the parachute to rip apart."

Thomas spoke up. "If all you want is to send them a radio, you don't have to use a crawler. Use one of the self-powered penetrator harpoons that Sam and I used on the twin moonlets, Zoroaster and Zwingli. Although they're designed primarily to gather subsurface temperature gradient and seismic data, they do have an external acoustic detector, so we can separate underground seismic vibrations from atmospheric vibrations like thunder and volcanic eruptions. That would be a perfectly adequate microphone. All we would need to do is add a speaker."

"And the best thing about the penetrators," added Sam, "is that they're rugged enough that they can pass through jet streams and storm clouds like they weren't there. Also, they are self-guiding, and as long as they can see a distinctive feature and match it with a preprogrammed map, they can hit any desired point on the surface within a few meters."

"Let's do it!" I said. "The sooner we give them a reply to their flaming cross signal, the better we all will feel."

"James?" said Sam to the imp riding on his shoulder. "Do you have a speaker that can take shock loads that we could add to a penetrator sensor suite?"

"Certainly," replied the computer voice back through his imp. "One of the standard options for the penetrator sensor package is an acoustic ranger designed for scanning the region around the landing point in order to more accurately determine the exact location of the penetrator with respect to surrounding surface features. Normally, a laser ranger is used, since it can be used as a crude video camera to build up a picture of the surroundings, but the acoustic option is available in case the atmosphere is expected to be opaque to laser light. The acoustic ranger has enough bandwidth that it would make a very adequate speaker."

"So we can either see, or talk, but not both," I said. "I already know what everybody looks like. I'll take the two-way talk option."

"Have the Christmas Bush get an acoustic ranger out of stores, and bring it down," said Sam. "Also, please send the shaft elevator to the Living Area Deck, so Thomas and I can use it to haul the penetrator down. We'll meet you near the airlock on the Control Deck."

"I'll come with you," I said, getting up to follow them.

We left the lounge and went to the central shaft. When the elevator arrived, we stepped on the donut-shaped platform.

"Level 14, please," said Sam, and the elevator rose up the long central shaft and came to a stop. Sam palmed open a panel. There was a honeycomb rack half-full of a dozen or so sharp-pointed metal tips. Thomas, having done this many times before, reached out and pulled at a small pointed tip centered in one of the hexagonal holes. Slowly, out came a meter-long metal spike about two centimeters in diameter. As he continued to pull, the tungsten carbide spike became thicker, then rapidly turned into a heavy exponentially tapered horn that was ten centimeters across. The metal spike was faired into the nose of what looked like a missile. The missile had a name painted in script on its side. The name was "Crash."

As Sam and Thomas took the long missile under their arms, James was filling the miniature memory of the penetrator missile with the optimum trajectory information, and a model of the surface features of the beaches around Crater Lagoon. Once the missile knew what its target was to be, it started looking for it.

"Where is it!?! I'm gonna CRASH right into it!"

"Just wait a few minutes, *Crash,*" said the lanky geophysicist. "We have to replace your ranging package first, then get you through the airlock." Just about that time, a portion of the Christmas Bush floated down the long central shaft of *Prometheus,* flying itself to a halt on the platform by the rapid motion of the thousands of tiny cilia on the ends of its bushed-out branches. It was carrying a cylindrical package that was the same diameter as the end of the missile. One end of the package had a male screw thread and the other end a matching female thread. Inset at four places around the perimeter of the package were four round ultrasonic senders.

"This screw-in segment replaces the laser ranger segment, the second from the end, between the acoustic sensor segment and the communications package at the rear," said the Christmas Bush.

With Thomas holding the spike, and I the nose, Sam unscrewed the communications cylinder, replaced the laser ranger with the acoustic ranger, and screwed the whole package back together again. By the time he had finished, the elevator platform had reached the command deck. Sam and Thomas hauled the missile over to the airlock, and Sam cycled the airlock controls. The Christmas Bush carried the harpoonlike penetrator missile through the airlock, and when the outer door opened, tossed it out into space. The missile fell slowly for a while until it was safely away from the habitat, then started its main engine.

"I've *got* it!" said *Crash*. "Here I go!"

Four hours later, I and the rest of the crew on *Prometheus* were at our consoles watching and listening as the telemetry signals from *Crash* sent back a crude video picture of what the missile was seeing with its seeker. The acoustic sensors in the tail returned the sound of a high-pitched scream that grew louder as the air grew thicker, until James was forced to lower the volume.

"It's found Crater Lagoon. . . ." said Caroline. "Now its locked on the remains of the burned-out cross. . . ."

I began to feel the excitement grow within me as this portion of the mission came to a successful conclusion. . . . I was soon going to be back in contact with Jinjur and the rest of my crew. . . . "It's going to hit right in the center of the X!"

The video return went black, but the whistling sound collected by the acoustic sensor in the tail of the missile exploded into a crack of thunder that rolled higher and higher in the heavens until it segued into a sonic boom. As the thunder rolled away, the sound of wind, light rain, and lapping water could be heard.

"The antenna boom has deployed," said Caroline from the communications console. "And James has hooked your imp up with the speakers on the tail."

My imp had left my shoulder and was now configured as a headset, with two sub-twigs acting as earphones, and another sub-twig out in front of my mouth, splayed to catch any acoustic nuance I might utter.

"Hello!" I said. "Is anybody there?"

Instantly I regretted the inane statement. Why hadn't I thought of something memorable to say, like—"Dr. Livingston, I presume?"

It seemed like an eternity, but it was actually much less than a minute before we heard the pounding of feet and somebody came panting up to the embedded penetrator.

"Well! You certainly announced your arrival with a bang!" came the voice of Jinjur. We could hear other people coming up around her. "It's great to hear a friendly voice. You'll be glad to know that we're all present and accounted for, including the flouwen. No injuries, but no equipment—except for what the flouwen were able to salvage for us, and that's not much."

"How's the atmosphere?" I asked. "Any breathing difficulties?"

"Outside of being thick, and hot, and humid, the air is breathable," replied Jinjur. "It's really not bad, once you get used to it, sort of like the Hawaiian Islands or Tahiti. Rather than being a Hell, it's more like Heaven."

Another voice intruded. It was Reiki. "Considering the primitive conditions, I would suggest it is more like Eden."

"How about food?" I asked. "Have you been able to salvage much? You shouldn't be touching the native foods. Never can tell which might be poisonous to humans."

"We've already had to go past that point," replied Jinjur. "Fortunately, nearly everything has been edible—some of it even tasty—like the pink clams with six legs."

"Clams got legs?" I splurted incredulously.

"That's not all," replied Jinjur. "Let me tell you about the snake that almost got Shirley. . . . Yes, Eden does have snakes . . . and I'll have to get Reiki tell you about meeting a Jolly Blue-Green Giant. . . ."

# ABANDONING

The tremendous boom of the landing penetrator shattered my sleep. I was on my feet before I was even awake, along with the rest. Jinjur, who had been awake on watch, was pelting down the sand ahead of us.

What a beautiful, beautiful sight! Plunged almost exactly into the intersection of our two long lines of sand and ashes was the gleaming shaft, its fins pointing at the sky. From the four round speakers in the sides came the wonderful sound of George's voice! Cool, authoritative, tremendously dear, but cracking slightly with urgency.

"Hello! Is anyone there?"

I missed the first several moments of excited responses, occupied with straining my eyes upwards, trying to penetrate the clouds as this visitor had done. My eyes are long-sighted, and several times I caught the faint but steady glow of the sail's reflected light. The view kept blurring, however; whether due to the intervening misty clouds or my own tears, I do not know.

Eagerly, we all clustered around the little missile. The excited voices back and forth went on and on, slowly transferring into the parent computer on

*Prometheus* all that we have learned so painfully about this strange world in the past few weeks. In camp the Jolly waited patiently; our hasty apologies were accepted gravely, and we returned to besiege the listening radio with descriptions, explanations, calculations. Surreptitiously, I once reached out a hand to stroke the gleaming sides of this precious link! And, occasionally, one of us breaks into the narrative to exchange a joyous greeting with a friend aboard the ship. We can almost hear the imps crackling on their shoulders as we talk! Even Deirdre broke her normal silence to send us a greeting—how clear the lilting voice sounded! The Celtic ancestry sings in her words—I longed to see my quiet friend and her equally quiet pet.

Jinjur, particularly, is enjoying this release from solitary command, and the access to the never-failing resources of James. Soon, a minicamp with a temporary shelter was set up around the finned metallic post stuck nose-deep in the sand. Everyone was reluctant to leave, fearing the loss of contact with home, and only left when it was their turn to gather wood or food.

I brought the Jolly down the sands so it could meet our comrades in the sky. I explained that the talking metal post played the part of a gatherer in passing speech back and forth, and it seemed to comprehend. The translator-intercommunication abilities of James began to bridge the gap between our languages with increasing speed. Interestingly, the Jolly seems to be learning our spoken language almost as fast as James translates; perhaps this will expedite our understanding of the giant plant—certainly we are much slower at learning a new language than it seems to be.

"I now wish we had found a way to put a camera on board the penetrator, too," George said during a pause in the conversation. "I'd really like to have a picture of that creature to send back to Earth."

"I have a video camera built into my recorder," I said, taking the versatile computer out of my pocket. "And I already have a number of still frames of the Jolly. If James will set up to receive in facsimile mode, I will program my recorder to transmit the images acoustically. What is the upper limit on the bandwidth of the acoustic sensors on the penetrator, James?"

"Thirty kilohertz. The ear can't hear as high as that."

"Then we can use the ultrasonic band for the video transmission, and the conversations between the two crews can continue on underneath." I programmed my recorder to transmit the images of the Jolly and the other flora and fauna on Zuni that I had taken and stored in its memory, and set the precious piece of machinery between the fins on top of the penetrator rocket. Automatically, I was back to talking with James, and handling data with him as fluently as I had when we were all together. The contrast between our primitive surroundings, and the cool discussion of high-technology transmissions, was being marveled at, somewhere in my mind, but consciously I was concentrating very hard on the work at hand.

"Is the reception okay?"

"The first few scan lines are coming up on my screen now," said George. "No noise, good color, and excellent resolution. Looks like the leaves of a palm tree. Not very interesting."

"That's just the top fronds of the Jolly, George," I chided. "Wait 'til you see the rest of the picture."

A few days later, the exploration crew had laboriously finished dictating the last of the meager information they had gathered up through the voice link into the memory banks on *Prometheus*. The entire contents of my journal had also been transferred to files in James's memory. The personal ones I had encrypted, and left the key with James in case I never returned to claim them.

The tension is increasing among those on the ground. We have heard no quick assurances of rescue—in fact, we have all talked and thought for days, and inexorably a conclusion has emerged. Even with all the technology at their disposal, neither computer nor human aboard our parent ship can devise a way for us to return—ever. For the rest of our lives, we shall be, at best, pioneers on this strange planet. None of us can really bear that truth yet. The desperate words continue, talking and talking, dealing lengthily with small and minor problems to avoid confronting the central, inescapable fact.

George then brought up a subject that had been bothering him. "Katrina is worried that, even if the food isn't poisonous and keeps you supplied with calories, it might not contain the right vitamins and minerals."

"John is worried about that too," said Jinjur. "But there isn't much we can do about it. Neither your team nor mine has been able to come up with any method of getting us off this planet short of waiting twenty-five years for the follow-on expedition. If we suffer from any vitamin or mineral deficiencies, they will certainly have shown up by then."

"I'm planning on loading up a crawler with as much as it can carry," said George, "then sending it down via aeroshell and parachute as soon as the weather clears and the winds aren't too bad. What do you want me to include?"

"John has a reasonable supply of antibiotics and other medicines in his bag," said Jinjur. "So there isn't any real urgency. How much can a crawler carry?"

"Each crawler has a cargo compartment about the size of a small trunk. If the cargo is dense enough, it can carry up to fifty kilos in mass without exceeding the aeroshell mass limits."

"How many vitamin pills in fifty kilos?" Jinjur wondered out loud, then turned to our small group, quietly listening to our leaders debating our fate. "John?" she asked. "How much does a vitamin pill weigh?" John's brow wrinkled as he tried to come up with an answer.

"I know how many milligrams of each vitamin is needed, but actual pills are mostly filler."

The voice of James intruded into the conversation. "Five grams. The fifty kilo mass limit of the crawler would mean it could carry up to ten thousand standard vitamin pills."

"That's pretty good," said Jinjur. "At ten pills a day, one a day for each of the ten people in my crew, a single crawler load would last a little over two and a half years. Nine or ten crawler loads would easily take us through the entire twenty-five years."

There was a long and increasingly dismal silence before George replied. "We've got only four crawlers and their aeroshells left. The Christmas Bush might be able to make some more crawlers in its workshop, but I don't think it has the capability of making a large ceramic aeroshell."

"I do not," came James' voice. "The temperatures required to fire the ceramic are beyond my capabilities."

"Then we had better be very careful about what we decide each crawler payload will be, to make sure every gram counts," replied Jinjur thoughtfully. There was a short pause, and then she continued on. Her voice now had the somber tone of carefully reasoned command authority, and the words were chilling to those sitting around the small fire burning in front of the makeshift shelter. A stormfront was approaching, and the intermittent rain showers from the scudding clumps of gray clouds were heavy and cold.

"You will withhold deployment of any crawlers until

we have further information," she ordered. "I will have John monitor our health periodically until we can determine exactly which supplements we need. The Christmas Bush can then make smaller pills with just the necessary compounds in them. That way, we should be able to double the number of doses each crawler can carry, so the four landers can suffice for the twenty-five year wait."

"At five years of supplies per crawler, that's only twenty years," George reminded her.

"I had taken into account that some of us would very likely die during the long wait," replied Jinjur flatly. "Either by accident or natural causes. Such events are highly probable in a group in this age bracket over a twenty-five year period of time."

"Oh . . ." replied George quietly. Those of us listening began to appreciate some of the more unpleasant aspects of being in command.

"So!" said Jinjur, putting a more cheerful tone in her voice, but keeping the tone of command authority. "There's no use in your hanging around here any longer. We have given you the information you need so you can prepare the report to Earth about the results of phase four of the mission. You now need to take *Prometheus* off and carry out phase five—a survey from space of the rest of the Gargantuan moon system. We'll continue the survey of this planet as we were meant to, only we'll have to use rafts or boats instead of a *Dragonfly* airplane. Won't be as fast, but we have plenty of time. After about six months, fly *Prometheus* back here and check up on us. By that time, John should have a good handle on what supplements we need, and you can send us our first crawler load. Then you can go back to your survey work until it's time for the next drop."

"Are you sure you have everything you need for that length of time?"

Strange feelings surged through me. George's voice, so familiar and admired—had it always been so cool? Was the detachment I heard in it simply due to the physical distance between us, or had he become somehow different? Had I? Jinjur's voice, replying to him, had been merry with relief on that first day, then had resumed its own cool assurance. Now, however, I could hear so clearly her dismay, anxiety, even fear, as she absorbed the finality of what she herself was saying.

"We are in good health, and are developing facilities and equipment satisfactory for our own use. We have made first contact with an intelligent alien, and plan to explore that intelligence. We have a great deal to do, plenty of time, though very little else . . . not that we won't miss you people . . ." The firm voice broke, and stopped.

I wanted to protest, but found no words. I could see protest in the faces around me—Arielle's tears were pouring—but none of us said a word.

"I don't want to abandon you like this . . ." protested George.

Jinjur took a deep breath. "You have your orders, Colonel Gudunov," came the brusque words.

"Yes'm," replied George coolly. "See you in six months." His voice changed tone to that of a commander, and we heard him give the order we all dreaded. . . .

"Mr. Roma, set our course for Zouave."

Slowly, but inexorably, the three-hundred kilometer diameter aluminum foil moon turned from a bright circle to an almost invisible ellipse in the clouding sky. Then *Prometheus* sailed away into distant space, leaving the ten of us marooned on Eden.

"They'll be within range for another few days, and even after that, we can always send a voice message by relaying it through the Zuni commsats," reminded Jinjur as she returned through the rain to the shelter and the warming fire, her jaw firmly set in an attempt to keep her welling tears from flowing. "Time for goodbyes before the round-trip delay time makes conversation impossible. You first, Reiki. The rest of us will give you some privacy while you talk. Take your time . . . we have plenty . . ."

I said farewell, one at a time, to those on *Prometheus*; acquaintances, co-workers, and friends. At the last, I talked to my dearest friend.

"Deirdre! Take my things to use, please!" I could make my voice say no more. . . .

# FLOODING

Richard watched, but made no move to help, as Reiki walked heavily up the path with the burden of water. She'd have refused any assistance anyway, he thought. But the sight of the straining shoulders angered him, just a little, and during dinner he spoke abruptly.

"On *Prometheus*, it didn't matter, because we had James to do all the work. But here, wouldn't it be fairer if we divided the work up more by who's most capable of doing it?"

Shirley sighed. "Make up a chart, or something, Richard?"

Jinjur understood the weariness. "Not only did James do all the work, he did the keeping track, too," she said. "Looks to me like all of us are pulling our own weight pretty well, these days. Do we really want a lot of 'whose turn is it now?'"

"I'm not thinking of assignments, or things like that," he protested. But hauling water . . ." He stopped, aware of Reiki's indignant stare.

Carmen chuckled. "On *Prometheus*, we always had James and the Christmas Bush to assist us. Technology personified. No job too difficult. Here . . ."

Shirley said thoughtfully, "It's been *years* since I've

considered it, but it's true. Technology like we were accustomed to made us all so equal we just accepted it. Now, without technology, some of us are . . . more equal than others!"

"I don't see why that should be any problem," argued David. "If it's work that needs to be done—something so routine and simple as fetching water—why don't we devise a technology to do it? We don't have to stay as primitive as we are!" There was a brief silence. So much had filled the eventful days that there had been no time for looking to a future. Now, perhaps, they could consider such a prospect.

"Running water—in camp?" Arielle's query was so joyful they laughed.

"I don't see why not!" exclaimed Shirley. "How difficult can it be to divert—"

John groaned. "Pretty damn difficult, with no shovels, or pipes. . . ."

"Why shovels?" demanded Jinjur. "Simple scoops of some sort, ten of us doing the job, a little at a time—Richard, how are you at surveying?"

As it turned out, Richard was particularly good at surveying. With a simply contrived level made from two pots and a long siphon made of plastic tubing the flouwen had brought up from the wreck, he found a nearby spring sufficiently elevated above the campsite, and routed a connecting channel. Intrigued by the always fascinating lure of playing with water, the crew joined in eagerly. It was not many days before the little rivulet, carefully lined with stones and bridged over gullies with lengths of hollowed out tree-trunk halves, delivered its small but steady flow to a sturdy catch-basin close to the fire.

The human delight in their achievement had an age-old effect: the desire for improvement. Not much was said, but the fire-place itself gradually acquired height, so that the various cooks no longer needed to bend to the ground. The judicious placement of certain rocks, as they were located, resulted in a rudimental chimney. The harmless tinkering continued, to everyone's satisfaction.

"You know, Shirley," said Carmen, some weeks after the completion of the water supply. "I've been thinking about what you said, back then . . . about equality being made possible by technology. I thought, at first, that was only so on *Prometheus*, but now, it looks like it works even better in a place as simple as this. The water's there, we all use it, and I know *I* really didn't enjoy lugging it!"

"Yes," said Shirley smugly. "And I've had *another* idea!" This one had been born of watching the laborious grinding of meal for breads, and utilized yet another of the bountiful streams with which the nearby countryside was supplied. The water mill was so simple to build that no one objected to the effort of its construction, and proved as fascinating for these sophisticated minds to observe as any spectacular technology of the past. Then it was decided it would be handy to have a wheeled cart, to carry various stores about, and once again Shirley was in her element, designing and engineering.

The small band of explorers, while still scrupulously compiling descriptions and analyses of the plants and animals of their new home, and sending off their recorded results each evening through the penetrator-to-commsat-to-Prometheus radio link, became absorbed also in the joys of furnishing their new home. The more routine tasks, such as keeping track of the whereabouts of tools, measuring the daily tides, replenishing the foodstuffs with just enough for each day's needs, became so automatic that no one actually paid much attention to them.

Nels walked briskly to the shore, calling to the flouwen hovering nearby, as he counted down the varicolored stones of the tide markers. "Nine . . . ten! Right." He made a quick note on a piece of bark with some charcoal, and turned to talk to the flouwen. How's the water, Little Red?"

"Water great! Big tide tonight! We'll be far out, come surfing in!"

"Fine—have fun!" Nels turned, then hesitated. Big tide? He'd better check. . . .

"I've lost track of the days, Jinjur. Is it a triple conjunction tide, tonight? Or one of those big quadruple conjunction ones?"

Jinjur turned to Reiki. "I've not been paying attention, either. Look it up in your journal, Reiki, will you?"

Nels's new piece of data was added to those already stored, and the journal then displayed a complex curve that showed the short record of tidal height versus time that had been collected since they started to keep tidal records. The complex curve showed the fifteen hour twice-a-day period of the small Barnard tides, the once-a-day medium-height tidal pulses from Zulu, and the larger pulses from Zouave as it passed in back of them every two-and-a-half days. It was obvious that the three peaks would be occurring near the same time, but the data was so sparse it was difficult to determine how close they would be together.

"It's hard to tell," concluded Shirley after inspecting the record. "What makes it difficult is that although we know that the tides on Eden are predicted to be as large as twelve meters or more, that only applies to an ideal planet with an ideal ocean with no island chains on it. It doesn't take into account the effects of ocean currents, prevailing winds, and local topography. The tides on this beach could be higher or lower than the nominal value."

Jinjur nodded. "I'll keep watch on it, myself, tonight, and make sure I mark it at its highest point," she announced. Accordingly, she settled down comfortably in the sand as the slow rise of the water began to grow. It was an unusually calm evening, with high clouds that hid the stars but let the light from Gargantua through to illuminate the beach. She could hear an occasional remark as the others went about the evening's small chores.

"We're running low on kindling, Shirley. Shall I collect some small stuff tomorrow?"

"You know, Reiki, it's not hard to cut up these big planks with a sharp-edged rock. They split easily enough, if you'd rather just bring an armload of them down."

"Very well, but I rather *like* picking up a big bunch of the twigs and things. Makes use of them, after all. And helps to tidy up the place!" Both smiled, a trifle wryly. After all the years of walking thoughtlessly on immaculate surfaces, they now forgot occasionally, and tripped and stumbled among the debris of the forest.

"Say, Cinnamon, maybe we could start a compost heap!" Nels was enthusiastic, but Cinnamon's voice was not.

"Maybe," she said. "But those things are tricky, Nels, especially when we can't monitor the heat inside, or the rate of deterioration. You have to add water from time to time, and keep the whole thing covered, and not dump in just everything. . . ."

"How can it be so tough?" he asked. "Stuff's going to rot, no matter what. Can't we just build a pile . . .?

"Nels, have you ever been downwind from a real dump?" Cinnamon said, in some exasperation. "Yes, eventually things rot, but the process . . ."

David's small flute began a tune, and Jinjur listened with more pleasure. A large shadow moved towards her, and John came to sit down nearby, with a sigh of relaxation.

"My turn to do the washing-up. Using sand for

detergent sure gets the fingernails clean—and keeps them filed down at the same time!" He grinned at Jinjur. She looked ruefully at her own hands.

"I know. I kept mine longer than this, even at boot camp. These grungy domestic jobs! Gives new meaning to the phrase 'galley slave,' don't they?"

He laughed, and stretched out. "Good thing there's ten of us. It's not so bad when it's not a daily thing."

Jinjur sighed, and leaned back on her folded arms. "That's right."

There was a silence. "You know," John said finally, "I never did any camping before. Our family vacations were as organized as the rest of the year, between conventions and campaigns, and once I got to college and began bouncing around between premed and engineering I didn't want to do anything but sleep in my free time. This whole thing is so new to me, I'm still reeling."

Jinjur was surprised. "I didn't notice," she said. "But then, I guess all of us are still reeling, in our own ways. Did you see Arielle this morning, when she was first up?"

He shook his head.

"I was just getting up, myself, and she was down at the shore, with a pot of some kind, and bending over it, and tilting it this way and that, and then finally she dumped it out into the sea and came stamping up the beach. Then she saw me watching her, and she gave me that look, you know, she has when she is truly disgusted, and said, 'Lousy mirror!' " Jinjur chuckled, and sighed again. There was another silence. Then John rose and dusted the sand from himself, and grinned down at Jinjur.

"*But*," he said softly, "this actually is tremendous fun!"

He walked away up the beach, and Jinjur turned her attention back to the rising tide, thinking about the things they'd accomplished today, the prospects for the morrow, all the details of this new life they were leading. As the water touched the ten-meter marker, and began to retreat, she sat up to watch carefully. Unfortunately, because of the high cloud cover, she couldn't see the shadows of the three moons as they lined up on the face of Gargantua. Because Gargantua was just a bright patch in the clouds, she wasn't quite sure of the time, although it was somewhere around midnight. They had all quickly learned to tell time during the night when Barnard was not in the sky, simply by the position of the terminator on Gargantua's face. At sunset one side of Gargantua was in half-moon phase, and at sunrise it was the other half that was illuminated, while at midnight, the entire face of the giant planet was lit. Fortunately, there was little wind that night, so the tidal mark that was reached was due to tidal effects only, with no assist—either positive or negative—from the wind.

With satisfaction and relief Jinjur got up to dust herself down. All was well, now. If that was the highest the tide would get in this region of the planetoid, and the next quadruple tide would not be for fifty-four days, then she and the others could concentrate again on all the work to be done instead of having to worry about moving their shelter.

John's words came back. . . . Yes, to be honest, this *was* enormous fun, and as far as Jinjur herself was concerned, their little Eden was made more so by all the challenges still to be met. She'd have been bored without problems to solve!

That was the trend of Shirley's thoughts, too, as she settled to sleep. Without the use of tools, or James, she had felt continual frustration for days. Now, however, she was relearning the skills of her own hands. As her eyes closed, she was not seeing the straggly thatch above her head, but a fine new roof of smoothed boards, and she smiled.

David reluctantly put away the little flute. The flouwen had been absent this evening, off on their surfing expedition, but he intended to meet with them again at the first opportunity. It had occurred to him to play some of the ceremonial sounds of the Jolly for the flouwen. It might just be that these two very different species of this star system might share some link in sounds. It was an exciting thought, and had only come to him today, as he strove to copy the Jolly's greeting, and remembered. Wasn't this little phrase part of the song Cinnamon and the flouwen had had such fun with, back in the tank on *Prometheus*? He curled on his side to rest, pleasantly weary from the day's exertions, and began to listen, as always, to the music that waited in his head.

Next to him, Arielle lay limp as a cat, and as relaxed. Her dark eyes, enormous in the gloom, moved slow and unconcerned over the drowsing camp. It was her watch. No doubt it would be as uneventful as every watch so far had been, but there was no question of not standing watches. With delight, she relived the glorious dives from the rocks she had found today; perfectly poised above the deep pool below, so that for a brief instant she was soaring, free from earth again!

Carmen and Richard were still talking, idly, by the fire. Both were tired, and were feeling just that little lassitude which makes one reluctant to make the effort to get up.

"Wonder if the Jolly could use a water mill to grind seeds, like we have?" Carmen said. "I know it doesn't make much power, but . . ."

"I think they eat what they eat pretty much as is," he said lazily. "Maybe they've some sort of gizzard arrangement. They seem pretty content, whatever."

"I know," said Carmen. "They do seem peaceful, and serene, and . . . happy." She speculated further. "They manage to keep busy, but they seem to feel they have everything they need, or want, for themselves and their young . . ." She was quiet.

"Well, of course, they've evolved here. This is their home, no wonder they're content. But for us, this is still howling wilderness. I hope! I like exploring, always did. And the mild weather makes it fun, knowing you're not going to freeze any minute. Kind of natural, to me, living like this . . ." His voice drifted off. A log cracked and fell apart in the fire, and the sound roused the two. Yawning, they stood and walked sleepily to the tattered shelter.

"Me and the Jollys," said Carmen. "I'm beginning to feel very much at home."

Almost unconsciously, Reiki's slim fingers pressed the last words into the chordic keyboard of her tiny recorder, and were still.

Eleven days later, things were not so tranquil. All morning, the wind had been increasing. From being an intermittent flutter of sound, the rattling of the thatch had become a steady clatter, almost obscuring the moan of the high winds in the treetops. Whitecaps foamed in the gathering grayness, lit by an occasional flicker of lightning from the approaching storm. Carmen and Reiki stopped their work at the little mill, and swept the flour and the unground grain hurriedly into waiting containers. Surveying the bending trees around them, they agreed to stow the precious pots right there, in the protection of some nearby boulders.

"And," said Reiki firmly, "we'll make a Scottish lid for them!" This, it turned out, consisted of several large rocks piled atop the ill-fitting lids, and Carmen approved. Already, the little mill had begun to splash more noisily as the storm moved towards them, bringing rain to the hillside above them.

Irritated by the racket, Shirley called John to help

her, and together they seized and tied down all the fluttering fronds they could reach.

"If this gets really bad, we may lose this roof, Shirley!" John raised his voice above the noise.

"Might be just as well," she shouted back. "I've got some ideas for a better one anyway."

The swirling smoke from the fire made Arielle cough, and she swore under her breath as she stirred the several pots, preparing their lunch, which they scheduled just prior to the midday eclipse of Barnard by Gargantua.

"Hand me bay, and thyme, and marjoram, please, Cinnamon? Damn smoke gets in my eyes!" Cinnamon thought of the song and started to sing, but a look at Arielle's red eyes silenced her and she reached quickly for the herbs. Actually, they were nothing like bay, or thyme, or marjoram, but Arielle had firmly labeled them with old names. "Close enough," she had said, "and those nice names."

Now she fumbled with the small boxes, and swore again as the dry leaves tried to fly upward with the smoke instead of falling into the pot.

Jinjur directed Richard, David, and Nels in the methodical securing of all their belongings which might be threatened by storm. Like the experienced commander she was, Jinjur had mentally worked out emergency plans for this camp well in advance, taking every contingency she could foresee into account.

"Nels, pile some rocks on the table as soon as we've finished with it, after dinner. Get a stack ready to hand. David, collect all the loose stuff you can see, and stow it in the shelter, topped with something that won't blow. Richard, let's move those heavy metal storage chests up there along the sides, they'll keep off some of the flying grit."

Indeed, the blowing sand was hindering everything they did. Their hurried midday meal was hot and good-tasting, but almost uneatable with grit. Cleanup was hurried, and then every utensil had to be packed into the chests. The wind was almost steady now, and blew chillier than anything they had felt so far on this strange world. It made the little crew huddle a little closer under the shelter. Shirley stared out over the dark ocean.

"Hope the flouwen are enjoying this," she said, "and that the Jollys are battened down."

Jinjur snorted. "The Jollys are the least of my concern," she said. "They know what's coming, and I'm not real sure. Did the flouwen mention a storm, recently?" No one spoke for a moment. Then Reiki said, "I talked with them two days ago, but that's the last I saw of them. When they left, Little Red was yelling about surfing, but then he frequently does. . . ."

"And no one's seen them since? Well, they're probably well out to sea, where they're safer anyway."

The fury of the wind increased, and the rain began with a rush that soon turned into a steady downpour. The colors in the sky looked different to the watching eyes.

"Look at the green, over there in the south," said David. "It's almost a glacier green, unusual for a sky illuminated by a red dwarf star." The strange color was not very apparent to the other humans, but the changing shades were fascinating to them all. They watched in silence, and relative comfort, as the roof above them stood sturdily in the storm. The lightning flashes increased in tempo, and soon the flashing strokes and rolling bangs were nearly continuous.

Before them, stretching to the horizon, the black ocean roared as loudly as the storm, and the incoming waves broke heavily on the beach, inexorably reaching further and further up the beach with each wave. It was John who said, a trifle uneasily, "Didn't we just have a peak high tide two weeks ago?"

Jinjur started, guiltily, when she remembered that she had measured that tide herself. "Yes, but it was just eleven days ago. The next peak high tide is not due for weeks yet. The water does look like its coming up pretty high though, doesn't it? I expect it's the storm, churning things up out at sea."

Nevertheless, they watched a little anxiously, as the frothing waves surged still further up the beach. It started to get even darker as Barnard started behind Gargantua for the midday eclipse. Suddenly Nels stood up, and plodded deliberately out into the pouring rain, heading for the carefully placed marker stones. The others watched as he carefully counted, and then walked quickly back to them through the gathering darkness. He stayed off the cushioning boughs, standing at the edge of the shelter, and his voice was rough.

"It's up *past* the ten-meter rock, Jinjur, and still coming! And it's not just the occasional breaker. I think there's something definitely going on!" Minds raced, searching for possibilities.

Shirley's eyes fell into a blank stare as she searched through her eidetic memory for an image she had seen many weeks ago on a screen on the control deck of Prometheus. With difficulty, for she had only looked at it once, and that briefly, she brought up the image and started looking at it carefully. "The triple conjunction tides occur every eighteen days, and they line up with the Barnard tide at either exactly midnight or exactly noon to form a quadruple conjunction tide every fifty-four days, but . . ." Here she paused as she looked even more carefully at the image in her memory. ". . . there is a 'false' peak in the tide that occurs eleven days *before* the true quadruple conjunction at midday. It occurs near midnight, but not exactly at midnight."

"There were clouds in the sky when I measured

that last high tide," said Jinjur. "I *thought* at the time it was midnight, but now I'm not so sure."

"The slope of the beach becomes shallower here where the shelter is," David reminded them. "A few extra meters in tide height means dozens of meters in additional beach coverage."

Just as he finished speaking, they were thrown into the pitch black darkness of the noon-time eclipse as the last bit of Barnard disappeared behind Gargantua, not to reappear for nearly two hours.

"That *does* it!" said Jinjur grimly. "I think, troops, we better move out. And up. Now!" With all her old authority, Jinjur directed the move of their precious possessions up the hill behind them. In the weak light of the banked fireplace, eager hands stacked and carried. Guided along the trails by the almost continual flashes of lightning, feet stumbled and hurried, while always in their ears was the hiss of the drenching rain, the roar of the rising tide, and the crack and rumble of the thunder. Within an hour, most of the little camp's salvaged belongings were high on the hill. There was now a new campfire, being carefully watched over by Cinnamon, who was getting soaked while keeping the fire dry. The others straggled along the dark muddy trail, breathing hard, and watching silently as the slightly phosphorescent waters continued their inexorable advance. When the waves began to swirl about the supports of their shelter, the people groaned, but there was nothing to be done. In a dismayingly short time, the wooden structure collapsed into the water, floating like some ungainly raft. The crew struggled to grasp and haul out the longest timbers, with Jinjur and Shirley shouting directions through the pouring rain and the crackling thunder, but the pull of the water and the weight of the logs made it impossible.

Jinjur yelled at the top of her voice. "Stop! Don't try to pull 'em. Just *hold* 'em if you can! The tide's turning!"

With desperation, the weary crew lined up along the remaining twisted structure, grasped its rough and slippery surfaces as tightly as they could, and fought for a footing in the shifting sand. Like contestants in some grotesque tug-of-war, they fought the sea for what was left of their flimsy house, but lost. The receding tide was slow, but extremely powerful, and the humans, battered by the continuing storm, one by one lost their grip and strength. At last, only Richard was left, clinging to the ridgepole grimly as he was forced, step-by-step down the sloping beach, until he was tripped up by a rolling rock, and fell into the surf. The sea, with a final triumphant breaker, seized the big pole and slid it smoothly and effortlessly out into the darkness.

Shirley and Nels, one on either side, helped the exhausted Richard back up the beach. With the others, they returned wearily to the pitiful heap of soggy belongings, and sank down to await the end of the noontime eclipse.

With the returning light, the wind died down to a gentle breeze. As the warmth of the surrounding sand increased, the people relaxed cramped positions, stretched out, and slept deeply. Shirley kept quiet as she stood and walked away, to wander about the littered shore, thinking and planning. The few traces of their encampment resembled a deserted play area in some vacant lot on Earth; a few stones arranged in a circle, a few more in an unnaturally straight line, the weighted table top still bearing its load of rocks but now sliding lazily in the shallows. With some care Shirley walked along the edge of the litter, seeking and marking as best she could the very highest limit of the water's advance.

One by one the rest awoke, stretched aching muscles, and rose. There was little talk, as kindling was sought, and a tiny fire laboriously relit from the rescued coals. By common, unspoken consent, the first efforts were made to produce the "coffee" they all enjoyed; it was comforting, filled empty stomachs temporarily, and could be sipped while talking. And a great deal of talking took place. These were people unaccustomed to failure, and the disaster which had placed them here was almost forgotten in the successes of their efforts at settlement.

"Boy, there's no arguing with Mother Nature, is there? Even in Eden." Richard looked at his new-scratched palms.

"Why did you try so hard to save that ridgepole?" asked John curiously. "We have plenty more trees around."

Richard shrugged. "I don't really know, just we'd worked hard on that lousy house, it *belonged* to us, I didn't like seeing it just . . . leave."

"Make like a tree and . . ." murmured Reiki.

Richard glared at her, and then chuckled.

Jinjur said, "I suppose you've been designing a new shelter, Shirley? Something with porticoes and flying buttresses, perhaps?"

Nels groaned, but Shirley said cheerfully, "Of course! But those only come much later. What I actually think we should build now is something very much like what we did the first time. It held up really well, until it was washed out from under. And it did shelter us, and it wasn't too hard to do. But, of course, we'll build it up here, above any possible tide."

"That sounds good," said David. "This time we know a little more about what we're dealing with, too. Should go easier." This optimistic prophecy was heartening, and while Shirley and Jinjur paced possible building sites, Richard and John headed for the woods to cut new timbers. Nels hauled in the table and other items drifting offshore, and Arielle and Cinnamon, as main cooks, discussed the best site for the new work area.

"Near water—I liked that, didn't you, Cinnamon?"

"Yes," she agreed. "But since the water channel washed out anyway, we can have it almost anywhere—just not too far uphill from before." It became apparent that the former site of their shelter was just about right for this.

"We'll put the table above, out of reach of the tide, and if the water covers the catchbasin next time we'll just sluice it out afterwards."

"Not 'if' water comes, '*when*,'" said Arielle with unusual grimness. "Somebody got to figure out." That issue was uppermost in Jinjur's mind, and when they next gathered, to eat and to plan the new construction, she spoke of it. "Reiki, I want you to take what records you can find we've mentioned, along with any data the rest of you recall. Talk with the flouwen, too, they may have been paying more attention than I have to the tides. Then calculate what we can expect, as far as we know. What we need," she said more slowly, "is a calendar, of all trivial things!"

Reiki nodded agreement, and began to turn over in her mind how to make some such thing, unaffected by weather.

"Rather unsettling, last night was," said John lightly. "High-tech humans, flooded out like field-mice!"

"It was dreadful," said Carmen flatly. "My father drowned in a flood."

"And it's awful, feeling there is so little a person can do," agreed Shirley.

"Well," said Nels, "we learned that there's a lot to learn. Again!"

"Still," argued David, "we got through this okay, again, and we can build what we need, again, and start over, again!"

"Sure!" said Jinjur. "For one thing, we've no other choice, and for another, we know we can do it!"

"Hooray," muttered John, but joined the others

willingly enough as, under Shirley's guidance, they began the new building.

The work went smoothly. Even in such primitive conditions, experience paid off. The new shelter, not quite so tall, but deeper, with longer sidewalls, and floored beneath the cushioning boughs, was not only more comfortable but also better looking than the first.

"Quite like Hawaii, or Tahiti!" said Reiki, standing back to admire.

"Ummm. I do like floor," purred Arielle, bouncing tentatively on the surface.

"I hope we don't get storms worse than that," said Carmen, looking rather anxiously at the gap between floor and roof, at the back. "Won't the wind come right through there?"

"Only if its a real howler, and then we *want* it to go through, not just push it over," explained Shirley. "At least," she said hopefully, "that's the theory!"

The communal feeling was one of modest triumph that evening, as they shared a rather dreary soup of hastily gathered vegetables.

"Something attempted, something done, in rather makeshift fashion," said Shirley. "At least this time we knew what to expect from the materials, and could work with them instead of trying to make them act like plastic or metal."

"*I* think it's lovely," said Reiki. "You all worked so quickly, and it just went together like every part was numbered, or something. Fast as I could bring a bit more timber, or whatever, it just vanished into the building! I was really impressed." There was a general sigh of satisfaction.

"Kind of fun, this time," admitted John.

"We'll have to rebuild the mill, too," said Carmen. "But you know, I think it might be better to make it smaller than before—we weren't using it all that much anyway."

"Well," said David thoughtfully, it is a source of free power—isn't there anything else we'd like to use that energy for?" There was a thoughtful silence, broken at last by a peal of delighted laughter from Carmen.

"It's fantastic! We can't think of anything! This place—it's so great we can't think of anything we need power for!"

Jinjur and Shirley started to protest. "Wait a minute, lights, pumps, tools . . ."

"What for?" asked Cinnamon, her dark eyes dancing. "Really, come right down to it, what for?"

"I'll think of something," frowned Shirley. But then grinned. "Maybe."

# EXPLORING

I woke slowly, to the sound of voices, and the rustle of the thatch overhead. Automatically, my fingers slid to my little recorder.

"Now that the rain's quit for a while, this breeze will have our stuff dry in no time!" Carmen felt the few spare garments we have with obvious satisfaction.

"I know," said Shirley. "And I'm going to replace this limp thing I'm wearing for that one with fewer stains. At least the sleeves are whole! And maybe it will save me a scratch or two on the on the trail—can't wait to start *really* exploring!"

"It makes a difference, doesn't it, knowing we're going to be here a long time," said Carmen thoughtfully. "In a way, it gives us a lot more freedom than thinking we'll be rescued."

Shirley agreed. "It's kind of a boost in a way, too, that George and the others seem to think we'll do all right on our own. They obviously didn't have any real worries about taking off and leaving us."

"We've got food, water, all the shelter we really need in this climate, plenty to explore, and all the time in the world to do it!" Carmen's voice had a new exultation in it, but then she was impossible to hear over the indignant bellow from the nearby beach. I rose to stroll down to the ripples with the others.

"George *gone*?" Little Red was very indignant. The flouwen had welcomed the arrival of the penetrator enthusiastically, but had grown bored with the endless talking, and gone off on their own pursuits for some days. Cinnamon and Richard were taking turns, explaining our new situation to the flouwen.

"Not much difference, really," she reassured them. "You'll still explore the waters, and help us to find out what lives there."

"And have plenty of time for play," added Richard.

Cinnamon and I lingered, talking with the flouwen about the strange plant life on the surface, especially the giant walking tree we had been recently interviewing.

"You know the plants that grow underwater? Seaweed, we call a lot of them, but there are all different kinds in some oceans," Cinnamon was saying.

"Yes, plants underwater here, too," Little White said. "Different from Rocheworld, here. Got six of things, floating around them."

"What things?" Cinnamon was startled. "Floating how?"

I didn't follow her thought, but instead began to explain to the flouwen about the giant land "plant" we had met being capable of moving about, and doing things on its own. Little Purple was interested.

"Maybe these plants in the water can move too," he speculated. "I never watched them long enough to see. Now I will." His speech is growing more like our own, as he grows in size and intelligence. Obviously thriving in the strange water, the flouwen communicate with us daily now, but briefly, preferring to spend their time out in the open ocean.

"Do the underwater plants have . . ." I hesitated. "Hedges? Walls of plants around them?"

"No," was the answer. "They grow among rocks and cave edges, right up close. But floating things come out and wander around, as far as their . . . things will let them." He hesitated, hunting for the right word. "Tentacles?" he tried.

"Yes, I know tentacles," I said. "You mean like long strings, holding . . ."

"Yes!" interrupted Little Red. "Tasty things come on tentacles!"

Little White explained further. "The plants don't have many leaves, mostly stem with clingers at the bottom. But the tentacles come out, two different kinds: one kind has tiny bumps on the ends, feeling all around; the other kind has swimming things, with nets in front, that scoop in lots of water." This sounded like it might possibly be the filter-feeder fish Nels had received from the flouwen, our first day. I asked about that, and was answered affirmatively.

"Biggest ones taste best!" Little Red was proud. "We bring you nice big one!" It had indeed been a substantial specimen. By now we have all tasted it, and both Nels and Cinnamon had been impressed with the meatiness, as well as the simplicity of structure of the creature.

"Where do these plants grow?" I asked, hoping to be able to dive for some.

"Down deep where the water is hot," said Little White. "Like Rocheworld, where hot water comes out of holes in bottom of sea, that's where most plants grow, and that's best place to find food, too."

"Volcanic vents," remembered Cinnamon. "Interesting . . . I need to talk to Nels," she said abruptly, and waded ashore. I followed more slowly, after enquiring gently about the well-being of our watery allies. I find it pleasant to talk with them; in their new freedom they visit us only if they wish, and it is curiously thrilling to have the silence of a swim broken by their cheerful presence. I floated, face down, to watch them for a few minutes as they moved easily through the water. I noticed below them a goodly cluster of the six-legged clams we had all enjoyed, and lifted my head to mark where they were, for later collection. Carmen was on the shore, waving me in, and I went to join her.

A discussion had apparently been going on for some time around the fire. I obtained a cup of the brew they were drinking; Arielle has named it coffee, but privately I feel that is a misnomer, principally because it tastes better than any coffee I have ever experienced.

Wasting no time, Jinjur was applying herself to organizing our situation and making plans.

"Our mission remains the same. We planned it out before we got here, and I've always found that the decisions made when we've been thinking rationally are best stuck to even when the situation . . . deteriorates." The crisp voice broke, momentarily only, but I felt with a quick pang of sympathy her genuine sorrow. She and George had shared so much! Strongly, she went on. "Whether it is our mission or not, we've got to learn as much about this world as we can, for our own purposes.

"Especially . . ." and real interest grew in her voice, "especially now that we have discovered the Jolly!"

"I've got some ideas . . ." began Nels eagerly.

"Wait until I tell you . . ." interrupted Cinnamon.

"Now!" said Jinjur loudly, reclaiming full attention. "Unlike most castaways, we've got few survival problems, so far. The climate means we don't need much shelter, or special clothing. . . ." (And we all, even I, have been gradually shortening sleeves and pantlegs, saving the precious scraps in a bundle.) "Food is available in such abundance we needn't worry about storage. And we've not met, yet, any threatening creatures. Not even mosquitoes!" True enough, although the defenses of the little clams had certainly been vigorous.

"Well, in general . . ." Jinjur stopped, and grinned at the mild pun. "That's the question, isn't it? How about it? Am I still to be *The General*? It looks to me like we are all, literally, in the same spot. In what manner shall we proceed?"

The question took us by surprise. We are so long accustomed to obeying orders! But our communal existence is already becoming more like that of a family, with comfortable familiarity the norm. Yet we are still individuals, desiring fairness and reasonable privacy. I was thankful that a few moment's thought brought us all to the same conclusion. It makes sense to have an acknowledged leader for the unforeseen situations we face; and Jinjur's good judgement, training, and automatic concern for the well-being of us all is something we can count on. But for our routine discussions and decisions? Do we simply expect each other's respect? Possibly . . .

"Reiki? How familiar are you with *Roberts' Rules*?" Jinjur's eyes were quizzical.

I took a deep breath. "Jinjur, there's a well-mannered precedent . . ."

"I knew it," she muttered.

"There was a group, similar in some few—*very* few!—ways to this, which operated successfully for quite some time on just two rules. One, nobody may interrupt. The other, nobody must remain around to listen! Perhaps that system, along with our general respect for you, may suffice. For instance, if you decide for some reason of your own that one of us needs washing—say, Shirley (obsessively clean Shirley!)—you may try to persuade us to do so. But you must obtain one hundred percent agreement! Otherwise, we will waste our few resources in fruitless arguing. As you argue, and as we walk away, you will eventually give up the argument, and Shirley can go unbathed. In cases of emergency, and where there is limited time for discussion, it makes sense for our leader to have authority by our consent. It does follow," I added slowly, "that the system must be acceptable to all. No fair ganging up on Shirley in the shower."

The total lack of a shower here made Shirley smile, without diminishing the point of my plan, which of course was my goal. Peace between ourselves is more possible than amongst many shipwrecked unfortunates, because we were selected for compatibility so many years ago, and have been through so much together. But we all know how tenuous can be the hold of civilization in such straitened circumstances as we presently are in!

"Where did that system come from?" asked David idly. "Japan?"

I shook my head, smiling, but said only, "Any etiquette system is only invented to help us keep our humanity presentable." And I sincerely hope no one will plumb the secret of the society of which I spoke, with its "Tw' Rules"! I think it is sufficiently obscure, and I hope it serves us longer than it did its founders!

Jinjur continued to lead the discussion, as we considered the days ahead of us. The mood seemed lighter, more relaxed; I noted with secret pleasure that Jinjur, knowing no one would interrupt her, stopped talking frequently, looking around for suggestions or questions. And there were plenty of suggestions!

"I want to record, somehow, some medical evaluation of everyone, so I can keep track of our health," John announced. The statement made us all turn to look at each other, consideringly, and the changes of the last few weeks were suddenly discernible.

David has grown a sandy beard and mustache—he

keeps the edges neatly squared with an obsidian blade, but seems almost proud of the thickness of the growth. His arms and legs are scratched by the tree trunks he climbs most days, but are firmly muscled. Arielle, too, shows marks and scratches, but her two belts fit no more loosely than before, and the big eyes are bright beneath the elfin cap of fair hair. Jinjur's uniform fits better now, not so clinging, and the trimmed edges are tidy and unfrayed. Carmen is slimmer too, and her rainwashed skin has a translucence that never showed under the heavy makeup. Shirley and Cinnamon look exactly the same as they always have, to me—I have noticed that they wander together along the beach every day, undoing their long braids, and talking cheerfully while the strands blow in the air before being replaited. In concession to the constant dampness, the braids are looser—not so tightly bound. The crisp coveralls favored by both women have softened considerably too, but they have sensibly refused to worry about lost buttons.

John and Nels look . . . tougher—their skins have darkened with exposure, and they swear companionably as they struggle to scrape their stubbly faces with obsidian—but they seem fit, moving easily with the heavy work that must be done, teeth gleaming in frequent laughter. I myself feel fine, although the black curls are becoming ominously long and seem to be developing an independent attitude which I deplore. At any rate, there doesn't look to be any need for medical concern among us.

"Check our belts," suggested Arielle. "See if they get tight or loose!" It sounds a practical and simple way to keep track. I had lost my belt in the crash, but Arielle handed over her regulation one with a grin, keeping her treasured one with the silver buckle. I took the firm fabric loop with inward trepidation, and was absurdly pleased when it fitted snugly.

Cinnamon and Nels were pleased with a private project of their own: "We sprouted some of Reiki's oats and barley," Cinnamon said happily. "We've been successfully propagating small batches on *Prometheus* for years, so it seemed worth a try."

"It's growing up along the ridge of that hill along with some of the native grains." Nels pointed. I remembered, now, seeing them examining those small sealed bags of grain so seriously some weeks before. "It's growing nicely, nothing seems to be trying to interfere with it, so we'll hope for another food crop."

"Great!" said Shirley. "From something the Jolly said, I gather it has some sort of food crop, too. Nels and I are going to spend today following that up." Several more voices offered to join her, and I was about to add my own when Jinjur said, questioning, "What's for dinner?"

"Soup," volunteered Arielle. "I make, using these roots."

"And I'll make those little cakes," added Cinnamon. I started involuntarily when she mentioned the cakes. Between them, Cinnamon and Carmen had devised a simple bread which had become a much-liked feature of our meals. Grinding some of the native seeds in primitive fashion between chunks of smooth stone, they experimented with the exact amount of water required to make a malleable dough. Both of them were adept at patting out thin, even little cakes which cooked beautifully on the open fire, acquiring a smoky flavor and a chewy consistency which we all enjoyed.

I had watched them carefully as they did this every night, and several days ago had resolved to try my own hand when I was alone. To my fury, it turned out to be much more difficult than I had expected! I had tucked the little pot of wet flour dough out of sight as David strolled into camp, and hurried to the shore to wash my hands of the sticky, uncontrollable mess before he saw. The little pot was still there—I could see it, under the bush, because I knew where to look—a cloth barely covered it. I decided quickly to find some other task for myself and return quietly later to dispose of that unfortunate experiment before its discovery.

"I spotted a nice bunch of those clams while I was talking with the flouwen this morning," I offered. "I'll get some to add to the soup, shall I?"

"Want some help?" Richard offered. I refused, I hoped politely, and as I headed for shore to collect a net and blade I noticed he did the same, but headed with long and silent strides up the hill into the forest.

I plunged happily into the warm salt water and swam strongly out to the area I had noted earlier. After so many years of not swimming at all, I find increasing pleasure in the support and caress of the water, and am steadily gaining in the speed and economy of my strokes. Now, nicely beyond the low breakers, I found a thick cluster of the six-sided clams and dove to them. The first few came away easily, but the next resisted, and I rose to the surface, gasping. They were lying deeper than I had realized, and I was exasperated at the time it took me to reach them. I knew what I needed, and headed back to shore, leaving my catch safely stowed in a shallow pool. Taking blade and net with me, I soon found some suitable thick leaves and slender vines, and returned to the shore to cut them into flippers. I cut a slot for my feet and fastened the things crudely to my ankles with the vine, and splashed into the water. It was soon obvious I had been much too lavish with my estimate, and I clambered awkwardly back out of the surf to trim the front edges. It took me many such trials and errors, but eventually I had formed a pair of very effective aids; uncomfortable to walk in, but enabling me to swim smoothly down through the water with only minimum effort behind the steady kicks. Further experimentation taught me the most efficient way to use this new tool, and by the end of the morning I had collected, with relative ease, enough of the shellfish to form a substantial part of a meal for the ten of us. I swam most of the way home, for further practice, and when I sat down to remove the flippers I was surprised to see Richard, grinning.

"Is *that* what you were doing, then!" he said. "I couldn't make it out—in and out of the water, splashing and whacking around in the surf, back into the ocean, swearing by the look of your shoulders. . . ."

"I didn't see you!" I said.

"I was hunting. Can't spot me when I'm hunting, of course."

"Then why were you watching me?" I demanded.

"It was fun!"

Quickly I reviewed my own actions, but was relieved to remember I had done nothing silly, I'd simply been busy. "Always pleasant, watching other people work!" I murmured, politely. "I do hope your prey didn't escape whilst you were—superintending?"

"Nope." The answer was assured and cordial—too late I saw the bulging game bag swinging at his belt. I marched past him a trifle stiffly, and joined the bustle of camp.

"Great stuff from the Jolly!" enthused Shirley. "Nels and I will enter it all in the recorder, Reiki, after we eat. He says . . ."

"After we eat," reminded Cinnamon, firmly.

"I'll just stir up those cakes. Where's that other little pot? It's just the right size. . . ."

I had forgotten again! Quietly I tried to edge away as Cinnamon hunted with increasing determination for that missing pot, but I had not got to safety when she pounced upon it.

"Here! But what's this? What *is* this stuff!" She bent to smell the mess, and gasped. "Shirley! Carmen! Did either of you do this?" Both women reached for the pot, denying having done anything, and sniffed in turn.

"Sourdough?" said Carmen doubtfully. "Yes! It's sourdough! But we've no yeast—how could it be—unless it just *sat* long enough . . ." Shrinking, I felt three pairs of eyes turning to me.

"Reiki!"

I stepped forward, my face burning. "I'm sorry, I know it's a waste. . . ."

"You've done it again! Sourdough's useful stuff. We can have biscuits and things now, Reiki, if I can remember how to keep the dough working!"

"There's another aspect I like," said John seriously. "If there's yeasts in the air which started that fermentation, maybe there'll be some of those complex B vitamins in the food—another nutrient we can use."

Nels and David looked at each other, an expression of unholy glee on each face. "Fermentation!"

I felt much better.

John has enjoined upon us all the most stringent demands for as much cleanliness as we can maintain. At his insistence, all of us scrub face and hands with water kept steaming at the side of the fire before every meal. Without soap, it's important to be thorough with these ablutions, and I not only enjoyed them but began to spend several minutes in a general sprucing up of my appearance at these times. Rather like a family of cats, we tidied ourselves vigorously and swiftly, before settling down.

But this time we were eager to share the interview with the Jollys. We hurried through the cleaning-up routine, which for the same hygienic reasons is never allowed to wait.

Nels began the report as I dutifully recorded it. Considering the vast differences between our life-forms, it is amazing how rapidly we are learning to communicate, and humbling to realize how much of the difference is being bridged by the giant plant. Most of the obtained data, of course, took much longer to hear and piece together than it took to relate, and I was impressed with the skill and tenacity of my fellow explorers.

"It appears the Jollys probably evolved from the same general plant structure that we first thought was the only one here—a main body with six outrigger plants," he said. "They're at the top of the local food chain, very intelligent, and very much aware of themselves and their environment. What's still difficult for me to comprehend is that, although they would still be classified as plants because they use photosynthesis, they are so active they need more food—in fact they're omnivorous—and in turn, they are able to get more food because they're so active!"

"Chicken and egg?" murmured David.

"Maybe." Nels shrugged. "They live, by choice, in those thorn thickets we've tried to get through, and they can make the thickets open up to them. I get the impression they're not afraid of anything, but they need to maintain a stable, upright position—you can see it'd be hard for them to get erect again if they toppled over!—and the thickets protect them from the wind as much as from any predator."

"How do they get other foods?" I asked curiously.

"It sounds to me like they have a sort of farm operation," said Cinnamon slowly. "The words are unclear still, and I keep thinking how unlikely that would be, but then I watch those thick roots pick up a knife . . ."

"And did you see that knife?" Carmen asked eagerly. "It's much better than anything I can make!"

"Yet the Jolly was really interested in my Mech-All," added Shirley. "After three or four of those gentle, pushy reachings for my belt-pouch, I got it out, switched it to a standard knife blade, and the Jolly examined every part of it."

"And did you notice how it did that examining?" said Jinjur. "I was fascinated—the root end felt it all over, like my fingers would, while one of those little owls hovered so close I could have touched it!"

"Those flying things really do appear to be eyes for the Jolly," Nels said. "But how they evolved into separate entities I can't figure out."

I remembered Cinnamon's curiosity about the underwater plants with their six mobile parts out on tentacles, and I glanced at her, but she said nothing, staring thoughtfully into the flames.

"As near as I can pronounce what the Jolly said, there is a creature called the jookeejook, which the Jolly controls, and uses for food," Shirley said. "I'm hoping I'll soon be able to ask to visit the thorn thicket this fellow calls home, if he does, and then we'll learn more."

"I'm taking it slow," she said to my quick question. "I think Reiki's right about the courtesy here, it just makes sense. We move so rapidly all the time, the Jolly might rightly feel threatened if we were anything other than calm and steady."

I was glad to hear this. I've seen how difficult it is for David, in particular, to move slowly, unless he is convinced of the necessity for it.

"How about those decorations?" I asked. "Did you get any explanation for them?"

"Not yet," Carmen answered. "It apparently has several different sorts, and uses them with obvious care, but they don't seem to serve any practical purpose. Like your laces, Reiki!" she added in surprise. I considered that—rather an appealing thought!

"Further," Nels went on, "I think that it's eating when the little animals bring stuff which goes into that hole in the trunk, and when it fetches out fruit and things from the pouches and puts them in the hole. The gurgly noises, for lack of a better term, rather indicate that. But the Jolly always covers the hole with that decorated cloth before the sounds begin—I've no idea why."

I gasped as a thought came to me, but my idea was too blatantly anthropomorphic to say aloud. But Shirley turned and gave me a quick and knowing grin.

"A napkin, Reiki?" she whispered.

"We did manage to ask a few simple questions about the trees and vines," she said aloud. "Mostly by showing them to the little owls, and letting David make interrogative sounds on the flute. It seems to know and use the fruit, when it can get it! But the interesting thing is the battle between the trees and the vines—I think the Jolly has a word that very definitely means war, and that it's going on all the time. We can't see it, or hear it, but it must be a bitter struggle—no holds barred!"

"Yes, I got that too," said Carmen. "They're all after the same thing, and I think it might be the treetop area."

"Yes," Nels agreed. "It looks like all the different sorts of trees live in family-type groups, and they're all struggling upward, probably to get as much light and rainwater as they can. In Earth's rainforests, there's a polite sort of distance between the various treetops, but perhaps because the light is poorer here, that space is literally up for grabs. The trees are always sending out exploring vines, or roots, or both, hunting for better terrain, and attempting to kill any other vine or root it meets and take over its area. When you and Arielle go up the trees using the vines you don't notice it—and I don't think the trees are cognizant, not like the Jolly—but the tree and vine you are scrambling over are actually locked in combat with each other!"

"How can you tell who wins?" asked Jinjur.

"Ultimately, by which survives," Nels answered.

"Or, at least, by which remains in control of that area," said Cinnamon, thinking it out. "I bet that's what started the plants moving in the first place. The simpler ones do it by shifting their main growth to the best place. The Jollys have evolved a lot further than that."

"What about the little animals that gather food for the Jolly?" I asked.

"They seem to be . . . just little animals that gather food," said Jinjur. "I got between one of them and the Jolly by mistake, this morning," she admitted. "Neither the animal nor the Jolly made any move toward me, but there certainly was an increase in the sounds between the animal on the ground and the animals inside the hole in the trunk! And the little thing shifted constantly until I was out of the way, and then headed straight and fast for the hole in the trunk."

There was not much more to add to the information, and my day in the water has left me drowsy. It is a rare clear night, and I wander down to the beach to watch the stars coming out. What an incredibly beautiful sight! There are only a few high clouds in the sky, and as I stand in the warm wind I can see the light of more distant stars, thick in the sky. But what fills the heavens is the gigantic glowing orb of Gargantua hanging overhead, bigger than my hand, and in "full-moon" phase. Richard came down to the beach to join me.

The night is peaceful—I might be in any tropical paradise but for the unearthly view above me. Hawaii, Pitcairn, Tahiti—but those places all have records of human violence. This place seems so innocent, and benign—perhaps it really is an Eden!

"What do you think would make life here better?" I asked Richard, curious. He started to speak, then stopped. Slowly, he said, "I'd be very reluctant to add anything at all, just yet. Any ecology is incredibly complex, and fragile—and here, where we're so . . . ignorant!" I liked hearing that.

I look up again at Gargantua. The shadow of Zapotec is already moving across the face of the planet, and is soon followed by our moon's shadow. It's very pleasant to stand thus, the little waves whispering over my feet, talking quietly with Richard—but I'm too weary to remain. I shall go to bed.

We learned so much today about the creatures of this new world that I am exhilarated! Any period of time spent in making discoveries is stimulating, of course—when my mind is absorbing new data I experience neither fatigue nor hunger for hours, and today was just such a joyous delight! It reminded me of early days at school, when some hitherto unknown realm of knowledge was suddenly available—a new field of literature or experiment to explore—and I could plunge into it with single-minded intensity!

This day began early. Jinjur agreed to a long interview with the giant alien, including David, Cinnamon, and Carmen; we hoped to expand our vocabulary, and to begin to suggest a visit to its territory. How much more we discovered than we had anticipated! But then, none of the information sent early to us by our landers had even hinted at the amazing development—even civilization!—of these peculiar plants.

We made a very formal start to our dialogue. David played the visitor's initial greeting-tune with great care, and we listened closely as it was returned, exactly similar to our ears, by one of the little animals standing at the entrance to the hole in the Jolly's trunk. We indicated our own selves by name, and then we received the first shock. Although it had only been hours since our last talk with this being, it apparently had spent the time in thought as rapid as its movement is slow, for it had absorbed so much of our language and vocabulary that we can now communicate with ease!

I asked, in tentative fashion, if the Jolly was comfortable: "Have you eaten? And rested?"

"Yes, thank you very much, Reiki. May I sincerely hope that all is well with you and the others also?" whistled a second animal who replaced the first one. Although the reply had a whistling or breathy tone instead of the humming tone generated by human vocal cords, it was definitely human speech and quite intelligible.

This amazing reply left us speechless! The creature then began, on its own initiative, to describe itself and the things about us in a mixture of English and Jolly words. When it used a word new to us, we were usually able to understand its meaning by context, and as the pace was slow, Cinnamon interpolated the words we would have been likely to use. At each such suggestion, the intelligent mind with us repeated it thoughtfully, and thereafter used it as we would. Our discussion was thus able to increase in speed and understanding with breath-taking alacrity!

As we had suspected, the "owls" are indeed the eyes of the creature; they fly out to gather information and are completely separate entities, but they are still simply eyes which must return to the plant very soon. There they reattach themselves to the prehensile teat Cinnamon had glimpsed within the "nests" or sockets, and the information they have obtained is instantly fed into the intelligence center, while the eye itself is nourished and sheltered simultaneously. The small animals living in the hole in the trunk serve as gatherers, or extra hands; they are capable of swift movement, and are dexterous in their ability to climb or dig to obtain food, but they have little more intelligence than our own hands. The coexistence of these parts serves to make a single, smoothly functioning individual, to which we can relate, although it is difficult to imagine our own hands or eyes operating independently at a distance from us!

At this point I had a most distressing thought. "Do you remember," I reminded Cinnamon quietly, "that we have caught—and eaten!—some of its eyes and hands?"

Her eyes widened in horror. "Shall we mention that?" she wondered.

"I think we'd better," I said. "It's not, after all, the minor sort of solecism one intelligent being might reasonably overlook from another! It must know we were ignorant, but not deliberately cruel."

Choosing words with care, I began. "We understand, now, that many days ago, when we captured and ate what we thought was an animal, and what we thought was a bird, we were wrong. We made a mistake. We did not intend to hurt or harm you. Please accept our apology." I kept on explaining and apologizing for some time in as many different words as I could, and the Jolly said nothing until I stopped. Then we heard another of the ceremonial-sounding melodies, followed by recognizable words:

"Your apology is accepted. I now grow a new eye"—here, it indicated a smaller nest in the canopy that contained an eye that was now open, but not yet mobile like the others—"and a new gatherer." It indicated then the central opening in the trunk, and Cinnamon got a quick glimpse within, to report that the teats for the gatherers are similar to the ones in the nests, and there was an immature gatherer attached to one of the teats inside.

The Jolly now reintroduced the subject of fire, and Cinnamon and Carmen demonstrated their techniques for starting a fire. The Jolly was quick to understand how to produce fire with bow and drill or flint and steel, but soon realized that both methods require rapid motions which would be difficult for it to emulate with its root-hands, although with a great deal of practice it might be able to some day carry out the fearful procedure using its gatherers. The eyes fluttered, watching intently as Cinnamon nursed the tiny spark along with bits of fuel and tinder, until it was a fair size. The giant began to back away from the bright yellow flames until Cinnamon, observing its trepidation, extinguished the fire. Instantly, the intelligence spoke of the implications of having heat as a tool—and then revealed to us that the only fires it had observed heretofore were full-grown affairs caused by lightning and lava flows. We could well understand how such a phenomenon would be a terror to the slow-moving plants!

Cinnamon then began to ask about the creature's home. She is so instinctively empathetic with any form of life, it was interesting to watch her. Moving slowly about the plant, bending occasionally to touch, ever so lightly, some curious portion of it, she crooned, rather than asked, her questions.

"Where do you rest? Have you offspring? Have you shelter from storms? I am interested in knowing how you live!"

The reply was startlingly quick, from so slow-moving a creature: "Come! I will show you!"

The Jolly began to move, and we watched, mesmerized by the unique stride of the big roots. Then we realized what it had said. Our opportunity had come! After a hurried discussion, David and Carmen moved up on either side of the Jolly and kept even with its slow progress, never stepping in its way or impeding the constant flights of the eyes. Cinnamon and I sped to collect the others, assuming correctly that everyone wanted to see whatever the Jolly could show us. Jinjur automatically began to think about leaving someone on watch, but a look around at our exceedingly sketchy encampment made her realize the absurdity of that. And as Arielle said, cheerfully setting aside the kettle, "If thief wants raw beans, he's welcome!"

It was a curious—in every sense of the word!—procession we formed. As we paced slowly to the north, we had ample time to roam the forest thickets at our sides, and bring specimens to the Jolly for comment or explanation.

Thus, we learned that the large low banyanlike trees with the bamboolike supports are peethoo trees. Nels had been right about their preferring leaf mass to trunk mass, and we had observed how their big spongy leaves, fragrant as cedar, soak up all the water that falls. But we had not appreciated fully their strengths. "Around the peethoo tree, taller trees can grow, and shade them from the light, and take the water from the sky. But the peethoo fight back! Roots hunt out invading roots, strangle and kill them."

The tentacle tree called the keekoo by the Jolly, whose root had attacked Shirley's braid, was another whose roots are warriors. In this case, they are specially developed and aggressive roots, always searching for food and running just under the surface of the soil for great distances. When the Jolly pointed out a keekoo root, Cinnamon attempted to entice it with the tip of her own braid, with Shirley standing by with the serrated blade on her Mech-All ready. The tentacle did begin to swell under the stimulus, and started to coil around the braid, but it moved so slowly Cinnamon easily avoided it. Such a runner could strangle other slower moving vines, or perhaps snare a slow-moving creature, but it's apparent now that Shirley's braid was ensnared on our first day only because she was motionless in her sleep.

The feebook plant, which we had referred to as "ivy," is ubiquitous on even the most barren-appearing soils, and has lemon-scented leaves which are virtually waterproof, collecting all the rain and funneling it to the central mass at the bottom of the creek beds. This dependence on rainwater for so many nutrients seems to bear out George's early speculations about the toroidal gas clouds that form in space around the orbits of Zouave and Zulu from the material that has escaped from their upper atmospheres. The gas drifts into Eden's orbit, is pulled in by Eden's gravity, and is enmeshed in the rains. All the storms and winds, which are only a hindrance to our activities are actually bringing vital elements to the native life—and ultimately to us, I suppose, if we continue to thrive here!

Through the upper canopies we occasionally glimpsed the gently smoking summit of the big volcano. I wondered aloud if the Jolly encompassed the mountains in the views with which its eyes supply it. The Jolly responded with great assurance that it knew a great deal about the Great Volcano Hoolkoor the Goundshaker and its sometimes violent habits. John listened to the Jolly's detailed explanation for some time.

"Sounds like a typical tribal interpretation of volcanic activity," he said. "Groundshaker's spear, Nightlight's insults . . ."

But Richard stated firmly, "Tribal interpretation or scientific analysis—they both describe what happens, with methods that can predict accurately, so what's the difference?"

I fell to thinking about the earthly coexistence of humans and volcanos, and how one result had been the formation of various taboos. Originally designed to protect human life, taboos often lost their purpose in the increasing complexities of daily routine over time, and unfortunately then became rigid limitations on individual freedom. As we shared our own views of the world around us with these strange natives, would we increase their appreciation of it? Certainly I hoped we would not disabuse them of any harmless beliefs!

We were now approaching a narrow but deep crevasse in the side of the volcano, down which a flow of still-smoking lava was moving sluggishly. The surface was crusted, but certainly impassable for either us or the Jolly.

"How will you cross this?" asked Jinjur curiously.

"I cannot cross here. I must move west until the flow is flat and not so hot." Patiently, the big plant set off.

"Wait!" cried Shirley. "How far must you go out of your way?"

"Sixth day march," came the answer. "And sixth day back to the route."

"But," protested Shirley, "It's not a wide crossing! A simple bridge . . ." The Jolly stopped, listening. While I explained the idea of a bridge, Shirley and the others quickly gathered some sturdy vines and planks.

Jinjur said, doubtfully, "Shirley, that giant must weigh a ton! Do you think this stuff will support it?"

"It'll be mostly rope mesh—or vine mesh, I mean!" explained Shirley. "These things are really tough, and we'll make it just wide enough for the Jolly's width, and put the planks along it for stability. We'll give it nice high "rails," draw the whole thing taut, and be on our way!"

I privately thought it would take as long to build a sufficiently sturdy bridge as to follow the lava stream to a fording place, but Shirley was excited at the chance to construct something. And, I must admit, with the skilled workers she had to hand and her own expertise, the project proceeded rapidly.

"I understand 'bridge,' " said the Jolly at my side, watching intently. The eyes were flying in an eager cloud above the workers, reporting back constantly.

"But how to get over, to start?"

"Just throw a line!" called Shirley, swinging a long light vine competently from one strong hand. The end of the vine was tied to the taproot of a small tree base that had thick forked roots branching out from the sides to make a grappling hook.

"Throw?" The word was obviously baffling. Shirley's first toss lodged firmly in some stout bushes on the opposite bank. The thought flashed through my mind that if the bushes were as intelligent as those of our friend here, we might find the construction sabotaged with some speed! But, fortunately, most of the plants have a response time more like that of the plants with which we are most familiar. The Jolly seemed to be searching for words.

"What you do . . . that is new . . . send things through the air like eyes!" It dawned on me, then, that this must be the first thrown object the Jolly had ever seen.

After the far anchor of the line had been thoroughly tested with the combined weight of Richard and Shirley, Arielle crossed hand over hand, a safety line connected to a branch overhead tied around her waist.

Quickly, the construction was complete, and a short but extremely stout bridge crossed the hot chasm. We started across, and the bridge did not even quiver. It is not surprising, however, that the Jolly stood hesitantly on the brink, feeling the first few planks in very doubtful fashion.

"Richard, John, Nels—give the Jolly a helping hand there!" said Jinjur. The three men recrossed, and as their combined weight made the planks tremble I saw the Jolly's roots retreat to the firm land.

"It's okay, old man!" Richard's shout was meant to be reassuring.

"We'll keep you upright," said John more practically. "We won't let you fall."

Obviously, the big plant had good reason to be frightened. There was absolutely nothing in its former experience to guide it in these circumstances, nor had it any justification for trusting us. It had seen us all together on the bridge, but must have been very unsure of its own safety on such a thing.

Cinnamon, watching closely, said suddenly, "It's going to try, because it is proud!" Impossible to know, but I rather think she was right. There was an almost tangible straightness and tension forming along the length of the trunk, and while the fluttering eyes maintained a vigilant surveillance of the scene, the ponderous roots moved out along the surface before it. The men braced their large hands firmly about the woody girth, and together the oddly assorted group moved slowly and steadily across the rude bridge. That strange picture is now one of the prized images in the memory of my recorder!

The crossing was uneventful, but the Jolly now spoke in different tones. I suspect it was pleased with itself! And its reaction was a friendlier feeling towards the creatures who had assisted it in the strange new adventure!

In any event, while we strolled our leisurely way, we continued to ask questions, and the answers came with not only increasing fluency but with more good will. The Jolly was picking up our language much more quickly than we were learning its own! But that made it easier, now, to praise the beauty of some of the tokens it had brought along as gifts. Among these were some irregularly shaped beads, strung along a length of vine. I fingered them, enjoying their warmth and color.

"What is this substance?" I asked.

"We find those in streams. Pretty. Easy to make holes in. Do not change color. Stay shiny." The answer was a sensible one, but John suddenly reached for the little strand, looked more closely at it, and hefted its weight in the reduced gravity.

"I think it's gold!" he said, in hushed tones.

Several heads lifted sharply, only to relax again as Jinjur said, with a laugh, "So what?"

I was glad to hear that. Unless we can think of a good, practical use for the metal, the little nuggets can remain as trinkets, and nothing more.

Carmen traced with a fingertip the intricate designs on the cloth which had also been a gift. "This is a perfect picture of the berry vine, isn't it, but how did you get the color?" The giant began to explain to her how the dye was made, from some sort of shell called the peekoo, but I was still puzzling over what purpose the cloth serves at all. The Jolly calls it a word meaning roughly mouthcloth, and it comes into use only when the plant is making eating noises, but it doesn't seem to be used to clean the mouth or hands, like a human napkin. It may very well be purely a cultural device.

The light was beginning to fade, indicating the approach of the midday eclipse. In our camp this was a pleasant hour of refreshment in the long day; the firelight is sufficient for a few things, but the intense darkness beyond it precludes any real activity. As the disk of Barnard set behind the black circle of Gargantua overhead, Shirley and Carmen found a pleasant site and quickly produced a small fire. Shortly after we had set out on this slow journey, John and David had gauged our speed, and returned to camp for a few foodstuffs. The Jolly watched the cooking process with great interest, its eyes steering carefully around the rising smoke. We offered it a bit of grilled fish, and some cooked vegetable. It accepted only tiny portions and politely refused more; we were similarly reluctant to sample much of the various items it proffered from its bulging travel net. There was one exception; a very tasty fruit indeed, according to Arielle, who was the designated taster. (We continue, understandably, to exercise great caution with unknown alien foods!) Arielle described the berry's sweetness enthusiastically, and our questions elicited the information that this is a crop which the Jolly harvests! It promised to show us the pens in which it keeps the plants which grow the fruit. The Jolly refers to them as jookeejook plants, and perhaps we too can use them as food. As we rested through the quiet darkness, we explained, as simply as we could, how we had arrived in this land, and why. The creature listened carefully, but I am sure—I think—it cannot comprehend the magnitude of our travels and differences, despite having seen and talked with the penetrator in our camp.

It said gravely, "When our fishing rafts drift far out to sea, they find strange plants floating in water. We never see these before. Perhaps you know them, and where they come from."

"I doubt it," Jinjur managed to convey. "What you describe are probably plants from another island, where they may have evolved in different surroundings . . . you understand how growing things can change from one generation to the next?"

"Certainly. Some jookeejook we grow for good fruit. Some jookeejook we grow for good meat. I show you jookeejook soon." The voice sounded a bit weary. "Then you understand."

For the last hour and a half of the darkness we relaxed, chatting idly among ourselves. The Jolly listened, but seemed to be resting also, for the eyes remained quiet in their nests, and the little gatherers were out of sight behind the mouthcloth.

When it was light enough to resume our slow but steady march, we did so. It was fascinating to see the small gatherers run ahead to the thorn thickets and signal our approach. With remarkable speed, considering their ordinary appearance, the spiky branches furled back upon themselves, and we all were able to pass through in a straight line as the gatherers lined our path, keeping the thorny coils back.

"The thook plants let us through, because we are members of their tribe," the Jolly remarked. "We help them, by cutting away any attacking vines or roots and keeping them supplied with water. We use them as protective walls around our sheds and workshops."

The mention of buildings was startling. We speculated briefly and fruitlessly on the possible nature of these things, and were soon to learn the reality; more fantastic, and yet simpler, than our imaginings!

The tedium of this journey was as hard on us as it was on the giant, I think. We could not help wishing for a faster pace, while the creature was making the best time of which it was capable. There was definitely relief in the Jolly's announcement that the thorn-thicket ahead of us was its home. The thorny walls rose higher and thicker than any we had seen, and we were glad to curb our impatience, and follow carefully into the central clearing. Here we stood silent, gazing around us at a scene of bizarre but sophisticated activity. There were indeed sheds, simple but very sturdy, containing shelves on which were stacked orderly piles of supplies. In front of one of them, another Jolly, smaller than our companion, was using those facile roots-hands to pressure flake a bit of obsidian in much the same manner Carmen employs, only, of course, much more slowly.

Ahead of us were pens made of flat stone, not unlike the Caithness flagstones that had kept the flocks of sheep penned in the fields in Scotland before the invention of barbed wire. We moved to look within these walls at the jookeejooks penned inside. I was intrigued at the sight of these—animals? Plants? I suppose, like the Jolly they resemble so much, they are both. They are much smaller than the Jolly, and they move about even more slowly, using all six legs. But their eyes! They are attached to long, stiff but flexible wire-like structures arcing up through the fronds, and so the eyes themselves flutter rather ineffectually about the canopy. The small gatherers are attached to them also, by something which resembles a vine, or possibly an umbilical cord, coming out of their mouth holes.

Like the Jolly gatherers, they seem to function as hands, and they move busily about the parent plant, but of course they cannot go far, and they seem content mostly to pick up bits of food from a long trough at one edge of their pen. It seems contradictory of us, but I think we have become so quickly accustomed to the sight of the Jolly's free-roaming eyes and gatherers that this more primitive form strikes us as stranger yet. Nels and I talked softly, exploring the idea that the fish we had eaten was an underwater version of this same structure. It seemed possible.

Another peculiarity of the small creature was the presence of globular growths, of various sizes, in clusters nestled among their fronds. While we watched, amazed, our host sent a gatherer to pluck one of these from the nearest jookeejook. It exhibited no distress, but went on placidly eating, while the Jolly offered us the fruit. It was the same sort Arielle had sampled previously, so with her encouragement, we tasted. The flavor was pleasant, and almost familiar, although I couldn't place it until Carmen exclaimed, "Strawberries!" She and Cinnamon began to ply the Jolly with questions about the cultivation and husbandry of these strange beings. I watched, in private mirth, Arielle studying the animals with hungry speculation—she looked like she was mentally carving! But Nels was totally enraptured, and reached a gentle hand to touch the strange growths on the jookeejook.

"I bet that's it!" he muttered. "The Jolly Giants must have evolved from a plant like this one, but their eyes and gatherers are intelligent enough to operate on their own and no longer need an attachment to the parent plant to function, although they still must return to the main plant periodically for life support."

The entire little village, if that is what it is, looks like a well-tended garden; the surrounding thorn bushes form a tidy wall, with no encroaching spines to brush against a passing Jolly, and the sheds and pens are connected by smooth and well-worn trails. Other Jollys nearby had instantly sent eyes to examine us rather closely, but no gatherers had approached.

I looked out through a thin patch in the thorn barrier where I could see the sparkle of water from a nearby lake, similar to the one near our camp, complete with sulfurous fumes rising from the center. Floating on the calm surface was a flat raft, and erect upon it were two Jollys. They were much slimmer than our acquaintance, and, between them, they were maneuvering a net much more finely woven than ours. However, I found I was paying little heed to the ponderous activities of the fishermen, my whole attention being fastened on the sturdy raft; and I realized I was coveting that awkward craft with surprising intensity! In honesty, I must admit I wanted such a thing not simply to improve my efficiency as a fisherman, but because I wanted to be out on the water with it.

I turned away reluctantly, and found Jinjur and Shirley still asking eager questions. Cinnamon was looking a trifle concerned, I thought, and in response to my question, she said, "I think the Jolly is a little tired of us, Reiki. The eyes keep starting off towards the sheds, only to come back reluctantly, it seems."

"I think you're right," I agreed. "I suspect we are in danger of overstaying our welcome—for a first visit! Jinjur . . ."

With some difficulty, I secured her attention, and

suggested it was time to go.

"But we need to know . . ." she began. "But not necessarily all at once," she conceded right away. "I understand. These are not creatures we could control, even if we wanted to, but they surely do seem to be creatures with a great deal to teach us! So we'll keep it polite—*you* can ask if we can return!"

I called David to stand beside me, and we waited in silence for the Jolly to finish his last explanation. Then David blew the formal meeting tune we had learned, and I began a rather florid farewell. I had already observed that while the speech pouring from the gatherers is rapidly becoming ever more precise and understandable, there is also a genuine enjoyment of language for its own sake. Certainly the creature's answer to my speech was both courteous and benign, and a future welcome was assured us as the Jolly had one of its gatherers repeat back one of my more lengthy declarations in its whistling tone:

"I sincerely hope we will have many more mutually beneficial consultations!"

With that, we felt ourselves dismissed, and headed in good order back to our own camp, discussing the implications of what we had learned. Nels, thinking aloud, developed an hypothesis explaining the evolution of the Jollys, and I listened with interest as he struggled with the evolutionary complexity of the mobile roots. We all joined in, making objections and compiling a list of the most important questions to put forward on our next visit. I had recorded all our observations, and this evening I will take my recorder down to the penetrator and transmit what we have learned back to James and the others on the now distant *Prometheus*.

Carmen, oddly enough, seemed to be thinking of something entirely different, and she spoke only once on our rapid hike.

"Jinjur! It's beginning to look like we have a comfortable future, finally, doesn't it? I mean, there's plenty of food, everything we really need—we even can have some time for our own pleasure! Not a bad place to spend the rest of our lives, don't you agree?" This is unlike Carmen, whose usual interest centers in the moment. Jinjur considered the question thoughtfully, and finally spoke with tentative pleasure.

"I think it's a little too soon to say, conclusively, that we really have an Eden here. But I'm hopeful, I honestly am."

With those cheerful words, we arrived at our spring, and I stopped here, to fill the jugs we shall want this evening.

# CHANGING

This day began so pleasantly, and ended in such a storm! I had thought our future, insecure and primitive as it has appeared these last weeks, to be reasonably under our own control, but *Carmen*, of all people, has unleashed feelings and ideas that threaten our very existence. I am resolved to combat these wild schemes and notions with every bit of my intelligence and strength—I hope desperately that I will succeed!

I had gone early to the shore, intending to fish, and was soon engaged in the work. My routine involves swimming slowly out to a likely area and surveying the bottom through the faceplate of a spacesuit helmet that the flouwen had salvaged from the *Beagle*. When I find a spot which seems to contain plants or shells, I mark it, return to shore to leave the helmet, and swim out again with knife and net and flippers. After a few deep breaths, I dive until I am tired or the net is full. The tenacious clams are so delicious I usually try to collect as many as I can of them first, for the curious filter-feeder fish are both easier and meatier; it is simply a question of locating the parent plant along a vent, and then harrying the attached "fish" until I can break it free and net it. I enjoy the work, but my mind continued to play with the idea of a simple boat from which to dive—it would save me the effort of swimming back and forth, and give me a place to rest between dives.

I resolved to discuss the project with Shirley at the first opportunity. I knew she would enjoy such a task, and I shall have to be firm about keeping the craft both light and simple; I hope this will be my own boat, and I shall want it to be of a size I can handle alone. I had begun to tire, and my thoughts veered off to the dreamy possibility of exploring other shores in my little boat, when I heard voices.

Little Red's shouts, as usual, came to my attention first, and, lifting my head from the water, I saw several people talking with the flouwen. It seemed a good time to stop work, and drift over to listen to the talk.

Nels was attempting to explain the nature and appearance of the Jolly Giants to the incredulous flouwen. After their own experiences on earlier expeditions, I would have thought the flouwen would have been more open-minded about unique new life-forms, but then I recall my own total disbelief at the sight of that moving plant, and I am more sympathetic.

"Plant has eyes that fly like Pretty-Smells?!" Little Red exclaimed, at his customary volume. Little Purple sounded rather wistful: "That sounds very strange, but very good too. That means they can look at things far away, without themselves having to move."

"We think that's how they see," Nels said. "But the idea is too new for us to understand fully, ourselves. There's a big gap between having eyes on your body, and having them free-moving."

"Want to see! Where is Jolly?" Little Red asked.

"Inland," said Cinnamon briefly. "They live near a big lake, so they can fish too, but they don't seem to care much for the ocean. And quite sensible that is, too," she added thoughtfully. "As slow-moving and top-heavy as they are, they'd have a lot of trouble coping with the waves, so they probably just avoid them altogether."

"We must arrange a meeting between the Jollys and the flouwen sometime, though," said Jinjur. "I'm all for expanding horizons between sentient beings!"

Privately, I hoped we took the time for considerable explanation to both parties before such a meeting; the Jollys had obviously found us interesting, but something of a disturbance.

At this point I waded out of the water and returned to camp, bearing my catch to what Arielle grandiloquently calls the "kitchen." We had indeed improved the cooking area with work surfaces, and here I found Shirley, grinding meal. She has already devised a more efficient mill, and is continually adjusting our crude tools for the better. As I expected, my new project captured her interest instantly.

"Yes! We can fasten those peethoo bamboo supports together, stop the ends with plugs of leaves—wait! Maybe a better idea would be to cut down one of those palms, and hollow it out! Make a dugout canoe!"

"Put in mast, and make sail? Then go farther, faster!" suggested Arielle. I was intrigued, myself, with the idea of a sail, but a little sorry to see my idea being so swiftly carried away from me.

"Could we start with just a little raft, please?" I requested. "It really would be a help in getting to good fishing spots."

"Okay, we'll do that tomorrow," agreed Shirley. "But a real boat, maybe an outrigger type, would be great for lots of other things too. I'll have to take a good look at that palm trunk—see what I can do with it." The palms are called boobaa by the Jollys, and bear the tough but useful fruits Arielle and David are so skilful in obtaining. Like so many other plants here, they grow in a sort of family arrangement. The attacking vines, reaching for the canopy space, are beautifully dealt with; in essence, the victim tree being climbed by the vine "retreats." It shrinks and transfers its energy to its allies. The vine thus uses its own strength in an unsuccessful attempt, because it is soon shaded out of any way to exist. The boobaa trunks are certainly wide enough for canoes, and if that is possible I hope we can do it! Discussion of various schemes for boatbuilding began our evening session, and by then Shirley had progressed to a scheme to build a fine dock out from Flouwen Beach.

We have all succumbed to the human tendency to name things, and Flouwen Beach marks not only our first landing place, but also the area where the water is deep enough for the friendly creatures to come close enough to hail us. I chuckled at Shirley's enthusiasm for a dock; the boulder on the beach where we had so unceremoniously draped Richard's half-drowned body was quite adequate to moor the modest craft I envisioned, but Shirley was already planning a ship the size of a young ocean-liner. It was easy to become excited at the prospect of a boat, however!

"With the boat, and guided by the flouwen, we can begin to do some real exploring," said Jinjur dreamily. "See if any nearby islands have these same plant forms, or different ones entirely."

"Bound to have some of the same, don't you think?" asked David. "The tides and currents would have transferred seeds and shoots."

"Unless the ones on each island are as aggressive and territorial as these seem to be," speculated Richard. "We might discover a regular beach patrol, resisting invaders!"

"We ought to survey the beaches around this island for that sort of thing," suggested Nels, half-seriously. "Although I'm not sure just what to look for. How does one spot a plant on guard duty?"

I was not listening too closely to this, because I was

considering the problem of navigation under these unfamiliar skies. I remembered having to relearn during the summer I spent on the schooner in Australian waters.

"Do any of you remember the charts on *Prometheus* well enough to steer by these stars?" I asked abruptly. To my surprise, Arielle answered.

"Never tried to learn them. But I spend watch, watching stars. I know how these move, I could steer by them. You want to learn?"

"Yes!" I declared. "Let's start tonight!" Arielle shook her head, her dark eyes somber. "Too cloudy. That always going to be big problem, here." From her remarks about making a sail for our proposed boat, I knew she too wants to set forth—the loss of the aerospace plane at the bottom of the lagoon means her own figurative wings are sadly clipped.

"We'd just have to wait for clear weather to set out . . ." I began.

"And clear weather to return," Jinjur reminded. "It might be a long time before you got . . . home."

There was a long silence.

"Is this home?" asked Cinnamon quietly. "For the next twenty-five years, are we going to wander, together or separately, or settle here?"

" 'Here' being *right* here?" asked John. "Right here in Town Square?" The term made me smile—anything less square than this sloping, uneven pile of rock has seldom been seen.

"What'll we call 'here,' then?" asked Shirley, avoiding more talk of plans. "Camp One? Base Camp? We've done an awful lot of talking, sitting around here—maybe . . ."

"Council Rock," said David definitely. Shades of Kipling! But it sounded rather pleasant. Jinjur's reference to this planet being an Eden returned to my mind. Perhaps it was more flattering a term than a truthful one, but civilizations have certainly been founded in more unpropitious surroundings.

And then it happened. Carmen, with a few brief words, shattered completely any prospects of tranquillity. Without preliminary, she announced calmly, "I want to have my home here. We've learned we can live comfortably right here, and I want to stay. And I want a child."

I could not believe I had heard her correctly.

"A . . . a child? Where will you . . ."

"I want to have a baby. Because I was a last-minute replacement on *Prometheus*, I was never made incapable of child-bearing like the rest of you. I want one of you men to reverse your vasectomy—John can help—and make me pregnant!"

I felt stunned and dizzy. "But, that's not possible!" I cried, at once. "We cannot start families, even if there were any way it could be done! We're explorers!"

Jinjur was quick to agree. "The reason we took the step to eliminate procreation in all of us before we left Earth, is that this is no life for a new generation. We knew that when we signed on!"

"But it *is* possible," insisted Carmen, so quietly that I knew she had given this a lot of silent thought. "I *can* have a baby, and I think this is a good place to raise a child—better than most places on Earth." She stopped then, and I saw with dread that she was expecting argument, and was prepared for it.

And argument there was!

"Childbirth requires hospital facilities, sterile surroundings, drugs—"

"Babies need special food, and soft warm beds, and clean surroundings—"

"Children could not survive in this wilderness, with danger all around—"

"Raising a child takes skills and learning we've none of us had—"

"Something is bound to go wrong, and then what?"

But Carmen just said, "Having babies and raising them is normal. It's human. In primitive societies, in ghastly places on earth, in wartime, people have borne children, and raised them. And I want to do that." I became more vocal than ever, seeing this as a genuine threat to the solidarity of our small community. Carefully, as each of us found words, we set forth the many reasons why Carmen's absurd desire must not attain fulfillment, and she listened, oh so politely, for more than an hour. Then, she suddenly stood, and following our own rules of conduct, she simply walked away from us into the gloom.

"Well! We'll just have to let it go for now, and resume pointing out the facts to her when we get the chance," said Shirley firmly. But I feel some most chilling qualms! For one thing, the men, after their initial expostulation, became very quiet and took no further part in the argument. For another, Cinnamon said, after Carmen's departure, "To have a real home, and a family—I knew I wouldn't have one when I signed on, but it does sound so pleasant—I'd like to think about it, myself, before we decide."

"I thought it *was* decided!" said Shirley, and my heart sank, for there was more hope than disapproval in the quick words.

"But how?" Arielle's question brought the discussion to a close—a most unsatisfactory one, to my way of thinking!

It is very late. I've been awakened by Arielle's hand on my shoulder—I was having the nightmare, and she is on watch and heard my moans. How long will I have that same dream? Unable to free myself from my bunk on the lander, while the water swirls higher—it must have been triggered by the dissension this evening, and my inability to resolve it. I lay sleepily for a while, thankful to have been wakened, and glanced around at the quiet forms, hoping I had disturbed no one. Automatically I counted them, as we all do from time to time. It is disquieting to see that two are missing! I turned to Arielle, and found her dark eyes regarding me calmly. Whoever is off in the night, she is not alarmed. What is happening?

I am absolutely exhausted. This week I have worked harder than ever in my life before, trying to persuade my formerly clear-thinking companions of their folly. To no avail! I cannot decide, myself, which is more galling; the idiocy of any attempt on our part to bring children into this incredible situation, or my own inability to convince anyone of that idiocy!

"For one thing, our ages are against this scheme," I said reasonably to Jinjur. "Even if our operations could be reversed, we women are surely past an age when we could possibly conceive."

"We are all still having our periods," she reminded me. "And John says that living so long in free-fall, and the No-Die we took for so many years, might have kept us fertile. But you may be right, I can't deny it. By the calendar, I am eighty-seven years old. Even subtracting thirty years for the time I spent on No-Die, my biological clock has been ticking for fifty-seven years. The youngest person we have in the crew is Cinnamon, and her effective age is forty-three."

"And if we did become pregnant, what of the effects of our ages on a pregnancy?" I argued. "None of us has ever been pregnant before, and we don't know how severe the strain might be. And giving birth! Here, in this wilderness! It's asking a great deal of a woman at the best of times, and in the best of circumstances—here, it is just suicidally dangerous!"

I think, to Jinjur, I should not have said that, because she began to look upon the prospect as a challenge. I continued, desperately, with the others, but met with frustrating obstinance. Shirley is intrigued with the technical difficulties, Cinnamon doesn't even seem to hear me, and Arielle thinks it would be "fun!"

As for Carmen, I followed her for a whole day, talking and talking. When she took to the water I followed, swimming easily next to her, and being my most logical and persuasive. I thought she was weakening until she lifted her head, looked straight into my eyes, and said, "If I have a boy I will name him after his father. If I have a girl, I shall name her 'Hope.' " Then she dove, and I drifted to shore, dispirited.

It quickly became obvious that Carmen had fastened on John as the one most likely to yield to her importunities. And he capitulated! Those nightly absences of the couple were not all spent in entreaty and denial; somehow, at who knows what agonizing cost to himself, John has reversed his own vasectomy, and is accommodating Carmen. She mentioned this, quite casually, at breakfast one morning, while John simply smirked, odiously. The rest of the time became uncomfortable in the extreme. Covert looks between the men; long, serious discussions among the women; John and Carmen being shunned but having much to say to each other—and only I have been sent to Coventry! As I adamantly continue to announce the undeniable facts confronting us in any attempt to proceed with this foolishness, I receive no word or acknowledgement from anyone—except the broad grin on Richard's face. I am baffled at the sight of seven intelligent people who have enjoyed the pleasures of carefree sex for so many years, now contemplating with envy the two who have given it up!

Still, I know that I can prevail—and prevail I must!—simply by holding out; I shall refuse to be part of a unanimous agreement.

* * *

This situation is, after all, too distressing for me to allow it to continue as it is. My obduracy, for I'm afraid that's how they envision it, is occasioning needless hardship on everyone but Carmen and John, whose individual actions are independent of us. I certainly need not become pregnant myself, nor take any part in this exercise of frivolity, but I cannot readily withhold my assistance in the technical difficulties confronting my friends. The matter was resolved, at least temporarily, in the quiet after-dinner darkness. I had resigned myself to the silence of the others, but I was sick of my own dreary arguments, and the tension in this small group of which I would, inevitably, always be a part could not be tolerated.

I advanced a hypothetical question, hoping to instigate some thoughtful discussion.

"Perhaps I don't fully understand our physical situation. Although it's evidently possible, relatively easily, to reverse the male vasectomy, I thought our tubal ligations could not be altered without major surgery. Is that not the case?"

My quiet question produced a quiet answer from John. "Both operations were deliberately done in a way so that they could be easily reversed. That was in case the mission was canceled, or one of us had to drop out for some reason. I myself am quite capable of performing the surgeries, but I could not, and would not, without certain minimum conditions."

"What are those?" Cinnamon's question was also quiet, and my heart eased a little, hoping yet to see us reach a sensible conclusion.

"Sterile surroundings, first of all, and anaesthesia. And the use of the right equipment—all that is available aboard the *Dragonfly*. It was planned years ago that in case the sick bay on the rocket lander was unavailable for any reason, the sleeping area on *Dragonfly* could be reconfigured as an emergency sick bay.

All the necessary equipment is stored in a sealed kit under the floorboards. With those facilities, and especially if I had the help of the Christmas Branch, I could not only reverse all the operations, I could check up on the status of the fertility of the person. But, of course, all of that is . . ."

"Under two hundred meters of salt water—and smashed," I said with finality.

"Not smashed too badly, remember," said David. "The computer on the *Dragonfly* is still intact, and probably functional, although it's powered down. We've been too busy to think about it, trying to survive here. Besides, we knew the computer wouldn't have been much help, since its motiles can only operate near *Dragonfly* where they can receive the laser signals that supply their instructions and motive power. That's why, until now, we've all automatically shelved the whole idea that the computer will be able to help us. With it being under two hundred meters of water, we can't reach it, and it can't reach us. But it's still there, if we can activate it."

"But how could one do that?" I asked, reasonably. "We'd have to get at it to activate it, and we can't survive a dive to that depth."

"We need a diving bell," said Shirley, but her voice was flat as she glanced around at our meager equipment.

John shrugged. "Without the Christmas Bush and those surgical instruments down there, I'll not take a chance on operating on anyone, unless it is an emergency, and this isn't. The Christmas Branch is the proper tool for the task—it's small 'fingers' can do perfect work without traumatizing even the most delicate tissues. And, while I know I'm good, I just won't interfere with any body other than my own without the right tools."

It was an uncompromising stand, and while I accepted it and was about to try to change the subject, other minds as determined as my own were concentrating fiercely on the problem.

Suddenly, David said, "*We* can't survive a dive to two hundred meters, but the flouwen can. And now that they've learned so much of our vocabulary, I might be able to teach them the voice commands that would reactivate the computer along with the Christmas Branch!"

"What good would that do?" John was still skeptical, for which I was glad. "The *Dragonfly* is stuck under the lander, with a damaged tail. The Christmas Branch can't operate out of sight of the communication lasers on the plane, so it has to stay down there, where its no good to us."

But David's mind was racing now. "If the flouwen were able to get Josephine awake and functioning, she and I would have the Christmas Branch to work with."

Shirley, who had been silently thinking all this time, spoke up. "We can't get away from the fact that, eventually, we still have to get down there ourselves, if there's going to be any operations done. We still need that diving bell! The only part of the ship I can think of with the right size and strength is the central storage tank column." I pictured it, myself. It originally contained storage tanks for water and high pressure air. We had added a tank to accommodate the flouwen, and shortened the water and air tanks to accommodate.

"The strongest part of that column was the high pressure air storage tank," recalled Jinjur. "It should be able to take the pressure at that depth, but of course it's down there, and permanently installed in the ship."

David's voice was insistent. "The Christmas Bush can do almost anything—with the tools it has available on *Dragonfly*, it would have no difficulty cutting metal—or welding it either!"

"We don't need to do either," said Shirley. "When I cut the tanks down to make room for the flouwen, I used flanged end-domes instead of the usual heliarc welded dome—made them easier to reinstall. So, if we unbolt the end-domes to the high pressure air tank, and put them flange to flange, we'll have a hollow, metal, one-person, underwater flying-saucer-shaped . . ." She paused, her eyes flickering. I could almost see the design drawings for the air tank flipping through her eidetic memory.

"Damn!" she said, finally. "The new flanges are over two meters in diameter. I designed that tank myself, and I know they're more. Not much, but we can't get them into the airlock on the *Dragonfly*. It's exactly two meters high."

I was relieved. Finally, my comrades would have to admit the futility of their irrational dreams.

"So, tilt it, " Jinjur suggested crisply.

"Of course! That'll work!" cried Shirley. Reluctantly, I could see even in my own mind's eye how such an object could slip through such a door. Even as I deplored the purpose behind this mental activity, I could not but enjoy its result; sitting empty-handed around a campfire, these people had little difficulty envisioning equipment and dimensions invisible to them.

"Then, if we can get the Christmas Branch to unbolt the end-domes, then the flouwen can bring them up. We'll need the nuts and bolts too, of course—and have them fetch a wrench!"

I fear the challenge of the problem is blinding my friends to the possible consequences of their project; it is their greatest weakness, as well as their greatest strength. David was already muttering voice commands for Josephine under his breath, with Arielle making suggestions.

"Reiki!" he said then. "Help me work out the very

minimum set of commands the flouwen will need . . ." He stopped, and looked uncertainly at me. In the sudden silence, I felt all their eyes upon me, and I thought frantically. To me, the motive behind the current proposal is absurd, even demented, but I do realize the tremendous value of getting access to, and the use of, the tools beneath the lagoon, and to that very desirable end I must contribute what I can. This task is full of risk, and I am dubious of its success, but we are so constituted—all ten of us!—that we must *try*.

I took a deep breath, and let it out in a long sigh. I hardly recognized my own voice, wavering, and very low.

"I think the self-check routine is the place to start . . ."

An echoing sigh sounded, all around the circle. Apparently I had not been the only one who had felt that awful tension! I spoke more steadily now, to mention another problem which had occurred to me.

"We can use the flouwen to activate the main computer, I think; it will simply mean rehearsing them until they have the commands perfectly memorized. But we can't depend on them for long, complicated technical messages back and forth. How can we set up some kind of direct communications link with Josephine?"

"Tell the Christmas Branch to drop the underwater sonar mapper from the cargo bay," suggested Richard. "The flouwen can haul it to the surface, and we can use that to talk back and forth with Josephine."

I agreed that was a good idea, and moved to talk it over with David. He and Arielle shifted along their log to make room for me, and it felt good to be working with them again. The magnitude of our disagreement had subtly shifted the growing familiarity of a family which we had been enjoying, making us into a society of individuals once more. My compromise had brought me back into the comfort of the family. We began to recall the words we had used to activate Josephine when we were aboard *Prometheus*, and then tried to simplify and shorten the commands. I became caught up in the problem myself, and we talked late. We hope to find the flouwen cooperative tomorrow!

The eight of us gathered for the evening meal tonight were quieter than usual. As always, I attempted to look as civilized as possible when we sat down, donning the laces that I now leave off during the rough work of the day, and trying to tame my increasingly unruly hair. Shirley and Cinnamon joined us with smooth fresh braids, and Arielle's shining cap swung just past her cheekbones as she served our nostalgic repast. The constraint we were all feeling was not due to formality; rather, I think, it was because we are so accustomed to being ten, that the absence of anyone feels very strange.

We had called the flouwen very early that morning. David and I had carefully selected the fewest possible commands for the flouwen to initiate the computer's activity, and were reviewing them anxiously once more when the opalescent blobs appeared, and we waded out to greet them.

"Hi! Hi! Let's play!" shouted Little Red immediately.

"Little Red is bored," explained Little White. "We swim along this coast all around. All the same. We catch food easily. We surf. We explore. But we find nothing new. When can we see Jollys?"

"Soon," promised Cinnamon. "We have a big job for you to do today, but as soon as it is done we'll ask the Jollys to come down to the shore to meet you." What a diverting thought—I hope most sincerely to be able to see that meeting!

"Job?" said Little Red dubiously. "Work?"

"More like a wonderful game," I said quickly. "Now that you can talk so well, and know so many fine words, maybe you can talk to the airplane pet; and maybe—just maybe—it will answer you."

"Great!" was the answering shout. "Let's go!"

"Wait!" called David. "You have to say just the right words, or it won't answer you."

"Hunh, pet dumb!" Little Red said sulkily. And, of course, he has a point.

"What words? Tell them to me," asked Little Purple eagerly.

Slowly, and with frequent repetitions, we gave the words of command to our alien friends, and they repeated them, memorizing. Finally they seemed to be word-perfect. We went through the routine a final time.

"Now," instructed David. "You go down to the airplane pet and put your body right onto the clear parts near the front. Then, you say, 'Self-check routine zero.' "

"Self-check routine zero," echoed Little White, in a creditable imitation of David's voice.

"Then, if you're lucky, the pet will answer! It will say, 'Seven-six-one-three-F-F.' But if it says anything else, or doesn't answer, come back and tell me."

"Dumb thing to say!" interjected Little Red.

"If it says, 'seven-six-one-three-f-f-,' then my turn to say 'self-check routine one,' " said Little White obediently.

"And when you hear a voice like this," I said, lowering my own to Josephine's husky accent, " 'Surface Excursion Module Four going through systems check' then you will know you are doing exactly right, and you say very quickly . . ."

"Emergency! Stop systems check! Lower sonar mapper!" ordered Little White firmly.

"Then I grab box and bring it up!" said Little Red eagerly.

"I carry the cable," added Little Purple importantly.

"Excellent!" said Cinnamon proudly. "You have learned very well."

"Off you go, then!" Jinjur waved, and the three flouwen swam from the shallows and dove into the depths of Crater Lagoon.

As we waited, we mentally went through the routine ourselves, and very shortly after we calculated that the exchange must be concluded, the three appeared again, bringing their precious cargo intact. There was a spontaneous cheer, and Shirley and David pounced upon the heavy black box covered with its array of ultrasonic senders, and quickly towed it ashore, the long power and communications umbilical trailing along behind. As they bent over it, speaking, I moved off to thank the flouwen for a job well done. They sped off and I turned to hear Jinjur's query.

"So! What's the status of the *Dragonfly*?"

David looked up from where he and Shirley were crouched before the sonar mapper, using it to talk with the airplane's computer. "Josephine was really upset at first, when she began to realize the situation. There were so many urgent damage control tasks to do at once, she didn't want to override any of them. But we told her to set the Christmas Branch to work on enough of them to allow her to go off emergency status. She was then willing to send out a sub-branch to begin unbolting the pressure tank domes."

"We also settled another worry I had," added Shirley. "I wasn't sure the Christmas Branch could function in the high pressure outside the airlock without a lot of short-circuits developing. But Josephine sent out a tiny imp first, and no problems developed. We've now got a sub-branch working on the bolts on the end domes. Perhaps, though . . ." The engineer's concern for her circuitry was back in force! "In case the salt water produces a long term corrosion problem, I think we should always keep most of the Christmas Branch inside, away from the seawater, and use the minimum portion of it necessary to do a job."

"Sounds good to me," I agreed. "David?"

He nodded. "I'll make that instruction part of Josephine's standard operation procedure with my next command," he said, and bent over the mapper again.

"Shirley," asked Jinjur seriously, "do you think there is any chance at all that we could raise the *Dragonfly*?"

Shirley's response was flat. She hates to be defeated!

"No. The lander is sitting right on top of it, and I don't think even the flouwen could rock it off. Besides, it doesn't have its wings on, and without the buoyancy supplied by the wing tanks, it would just sit there. The wing segments, and the rudder, and the liquid metal radiator loop in the rudder, were all destroyed by the engine burnthrough and crash. The radiator loops in the two horizontal stabilizers do still work, so the nuclear reactor is properly cooled, and that means there's still lots of power. It's just all on the inside of the plane, is all," she ended sadly.

John grunted. "I'm just glad it's right side up. The deck angle doesn't seem to be too steep. I should be able to work, if I can get down there."

The water roiled behind me, and I put an ear below the surface to hear Little Red complaining.

"Heavy! I do all hard work."

Quickly I called some others and between us we relieved Little Red of the burden of the detached dome.

"Did you bring the O-rings?" asked Shirley anxiously.

"Here are small hard things, and thin torus thing," came the voice of Little White, as he held out the nuts, bolts, washers and O-rings. "Now I go down to help Little Purple with the other heavy thing."

With the safe landing of the two domes, the flouwen moved off to watch, commenting freely on Shirley's activities. It took several pairs of hands, working carefully under Shirley's direction, to position the two domes together.

"I really hate to rely on a seal between two O-rings," fussed Shirley.

"Yes," agreed Carmen. "Having a flat surface on one would certainly help. Thank goodness there's still plenty of silicone grease in this groove. We'd better be really careful not to get any sand into it!"

"Richard? Nels? Help us get this thing into the water for a test dive!"

The assembly seemed to me to have gone with amazing speed, but I suppose it's because this device is so extremely simple, without the complicated technology to which I am accustomed.

"How deep are you going to send it for a test?" I asked.

Shirley considered. "At least fifty meters deeper than the plane," she said slowly. "And then we should have a complete, timed run-through, with the Christmas Branch removing the bolts and opening the bell while it is inside the airlock. The air in the bell will be limited and we need to know how long it will take."

"Wait a minute," interjected David. "There are spare suit air tanks in the airlock. I can direct the Christmas Branch to put one of them in the bell, this first trip. That way there'll be an emergency air supply right inside."

"Good idea," said Jinjur. "And if it can locate a flashlight to include, tell it to get that in too. Nice to have light if you need it."

"Lunch?" Arielle's voice was hopeful. Shirley began to protest.

"The dive will only take few minutes!" But Arielle's

comment made me think of something.

"As long as the diving bell will be empty on this first trip, why not take advantage of the chance to carry a cargo that's expendable, like some decent food and spices from the galley?"

"Sounds good to me," agreed David. "I can have the Christmas Branch send up ten or twenty of our special meals."

Shirley's expression revealed a sudden recollection of her favorite shish-kebab feasts, and she readily agreed to utilize the first trip of our improvised vessel for a frivolous cargo.

After briefing Josephine on our plans, we called the flouwen and sent them plummeting downward, tugging the now completed diving saucer between them. The trip was made without apparent incident, and all the seals proved, to Shirley's relief, to have been opened and resealed with no leakage. The "payload," if I may apply such an official title to the motley collection of packages which lay before us, was in perfect condition, and Carmen and Nels happily divided the packages up between them and carried them up the hill.

Shirley was still examining the inside of the metal domes. An airtank and flashlight were neatly held down inside by straps glued to the metal, and there was just enough room for one person left. The closeness of the fit was a bit of an advantage, as it meant the passenger would be less likely to be bumped around; however, the thought of a dizzying tumble down in the darkness was distinctly unpleasant.

"We really ought to have a lot more test-trips," fretted Shirley. "I'm still not happy about those O-ring seals. But since we don't have a back-up bell anyway, we might as well proceed to a manned dive. I'll go first."

John was quick to disagree with this. "The main reason we're planning these descents is to get to that sick bay and do the operation reversals. It's essential that I be there, so I'll go down first. I'll need to set up the sick bay and get ready. First I'll check out my control of Josephine's surgical capabilities by having the Christmas Branch hook up the left side of me using a local. Then I'll pass the word up. Nels and Richard and David should come down next, one at a time. It's been quite a while since I attempted even minor surgery using the Christmas Branch, and I'd prefer to start with . . . the simpler operations. I can do all three of those today." He paused, and the immediacy and risk of this appalling project sank into my mind anew. "The women will each need to stay down for a full day, to be monitored during recovery for any complications. But I don't anticipate any trouble."

So saying, John stepped over to the little bell, and turned to look at us appraisingly. I think, even now, we might have sensibly reconsidered, but there was something just faintly superior in the smile he directed at the three men. I felt, rather than actually saw, the little ripple of jealousy that swept through them, and then Richard's voice spoke, a trifle harshly.

"Well, go ahead, make yourself comfortable and we'll seal you up!" Nels moved to help, and the diving bell was quickly released to the waiting flouwen.

They were soon back—they have already become adept at handling the diving saucer, and each trip became swifter. Through the sonar mapper we heard John's voice, assured but tinny, as he located and set up his small surgery.

When at length he pronounced himself ready, his first patient sped on his way, followed rapidly by the other two men. It was apparent immediately that John had not exaggerated his own skill, nor that of the Christmas Bush. With the assistance of the incredibly strong but minute "fingers" on the ends of its branches, only the tiniest incision is necessary, and the men each returned obviously relieved. Shirley wanted very much to make the next descent; she insisted it is because she wants to recheck the safety of the little vessel and the aerospace plane itself, and, politely, we didn't contradict her.

Our dinner that evening, then, was a strange occasion, with John and Shirley absent at the bottom of the lagoon. We all enjoyed a full meal of our most favorite dishes, and the aroma of Richard's corned beef and cabbage was as unique on the warm wind of this alien world as that of Cinnamon's garlicky pasta. My own spicy chili, rich with meat and peppers, tasted better than ever it had aboard *Prometheus*, but I was not particularly hungry for it. I offered to share it with the others, something we have never done with our "specials" before. Of course, always before these special meals were designedly selfish; purely personal treats, for those occasions when one felt the need for a little self-indulgence. Now, in these primitive surroundings, it seemed a final, formal celebration of a past from which we were forever separated. The thought of sharing the varied tastes was a surprise to the others, but they agreed quickly, and the little tidbits were ceremoniously passed around. I think everyone was a little curious about the other dishes, but mainly partook of this strange buffet because they know such an opportunity will not occur again. I myself enjoyed all the wildly different flavors, but took only the tiniest of tastes of each, as one after another tasted my chili and reached hastily for the water bucket! Arielle, indeed, reached out a slender hand to touch my throat, and murmured, questioning, "Asbestos?"

We lingered long, savoring the last of those flavors so reminiscent of a world millions of miles away. In the back of our thoughts, the welfare of John and

Shirley, deep in the dark waters of the lagoon, was a constant concern. Occasionally we heard a casual remark from the sonar scanner, but all seemed serene.

Finally, I got up briskly to begin the dreary but essential cleaning up. We take the task in strict rotation, and because I dislike it so, I have become swift and efficient, and it was quickly done. I returned to my place with a sigh, then, to listen as David's fingers moved over the holes in his tenor recorder, rescued by him from the lander, bringing forth old, old songs—simple songs, old even on earth, of home, and love, sorrow and joy. Nearby, Nels's pencil hovered over some of his precious paper, sketching with meticulous precision the structure of the Jolly. Cinnamon stood, and stretched, and moved to add wood to the fire, making the bright sparks leap upward from the blaze. Arielle and Jinjur chuckled softly over some small joke, sipping from steaming cups, and Richard moved his feet closer to the warmth, and lay back, yawning contentedly.

As I studied the little group, I heard, without really noticing, the differences in the sound. David was trying first the professional recorder he had salvaged from the lander, and then the primitive small flute he had made. The pure, dispassionate perfection of the notes from the more sophisticated instrument contrasted sharply with the breathy softness of the short range of which the simple one was capable. With a sudden surge of feeling, I realized I preferred the more human, imperfect tones! But I said nothing.

Shall I take my turn, when it comes? Shall I join the others in their plan to bring children into Eden? No one would blame me, if I choose to remain apart. But, if I choose to participate, possibly to regain the potential for having a baby, I must do so *soon*. I have only a few days! I have stayed awake most of this night, thinking and thinking, and I am so tired. But I have decided.

I cannot separate myself from these people. They are all I have, and they are important to me. Maybe I shall never become pregnant. Maybe, if I ever do, it will be very bad. Maybe we are taking foolish risks. But I shall join my people in their risk-taking, and I shall do it the minute Shirley returns.

# COURTING

Well, it was not particularly traumatic, after all. The trip down in the diving saucer was dark, cramped, and dizzying, but mercifully brief. And the surgery was almost as brief! There was no pain, although it felt peculiar in the extreme, after weeks of independence, to allow the intrusion of the Christmas Branch. John's remote manipulation of the various tiny tools was swift and as non-invasive as possible, and I made an effort to trust their expertise and relax.

John's manner to me was grave and polite, as always, and I maintained a cheerful composure I was far from feeling. John sensed this, I think, for he did ask, suddenly, "Aren't you being hypocritical, Reiki? You must be still reluctant about this whole project, so are you just pretending to be agreeable?"

"Certainly!" I answered, startled into honesty. But I did explain a little: "It helps, you know. More false cheer and less honest griping makes it easier all round."

It seemed very strange to be back in the *Dragonfly*, and to know it was so hopelessly submerged by the dark water. I tried not to look at the black windows, and as soon as Josephine had completed the battery of tests and examinations she required of me, I turned my attention to the accessible ship's lockers.

For most of my day of recuperation and observation I was busy, sorting and selecting objects suitable to take back with me. We are all doing this, and it calls for considerable thought; the items must fit within the diving bell, and be of genuine worth in our present non-technological situation. With regret, I passed over my discs of favorite books and music, in favor of coils of useful wire and sturdy containers. Of course, I had no way of playing those discs in Eden—I should have to manage without the precise directions for creating true Valenciennes, and without the rules of Victorian fan etiquette! These volumes of such exquisite refinements had made me chuckle, and I had never longed for a society in which women were placed so protectively on pedestals that they could not take a free step; but my current style of living seemed to give new meaning to the term "rude." Considering this, I firmly added yet another lacy collar to my choices. Then, more sensibly, I gathered an armful of fresh, unworn slippers and sandals. Fitting the practical bits and pieces compactly around me, I submitted again to the confinement of the bell, and was soon scrambling out onto the shore. Arielle was waiting, ready and relaxed.

"I want to play with little sub, later!" She smiled.

Five days later it was all over, and John returned to the surface. That night, as we rested, he addressed us women in his coolest clinical tones:

"You all probably know this, but I'm going to remind you anyway, since things are slightly different here on Eden. Living so closely together on *Prometheus* tended to synchronize your menstrual cycles, and they haven't drifted too far apart yet, so all of you were just past your normal ovulation time when Josephine and I did the operation. It is very unlikely you will get pregnant between now and your next period. You will then be fertile, if everything proceeds as we planned it, between fourteen and sixteen *Earth* days after your period is over. However, since the day is thirty hours long on Eden, that will be eleven to thirteen *Zuni* days, subject, of course, to individual variation. You know your own cycles better than I do, and living in the open air will tend to increase the variables, so your behavior will be governed by your own judgement."

During the silence that followed this pronouncement, I thought, rather sourly, that judgement had not recently been much help. I had sincerely hoped that with the conclusion of the restorations to full manhood and womanhood, we would resume our normal work and pastimes completely, but I was rather too sanguine. Not that there was anything overtly different immediately, or that my friends altered their behavior drastically, but subtle inflections, glances, and casual touches began to occur. They were so slight I fancied I was imagining them, at first, but I should have known I am never wrong about such things. The alteration showed itself in such minor ways!

Fortunately, there is no real indication anyone is in a hurry actually to become pregnant. Even Carmen is now reconsidering, more realistically, the possible difficulties inherent in childbirth. The talk of the responsibilities of raising children has also become more serious.

"Cuddling a tiny baby is so nice!" said Cinnamon dreamily. "But trying to soothe a screaming toddler—I never felt that was any fun at all."

Sometimes the expression of new feelings brought us all pleasure; Arielle, and Carmen too, have begun to dance for us more often. David had brought up, from his own trip to the Dragonfly, his tenor recorder and some excellent strings for a much better harp. As he played, the two women sometimes improvised their own dances, although never together. Arielle's lithe and graceful movements are nothing like the earthy rhythms of Carmen's flying feet, but both are exciting to watch. They create a tension in us, the audience, that is both pleasant and unsettling. I noticed the growing electricity first a week or so ago; the dancers had stopped, but David's lilting music continued, and suddenly I heard Richard's voice very soft beside me.

"Would you care for a stroll in the moonlight, ma'am?"

I was quite startled, but managed to smile as I refused.

At the same time, conversely, our fireside evenings are more relaxed. We have settled down to daily routines that are satisfying, as we work to explore and understand Eden's ecology, and physically very strenuous, as we carry out the labor of necessary daily chores. Without any necessity for arbitrary assignments, we seem to have developed a division of responsibilities that is both fulfilling and busy. For a time I feared that the change in our sexual capabilities might make for jealousies or dissension, but so far, at any rate, that has not occurred. A rather spicy hint of flirtation has quietly crept into some behavior, but it is only a hint. There is private speculation, I'm sure, because there are four men to six women; it's rather amusing to listen to the calm academic discussion of gene pools and hybridization concerning the gardens we have begun!

And the men, especially, are transparently posturing when there is anyone to watch. When I arrive at the edge of camp with a load of either firewood or fish, one or another is instantly at my side, gallantly taking the burden from my hands! David and Richard vie with each other in their fearless climbs, and John and Nels revel in hauling massive nets ashore, although frequently most of the catch must be released, because it is more than we can consume!

Cinnamon's shyness so far disappeared that she clings openly to Nels's arm, while Shirley's former forthrightness with male and female alike has changed into a coy helplessness that make me, personally, want to throw something at her. The men, responding to all the melting glances and soft touches, are now showing off like stags in the rutting season—I suppose we can only be thankful they have too much sense to do physical battle!

It is particularly irritating to watch David, whose long friendship with Arielle has obviously turned into something much more intimate, keep the girl very much under his wing, while still casting a roving eye at the rest of us! And Nels, with all his tenderness towards his adoring assistant, still is eager to lift Jinjur, or Carmen, when their short stature makes this desirable—and both lifter and liftee prolong the contact with evident pleasure! John and Richard are, frankly, strutting—and all the conversations that used to flow so factually and easily are now brimming with innuendo:

"The bark of this tree has a curious aroma, doesn't it, John? It smells like a really good soap—shall I try steeping a bit of it, and scrubbing, oh, say, someone's back with it?"

"Ummm," responded John. "Of course, it really might be . . . safer . . . to do that, than to try it on skin as soft as yours!"

Only Arielle reacts to all this nonsense with such genuine laughter that I, too, can smile—especially when that "soft soap" produced an itchy, though temporary, rash!

There is obviously some serious courting going on, as well. Our duties are not so stringent as to disallow private conversations. And certain advantages are taken, when the occasion arises; Arielle seldom finds herself alone among the high branches where the ripe fruit grows, and when I return to the surface after my deepest dives, I frequently find company awaiting me aboard the raft.

We have found another mutual pleasure, simple in the extreme but thrilling—it is singing! It began with some of the songs David was playing one night, when Shirley began, struggling to remember the words. Her voice is very sweet, and soon Cinnamon's lower voice began a harmonic addition. Nels' surprising tenor, and Richard's booming deep notes were added, and, to my own surprise, I heard myself in the high descant I had been born with, and which is so different from the husky tone when I speak. It was glorious, making such splendid sounds into the gloom around us. But it was very brief, because, apart from a few Welsh hymns and American folk songs, we could remember so little. David was delighted, however. One of the songs we had recalled was a Christmas carol, and after we'd finished, Jinjur said abruptly, "We ought to have a holiday."

"Why?" asked John.

"Why not? For fun!" said Arielle.

"We can make up whatever we'd like, of course," said Jinjur, "And celebrate any way we want."

"Birthdays!" said Carmen. "And Christmas and anniversaries, and . . ."

"And dress up and act polite!" said Richard, glancing at me with a laugh.

"Why not?" I retorted. "Refreshing, any change in a routine!"

"How about the anniversary of the day we crash-landed?"

"Rather grim, wouldn't that be?" responded Shirley to Jinjur's suggestion.

"I think that's the most important one of all," said Cinnamon quietly. "And I think I'd be thinking about it anyway."

"Traditions have a way of forming themselves, in time," I said comfortably. "We can start by remembering the dates, from my little journal. Any celebration can be left to inspiration!"

Richard's invitations for a nightly stroll steadily persisted, and I continued to decline them. I am not sure, in my own mind, whether I do so out of genuine disinterest, or a hitherto unfamiliar perversity—I cannot deny I rather enjoy the invitations! All about me the little games go on and on, but I try to maintain my long-standing resolution: to be responsible for my own behavior, and not worry about that of others.

However, when I last went foraging for firewood, I made an unsettling discovery. I had followed my favorite little stream for quite a distance, and plunged into a small clearing along its banks. What first caught my eye was one of our few blankets, neatly folded, and hanging over a low limb. As I stared around, I realized that the soft pile of leaves and branches in the center of the clearing was, literally, a sort of nest; a comfortable cushion for two people, private and secluded, and within the sound of the noisy ripples. I felt oddly shaken by the sight of this little retreat, and turned to leave, when I saw the imprint of a large bare foot in the soft earth. I bent over it to look more closely—there was no mistaking that distinctive shape, with only four strong toes!

I straightened, and returned to my task. Arielle had requested a supply of a particular sort of wood—it burns very hot and is perfect for grilling fish. It is also difficult to cut, being very tough, but I found it much easier on this occasion! It was unreasonable of me to be so angry, and I was only thankful that I was out of sight and hearing of anyone, so that my helpless stamping could go unnoticed. I was still upset when I returned with my burden, dropped it beside the cooking fire, and walked away at some speed, determined to stay away until I was calm.

I was soon on the shore of Rain Lake, and thought a swim might be therapeutic, but on impulse I stopped, and bent to see my reflection in its flat surface. I was dismayed to observe that the black curls I had been struggling to keep under some sort of control had got completely out of hand, writhing about my head until I bore a definite resemblance to portraits of Medusa. It had a barbarian aspect which distressed me very much, and I determined to enlist the assistance of the first person I met. Accordingly, I returned straightway to camp, found Shirley's scissors, and looked about. Richard was standing by the catch basin, dipping water into our biggest container. I quailed momentarily, but then my irritation returned and I marched briskly to him, and thrust the scissors into his hand.

"Here! Please! Just pull on a curl, and when it's a couple inches from my head, cut it off!"

"Cut off your head?"

"Uurrgh!"

"Okay, okay! Sit down and hold still."

Tensely, I huddled on the rock while Richard was silent, lifting one lock and then another. Finally, joyfully, I heard a snip, and then another, and when he began to whistle idly, I relaxed, while the black pile grew around me. Finally he stopped, and I turned to face him.

"Thank you very much! Does it look alright?" I asked anxiously, while he surveyed me coolly, grinned, and then grabbed my head and kissed the top of it. I was most inordinately pleased! However, I refused his invitation that evening with distinct coolness.

We began a series of daily visits to the Jolly Giants, taking turns in pairs, and carefully selecting our most urgent questions. Useful information began to accumulate rapidly in my journal as the reports came in.

"The slopes of the sides of the volcanoes look to be our best bet for a big garden," Nels enthused. "The soil is rich there, and the Jollys don't like to cultivate on such a slanting surface, so we won't be taking space they'd want."

"Won't the heavy rains wash all the seedlings away?" asked Carmen. It was raining again, but not torrentially as before.

"The Jollys say, if we plant now, the seedlings will be well established soon. This particular season brings only light rains, and by the time we get real storms, in about forty-five days, the new plants will have strong roots and be ready to assimilate all the moisture."

From my own questioning, I had learned that the fishing in Sulfur Lake was equal to that in the ocean, and easier. Jinjur and John had, on the Jolly's advice, begun a small husbandry of the jookeejooks for our own use.

In addition, Arielle and I had examined some of the cloths the big plants use for ceremonials; these are not woven, but are somehow formed from pounded sheets of bark, somewhat like the tapa cloth of Earth's Polynesia. It is very soft and almost white, and light and cool against the skin. Our own garments are becoming woefully threadbare; the fabric was never meant to be particularly durable, when the Christmas Bush was so capable of supplying more on demand. And, while the hot climate encourages us to shed excess clothing, none of us is willing to abandon it altogether! There are likely looking fibers in the bamboolike peethoo supports, but spinning and weaving them would be dauntingly time-consuming; we'd much prefer to use the bark-cloth. I held up one of the long sheets, studying it.

"Look, Reiki!" Arielle summoned me to see her instant creation. I had been thinking along the lines of a simple tunic, possibly with straps of vine—there are plenty of sharp thorns to fashion into needles, and the peethoo fibers make serviceable thread. But Arielle had draped and folded the supple fabric into a sarong, as easy to move in as air, and endlessly adaptable. I was delighted.

"Perfect, Arielle! And the dyed design along the border—I've never seen anything lovelier!"

The fashion was an instant success, and we are eager to learn how to make the cloth ourselves, and how to obtain the bright dye from the clamshells.

"Maybe we could trade something with the Jollys for a supply of the cloth, and for instructions in how to make it," suggested Jinjur. "But what?"

We considered the problem in silence, once more on Council Rock. Many of the hands are busy, now, in these nightly sessions, but all of the minds pounce as eagerly as ever on any new topic for discussion.

"Let's see, we made the bridge," mused Shirley. "But though we've used it every day, I doubt if a Jolly will ever enjoy it!"

"And they already have better knives and tools than we can make yet," said Carmen, looking ruefully at her own latest effort. John frowned over the meshes he was tying, sitting very close to Carmen.

Our crude handicrafts must go on, despite the frivolity of the vanilla-scented flower tucked behind Cinnamon's ear, or the oh-so-casually twisted strip of cloth around Nels' massive biceps! I patted my own neatened head with curious pleasure.

"That's the difficulty, isn't it," said John. "We've no idea of their needs, or even if they'll like anything we can do. What don't they have that we are used to having?" There was a brief silence, and then Jinjur and Cinnamon spoke at once.

"A wheel!"

"Of course!" said Shirley. "There's always a use for some sort of cart to haul things around in, isn't there!"

In the old days, computer screens would have been instantly covered with experimental models; now, however, there were only wrinkled brows and quick suggestions:

"Large spoked wheels, with wide rims, to move over this rough ground . . ."

"Pull instead of push for easier steering . . ."

"Just a deep bin with two wheels in the back and two drawbars in front . . ."

"A belt between the drawbars for their 'waist' so they can use all six legs for walking . . ."

As in so many of our projects, enthusiasm and intelligence made up for lack of tools, and the resultant cart was soon completed. It went sadly against Jinjur's training to have no way to paint it!

Although the Jolly's eyes had kept our construction effort under surveillance, we had not mentioned our purpose aloud, and when we trundled the bulky but maneuverable vehicle to the Jolly enclave, the plant's surprise and pleasure were apparent—the giants ripple visibly when having emotional feelings. Very shortly, the new device was in constant use in the Jolly camp, hauling food and other materials here and there.

While the goodwill engendered by our gift was still most noticeable, we broached two subjects; one was our desire for some of the precious cloth, and help in creating some of our own, and the other was the proposed introduction to the flouwen. Both topics seemed agreeable to our large new friends.

We had decided that there was no real need to explain the flouwen to the Jollys, nor the other way around, even if we were capable of doing so. The two aliens would have to work out their own relationship in any case, and would probably do so more quickly left to their own intelligence. Accordingly, Nels simply escorted three of the more curious Jollys down to the shore, at a place where the beach ran long and flat.

Meantime, Jinjur and I went quickly to Flouwen Beach and summoned them; they had been staying close to the area for several days, hoping for just such a meeting.

By the time the Jollys had approached the water as closely as they cared to, the flouwen had each formed an eye so they could look at things outside the ocean and were waiting with obvious delight, looking with their eyes at the approaching Jollys while at the same time trying to see the insides of the giant plants with their high-pitched ultrasonic pings.

"Wow! *Funny*-looking plant!" chortled Little Red. The Jolly's eyes fluttered low over the water, and Little Red splashed playfully as he bombarded them with questions. "How do your eyes tell what they've seen? Do the pictures come up, like on the screens we saw on *Prometheus*? Do you see when eyes fly back, or all the time? How do you tell the eyes where to go?"

Little Purple also spoke. "Greetings, strange creature! I must seem a strange creature to you, too, living in the water while you live always on land. I would like to know more about you, please!" Little Purple's sonorous words thrilled me; he is learning the arts of diplomacy! And, to my satisfaction, the Jolly elected to respond to him, ignoring the shouted comments of Little Red.

"Greetings to you, there in the water! In all my life my eyes have not observed creatures like you in these seas!"

Little White hurried to explain that they were newcomers indeed, modulating his tones and adopting the gentle courtesy of the other. While we listened, saying little, the amazing dialogue continued. The tall civilized plant then extended a root out over the water, to touch lightly the translucent color of the fluid civilized ocean-dweller. It was a sight to store with great care in our own minds, and I made sure to insert a number of still frames in the memory of my journal.

At length, the meeting ended in mutual agreement to meet again. We may find ourselves serving as intermediaries, or the two species may simply seek each other out, but I am well pleased with their initial confrontation. It had been a conference with some possibility for misunderstanding, and I am relieved that it is successfully concluded.

Richard's gentle invitations of an evening persisted, and I rejected them with increasing asperity—the memory of that pretty little private nest continues to rankle! Last night I could bear it no longer, and I declined, politely, and then burst out with a remark that I was "sure he could find more accustomed companionship, even perhaps in his very own—gazebo!" It was a stupid thing to say—I cannot understand myself these days!—and I was heartily discomfited when his eyes widened, and he retorted indignantly:

"*My* private . . . Do you mean the little nest I saw you leaving, up there where you walk so often for . . . firewood?"

The dark eyes were very serious, and I stammered some quick denial and ended the conversation abruptly.

The confusion, and the shifting alliances all around, are disturbing. The lovely hours of single-minded work, and peaceful evening discussions have been altered, perhaps permanently, by all this physical uncertainty. Within a week, of course, the situation may settle down temporarily, but I foresee the whole absurd cycle will have to be gone through again and again. Almost I wish they would all get pregnant soon, if that is what they wish, so that we could have peace! Struggling with these elemental drives is so much harder than coping with the mild demands this gentle world places upon us!

My little boat has been my own delight, and escape—I'm drifting on it at the moment, contemplating the shifting water beneath me with calming mind and heart. The boat was a tremendous joy from the very beginning! At my determined insistence, Shirley kept it both small and very flexible.

"But, Reiki, that's not big enough to hold more than . . . two"—she gave a sidelong glance at John—"and, just flat like that, you'll be right out in the open, sort of vulnerable . . . exposed . . ." I could have smacked her!

"It's just perfect, Shirley!" I said sweetly. "I only need it for a diving platform, mostly, and I know you're anxious to get to work on building that outrigger from the boobaa treetrunks!"

From her expression, I saw she had completely forgotten that earlier idea. For Shirley, the passionate engineer, to have become so dreamy as to abandon a new project was such a shock to me that I instantly forgave her—she really is helpless, just now. I left, quietly, tugging my new little raft into the shallows, while behind me John began talking in deep tones about cutting down the largest tree single-handed with an obsidian axe.

Since then I've spent happy hours tinkering with the small craft. The slender poles bound together with strong vines make it both light and limber, and it was not too difficult to shape the front and the back into an upcurving sheaf. The low box along one edge serves as both seat and storage. I succeeded in stepping a short mast, and affixed an even shorter boom, but the skimpy sail is not very satisfactory, and without a keel my control over my direction is sporadic at best. Still, it is endlessly fascinating to play with, and has served, at any rate, to give myself the appearance of industrious activity, while absenting myself a little from the group idiocy.

But I must begin, now, to try to sail home for the

night—it's growing late, and I fled early today. I've come a fair distance—my view of the volcano shows that—but the wind has shifted and will speed me homeward. Perhaps there'll be some change—my own menstrual period is already seriously delayed, no doubt due to the recent operation—but if one of the others' is beginning, there may be a resultant improvement in behavior. I dearly hope so!

I heard the laughter before I landed and moored the raft. It was so relaxed and delightful-sounding I hurried, hopefully, to the group about the fire.

"Here's Reiki! Home is the sailor, home from the sea—or lake, whatever. We've a discovery for you, Reiki, come have a drink!"

I stopped, startled. I'd been heading for the shelter to tidy myself for the evening, but this new statement called for investigation.

"A drink?" David was extending a cup to me, and I saw everyone was holding something—the liquid within was clear and pale, and I took a cautious sip. It was pretty bad—rather worse than the homemade parsnip wine I had once had from a villager in France—but it was most definitely wine.

"Where on earth—or Eden—did you get this?" I asked, incredulously.

"We made it! Ourselves!" David laughed. "Nels, and John, and I—and Jinjur helped. But you deserve some credit too, Reiki!"

"That's right!" Richard boomed. "You know those bitter little grapes we found, growing next to the sour fruits? Well, they both seemed pretty hopeless, so we decided to try the Reiki Technique!"

I heard the capital letters, but was too puzzled to interrupt.

"Yes, Reiki," said Jinjur, chortling. "We added some water to the little grapes, and went off and left 'em for a week. Then we took the sour things and boiled them until they were unrecognizable!"

I was a trifle miffed at that, but couldn't think of much of a reply. Fortunately, Cinnamon took pity on me and explained.

"The grapes fermented, Reiki, and these clever people just let the process go along naturally. The sour things cooked down into a sort of syrup, oddly enough—it's really too bland and cloying to be good on its own, but it's going to be very useful as sweetening—and it certainly helped the wine!"

I took another, more generous sip. The stuff tasted better, now, and its warmth was very pleasant going down.

"I like it, too," said Richard cheerfully, and I glanced at him with a twinge of alarm. He caught my glance—obviously the intensified awareness is still around—and spoke calmly. "The supply of grapes is so limited, we'll none of us be liable to have any problems with the wine—there just won't be much of it! But it's nice to have now, isn't it?"

I agreed, and went off to complete my dressing for dinner, if one may refer to such primitive procedures by so grand a title. When I returned to the circle I found the mellow mood to have increased. The others were waiting for me before beginning the meal, and I was oddly touched by that. We sipped the wine companionably, and the easy talk became relaxed and carefree.

"I don't want to embarrass anyone," said Jinjur quietly, "but unless somebody's managed to be a lot more discreet than I ever suspected, there's something screwy about our female cycles."

There was silence, and quick little questioning glances flashed around the circle.

"Now . . . no doubt there could be many reasons for that," continued Jinjur. "But in my case, the only one I can think of is that Josephine's surgery somehow interfered with the pattern I'm accustomed to."

I spoke up, trying to make my own words as clear and still impersonal as Jinjur's, to say that I, too, had not yet begun any menstrual flow. To my surprise, the others joined in! With the exception of Carmen, the other women were puzzled, but completely sure they had not conceived—they had been enjoying the processes of flirting and courting so much, they had deliberately postponed the inevitable conclusions, while of course having every intention of selecting a mate in the next month or so. The five of us stared at John in consternation.

"I don't understand that, at all," he said hastily. "I'd better ask Josephine some serious questions. David, can you set up the sonar scanner so I can talk to Josephine? We'll do it at next light."

The meal resumed, and we passed a normal night, but I was grateful for the relaxation of the wine—I might have otherwise found sleep difficult.

In the morning I joined David and the others at the sonar mapper. It was now safely ensconced in a rock crevasse situated well above high tide, with its long umbilical cord leading down the shore into the depths of Crater Lagoon and to Josephine in the *Dragonfly*.

"Josephine. Current activity status report, please." I addressed my old ally confidently.

"Current activity: Proceeding with emergency repairs. Number of repairs completed, thirty-two. Estimated number of repairs still to do, eighteen." Josephine's voice was warm and reassuring; I had designed her to be so in these circumstances, with all the emergency repair work still to be done.

"Request access to file of medical procedures, most recent, Josephine," David stated. There was a brief pause.

"Access granted, but John should be available for interpretation, if necessary."

"I'm right here, Josephine," said John. "What is the report on the sperm, ova, and tissue samples you kept for analysis?"

"Positive." Again, that brief and noncommittal answer!

"Josephine, we'd like a much more detailed summary of your findings, please," I directed. "John shall explain any terms we cannot understand, but we need to know the results of your examination and procedure. Are all of us returned to normal sexual functions? Are all of us in good health, and are the women capable of child-bearing? When can we expect ovulation?" I knew that my voice was harsher than I had used in some time to Josephine. In her programmed care for us she sometimes kept what she considered to be unnecessary or unpleasant details to herself. However, the words came readily enough at my command:

"All health checks are normal. All functions are normal. Ovulation for women will resume at conclusion of current pregnancy."

"WHAT?" Our voices screamed the word.

"Repeat that report, Josephine," David sternly commanded. "And clarify statement regarding 'current' pregnancy!"

To my horror, I heard the mechanical voice continue, repeating the report, and then came these dreadful words:

"While conducting requested operations designed to return the crew to complete human sexual function preliminary to breeding, I analyzed all combinations available from the limited gene pool. Best selections for each female were matched with best available male. Ova were selected and fertilized using the available sperm saved from the prior sperm-count analysis samples gathered from the males, then implanted along with hormones to initiate pregnancy cycle."

I stared helplessly at the sonar mapper, at David, at John . . . John!

"What did you do to me?" I shrieked at him. His face was white, and his eyes blank with astonishment.

"Josephine!" he shouted. "Why did you initiate pregnancy? That was not part of your instructions from me!"

Almost, I could hear the unemotional intelligence shrug: "The obvious objective to the directed procedure was to reproduce. So the best and most efficient reproduction objective was calculated and implemented. Consideration was given to possible implantation of two each foeti in each female using sperm from different males, but decision was made to simplify pregnancy and birth by limiting infants to one each female. All findings indicate pregnancies will be normal in duration, and deliveries will be uncomplicated. Expected date of births will be two hundred fifteen Zuni days from now."

In terror, I stared at Jinjur, and Shirley, and Cinnamon, and Arielle—eyes wide and faces pale—*all* of us were pregnant? By computer?

I got to my feet, somehow, and fled. By the time I reached the shore and fumbled loose the mooring rope, my tears were pouring, and blindly I released the small craft and flung myself upon it in despair.

While it drifted aimlessly, I wept, the tears going through the deck unnoticed into the sea. I felt I had been betrayed, even raped, by an intelligent monster at least partly my own creation! With hideous efficiency, the expert skill of the unfeeling computer had succeeded in an accomplishment which might well have been beyond our human ability. To have successfully impregnated all five of us was a task I should have doubted could be done, even had such an awful eventuality entered my mind. My feelings were chaotic, hysterical, wildly frantic as I realized the enormity of what had happened to me! I stormed aloud, then raged in silence, back and forth in desperate fury. I've no idea how long I howled my woe, but inevitably, eventually, I subsided in exhaustion and lay limp and miserable.

I had not drifted far, I saw through swollen eyes. The light had nearly faded, and the sea around me was flat and calm. I sat up, trying to catch my breath, and to return to some sort of normal state of mind. However, I couldn't think at all, and simply stared at the little waves behind me. I felt betrayed, frightened, and, now that my anger was worn out, desperately lonely. Then I heard the sound of rhythmic splashing; it came steadily nearer, but I didn't move as Richard's face, dripping, confronted my own. His eyes were worried, and gently he put both big hands around my head.

"Reiki? Let me help." The sound of human compassion brought fresh tears, but the weeping was less painful now. I lay, held tightly against another living heart; and when this shower passed I felt able to return to the darkening shore.

I discovered that my friends had undergone, in varying intensities, all the same passions I had experienced, and were trying to assimilate all the implications of Josephine's thoughtless interference. However, they had gone beyond me in their decision-making, and were beginning to accept what had happened as fact.

"Josephine absorbed a lot of outraged yelling, after you left," Jinjur told me. "Apparently she's programmed to react, because she wouldn't speak a word for hours. Her persona was replaced by a mechanical voice."

"Yes, that was part of the program," I admitted. "If there's a real overload of anger from us, it means she needs to recalculate her entire position before she interacts again, so she was going through that."

"I wish that electronic moron had a head so I could knock some sense into her," muttered Shirley. I gripped her hand tightly, unable to speak. It felt good to realize I really was not alone in this predicament! As we went through a semblance of our normal routines, we talked, slowly beginning to comprehend what lay ahead of us.

We plied John with questions; we are all so ignorant, and feel so helpless!

"What will it be like?"

"How will I know when the baby is ready to be born?"

"Should I be doing anything different?"

John looked like he was trying very hard to be soothing, and knew he was not succeeding very well: "You just go on, living as usual, and when the babies come . . ." Here he looked definitely frightened. " . . . they come." Far from reassuring!

"There is one good thing, though," continued John. "You won't have to worry about infections in either you or your baby—unlike on Earth, where going to the hospital exposes you to drug-resistant germs. I took a sample of soil down with me and had Josephine analyze it. As I suspected, although there are the Zuni equivalent of bacteria and viruses in the soil, the bacteria have no defenses against our white blood cells, and the viruses are unable to use our cells internal machinery to replicate themselves—they use a different genetic code."

"I think I should tell you," said Carmen, later, "that I'm quite sure I'm pregnant too. I'm not so sure of my own due date, but I also think I should tell you that *I'm* pleased about it."

That produced a heavy silence, and I reluctantly faced reality, squarely. The men had said nothing at all, but now David cleared his throat, and spoke huskily.

"When Josephine is ready to talk with us again, she may reveal who is the father of each—baby," he said tentatively.

I looked around at the serious faces, and sighed.

"Well, I suppose that will matter to me, sometime. But all I can bring myself to do now is accept the fact that a baby is begun, and I'll do my best to do the thing right."

There was a soft murmur of agreement. Any alternative is more unthinkable than these present unthinkable circumstances! Each of us was busy with our own thoughts after that, although David found comfort, as always, in music. The soft melody of the little flute seemed unbearably sweet tonight, and if I had had any tears left I would have wept. But the gentle sound went on, and my sore heart eased as I listened to the beautiful song.

I was startled, yet again, at Richard's low voice in my ear. "Would you care for a stroll, ma'am?"

I stood to look at the man. Oddly enough, it was then, as I realized that there was no need for me either to avoid Richard or to seek him out, no pressure to conform or to rebel, that all my barriers came down. With no hesitation, I smiled up at the dark face above me, and said, "Thank you very much, I should enjoy that."

I think the polite response startled him, after the weeks of cool rebuffs, but he reached for my arm with a gentle force that made me melt against him as we walked away into the quiet darkness. It was not far along the trail before the whole of me was engulfed in that embrace, which made it extremely difficult to walk, but which I confess I enjoyed greatly.

# BIRTHING

As I begin this entry, I can feel my unborn child moving within me. It's pleasant to rest here, recalling that stormy time, secure in the private and comfortable little nest that I sometimes share with Richard now. Shortly I must make my way down to Council Rock—our evening meals are much eased as we continue to share the work, particularly now that we are all so cumbersome! As Shirley said, "Now that I get tired quickly, and can't use tools on my lap because I haven't *got* any lap, I can see just how easy it was, to work with James and the Christmas Bush."

Jinjur agreed. "I used to get a tad annoyed when one of my sergeants went off on maternity leave—throwing away your career, I felt! But I'm going to be just as capable, and so are you, Shirley, when this is over. I'm glad, now, in a way, that we're all vulnerable at once—sort of points out, doesn't it, that it can happen to anybody!"

Having reconciled ourselves, finally, to the prospect of becoming parents, we have been very busy with plans and preparations. It won't be long, now, before the births are due, and we intend to be ready. John's expression, as he watches six heavily pregnant women, clad in billowing sarongs, strolling past him on the beach, is so funny it gives us all a rather wicked pleasure, although of course it's followed by private worries. We are all thankful, yet again, for the careful screening we had undergone at the start of this mission; our collective health is extremely good, and our genetic histories are sound. For years we were monitored by James, and even now we were living a healthy balance of exercise and diet. This, of course, did not excuse in any way Josephine's imprudent actions, and each of us pointed that out to her in various vigorous ways. Jinjur's "Boy, you really screwed us up, you dumb piece of junk!" was perhaps the mildest.

Interestingly, we have slowed down the pace of our existence; not to the Jolly's level, of course, but significantly more leisurely than when we first began our settlement. I admit the easier life is very pleasant! The brisk walk has become a relaxed amble; swimming in the warm water is a restful interlude, with the water relieving us of the weight we carry; and I can see that, becoming absorbed in what is taking place within our bodies, we are less concerned about the intensity with which we are studying this planet. The prospect of giving birth we contemplate with what may be too much optimism, and a rather easy confidence.

Our concerns about the nutritional adequacy of the foods here were also eased. After watching us closely for many weeks, John came to the conclusion that the food here is nearly adequate, although lacking in fat, and, according to Josephine, low in Vitamin B-12. Accordingly, he directed us to adopt the rather more slow-moving pace that this tropical atmosphere seems to induce, and Josephine instructed *Prometheus*, when it returned, to load the crawler with smaller, more specific vitamins. This left room aboard the crawler for the obstetrical forceps John wanted to have on hand just in case (they had to be specially fabricated by the Christmas Bush on *Prometheus*, since they certainly hadn't been included in the original supply of medical tools), a few child-sized medical instruments, and some personal items. Among these was a supply of very thin, tough paper for John, several pairs of scissors made of a non-rusting alloy, and a gift from Deirdre: my eyes blurred as I recognized her warm thoughtfulness—it was a laminated photograph of the crew left aboard. I'm not the only one to spend delighted minutes poring over those beloved countenances!

Our easier life has lead to some genuine play—rather fun to watch, and even to participate in. Nels used a bit of burnt stick to draw, upon some large flat stones, various targets, and the men instantly began to try to hit them with every sort of missile and projectile afforded by our surroundings. Little pebbles, hard shards of obsidian, even leftover nutshells were hurled from varying distances with varying techniques, and much boasting and betting accompanied their trials. Practice at these games of skill continue yet, but in a calmer way, as it was determined inevitably, that the real champion, with whatever ammunition, is Jinjur! Her aim is uncanny, and Shirley is a very close second. The men must vie, rather halfheartedly, for third place. To give them credit, their force is tremendous, and several targets have been completely shattered!

I discovered, to my joy, that the finer strands of fiber from the peethoo tree are equal in strength and fineness to the linen threads in my favorite laces, so I can not only keep them in good repair, I can create new ones. They are not as purely white as some of the originals, nor is my skill nearly as fine, but I enjoy making some narrow edgings for the borders of my sarong, saving the lovely pieces I brought with me for the special occasions when I can wear them as Richard likes, with no other garments at all!

The sarongs, and the pareus worn by the men, increase our resemblance to a tribe in the South

Pacific. Our outdoor life has altered our appearances, as it has increased our physical strength, and we are having, somewhat to our surprise, a great deal of fun.

Recently, I set out early to gather firewood, and explored far up the little stream. To my delight, I found a spot where it fell some thirty feet into a pool, surrounded by large rocks. It became a favorite retreat, a place to stand, bemused, while the water poured unceasingly over one's head! The only drawback, possibly, was the distance from Council Rock; Shirley had finally to give up on the idea of constructing such a shower closer to home, after examining the terrain minutely.

Her latest creation was a small but extremely sturdy floating dock. It rises and falls smoothly with the various tides, and provides the visiting Jollys with a trustworthy platform from which to communicate with the flouwen. The flouwen have been tremendously inquisitive every since we've known them, but I was a little surprised to see how eagerly the Jollys come to question them! Their conversations range over all that is on this world and all the flouwen can share of other worlds. Some of the most entertaining conversations that we hear, deal with their evaluations of us!

"The sky-people still move with particularly unnecessary rapidity," said Seetoo. "Their excessive speed frequently results in significant errors and miscalculations. It is obvious that slowing their pace would be considerably more efficient and make much more efficacious use of effort. Have you seen the one they call 'Daaveed' make those laborious ascents to the top of the boobaa tree for fruit, only to have it rejected by the one they call Seeneemaan?"

"Dumb! Too much working anyway!" was Little Red's verdict. "Always asking questions, trying out, lifting, piling up, digging, moving things around with hands . . . but slow and clumsy in water!"

"Most extraordinary!" agreed the Jolly.

As comfortable as the two beings sound together, the fact of their own peculiarities doesn't seem to occur to them as they, so to speak, shake their heads over our own oddities.

Cinnamon's gardening desires have led her to plant flowering bushes and specimens all around the Big House, and at every vantage point along the paths we take. Jinjur's long-frustrated desire to be a farmer has resulted in cages of every sort of small animal. Her detachment from these specimens is far from truly agricultural, however; she is forever taking them out to play with or train, so that we are surrounded now by a private zoo of pets. But we are so few, and this world is so large, that we have tacitly accepted it as our own Eden, to enjoy and play with in great freedom.

My journal serves to remind us of anniversaries of various sorts, as they occur, and sometimes we decide to celebrate in some fashion. With our limited resources, this usually amounts to no more than a few words of congratulation, or the occasional small gift. For my birthday, Richard surprised me with a pretty little thimble, carved out a bit of nut-husk, and smoothed with fine sand until it was as silky to touch as finely polished ebony. I was most pleased and touched, although he admitted readily that the idea was Carmen's!

So our days and nights continue in harmony, with our surroundings and with each other. We are fortunate to have what we need so easily available, and what we might only desire so completely unattainable. Those two facts, coupled with the generous size of our domain, serve to keep us content, and willing to live at peace with ourselves and our alien friends.

Our first crop of grain was successfully harvested just yesterday. It was deliberately small, as storage is more difficult than cultivation, and successive crops are already in the ground. Our friend Seetoo the Jolly was interested in our success; his eyes hovered above the harvest, and we learned, later, from the Giant himself, that what had most intrigued him was the planting of the grain in straight lines! Such a procedure was so automatic with Nels and Cinnamon, that they gave it no thought, and the Jolly is taken with the aesthetics of the line. He was more excited than I had ever seen him, and I anticipate an entire new art form for the Jolly, as the delights of geometry are revealed—both by us and by the flouwen, who are also enjoying their meetings of minds.

Our domestic interests have by no means obviated our curiosity about the mysteries of our new home. Nels and John, after a great deal of careful observation of the jookeejooks, and thoughtful questioning of the Jolly, have hypothesized that the one evolved from the other. At some point in their development, the Jollys severed the connections between trunk and eyes and hands, much as a human umbilical cord is severed, while still maintaining the functions of the freed appendages. How this transition managed to occur is still a puzzle.

The jookeejooks, themselves, are proving as useful to us as they are to the Jollys. Jinjur's little farmyard provides us with both fruit and the "steaks" Arielle was contemplating, although they are rather more similar to a vegetarian version of a steak than actual meat. The protein they supply us seems adequate, and even tasty. Years of living on the products of Nels's laboratory have made us none too critical of flavor, and Nels is, I think, glad to be free of that task and out in the open fields.

I still work at the fishing, though less vigorously than I did; no doubt my strength for the job will return after the child's birth. At present, I am grateful for Richard's assistance, with even so small a boat as mine—and even more grateful for his construction of a small rudder. I could almost become philosophical about my direction coming under control!

It became apparent immediately that, although we could not alter Josephine's preemptory accomplishment, we could indeed determine the identity of the father in each case; Josephine concurred that such information was vital to assuring a knowledgeable use of the tiny gene pool among us. It was quietly satisfactory to me to learn that Richard is the father of the child I carry; as it was for Arielle to know that David was the one selected for her, and Cinnamon's male was Nels. The pairing of these three couples was already a matter of affection as well, although we have no assurance of their permanence: Jinjur declared, without being asked, that she would not perform a marriage for anyone at any time, so any commitments that exist are private, which is probably as it should be!

John is anticipating being the father of two children: Carmen's baby, which he expected, and Jinjur's, which he did not! I think Jinjur is secretly delighted at the prospect of becoming a mother. And Shirley, whose unchosen mate was Nels, is thinking pleasurably of rearing a young Viking; I notice some speculative glances at the other men, as well!

Shirley's considerable energies turned toward nest-building with enthusiasm. I heard her just a short time ago, exhorting and supervising:

"John! You and Nels, place the bottom of that pole right here, and walk it upright! Are you ready up there, David? Grab the top and straighten it! Straight! To your left just a bit! That's good, now, take a bight around the roof-ridge . . . Richard! The floor's beginning to slope again towards the back! It's got to have a tiny slope the other way, or the rain . . ."

She is enlarging the Big House, so that the front of

it is an open, roofed, porch sort of arrangement, well above the slope of Council Rock. The work is going nicely under her determined leadership. She looks magnificent, these days, swelling with pregnancy as a Norse goddess would swell. The Big House will soon be spacious and airy, and complete until she decides it needs more work!

The Big House even has a front patio—flat flagstones where we can clean the mud and sand off our feet before stepping inside—and a small "lawn" of "moss," usually found only on rocks on the rain-drenched volcanic slopes, but now living comfortably on flagstones where Cinnamon makes sure it gets watered every day it doesn't rain. Set in the sand in front of the lawn is a neat sign, saying: "Keep Off The Grass!"

Our private retreats are much more humble, although Arielle's resembles that of a bowerbird, as the adoring David fetches ever-changing decorations of flowers, shells, and bits of driftwood for her to arrange. My own nest is soft, and dry, and small—I am as fond of comfort as a cat, and this is cozy and private, and ample for our needs; I have no desire for a structure which requires maintenance chores, and neither does Richard.

The flouwen have been visiting us only occasionally, when it is necessary for them to replenish their internal store of ammonia. Last time, Little Red (no longer so little!—life here evidently agrees with the creatures, and he is bigger and louder than ever) began shouting to us while still far out in the water.

"Hi! Hi! Hi! We've been fighting! I won!"

Jinjur and I straightened from our task, and looked out in concern. The rapidly approaching flouwen looked as usual. At a more reasonable distance, Little Purple's calm tones announced, "Little Red is bragging. We found a large shark eating the filter-fish. It had six eyes that swam ahead of it, and six gatherers that herded the filter-fish into its mouth. It was quite large, with many sharp teeth in its mouth, and could have eaten enough of us in one bite to turn us into a youngling. But we attacked its eyes and gatherers with focused sonar bursts and drove it away."

"Big fight! Big shark!" bragged Little Red, loudly.

"Big, yes, and *very* carnivorous!" agreed Little White, then added thoughtfully, "The shark was quite similar in design to a Jolly. Both have six freely moving eyes that return to the main body periodically to report their observations, and both use six freely-moving gatherers as hands to gather in food. Perhaps they have a common ancestor despite the fact that one is designed to operate on land and the other in water."

"Humans and dolphins are similar in the same way," I remarked. "Despite one having legs and the other having fins, they are both mammals and have high intelligence. Since the Jollys are intelligent, perhaps these sharks are too."

"This shark did not have intelligence," replied Little White.

"Shark dumb!" interjected Little Red.

Ignoring Little Red's outburst, Little White continued on, "As we approached the shark, I listened carefully to the sounds it was making. The main body, the eyes, and the gatherers were emitting only simple clicks and chirps, sufficient only to see each other and their prey with sonar sight. There was no evidence of any complex sound variations such as would be needed to use sound for talking. Since they don't talk, they must not be intelligent."

"You are probably correct in your observations," I replied. "Although dolphins and whales use clicks and chirps for seeing underwater, they also are able to make other sounds that are for communication. We still don't understand the language, but we do know they are talking to each other."

I noticed with pleasure Little White's careful use of language, as he describes to us what he has observed. This scientific attitude means that his evidence is genuinely useful, and he and Nels spend much time together these days, more or less comparing notes. However, this particular visit was unusually brief.

"Come on! Come on! I'm feeling too bulky, let's . . ." The final word was new to me—a strange conglomeration of hissing consonants.

"What's that?" I asked. "What does that word mean?"

But they were gone.

How long it has been since my last entry! And why, when I have always been so meticulous in chronicling everyday mundane matters, have I not taken the time to describe the tumultuous events of the past few weeks? Perhaps because, although they are vivid to those who live through them, the events are only part of the age-old human cycle, and the arrivals of six new people into the world we share is only important to ourselves. But I have just taken a quiet look around, and want to record what I see.

Nearest by, Richard is holding our small son, with that over-careful, masculine awkwardness that has melted tougher hearts than mine. Just out of sight, I can hear Jinjur admonishing her son. . . . "Every meal a banquet! Every task an honor! Every . . ." The wee lad is already in the Corps!

In the glow of the firelight, Cinnamon is sitting in the curve of a vine suspended from the rooftree, keeping up a slow swinging with one brown foot, and singing. To my surprise, I hear the notes are minor, and it dawns on me she is singing an Inuit song to the baby she is nursing. Across from me, David sits crosslegged on the porch, the harp in his lap making an accompaniment to Cinnamon's song. At a little distance, Shirley is curled around her baby in the comfortable hammock she built, peacefully asleep. John, too, lies in a hammock, awake, and with the strange expression of pride and dismay that has so often been on his face since the births of his children! Arielle is arranging something by the fire, her baby held so much more gracefully than Richard's, and prattling to the infant in French, of a sort. Nels is watching Cinnamon, more awe on his face than was there with the completion of his new legs. And Carmen looks radiant, content to stare dreamily into the fire as she cradles her child. Perhaps she is the most happy? No, I think it must be I; I am utterly content, to be marooned on Eden.

Our lives are now flowing in simple routines; domestic affairs take some attention, but we are resolved to keep unnecessary tasks from multiplying; the small ones's needs are basic and simple, so we tend to those. We're also resolved to enjoy every minute, and are fortunate that we still have all the curiosity and intelligence for which we were chosen. Therefore, every day is different, while every day's the same—the ease of living, our mutual amicability, the constantly unfolding tapestry of the world around us—all make for happiness, and it will be our delight as well as our responsibility to share it with, and maintain it for, our children.

Today we took the babies to show to the Jollys. They listened, with grave interest, to Jinjur's graphic description of their births.

"Tell me, please, Commander Major General Jinjur . . ." (I think the Jollys treasure titles for their own sakes.) "Did not the experience cause you physical pain?"

"Wow! Did it ever!" agreed Jinjur, and became more graphic yet.

"I think," declared the Jolly, "that, on the whole, I prefer the more civilized methods we employ among ourselves. Seeds can be nurtured with so much more—cultivation, can they not?"

It rendered Jinjur speechless, temporarily.

Upon our return to Council Rock, we found the flouwen waiting for us. We went down to display our offspring, proudly. Richard stepped into the calm warm water, and gently laid our child upon Little Red's surface. The baby squalled at the change, and Little Red, after a quick sonar exploration of the small body, passed him to Little White.

"Make sure you keep his mouth and nose out of the water," warned Richard.

"Is that the noisy part? I can hear that from the outer edge of the lagoon!" said Little Red.

"It certainly is built like a miniature human," said Little White, exploring the interior of the baby with sonic vibrations. The vibrations soothed the baby, and he began to coo. "Except the head is too big for the body, and some of the smaller sticks inside are still soft."

"Wherrre small noisy thing?"

I gaped in astonishment. A small pink blob had suddenly appeared between the bigger flouwen! Little Purple sounded proud, as he performed the introduction:

"Reiki, Richard, this is our youngling!"

"Rrrrreiki, Rrrrichard?"

Startled, I giggled, but instantly quashed it. I had not heard "r"s so rolled since I left Scotland!

Little White explained, "It will learn better speech, but it does say that particular sound in a repetitive way. We call this youngling Warm Chirring Pink!"

"We all have younglings now," said Little Purple

calmly, as it carefully placed the tiny pink human child on top of the large pink flouwen youngster so it could scan the baby.

"Our young bigger than your young!" bragged Little Red.

"Be quiet, Little Red!" chided Little White. "That is not polite!"

Little Red ignored the reproof.

"Our young can talk!" Little Red said proudly. "Human young can't talk. Human young DUMB!"

Little Red glided the baby off the pink youngster and back to Richard's waiting hands, then started moving off toward the mouth of the lagoon.

"Come on!! I feel a storm coming up . . . let's go SURF!!!"

"Watch out for the sharks!" I called after him. Then I felt a strange foreboding as I gathered my baby from Richard's strong arms. This world is like Eden, but the inhabitants of the original Eden had come across animals that had introduced death to their hitherto deathless world. We have only explored part of one small island on this Edenlike world and we know only a few of the animals that must inhabit it. The recent discovery of the existence of the sharks is but one example of our ignorance. What other creatures and what dangers will we and our children encounter as the years go by? I shudder and hold my baby close as I face the unknown future.

*(To Be Continued)*

Technical Report BSE-TR-71-0868
July 2071

---

# BARNARD STAR EXPEDITION
# PHASE IV REPORT

## VOLUME I-EXECUTIVE SUMMARY

Submitted by:

George G. Gudunov, Colonel, GUSAF
Acting Commander, Barnard Star Expedition

## INTRODUCTION

This Volume I is the Executive Summary of the information collected to date by the Barnard Star Expedition, especially the more recent information gathered during Phase IV of the expedition, which primarily consisted of the landing of an exploration crew on the Gargantuan moon Zuni. Although the mission could not be considered a complete success because the landing rocket crashed and sank on arrival at the surface, the exploration crew did manage to survive and return a significant amount of information on the life-forms found there. This Executive Summary is a brief condensation of the highly technical material to be found in the companion volume, Volume II—Technical Publications. Volume II, as well as similar publications that followed Phases I through III, contains a series of technical papers and reports on various aspects of the mission, each of which runs to hundreds of pages, including tables. These papers are intended for publication either in archival videojournals or as scientific or technical monovids, and contain many specialized terms that would be understood only by experts in those particular fields.

For the benefit of the reader of this volume, who is assumed to be interested only in a brief summary in non-technical language without extensive numerical detail, the more precise specialized words and phrases used in the technical reports and papers have been replaced in this summary with common words, and most of the numerical data have either been eliminated or rounded off to two or three places. In addition, to assist those readers of this Executive Summary who may not have read the previous summary reports, pertinent background material from those reports has been included here.

The three major topics discussed in this Executive Summary are covered in three sections:

Section 1—Equipment Performance. A report on the configuration and performance of the technical equipment used to carry out the Barnard Star Expedition.

Section 2—Barnard System Astronomical Data. A summary of the pertinent astronomical data concerning the Barnard star planetary system, with emphasis on the moons around the giant planet Gargantua, and specific emphasis on the moon Zuni, the site of the fourth landing.

Section 3—Biology. A summary report of the biology of the alien life-forms discovered on Zuni.

## SECTION 1
## EQUIPMENT PERFORMANCE

Prepared by:
Caroline Tanaka—Acting Chief Engineer
Anthony Roma, Captain, GUSSF—Chief Lightsail Pilot
Thomas St. Thomas, Captain, GUSAF—Chief Lander Pilot
George G. Gudunov, Colonel GUSAF—Acting Chief Aircraft Pilot

### Equipment Configuration at Launch

The expedition sent to the Barnard star system consisted of a crew of twenty persons and their consumables, a habitat for their long journey, and four lander vehicles for visiting the various planets and moons of the Barnard system. This payload, weighing 3000 tons, was carried by a large reflective lightsail 300 kilometers in diameter. The lightsail was of very lightweight construction consisting of a thin film of finely perforated metal stretched over a sparse frame of wires held in tension by the slow rotation of the lightsail about its axis. Although the lightsail averaged only one-tenth of a gram per square meter of area, the total mass of the payload lightsail was over 7000 tons, for a total mass of payload and lightsail of 10,000 tons. Light pressure from photons reflected off the lightsail provided propulsion for the lightsail and its payload. The lightsail used retroreflected coherent laser photons from the solar system to decelerate the payload at the Barnard system, while, for propulsion within the Barnard system, it used incoherent photons from the star Barnard.

At the time of launch from the solar system, the 300 kilometer payload lightsail was surrounded by a larger retroreflective ring lightsail, 1000 kilometers in diameter, with a hole in the center where the payload lightsail was attached. The ring lightsail had a mass of 72,000 tons, giving a total launch weight of lightsails and payload of over 82,000 tons.

## Interstellar Laser Propulsion System

The laser power needed to push the 82,000 ton interstellar vehicle at an acceleration of one percent of earth gravity was just over 1300 terawatts. This was obtained from an array of 1000 laser generators orbiting around Mercury. Each laser generator used a thirty kilometer diameter lightweight reflector that collected 6.5 terawatts of sunlight. The reflector was designed to pass most of the solar spectrum and only reflect into its solar-pumped laser the 1.5 terawatts of sunlight that was at the right wavelength for the laser to use. The lasers were quite efficient, so each of the 1000 lasers generated 1.3 terawatts, to produce the total of 1300 terawatts needed to send the expedition on its way.

The transmitter lens for the laser propulsion system consisted of rings of thin plastic film stretched over a spiderweb-like circular wire mesh held in tension by slow rotation about the mesh axis. The lens was designed with circular zones of decreasing width that were alternately empty and covered with plastic film whose thickness was chosen to produce a phase delay of one half a wavelength in the laser light. This huge Fresnel zone plate, 100 kilometers in diameter, collimated the laser beam coming from Mercury and sent it off to Barnard with essentially negligible divergence. The relative configuration of the lasers, lens, and lightsails during the launch and deceleration phases can be seen in Figure 1.

The accelerating lasers were left on for eighteen years while the spacecraft continued to gain speed. The lasers were turned off, back in the solar system, in 2044. The last of the light from the lasers traveled for two more years before it finally reached the interstellar spacecraft. Thrust at the spacecraft stopped in 2046, just short of twenty years after launch. The spacecraft was now at two lightyears distance from the Sun and four lightyears from Barnard, and was traveling at twenty percent of the speed of light. The mission now entered the coast phase. For the next 20 years the spacecraft and its drugged crew coasted through interstellar space, covering a lightyear every five years, while back in the solar system, the transmitter lens was increased in diameter from 100 to 300 kilometers. Then, in 2060, the laser array was turned on again at a tripled frequency. The combined beams from the lasers filled the 300 kilometer diameter Fresnel lens and beamed out toward the distant star.

After two years, the lasers were turned off, and used elsewhere. The two-light-year-long pulse of high energy laser light traveled across the six lightyears to the Barnard system, where it caught up with the

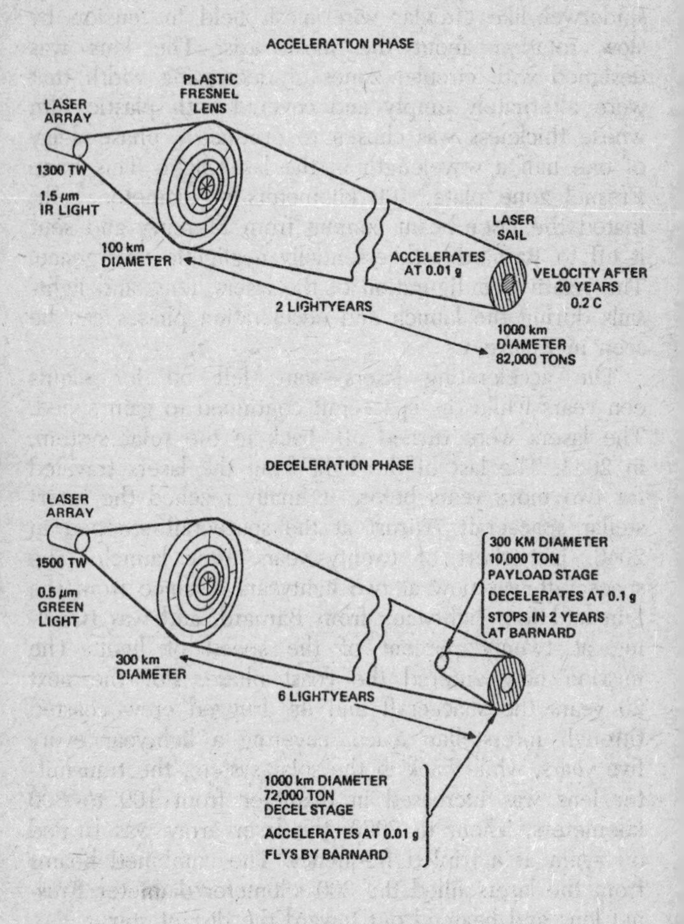


*Figure 1*—Interstellar laser propulsion system.
[*J. Spacecraft*, Vol. 21, No. 2, pp. 187-195 (1984)]

spacecraft as it was 0.2 lightyears away from its destination. Before the pulse of laser light reached the interstellar vehicle, the revived crew on the interstellar vehicle had separated the lightsail into two pieces. The inner 300 kilometer lightsail carrying the crew and payload was detached and turned around to face the ring-shaped lightsail. The ring lightsail had computer-controlled actuators to give it the proper optical curvature. When the laser beam arrived, most of the laser beam struck the larger 1000 kilometer ring sail, bounced off the mirrored surface, and was focused back onto the smaller 300 kilometer payload lightsail as shown in the lower portion of Figure 1. The laser light accelerated the massive 72,000 ton ring lightsail at one percent of Earth gravity and during the two year period the ring lightsail increased its velocity slightly. The same laser power focused back on the much lighter payload lightsail, however, decelerated the smaller lightsail at nearly ten percent of Earth gravity. In the two years that the laser beam was on, the payload lightsail and its cargo of humans and exploration vehicles slowed from its interstellar velocity of twenty percent of the speed of light to come to rest in the Barnard system. Meanwhile, the ring lightsail continued on into deep space, its function completed.

### Prometheus

The interstellar lightsail vehicle that took the exploration crew to the Barnard system was named *Prometheus*, the bringer of light. Its configuration is shown in Figure 2, and consists of a large lightsail supporting a payload containing the crew, their habitat, and their exploration vehicles. Running all the way through the center of *Prometheus* is a four-meter-diameter, sixty-meter-long shaft with an elevator platform that runs up and down the shaft to supply transportation between decks. A major fraction of the payload volume was taken up by four exploration vehicle units. Each unit consisted of a planetary lander vehicle called the Surface Lander and Ascent Module (SLAM), holding within itself a winged Surface Excursion Module (SEM).

The largest component of *Prometheus* is the lightsail, 1000 kilometers in diameter at launch, and 300 kilometers in diameter during the deceleration and exploration phases of the mission. The frame of the lightsail consists of a hexagonal mesh trusswork made of wires held in tension by a slow rotation of the lightsail around its axis. Attached to the mesh wires are large ultrathin triangular sheets of perforated reflective aluminum film. The perforations in the film are made smaller than a wavelength of light, so they reduce the weight of the film without significantly affecting the reflective properties.

Capping the top of *Prometheus* on the side toward the direction of travel is a huge double-decked compartmented area that holds the various consumables for use during the 50-year mission, the workshops for the spaceship's computer motile, and an airlock for access to the lightsail. At the very center of the starside deck is the starside science dome, a three-meter-diameter glass hemisphere that was used by the star-science instruments to investigate the Barnard star system as *Prometheus* was moving toward it.

At the base of *Prometheus* are five crew decks. Each deck is a flat cylinder twenty meters in diameter and three meters thick. The control deck at the bottom contains an airlock and the engineering, communication, science, and command consoles to operate the lightcraft and the science instruments. In the center of the control deck is the earthside science dome, a three-meter-diameter hemisphere in the floor, surrounded by a thick circular waist-high wall containing racks of scientific instruments that look out

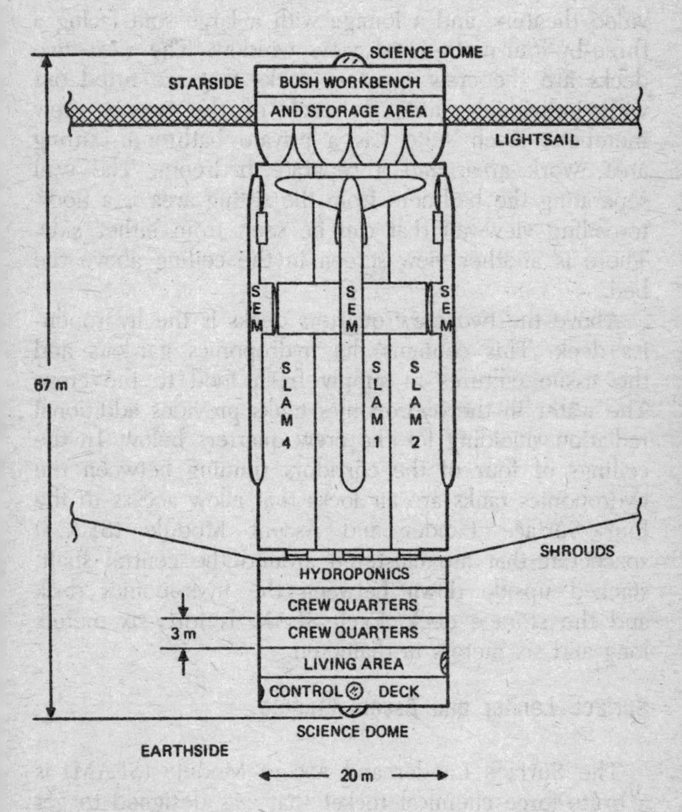


*Figure* 2—Prometheus

through the dome or directly into the vacuum through holes in the deck. Above the control deck is the living area deck containing the communal dining area, kitchen, exercise room, medical facilities, two small video theaters, and a lounge with a large sofa facing a three-by-four-meter oval view window. The next two decks are the crew quarters decks that are fitted out with individual suites for each of the twenty crew members. Each suite has a private bathroom, sitting area, work area, and a separate bedroom. The wall separating the bedroom from the sitting area is a floor-to-ceiling viewwall that can be seen from either side. There is another view screen in the ceiling above the bed.

Above the two crew quarters decks is the hydroponics deck. This contains the hydroponics gardens and the tissue cultures to supply fresh food to the crew. The water in the hydroponics tanks provides additional radiation shielding for the crew quarters below. In the ceilings of four of the corridors running between the hydroponics tanks are air locks that allow access to the four Surface Lander and Ascent Module (SLAM) spacecraft that are clustered around the central shaft, stacked upside down between the hydroponics deck and the storage deck. Each SLAM is forty-six meters long and six meters in diameter.

## Surface Lander and Ascent Module

The Surface Lander and Ascent Module (SLAM) is a brute-force chemical rocket that was designed to get the planetary exploration crew and the Surface Excursion Module (SEM) down to the surface of the various worlds in the Barnard system. The upper portion of the SLAM, the Ascent Propulsion Stage (APS), is designed to take the crew off the world and return them back to *Prometheus* at the end of the surface exploration mission. As is shown in Figure 3, the basic shape of the SLAM is a tall cylinder with four descent engines and two main tanks.

The Surface Lander and Ascent Module has a great deal of similarity to the Lunar Excursion Module (LEM) used in the Apollo lunar landings, except that instead of being optimized for a specific airless body, the Surface Lander and Ascent Module had to be general purpose enough to land on planetoids that could be larger than the Moon, as well as have significant atmospheres. The three legs of the Surface Lander and Ascent Module are the minimum for stability, while the weight penalties for any more were felt to be prohibitive.

The Surface Lander and Ascent Module (SLAM) carries within itself the Surface Excursion Module (SEM), an aerospace plane that is almost as large as the lander. Embedded in the side of the SLAM is a long, slim crease that just fits the outer contours of the SEM. The seals on the upper portions were designed to have low gas leakage so that the SLAM crew could transfer to the SEM with minor loss of air.

The upper portion of the SLAM consists of the crew living quarters plus the Ascent Propulsion Stage. The upper deck is a three-meter-high cylinder eight meters in diameter. On its top is a forest of electromagnetic antennas for everything from laser communication directly to Earth to omni-antennas that broadcast the position of the ship to the orbiting relay satellites.

The upper deck contains the main docking port at the center. Its exit is upward, into the hydroponics deck of *Prometheus*. Around the upper lock are the control consoles for the landing and docking maneuvers, and the electronics for the surface science that can be carried out at the SLAM landing site.

The middle deck contains the galley, lounge, and

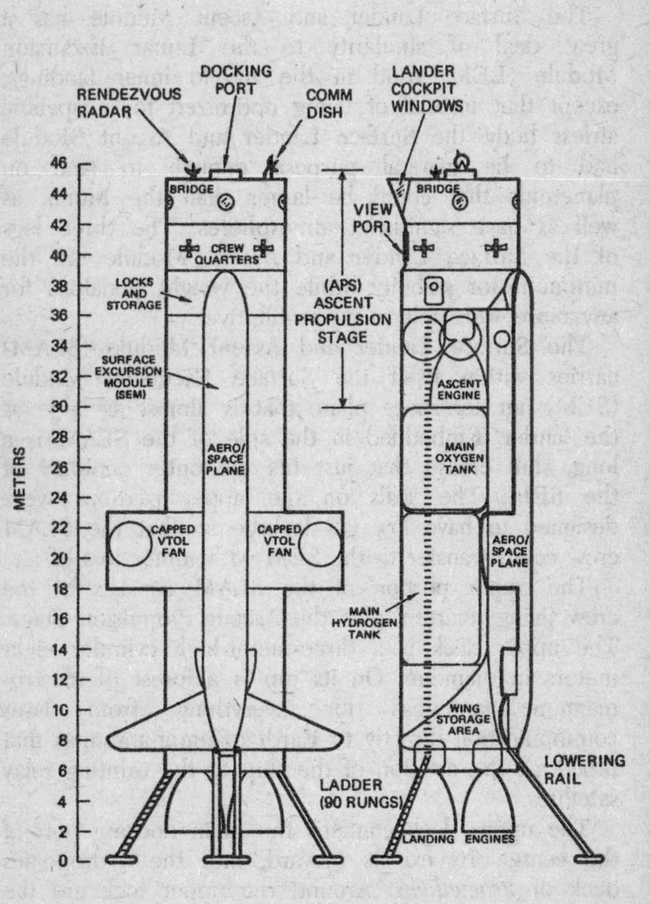


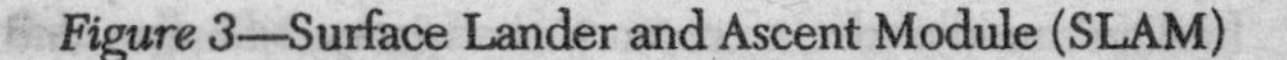

*Figure 3*—Surface Lander and Ascent Module (SLAM)

the personal quarters for the crew with individual zero-gee sleeping racks, a shower that works as well in zero-gee as in gravity, and two zero-gee toilets. After the SEM crew has left the main lander, the partitions between the sleeping cubicles are rearranged to provide room for a sick bay and a more horizontal sleeping position for the four crew members assigned to the SLAM.

The galley and lounge are the relaxation facilities for the crew. The lounge has a video center facing inward where the crew can watch either videochips or six-year-old programs from the Earth, and a long sofa facing a large viewport window that looks out on the alien scenery from a height of about forty meters. The lower deck of the SLAM contains the engineering facilities. Most of the space is given to suit or equipment storage, and a complex air lock. One of the air-lock exits leads to the upper end of the Jacob's ladder. The other leads to the boarding port for the Surface Excursion Module.

Since the primary purpose of the SLAM is to put the Surface Excursion Module on the surface of the double-planet, some characteristics of the lander are not optimized for crew convenience. The best instance is the "Jacob's Ladder," a long, widely spaced set of rungs that start on one landing leg of the SLAM and work their way up the side of the cylindrical structure to the lower exit lock door. The "Jacob's Ladder" was never meant to be used, since the crew expected to be able to use a powered hoist to reach the top of the ship. In the emergency that arose during the first expedition to Rocheworld, however, the Jacob's Ladder proved to be an adequate, although slow, route up into the ship.

One leg of the SLAM is part of the "Jacob's Ladder," while another leg acts as the lowering rail for the Surface Excursion Module. The wings of the Surface

Excursion Module are chopped off in mid-span just after the VTOL fans. The remainder of each wing is stacked as interleaved sections on either side of the tail section of the Surface Excursion Module. Once the Surface Excursion Module has its wings attached, it is a completely independent vehicle with its own propulsion and life support system.

## Surface Excursion Module

The Surface Excursion Module (SEM) is a specially designed aerospace vehicle capable of flying as a plane in a planetary atmosphere or as a rocket for short hops through empty space. The crew has given the name *Dragonfly* to the SEM because of its long wings, eyelike scanner ports at the front, and its ability to hover. An exterior view of the SEM is shown in Figure 4.

For flying long distances in any type of planetary atmosphere, including those which do not have oxygen in them, propulsion for the SEM comes from the heating of the atmosphere with a nuclear reactor powering a jet-bypass turbine. For short hops outside the atmosphere, the engine draws upon a tank of monopropellant, which not only provides reaction mass for the nuclear reactor to work on, but also makes its own contribution to the rocket plenum pressure and temperature.

Unfortunately, the SEM IV aerospace plane was damaged and sank under 200 meters (600 feet) of water during the rocket engine burnthrough and subsequent crash of the SLAM IV lander during an attempted landing on Zuni. Fortunately, the entire crew of ten humans and three flouwen buds managed to survive the crash and are still on Zuni, but without the flying ability of the SEM, the exploration range of the humans is limited to a single small island on the large moon.

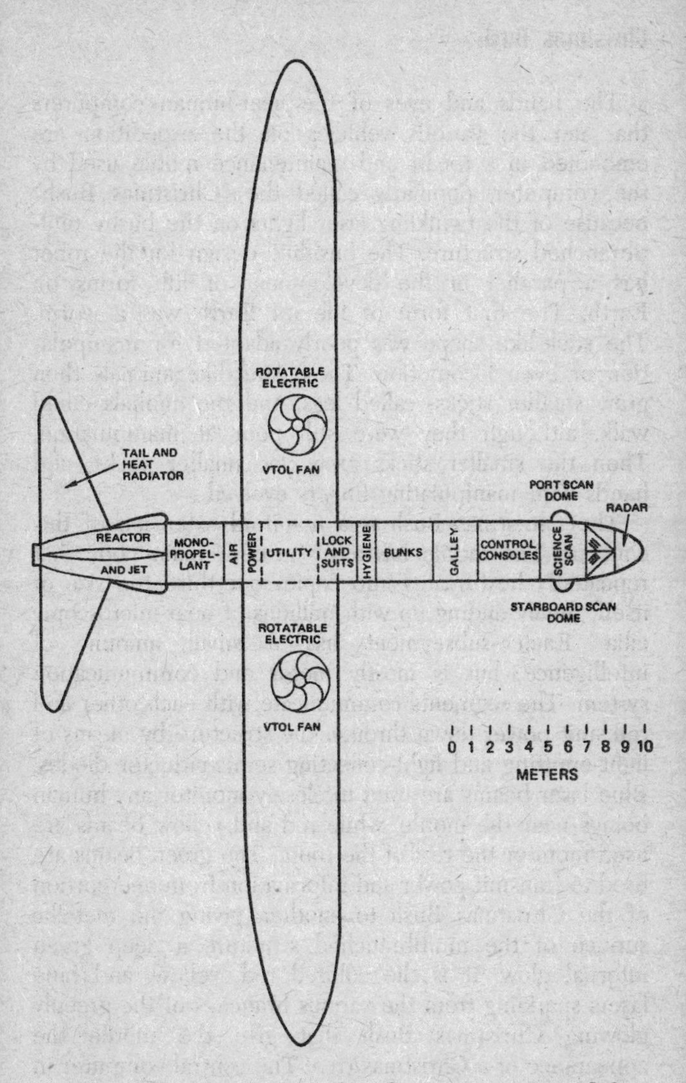


*Figure 4*—Exterior view of Surface Excursion Module (SEM)

## Christmas Bush

The hands and eyes of the near-human computers that ran the various vehicles on the expedition are embodied in a repair and maintenance motile used by the computer, popularly called the "Christmas Bush" because of the twinkling laser lights on the bushy multibranched structure. The bushlike design for the robot has a parallel in the development of life forms on Earth. The first form of life on Earth was a worm. The stick-like shape was poorly adapted for manipulation or even locomotion. These stick-like animals then grew smaller sticks, called legs, and the animals could walk, although they were still poor at manipulation. Then the smaller sticks grew yet smaller sticks, and hands with manipulating fingers evolved.

The Christmas Bush is a manifold extension of this concept. The motile has a six-"armed" main body that repeatedly hexfurcates into copies one-third the size of itself, finally ending up with millions of near-microscopic cilia. Each subsegment has a small amount of intelligence, but is mostly motor and communication system. The segments communicate with each other and transmit power down through the structure by means of light-emitting and light-collecting semiconductor diodes. Blue laser beams are used to closely monitor any human beings near the motile, while red and yellow beams are used monitor the rest of the room. The green beams are used to transmit power and information from one portion of the Christmas Bush to another, giving the metallic surface of the multibranched structure a deep green internal glow. It is the colored red, yellow, and blue lasers sparkling from the various branches of the greenly glowing Christmas Bush that give the motile the appearance of a Christmas tree. The central computer in the spacecraft is the primary controller of the motile, communicating with the various portions of the

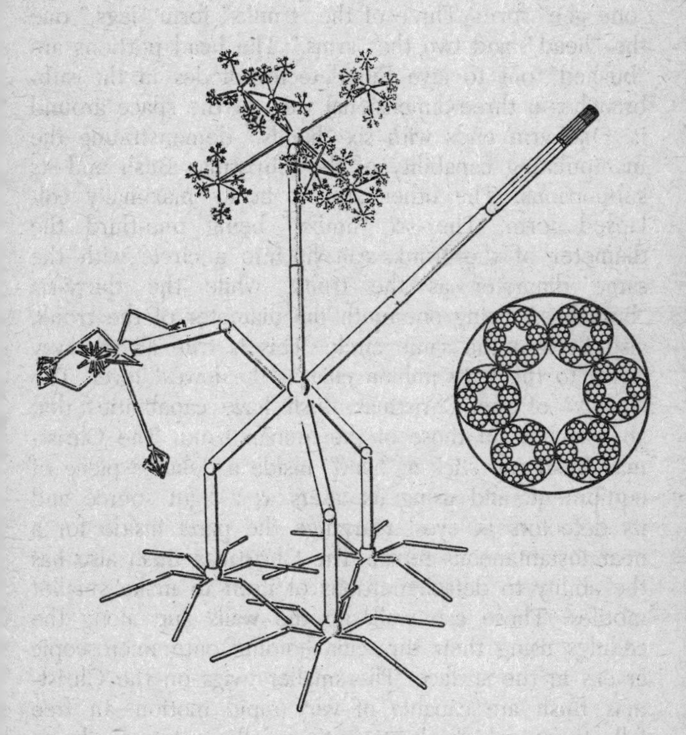

*Figure 5*—The Christmas Bush

Christmas Bush through color-coded laser beams. It takes a great deal of computational power to operate the many limbs of the Christmas Bush, but built-in "reflexes" at the various levels of segmentation lessen the load on the main computer.

The Christmas Bush shown in Figure 5 is in its "one gee" form. Three of the "trunks" form "legs," one the "head," and two the "arms." The head portions are "bushed" out to give the detector diodes in the sub-branches a three-dimensional view of the space around it. One arm ends with six "hands," demonstrating the manipulating capability of the Christmas Bush and its subportions. The other arm is in its maximally collapsed form. The six "limbs," being one-third the diameter of the trunk, can fit into a circle with the same diameter as the trunk, while the thirty-six "branches," being one-ninth the diameter of the trunk, also fit into the same circle. This is true all the way down to the sixty million cilia at the lowest level. The "hands" of the Christmas Bush have capabilities that go way beyond those of the human hand. The Christmas Bush can stick a "hand" inside a delicate piece of equipment, and using its lasers as a light source and its detectors as eyes, rearrange the parts inside for a near instantaneous repair. The Christmas Bush also has the ability to detach portions of itself to make smaller motiles. These can walk up the walls and along the ceilings using their tiny cilia holding onto microscopic cracks in the surface. The smaller twigs on the Christmas Bush are capable of very rapid motion. In free fall, these rapidly beating twigs allow the motile to propel itself through the air. The speed of motion of the smaller cilia is rapid enough that the motiles can generate sound and thus can talk directly with the humans.

Each member of the crew has a small subtree or "imp" that stays constantly with him or her. The imp usually rides on the shoulder of the human where it can "whisper" in the human's ear. Some of the women use the brightly colored laser-illuminated imp as a decorative ornament. In addition to the imp's primary purpose of providing a continuous personal communication link between the crew member and the central computer, it also acts as a health monitor and personal servant for the human. The imps go with the humans inside their spacesuit, and more than one human life was saved by an imp detecting and repairing a suit failure or patching a leak. The imps can also exit the spacesuit, if desired, by worming their way out through the air supply valves.

## SECTION 2
## BARNARD SYSTEM ASTRONOMICAL DATA

Prepared by:
Linda Regan—Astrophysics
Thomas St. Thomas, Captain, GUSAF—
Astrodynamics

### Barnard Planetary System

As shown in Figure 6, the Barnard planetary system consists of the red dwarf star Barnard, the huge gas giant planet Gargantua and its large retinue of moons, and an unusual co-rotating double planet Rocheworld. Gargantua is in a standard near-circular planetary orbit around Barnard, while Rocheworld is in a highly elliptical orbit that takes it in very close to Barnard once every orbit, and very close to Gargantua once every three orbits. During its close passage, Rocheworld comes within six gigameters of Gargantua, just outside the orbit of Zeus, the outermost moon of Gargantua. It has been suggested that one lobe of Rocheworld was once an outer large moon of Gargantua, while the

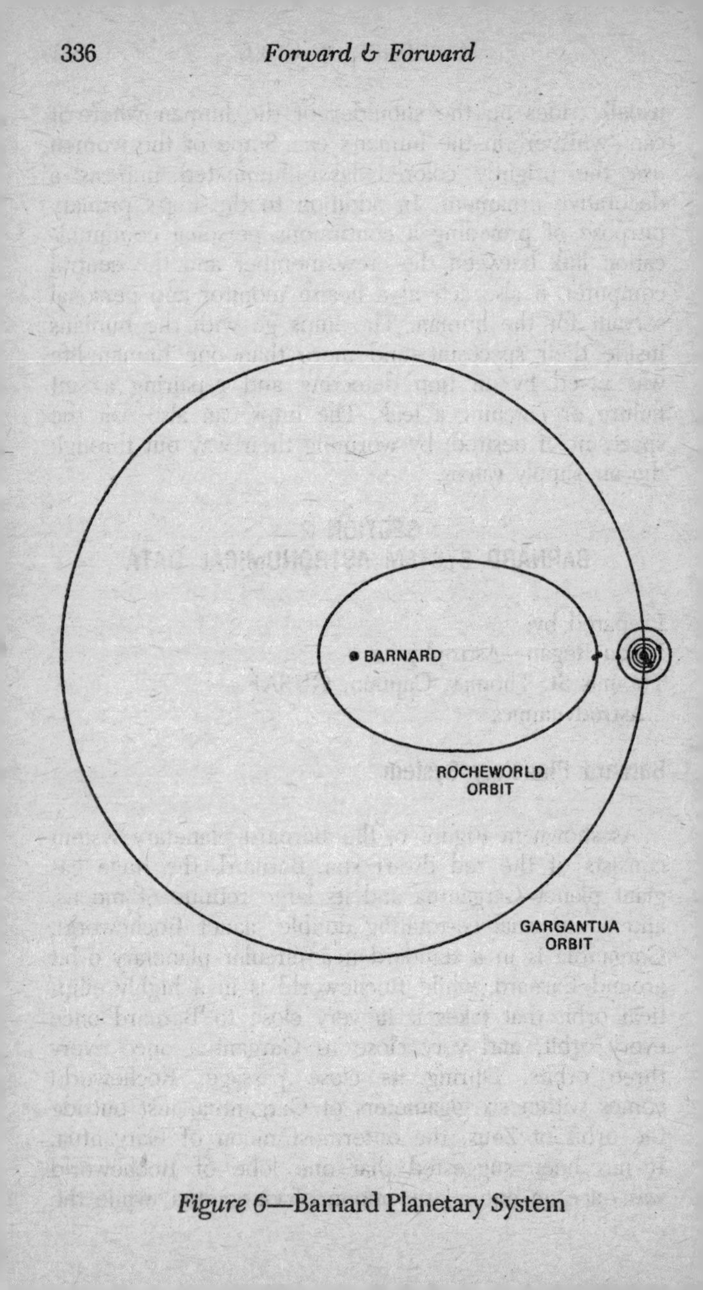


*Figure 6*—Barnard Planetary System

other lobe was stray planetoid that interacted with the outer Gargantuan moon to form Rocheworld in its present orbit. Further information about Barnard, Rocheworld, and Gargantua and its moons follows:

## Barnard

Barnard is a red dwarf star that is the second closest star to the solar system after the three-star Alpha Centauri system. Barnard was known only by the star catalog number of +4$^{0}$ 3561 until 1916, when the American astronomer Edward E. Barnard measured its proper motion and found it was moving at the high rate of 10.3 seconds of arc per year, or more than half the diameter of the Moon in a century. Parallax measurements soon revealed that the star was the second closest star system. Barnard's Star (or Barnard as it is called now) can be found in the southern skies of Earth, but it is so dim it requires a telescope to see it. The data concerning Barnard follows:

**BARNARD DATA**

Distance from Earth = $5.6 \times 10^{16}$ m (5.9 lightyears)
Type = M5 Dwarf
Mass = $3.0 \times 10^{29}$ kg (15% solar mass)
Radius = $8.4 \times 10^{7}$ m = 84 Mm (12% solar radius)
Density = 121 g/cc (86 times solar density)
Effective Temperature = 3330 K (58% solar temperature)
Luminosity = 0.05% solar (visual)
= 0.37% solar (thermal)

The illumination from Barnard is not only weak because of the small size of the star, but reddish because of the low temperature. The illumination from the star is not much different in intensity and color than that from a fireplace of glowing coals at midnight. Fortunately, the human eye adjusts to accommodate for both the intensity and color of the local illumination source, and unless there is artificial white-light illumination to provide contrast, most colors (except for dark blue—which looks black) look quite normal under the weak, red light from the star.

Note the high density of the star compared to our Sun. This is typical of a red dwarf star. Because of this high density, the star Barnard is actually slightly smaller in diameter than the gas giant planet Gargantua, even though the star is forty times more massive than the planet.

## Rocheworld

The unique co-rotating dumbbell-shaped double planet Rocheworld consists of two planetoids that whirl about each other with a rotation period of six hours. As shown in Figure 7, the two planetoids or "lobes" of Rocheworld are so close together that they are almost touching, but their spin speed is high enough that they maintain a separation of about 80 kilometers. If each were not distorted by the other's gravity, the two planets would have been spheres about the size of our Moon. Because their gravitational tides act upon one another, the two bodies have been stretched out until they are elongated egg-shapes, roughly 3500 kilometers in the long dimension and 3000 kilometers in cross section.

Although the two planetoids do not touch each other, they do share a common atmosphere. The resulting figure-eight configuration is called a Roche-lobe pattern after E.A. Roche, a French mathematician of the later 1880s, who calculated the effects of gravity tides on stars, planets, and moons. The word "roche" also means "rock" in French, so the dry rocky lobe of the pair of planetoids has been given the name Roche, while the lobe nearly completely covered with water was named Eau, after the French word for "water." The pertinent astronomical information concerning Rocheworld follows:

## ROCHEWORLD DATA

Type: Co-rotating double planet
Diameters: Eau Lobe: 2900x3410 km
Roche Lobe: 3000x3560 km
Separation: Centers of Mass: 4000 km
Inner Surfaces: 80 km (nominal)
Co-rotation Period = 6 h
Orbital Semimajor Axis = 18 Gm
Orbital Period = 962.4 h
= 160 rotations (exactly)
≈ 40.1 Earth days
Axial Tilt = $0^{o}$

One of the unexpected findings of the mission was the resonance between the Rocheworld "day," the Rocheworld "year," and the Gargantuan "year." The period of the Rocheworld day is just a little over 6 hours, or 1/4th of an Earth day, while the period of the Rocheworld "year" is a little over 40 Earth days, and the orbital period of Gargantua is a little over 120 days. Accurate measurements of the periods have shown that there are exactly 160 rotations of Rocheworld about its common center to one rotation of Rocheworld in its elliptical orbit around Barnard, while there are exactly 480 rotations of Rocheworld, or three orbits of Rocheworld around Barnard, to one orbit of Gargantua around Barnard.

Orbits such as that of Rocheworld are usually not stable. The three-to-one resonance condition between the Rocheworld orbit and the Gargantuan orbit usually

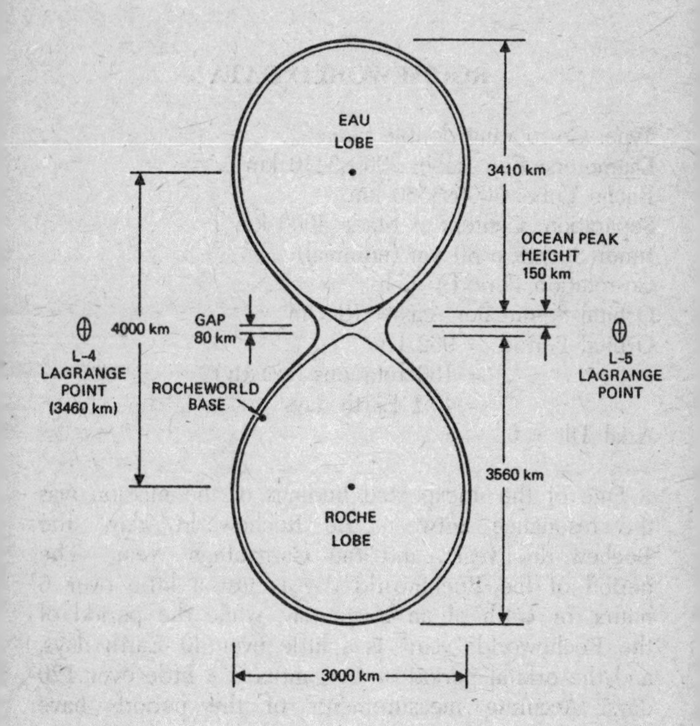


*Figure 7*—Rocheworld

results in an oscillation in the orbit of the smaller body that builds up in amplitude until the smaller body is thrown into a different orbit or a collision occurs. Due to Rocheworld's close approach to Barnard, however, the tides from Barnard cause a significant amount of dissipation, which stabilizes the orbit. This also supplies a great deal of heating, which keeps Rocheworld warmer than it would normally be if the heating were due to radiation from the star alone. Early in the expedition, both Rocheworld and Gargantua were "tagged" with artificial satellites carrying accurate clocks, and the planets have been tracked nearly continuously since then. The data record collected extends for almost four years. The 480:160:1 resonance between the periods of Gargantua's orbit, Rocheworld's orbit, and Rocheworld's rotation, is now known to be exact to 15 places.

Rocheworld was explored extensively in landings made during Phase I and Phase II of the mission, and more detailed information about the double-planet, and its interesting astrodynamics, can be found in the Phase I and Phase II reports.

## Gargantua

Gargantua is a huge gas giant like Jupiter, but four times more massive. Since the parent star, Barnard, has a mass of only fifteen percent of that of our Sun, this means that the planet Gargantua is one-fortieth the mass of its star. If Gargantua had been slightly more massive, it would have turned into a star itself, and the Barnard system would have been a binary star system. Gargantua seems to have swept up into itself most of the original stellar nebula that was not used in making the star, for there are no other large planets in the system. The pertinent astronomical information about Gargantua follows:

## GARGANTUA DATA

Mass = $7.6x10^{27}$ kg (4 times Jupiter mass)
Radius = $9.8x10^{7}$ m = 98 Mm
Density = 1.92 g/cc
Orbital Radius = $3.8x10^{10}$ m = 38 Gm
Orbital Period = 120.4 Earth days (3 times Roche-world period)
Rotation Period = 162 h
Axial Tilt = $8^{0}$

The radius of Gargantua's orbit is less than that of Mercury. This closeness to Barnard helps compensates for the low luminosity of the star, leading to moderate temperatures on Gargantua and its moons.

*Gargantuan Moon System*

There are nine major moons in the Gargantuan moon system. Their orbital and physical properties are listed in the following table. The five smaller moons are rocky, airless bodies, while the four larger moons have atmospheres and show distinctive colorings. All the moons are tidally locked to their primary.

| Name | Sol Equivalent | Orbital Radius (Mm) | Orbital Period (h) | Mass ($10^{20}$ kg) | Radius (km) | Surface Gravity (gee) |
|---|---|---|---|---|---|---|
| Zeus | Asteroid | 4850 | 828.0 | — | 12 | — |
| Zapotec | Mars | 1650 | 164.3 | 4500 | 3000 | 34% |
| Zen | Oberon | 1440 | 134.0 | 10 | 400 | 4% |
| Zion | Iapetus | 1210 | 103.2 | 22 | 550 | 5% |
| Zouave | Titan | 730 | 48.3 | 3100 | 2900 | 25% |
| Zuni | Earth | 530 | 29.9 | 1500 | 1900 | 28% |
| Zulu | Ganymede | 330 | 14.7 | 2100 | 600 | 21% |
| Zoroaster | Asteroid | 250 | 9.7 | — | 30 | — |
| Zwingli | Asteroid | 250 | 9.7 | — | 32 | — |

Figure 8 presents a comparison of the orbits of the four large moons in the Gargantuan system with the orbits of the four large moons in the Jovian system. The Gargantuan system is seen to be quite similar to the Jovian system, although a little more compact.

| Jupiter | Io | Europa | Ganymede | Callisto | |
|---|---|---|---|---|---|
| 71 | 420 | 670 | 1070 | 1880 | Mm |
| ( ) | o | o | o | o | |
| ( ) | o | o | o | o | |
| 98 | 330 | 530 | 730 | 1650 | Mm |
| Gargantua | Zulu | Zuni | Zouave | Zapotec | |

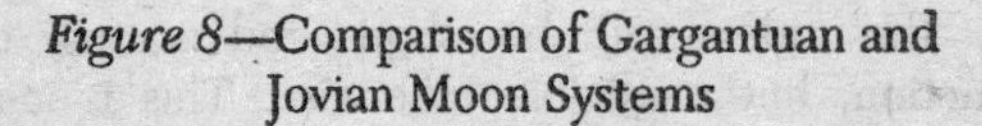

*Figure 8*—Comparison of Gargantuan and Jovian Moon Systems

*Conjunctions*

The three inner large moons, Zouave, Zuni, and Zulu, can exert significant tidal effects on each other. This happens during a conjunction, when the distance between the two moons is a minimum. After a conjunction has once occurred, it will reoccur when after a certain time period, the inner moon (which always revolves faster than the outer moon) has rotated exactly one revolution more than the outer moon. The joint conjunction periods for the three innermost large moons of Gargantua are:

| | |
|---|---|
| Zulu/Zouave | 21.1 h |
| Zulu/Zuni | 28.9 h |
| Zuni/Zouave | 78.4 h |

Triple conjunctions, when all three moons are nearly in alignment, are much rarer. The triple conjunction period is about 549 hours (about 23 Earth days). This triple conjunction occurs every 26 conjunctions of Zulu with Zuni, 19 conjunctions of Zulu with Zouave, and 7 conjunctions of Zuni with Zouave.

Quadruple conjunctions, when all three moons and Barnard are nearly in alignment, are even rarer, occurring every third triple conjunction. The quadruple conjunction period is about 1646.8 hours. This is about 68 Earth days, 55.5 Zuni days, 111.5 Zulu days and 33.5 Zouave days.

*Intermoon Tides*

Since the tidal force exerted by one moon on another goes as the inverse cube of the separation distance, the tides will be short and strong during conjunction, but negligible otherwise. This is a different situation than the tides on Earth, where the distance from the Earth to the Moon and the Sun stays nearly constant with time. Because the distance from the Earth to the tide-making body stays roughly constant, the dual oceanic tidal bulges (one bulge toward the body making the tide and a matching bulge in the opposite direction) from the tidal effects of the Moon and Sun stay roughly constant in height. The lunar tide turns out to be roughly twice the height of the solar tide because the closer proximity of the Moon more than makes up for its smaller mass. The approximately twice daily variations in tides that are observed on the Earth comes from the Earth rotating its continents around underneath the two oceanic bulges one each day. The seasonal variations of spring tides and neap tides occurs because the Sun and Moon tidal bulges move with respect to each other from new moon to full moon, and season to season, sometimes reinforcing each other and sometimes partially canceling each other.

On Zuni, there are calm seas most of the time with

a single modest periodic tide from Barnard that is 1.5 times the height of a high tide on Earth (about 1.5 meters). This Barnard tide comes every 15.1 hours or twice each Zuni day of 30.2 hours. On top of this periodic tide from Barnard there are superimposed sharp impulse tides caused by the close passage of Zuni by the nearby moons Zulu and Zouave. There is a conjunction with Zulu every 28.9 hours or slightly less than once a day. The Zulu tide is 4.5 meters or 4.5 times the height of an Earth high tide but the surge only lasts 3.4 hours. For the remaining 25.5 hours until its next passage, the tidal effects of Zulu on Zuni are negligible. There is also a conjunction with equally nearby Zouave every 78.4 hours, or 2.6 Zuni days. The Zouave tide is 6.5 meters or 6.5 times the height of an Earth high tide. The surge lasts for 6.2 hours out of the 78.4 hour interval between surges. When there is a triple conjunction, with Zulu and Zouave both passing by Zuni at the same time, the tides can become very large, with tides greater than ten times an Earth high tide. The maximum tidal effect experienced during a triple conjunction varies, since the alignment of the three moons is more precise during some triple conjunctions than others. Then, when Barnard is also lined up with the three moons, its periodic tide adds to the impulse tides of the two moons. The triple conjunction tides reach a maximum every 20,078 hours (about 2.3 years) of 12.4 times an Earth high tide. This produces a tidal surge with a height of nearly 13 meters (40 feet).

*Illumination*

The major source of illumination on Zuni is from the star Barnard. Barnard, however, not only has a weak luminosity of 0.05% that of the Sun, but it has an angular diameter of only 0.25 degrees in the skies of Zuni, which is half the diameter of the Sun in the skies of Earth. Gargantua is so large and so close to Zuni that it covers 21 degrees in the sky over Zuni. As a result, a substantial amount of illumination comes from the planet in addition to the light from Barnard. On Zuni, at "full moon," when Barnard is over the outer pole, the light from Gargantua is 1.5 percent of the light from Barnard. For comparison, the light flux from the Earth's Moon is only one-millionth that of the Sun, because the Moon has a low albedo and covers only a half-degree in the sky, while Gargantua has a high albedo and covers 21 degrees in the sky.

The illumination from Gargantua is most noticeable at a site on the inner pole of Zuni, where there is nearly always light, either from Barnard or from Gargantua. A site on the outer pole of Zuni, however, never seeing Gargantua anyway, is only illuminated by the light from Barnard, and so therefore has a normal day-night cycle (although 30.2 hours long instead of 24 hours long).

There is also illumination from the other large moons around Gargantua. From Zuni, at an orbital distance from Gargantua of 530 Mm, the inner moon Zulu, with an orbital distance of 330 Mm, looms to 1.5 degrees in size as it passes over the disk of Gargantua (three times as large as our Moon in the Earth sky) at the time of conjunction and high tide and is still 0.35 degrees in diameter at opposition, just before it goes behind Gargantua. The next moon out, Zouave, at 730 Mm from Gargantua, varies from 1.66 to 0.26 degrees in angular diameter between conjunction and opposition, while Zapotec, at 1650 Mm from Gargantua, varies from 0.17 to 0.26 degrees.

### *Shadowing*

Zuni experiences an eclipse of Barnard by Gargantua once every rotation. The eclipses are most noticeable for a site on the "Inner" side of the moon. Since Zuni is tidally locked to the planet, this is the side that always faces Gargantua. At the Inner site, the eclipse occurs at high noon and cuts 1.8 hours out of the 15.1 hour Zuni daylight period. If the site is on the "Leading" side of the moon, the side that always faces the direction of the motion along the orbit and where water vapor from Zulu and carbohydrates from Zouave fall out of the sky, then Gargantua hangs perpetually on the sunrise side of the horizon, cut in half by the horizon. Barnard rises from behind Gargantua, causing a late sunrise. For a site on the "Trailing" side, there is an early sunset as Barnard sets behind Gargantua hanging perpetually halfway down the sunset horizon. For sites on the "Outer" side of the moon, always facing away from Gargantua, the eclipse occurs at local midnight, off on the other side of Zulu, so nothing really noticeable is observed.

## SECTION 3
## BIOLOGY

Prepared by:
Katrina Kauffmann—Biology
Deirdre O'Connor—Zoology and Botany

With Contributions By Zuni Explorers:
Cinnamon Byrd—Zoology
John Kennedy—Physiology
Nels Larson—Botany and Genetics
Reiki LeRoux—Anthropology
Little White Whistler—Oceanic Life-forms

### Introduction

Alien life-forms were found in both the land and ocean regions of Zuni, the fourth moon of Gargantua.

In addition, three members of the exploration team were intelligent alien life-forms from the double-planet Rocheworld, called flouwen. The biology of the Rocheworld flouwen will be summarized first, followed by a discussion of the Zuni life-forms.

## Flouwen

The dominant species on the Eau lobe of Rocheworld have been given the common name of "flouwen" (singular "flouwen," taken from the Old High German root word for flow). The flouwen are formless, eyeless, flowing blobs of brightly colored jelly massing many tons. They normally stay in a cloudlike shape, moving with and through the water. When they are in their mobile, cloudlike form, the clouds in the water range from ten to thirty meters in diameter and many meters thick. At times, the flouwen will extrude water from their bodies and concentrate the material in their cloud into a dense rock formation a few meters in diameter. They seem to do this when they are thinking, and it is supposed that the denser form allows for faster and more concentrated cogitation.

The flouwen are very intelligent—but non-technological—like the dolphins and whales on Earth. They have a highly developed system of philosophy, and extremely advanced abstract mathematical capability. There is no question that they are centuries ahead of us in mathematics, and further communication with them could lead to great strides in human capabilities in this area.

The flouwen use chemical senses for short-range information gathering, and sound ranging, or sonar, for long range information gathering. Since sonar penetrates to the interior of an object, especially living objects such as flouwen and their prey, sonar provides "three-dimensional sight" to the flouwen and is their preferred method of "seeing." The bodies of the flouwen are sensitive to light, but, lacking eyes, they normally cannot look at things using light like humans do. In general, sight is a secondary sense, about as important to them as taste is to humans. One of the flouwen learned, however, to deliberately form an imaging lens out of the gel-like material in its body. It used this lens as an "eye" in order to study the stars and planets in their stellar system. Called White Whistler by the humans, this individual was one of the more technologically knowledgeable of the flouwen. White Whistler has since taught the eye-making technique to the rest of the flouwen.

In genetic makeup, complexity level, and internal organization, the flouwen have a number of similarities to slime-mold amoebas here on Earth, as well as analogies to a colony of ants. The flouwen bodies are made up of tiny, nearly featureless, dumbbell-shaped units, something like large cells. Each is the size and shape of the body of the tiny red ants found on Earth. The units are arranged in loosely interlocking layers, with four bulbous ends around each necked-down waist portion, two going in one direction and two going in the other, so that the body of the flouwen is a three-dimensionally interlocked whole.

Each of the dumbbell units can survive for a while on its own, but has minimal intelligence. A small collection of units can survive as a coherent cloud with enough intelligence to hunt smaller prey and look for plants to eat. These small "animals" are the major form of prey for the flouwen. Larger collections of units form into more complex "animals." When the collection of units finally becomes large enough, it becomes an intelligent being. Yet, if that being is torn into thousands of pieces, each piece can survive. If the pieces can get back together again, the intelligent individual is restored, only a little worse for its experience. As a result, a flouwen never dies, unless it is badly damaged in an accident (boiled by a volcanic eruption or stranded on dry land a long distance from water).

Reproduction for the flouwen is a multiple-individual experience. The flouwen do not seem to have sexes, and it seems that any number from two flouwen on up can produce a new individual. The usual grouping for reproduction is thought to be three or four. The creating of a new flouwen seems to be more of a lark or a creative exercise like music or theater than a physically driven emotional experience. The explorers on the first expedition to Rocheworld witnessed one such coupling put on for their benefit by four flouwen. They each extended a long tendril that contained a substantial portion of their mass, estimated to be one-tenth of the mass of each parent. These tendrils, each a different color, met at the middle and intertwined with a swirling motion like colored paints being stirred together. There was a long pause as each tendril began to lose its distinctive color, indicating that the liquid layers between the units were being withdrawn, leaving only the units.

Then finally the tendrils were separated from the adult flouwen bodies, leaving a colorless cloud of gel-like units floating by itself, about forty percent of the size of the adults that created it. After a few minutes, the mass of cells formed themselves into a new individual, which took on a color that was different than any of its progenitors. The adults then take it upon themselves to train the new youngster. The adults and youngsters stay together for hunting and protection, the group again being very much like a pod of whales or porpoises.

Since a small portion of a flouwen can function like a full-sized flouwen, except for decreased physical and mental capabilities, it was found that a small portion of a flouwen, weighing only a fifth of a ton (200 kilograms or 440 pounds), can bud off from the multi-ton main flouwen body, get into a specially built spacesuit with lenses built in the helmet visor to serve as eyes, and ride in human space vehicles in order to take part in joint expeditions with the humans. These sub-flouwen are somewhat more intelligent than humans, and have already proved to be valuable exploration partners on those worlds containing oceans, such as the moons Zulu and Zuni.

## Zuni Life-forms

The sub-categories of fauna and flora are not appropriate for the life-forms on Zuni, especially since the dominant predator life-form, the Jolly, may act like an animal in function but is more like a plant in form. Since Barnard has weak illumination, the plants cannot survive on photosynthesis alone, unless they are very large in light collecting area (many acres). Fortunately, the moon Zuni is situated between the moon Zulu, which emits water into space, and the moon Zouave, which emits hydrocarbon smog into space. These materials stay in orbit around Gargantua, forming large torus-shaped clouds, one of water and one of smog. The water molecules and hydrocarbons are acted on by the light and particles from Barnard, producing energetic compounds. Zuni passes through the outskirts of these clouds and collects this energized water and "fertilizer" on its leading pole. The periodic strong impulse tides from the close passage of Zuni to Zulu and Zouave also keep the volcanoes on Zuni active, which throws more energetic gasses, compounds, and particulates into the air. These energy-bearing materials then fall as enriched rain on the plants.

Thus, the "flora" on Zuni are those plants that live mostly by developing large structures with lots of surface area to collect as much rainwater as possible, while the "fauna" are plants that get some or all of their nutritional needs from attacking other plants and sucking their sap or eating their leaves, limbs, and or fruits. It seems, however, that nearly all life-forms on Zuni are predators at some level of activity.

In the lakes and oceans of Zuni are additional life-forms being studied by the three flouwen members of the expedition. Most of the underwater life exists only in and around volcanic vent fields, again because photosynthesis is so weak that algae and other forms of plant-like plankton cannot thrive without another energy source, such as hydrogen sulfide and other compounds emitted by volcanic vents.

The following life-forms are listed in approximate order of intelligence or importance to the human explorers. There are certainly many more life-forms to be discovered, not only on the island where the explorers are located, but on other islands and in other oceans of Zuni.

*Jolly*—The dominant life-form on Zuni seems to be a large, intelligent, omnivorous, mobile plant. The humans have named the plant type a "Jolly," after the "Jolly Green Giant" animated character used in Del Monte vegetable television commercials. The Jolly's name for themselves is their tribal name "Keejook," with the neighboring tribe called the "Toojook." The word "jook" seems to be a generic name meaning roughly "person." An adult Jolly is typically four meters (13 feet) tall, has a large trunk a meter in diameter, a canopy ("hair") of blue-green fronds, and six legs. The legs of a Jolly have no joints, but are moved by differential internal hydraulic pressure, which makes them prehensile like the trunk of an elephant, or giant cloth-covered slinky toys. The legs can expand and contract in length, and are moved in two sets of three. One set consists of one leg at the very front, and two at right and left toward the rear. The other set consists of two legs toward the front at right and left, and one at the very rear. This way, the Jolly is always securely balanced on one set of three legs while the other set of three legs slowly "steps" forward by contracting in length, swinging forward, then extending in length to touch the ground. The body weight is shifted by the extension of the back set of legs, while the new ones contract slightly until they are supporting the body weight overhead. The process of taking two steps to return to the original state takes a whole minute for a roughly one meter pace. This translates to sixty meters per hour, or two kilometers of travel each thirty hour Zuni day.

When balanced on three of its feet, the Jolly can use the other three feet as arms. Its root-like feet are strong and capable hands that can manipulate its stone-age tools, like knives, scrapers, diggers, etc. It carries its tools in loops or pouches hung from a belt made of dried vines, or in a carrying net used as a pack for long journeys.

In the central body or "trunk" of the Jolly, just above the hips, is a mouthlike hole. This is the home of a number of scurrying little molelike creatures or "gatherers," with blue-green hairy fur, six strong jointed legs, a single large eye, long mole-like nose, and a small toothless hole at the back of the head for a mouth. The front two legs have six opposable "fingers" with sharp claws that are used for grasping, tearing, and digging. The gatherers scamper down the legs of the host Jolly, climb up trees to harvest nuts and fruits, dig into the ground to find grubs, kill smaller animals and plants, and haul their finds back to the mouthlike hole, using their front two feet to hold the food, while walking on the rear four. These gatherers have minimal gut and brain, and act as mobile "hands" of the Jolly. They bring food to the

Jolly and put it into a "throat" in the back of the "mouth" hole in the trunk that leads to a "gizzard." The Jolly digests the food, and in turn feeds the gatherers the enriched "milk" they need through a long prehensile "teat" or "umbilical cord" extending down from the ceiling of the mouth-hole. The same umbilical is used as a "data" line to "download" a "program" into the semi-intelligent gatherer before sending it out on another foray. The Jollys speak through their gatherers by downloading a sentence into the gatherer through the umbilical. The gatherer then releases the teat and "whistles" the sentence while the Jolly is downloading the next sentence into another gatherer. Because of the lack of vocal cords to make humming sounds, and the structure of the feeding orifice on the gatherers, Jolly speech is limited to whistling or hissing vowel sounds and various stops for consonants.

Hanging from the fronds growing from the top of the trunk of the Jolly are nestlike structures, each the home of a small owl-like creature consisting of a single large eye and two blue-green wings with three stiffening struts each. The "owls" have no visible feet or beak, but there is a small toothless hole for a mouth, again in the back of their head. They have minimal gut and a large brain, mostly concentrated behind the retina of the single eyeball. These owl-like creatures flutter about the canopy from nest to nest. Occasionally one of them will dash off into the distance, fly around and inspect some object at a distance, then flutter back to a nest. These "owls" are the eyes of the Jolly. They bring back pictures to the Jolly, who uses them to assemble and maintain in its mind a three-dimensional "view" of the world around it.

This three-dimensional view of the world "seen" by a Jolly is probably very different from the moving two-dimensional imagery as seen by a human. First, the view is a stored three-dimensional image, so that the Jolly mind can "walk around" the image and inspect it from any point of view at any time. Second, the view stays static until an "owl" comes back to a nest and supplies an updated version of one portion of the whole view.

Nothing definite is known about the sex life of the Jolly. Since they obviously have fruiting bodies hanging from their fronds, they may be bisexual, like most plants, or of a single sex, like holly trees and a few other plants. The children are planted as seeds and are started as rooted plants surviving on the nourishment of the fruit pulp. They are weaned to partially digested and regurgitated adult food as soon as their mouths and eyes are open. Once weaned, they pull up their roots, walk away from the nursery bed, and go to school where they are taught by the tribal elders the skills needed to become adult members of the tribe.

*jookeejook*—The "pig" of the Jolly food chain, but the "chimpanzee" from an evolutionary point of view. The Jolly word "jookeejook" means literally "person that is not a person." The jookeejook is a cultivated omnivorous mobile plant that has been bred by the Jollys to eat garbage and produce delicious fruits and meat. A jookeejook is built along the lines of a Jolly, with a trunk, vestigial leaf crown, mouth, and six legs, but the jookeejook always walks on all six legs and seldom uses a leg as a "hand." Its eyes and gatherers are connected to the main body by semipermanent umbilical cords connected to the back of the heads of the motiles, which severely limits the range of the motiles. The umbilicals to the eye motiles are like fine stiff wires that arch up through the fronds to partially support the eye out at the tip. The eyes have wings so they can move around to change their view, but the wings are not large enough for the eyes to fly well.

A jookeejook eye or gatherer motile is normally permanently attached to its umbilical. If the motile is pulled upon or becomes caught in something, however, the motile will detach from the umbilical, somewhat like the disposable tail of some earth lizards, except that the motile can be reattached to the umbilical. When separated, however, the jookeejook motile is incapable of independent purposeful action, unlike the more intelligent motiles of the Jollys. Although it is difficult to see exactly how it happened, it is expected that future studies of the comparative physiologies of the jookeejook and Jolly will help establish how the Jollys evolved their semi-intelligent free-roaming eyes and gatherers.

*peethoo*—The banyan tree of Zuni. A large low tree covering many acres. The long limbs from the main trunk are supported by "saplings" that grow down from the bottom of the limbs to the ground. The leaves are large and spongy, and soak up all the water that drops on them. By staying low to the ground and using multiple trunks, the peethoo tree minimizes trunk mass versus leaf mass. They are susceptible to taller trees shading them at the edges, but once they have become large enough, the leafy area in the center keeps the whole tree going while the outer edge engages in subterranean root-killing warfare with the neighboring trees.

*thook*—A semi-intelligent thorn thicket that is cultivated and trained by the Jolly tribe to protect the Jollys from raids by tentacle trees and other Jolly tribes. The thook branches grow in coils that can be hydraulically contracted and expanded quite rapidly (from a Jolly point of view), impaling an intruder on the sharp thorns. Humans can usually move fast enough through a large hole in the barrier to avoid being caught. The thook thicket recognizes the members of the tribe, and automatically coils its branches back out of the way to allow the Jollys of the tribe and their gatherers through.

*boobaa*—The Zuni equivalent of a coconut palm tree. The boobaa is a very tall tree with a bare trunk, large leafy crown, and large spongy tough fruits. The boobaa trees live in interconnected "families." Their crowns meet at their edges and cover a wide area. They live off the energy-rich nutrients in the rainwater like most plant life on Zuni. When one of the boobaa trees is attacked by a climber vine attempting to take over the canopy area, that tree passes on its stored resources to its neighbors through their interconnected root system, deliberately shrinks in size, and lets the neighboring boobaa trees grow to shade it. This results in the killing of the climber vine by making it use up its stored resources climbing the trunk while not allowing it to gain anything in the end for all its effort. The tree grows fruit up high which it drops during severe windstorms, hoping that the fruit will roll to a place where some tree has been uprooted, so it can take over the space.

*keekoo*—The keekoo, or "tentacle tree" as the humans call it, sends out very fine threads along and under the surface of the ground to great distances. Upon finding a source of nourishment, such as a dropped fruit, dead plant, or dead animal, the tree pumps resources to that section of thread, which turns the thread into a strong snake-like tentacle that grabs the food object, constricts to kill it if necessary, and then transports the object back along the thread to the main trunk to nourish the root system.

*feebook*—The "ivy" plant of Zuni. The feebook plant grows in soilless steep areas and rocky creek beds where normal plants and trees cannot grow. It spreads out wide, waterproof leaves over the rocks and barren ground that form a groundcover. The large waterproof leaves prevent the nutrient rain from soaking into the ground, and funnels the rainwater to the central plant at the bottom of the creek bed.

*peekoo*—An edible bivalve shellfish with a soft pink body and six legs with pincer claws. The bivalve shell is not symmetric, but instead is constructed with a flat bottom shell and a domed upper shell, somewhat like a six-legged headless and tailless tortoise. It detects the approach of predators with an array of small scallop-like eyes peering out from under the shell, and either scampers away on its six long legs or holds fast to a rock using a combination of claws and suction.

# CASTING

## HUMANS

The initial crew of the Barnard Star Expedition consisted of twenty people when it left the solar system in 2026. One of the crew, Dr. William Wang, during the long process of curing the rest of the crew from an infectious type of cancer, died from the same cancer while en route to Barnard. Although the crew spent forty calendar years traveling from the solar system to Barnard, their aging rate during the long journey was slowed by a factor of four through the use of the drug No-Die. As a result, upon arrival at Barnard in 2066, the effective biological age of the crew had only increased ten years over their age at the start of the mission. The crew spent the next two years decelerating to a halt in the Barnard planetary system, then three years surveying the entire system from space, exploring the surfaces of the two lobes of the double-planet Rocheworld, and exploring the surface of the Gargantuan moon Zulu, before moving on to the surface exploration of Zuni. The ages for the humans are given in terms of their effective biological age at the time of their crash landing on Zuni, now known as Eden, in 2073.

*Landing Party*

The landing party for the surface exploration of Zuni consisted of ten crew members:

**Major General Virginia "Jinjur" Jones**—Commander of the Barnard Star Expedition. Height: 158.5 cm (5′2″). Weight: 61 kg (135 lbs). Effective Age: 57 years. Jinjur is short and solid with dark-black skin and a no-nonsense black pixie Afro haircut. She graduated high in her class at the U.S. Naval Academy and chose the Marines. During her first tour of duty with the Marine Recruit Training Command, she distinguished herself in the Greater San Diego tourist riots in 2009. She rose to become commander of a Space Marine fleet of lightweight solar sailcraft that kept the spacelanes swept of debris, inspected foreign spacecraft for compliance with the Space Treaty, and resupplied and protected the Laser Forts. Jinjur's nickname (bestowed on her by her Space Marines) was taken from the name of the spicy female general that conquered the Emerald City in one of the lesser-known Oz books.

**Reiki LeRoux**—Computer programmer and anthropologist. Height 163 cm (5′4″). Weight: 53 kg (117 lb). Effective Age: 44. Reiki is the daughter of a Japanese woman of good family, who met and fell in love with a US Navy aircraft carrier pilot stationed in Japan. His family were oil-rich Louisiana Cajuns. The couple married, but he was killed in a training crash before Reiki was born. Reiki spent her childhood in Japan among a large family, who loved her, but found her alien appearance constantly unsettling in the community. Her skin is almost apricot, her black hair is curly, and her dark eyes are round. With money no problem, she was sent early to a good boarding school in Scotland, where she pursued a wide variety of courses and excelled in them all. She specialized in computer programming and anthropology at Glasgow University, graduating with honors. Of medium size and pleasantly curvy, she has had lots of experience with many different kinds of people, and has learned the skills of cooperation to a high degree. This manifests itself in a passion for etiquette, which the others find entertaining. She is a quiet person, very good at her work, which is designing user-friendly computer interfaces, and keeps a detailed diary in her slim electronic journal that goes with her everywhere.

**Shirley Everett**—Chief engineer and pilot. Height: 190 cm (6′3″). Weight: 85 kg (185 lbs). Effective Age: 48 years. Shirley is the epitome of a tall, strong, tanned, blue-eyed, blond-haired "California Surfer Girl." At USC, she obtained a B.S. in electrical engineering with minors in nuclear engineering and mechanical engineering. She played on both women's and men's basketball teams in college, and became the third woman to play on a men's professional basketball team, but gave up her pro-basketball career as a second-string forward for the Los Angeles Lakers to return to USC to get an Engineering Doctorate. After learning to fly, she went to work for the company that designed and built the aerospace planes used on the Expedition. With her eidetic memory, Shirley knows everything about the spacecraft they fly, except details of the computer software programs, where David Greystoke takes over. She can fix anything, not with the proverbial hairpin—she is too well trained and equipped for that—but could if she had to.

**Cinnamon Byrd**—Levichthyhusbandry specialist, medic, and pilot. Height: 172 cm (5′8″). Weight: 53 kg (117 lb). Effective Age: 43 years. Tall and skinny, Cinnamon wears her long straight black hair in two low braids to cover her large ears. Cinnamon was born in Alaska to an Eskimo woman and her outback doctor husband, altruistic scion of a prominent East Coast family. By 16, Cinnamon had become both a pilot and an emergency medical technician in order to help her father during emergencies. She studied oceanic fish-farming (ichthyhusbandry) at the University of Alaska. Through the International Space University, she did graduate work in levichthyhusbandry at Goddard Station, where she met Nels Larson and proved to be invaluable to him. She was brought along on the Expedition largely at Nels's request, although it helped that she aced the GNASA piloting tests and qualified as a back-up pilot for both the rocket landers and the aerospace planes.

**Richard Redwing**—Planetary geoscientist. Height: 195 cm (6′4″). Weight: 110 kg (225 lbs). Effective Age: 49 years. Richard is a very large, very strong outdoorsman of American Indian heritage. He was a college champion weight lifter and won a gold medal in the 2012 Olympics. He earned his B.S. in geophysics in 2014 and started work for a mining company in the Alps. He was also a part-time mountain-climbing guide who distinguished himself in a mountain rescue that cost him his two little toes. He grew tired of the lack of mental challenge and returned to school to get his Ph.D. in planetary physics and geophysics. He did his post-doctoral field training on the Moon and Mars, participated in the Ceres and Vesta expeditions, and was part of Callisto field crew when he was accepted for the Barnard Star Expedition.

**Carmen Cortez**—Communications engineer. Height: 165 cm (5′5″). Weight: 80 kg (176 lbs). Effective Age: 43 years. Carmen is a chunky, very feminine Spanish señorita, with black, nearly-afro, curly hair. She always wears makeup and a tightly tailored uniform. She went to the University of Guadalajara in 2015, and became president of the College Radio Amateur Club. She was in charge of the generator-powered base station during a radio field day, when the 9.1 magnitude earthquake struck Salamanca, Mexico in 2018. For 48 hours she ran the only operational emergency communication services in West Central Mexico. She obtained her B.S. in Engineering from the University of Guadalajara in 2019, then a Doctor of Electrical Engineering *magna cum laude* from University of California, San Diego in 2022. She applied for the Barnard Star Expedition upon graduation and was placed on the back-up list. She was in training on Titan for the Alpha Centauri Expedition when she was activated for the mission at the last minute in order to replace a primary crew member who had to return to Earth for health reasons.

**Arielle Trudeau**—Aerodynamicist and aerospace-plane pilot. Height: 165 cm (5′5″). Weight: 50 kg (110 lbs). Effective Age: 50 years. Arielle is thin, delicate, beautiful, shy, and fair-skinned, with short, curly light-brown hair and deep-brown eyes. She was born and raised in Quebec, Canada before the secession of Quebec from Canada. She emigrated to the United States and became an American citizen after the absorption of the rest of the Canadian provinces into the Greater United States of America in 2006. Her father taught her how to fly at an early age and she has hundreds of hours experience in a glider. She obtained a Ph.D. in aerodynamics at CalTech and entered the space program as a non-pilot mission specialist. On her first flight into space, there was a cockpit explosion that killed both Super-Shuttle pilots. Single-handed, encumbered by a spacesuit, she brought the crippled Super-Shuttle safely down in the smoothest landing ever recorded in the shuttle program. Arielle was given special dispensation to take Super-Shuttle pilot training after public acclaim, later became one of the best shuttle pilots. She was training for lunar pilot status when the Barnard Star Expedition let her travel to the stars.

**John Kennedy**—Engineer and nurse. Height:

183 cm (6′0″). Weight: 80 kg (176 lb). Effective Age: 47 years. John bears a striking resemblance to his distant relative. He tried the premed curriculum at USC, but gave it up when he didn't get a high enough score on the MSATs, and went on to get a Ph.D in electromechanical engineering. He didn't feel satisfied working solely on machines and went back to get his R.N. His strange mix of talents just fit a slot on the Expedition.

**Nels Larson**—Leviponics specialist. Height: 178 cm (5′10″). Weight: 75 kg (165 lb). Effective Age: 48 years. Nels has very muscular arms, a barrel torso, and a large handsome head with a strong jaw, light-blue eyes, and long yellow-white hair that he combs straight back. When Nels was born with flipper-like feet in place of legs, his parents quit their jobs on Earth and moved to Goddard Station where Nels grew up. He took college courses by video and apprenticed in levibotany and levihusbandry at the Leviponics Research Facility on Goddard. He initiated the famous Larson chicken breast tissue culture ("Chicken Little" to most astronauts) and many new strains of algae with various exotic flavors. Nels's initial primary duties were on *Prometheus*, where, with its near free-fall environment, legs were more of a handicap than a help. While on Rocheworld, Nels was instructed by the flouwen on a method for regeneration of limbs in advanced species. Using this knowledge, Nels built a custom-made hydroponics "bed" where he grew himself a new pair of legs.

**David Greystoke**—Electronics and computer engineer. Height: 158 cm (5′2″). Weight: 50 kg (110 lbs). Effective Age: 50 years. David is short, thin, and redhaired, but quiet and calm in temperament. He has perfect pitch and perfect color sense, and can see color differences in the flouwen that others cannot see. An undergraduate at the prestigious liberal arts college at Grinnell, Iowa, he went on to Carnegie-Mellon University for a Ph.D. in robotics and computer programming, with a minor in music. He wrote most of the programs used on the computers operating the various vehicles. David's hobby is creating computer generated animated art-music forms and laser light shows.

*Sailcraft Crew*

The backup crew in space, on *Prometheus*, consist of:

**Colonel George G. Gudunov**—Second-in-Command of Barnard Star Expedition, commander of the sailcraft *Prometheus*. Height: 185 cm (6′1″). Weight: 100 kg (220 lbs). Effective Age: 66 years. George is the oldest person on the mission. He obtained an Air Force ROTC commission from University of Maryland and was first in his class in flight school. His first assignment was with the Space Command Laser Forts project. When a twenty-three-year-old Captain, he suggested testing the laser fort system by using them to send interstellar probes to the nearest star systems. When a number of space laser forts suffered catastrophic failure under this two day test, he was commended by Congress for exposing the problems, but the military brass never forgave him. When the positive reports from the Barnard probe came in twenty-four years later, he had only just made Lieutenant Colonel. Despite his age, he was promoted to Colonel and allowed to go on the Expedition.

**Katrina Kauffmann**—Nurse and biochemist. Height: 150 cm (4′11″). Weight: 45 kg (99 lbs). Effective Age: 55 years. Katrina is a small, compact, efficient no-nonsense scientist with a short cap of straight brown hair. Trained in Europe, she had started out in a nursing school, but after getting her R.N. she found she liked working more on scientific problems than working with sick people, so switched professions. She received a Diploma in Biophysics at the University of Frankfurt a.M., Germany in 2010, and went on to get a Ph.D. in Biochemistry. She came to the Greater United States on a post-doctoral fellowship and stayed until picked for the mission.

**Captain Thomas St. Thomas**—Astrodynamicist and lander pilot. Height: 188 cm (6′2″). Weight: 85 kg (187 lbs). Effective Age: 48 years. Thomas is good looking and clean shaven, with Air Force trim short black hair, and a light-brown skin from a Jamaican heritage. After graduation from the U.S. Air Force Academy, he became a Rhodes scholar in 2014, and obtained his Ph.D. in astrodynamics at Oxford in England. On return, he went into Air Force pilot training and became a heavy-lift rocket pilot in 2019. He had over five years of experience raising and lowering the heavy, cumbersome rockets in Earth's gravity before joining the Barnard Star Expedition. He is also an amateur photographer who takes strikingly artistic photographs of the exotic locales visited by the Expedition.

**Caroline Tanaka**—Fiber-optics engineer and astronomer. Height: 165 cm (5′5″). Weight: 60 kg (132 lb). Effective Age: 48 years. Caroline has long dark-brown hair, brown eyes, and light-brown skin from a mixed Hawaiian heritage. Although moderately good-looking, she is an intense, hard-working engineer who pays no attention to her looks. Caroline did all the design, fabrication (with the help of the Christmas Bush), installation, and check-out of a laser communicator that was left behind for use by the flouwen on Rocheworld after the humans had departed their world. The flouwen use the laser to communicate with the Expedition crew on the lightcraft *Prometheus*, as well as human scientists back in the solar system.

**Captain Anthony "Tony" Roma**—Lightsail and

aerospace plane pilot. Height: 168 cm (5′6″). Weight: 70 kg (155 lb). Effective Age: 45 years. Tony is small and very handsome, with a dark complexion, dark eyes, dark wavy hair, and a neat mustache. He was a cadet in the first class at the Space Force Academy and went directly from aircraft pilot school into lightsail pilot training. When picked for the mission, he was on assignment as a pilot in General Virginia Jones's Space Marines Interceptor Fleet, where he invented a number of new lightsail maneuvers.

**Elizabeth "Red" Vengeance**—Asteroidologist and lander pilot. Height: 178 cm (5′10″). Weight: 70 kg (154 lbs). Effective Age: 53 years. Red is tall and thin, with an aristocratic nose, a short, straight cap of red hair, green eyes, and the typical redhead complexion with freckles resulting from an Irish heritage. She has over 150 hours of credits in mining and mineralogy from University of Arizona but no degree. Elizabeth was one of the first independent prospectors in the asteroid belt. She struck it rich, became a billionaire, and then realized that there were more interesting things to do than loafing for the rest of her life. Her extensive space experience as an asteroid prospector and heavy-lift asteroid-tug operator got her selected for the Barnard Star Expedition.

**Sam Houston**—Planetary geoscientist. Height: 200 cm (6′7″). Weight: 80 kg (176 lbs). Effective Age: 60 years. Sam is very tall and very thin, with pale face and skin, long bones with knobby joints, gray-blue eyes, and long graying hair. He does not have a doctorate, but instead has years of experience in the field. He started field exploration in 2003 on the Canadian shield with Exxon. By the next decade, he had worked on all the continents, both poles, and the continental shelves of five of the seven seas. One of the first full-time geologists on the Moon, he spent 2015 making a preliminary geological map of the backside, then spent two years on Mars with the first Mars colony. He was the lead geologist on the 2018 "Big-Four" asteroid mapping expedition, and his experiences on Ceres, Vesta, Pallas, and Juno, followed by two moons of Jupiter—Ganymede and Callisto—made him an obvious choice for the Barnard Star Expedition.

**Linda Regan**—Solar astrophysicist. Height: 155 cm (5′1″). Weight: 55 kg (121 lb). Effective Age: 46 years. Linda is a short, stocky, bouncy "cheerleader" type, with sparkling green eyes, curly brown hair, and lots of energy. She took physics at USC, went on to get a Ph.D. in astronomy at CalTech, and earned her way to a position at the Solar Observatory around Mercury, then onto the Barnard Star Expedition.

**Deirdre O'Connor**—Biologist and Levihusbandry specialist. Height: 168 cm (5′6″). Weight: 60 kg (115 lb). Effective Age: 43 years. Pale green eyes and long reddish-brown hair pulled back into a ponytail. Her short ecstatically happy marriage ended with the accidental death of her husband, whom no one can replace. Her animal companion is a "woosel," a hitherto unknown weasel-like marsupial with a prehensile tail Deirdre found in the Amazon Basin. When the only known female died in an accident with six rice-grain-sized young hanging from teats in its pouch, Deirdre showed it was possible to deep freeze the young, transport them out of the jungle wilds, and construct an artificial teat that would nourish the embryos until they could cope on their own, saving the species. Now, one of their many great-grandchildren has joined her on this interstellar mission. It was kept as a frozen embryo for forty years while Deirdre and the others were "living" on No-Die, and brought to life to enjoy the care and attention of the savior of its species—and its friend.

# ABOUT THE AUTHORS

**Dr. Robert L. Forward** writes science fiction novels and short stories, as well as science fact books and magazine articles. Through his scientific consulting company, Forward Unlimited, he also engages in contracted research on advanced space propulsion and exotic physical phenomena. Dr. Forward obtained his Ph.D. in Gravitational Physics from the University of Maryland. For his thesis he constructed and operated the world's first bar antenna for the detection of gravitational radiation. The antenna is now at the Smithsonian museum.

For 31 years, from 1956 until 1987, when he left in order to spend more time writing, Dr. Forward worked at the Hughes Aircraft Company Corporate Research Laboratories in Malibu, California in positions of increasing responsibility, culminating with the position of Senior Scientist on the staff to the Director of the Laboratories. During that time he constructed and operated the world's first laser gravitational radiation detector, invented the rotating gravitational mass sensor, published over 65 technical publications, and was awarded 18 patents.

From 1983 to the present, Dr. Forward has had a series of contracts from the U.S. Air Force and NASA to explore the forefront of physics and engineering in order to find breakthrough concepts in space power and propulsion. He has published journal papers and contract reports on antiproton annihilation propulsion, laser beam and microwave beam interstellar propulsion, negative matter propulsion, space tethers, space warps, and a method for extracting electrical energy from vacuum fluctuations, and was awarded a patent for a Statite: a sunlight-levitated direct-broadcast solar-sail spacecraft that does not orbit the earth, but "hovers" over the North Pole.

In addition to his professional publications, Dr. Forward has written over 80 popular science articles for publications such as the Encyclopaedia Britannica Yearbook, Omni, New Scientist, Aerospace America, Science Digest, Science 80, Analog, and Galaxy. His most recent science fact books are *Future Magic* and *Mirror Matter: Pioneering Antimatter Physics* (with Joel Davis). His science fiction novels are *Dragon's Egg* and its sequel *Starquake, Martian Rainbow, Timemaster, The Flight of the Dragonfly* (published by Baen Books in a longer version as *Rocheworld*), and *Camelot 30K*. He is presently in the process of writing four sequels to *Rocheworld* with members of his family. The first sequel, *Return To Rocheworld*, was written with his daughter, Julie Forward Fuller, while this sequel, *Marooned On Eden*, was written with his wife, Martha Dodson Forward. The novels are of the "hard" science fiction category, where the science is as accurate as possible.

Dr. Forward is a Fellow of the British Interplanetary Society and former Editor of the Interstellar Studies issues of its Journal, Associate Fellow of the American Institute of Aeronautics and Astronautics, and a member of the American Physical Society, Sigma Xi, Sigma Pi Sigma, National Space Society, the Science Fiction Writers of America, and the Author's Guild.

**Martha Dodson Forward** obtained a Bachelor of Arts degree in English from the University of South Carolina in 1956 and took graduate courses at UCLA. Her primary literary output consists of letters to a wide circle of family and friends, some of whom save them assiduously with the fond and foolish hope of becoming wealthy from their publication after her demise.

# POUL ANDERSON

Poul Anderson is one of the most honored authors of our time. He has won seven Hugo Awards, three Nebula Awards, and the Gandalf Award for Achievement in Fantasy, among others. His most popular series include the Polesotechnic League/Terran Empire tales and the Time Patrol series. Here are fine books by Poul Anderson available through Baen Books:

**THE GAME OF EMPIRE**

A *new* novel in Anderson's Polesotechnic League/Terran Empire series! Diana Crowfeather, daughter of Dominic Flandry, proves well capable of following in his adventurous footsteps.

**FIRE TIME**

Once every thousand years the Deathstar orbits close enough to burn the surface of the planet Ishtar. This is known as the Fire Time, and it is then that the barbarians flee the scorched lands, bringing havoc to the civilized South.

**AFTER DOOMSDAY**

Earth has been destroyed, and the handful of surviving humans must discover which of three alien races is guilty before it's too late.

**THE BROKEN SWORD**

It is a time when Christos is new to the land, and the Elder Gods and the Elven Folk still hold sway. In 11th-century Scandinavia Christianity is beginning to replace the old religion, but the Old Gods still have power, and men are still oppressed by the folk of the Faerie. "Pure gold!"—Anthony Boucher.

**THE DEVIL'S GAME**

Seven people gather on a remote island, each competing for a share in a tax-free fortune. The "contest" is ostensibly sponsored by an eccentric billionaire—but the rich man is in league with an alien masquerading as a demon . . . or is it the other way around?

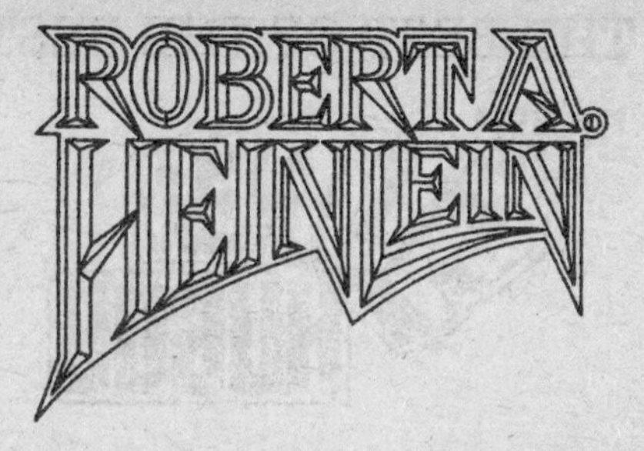
ROBERT A.
HEINLEIN